Donna Baker was born in Hampshire just before the outbreak of war, and is the youngest of four children. She began writing magazine and newspaper articles in 1973, moved on to short stories and has written a number of romantic novels under a pseudonym. She is married and has two children, and now lives in the Lake District. The first title in *The Glassmakers Saga*, *Crystal*, is also available from Headline.

Reviews for *Crystal*:

'. . . the novel is well conceived and the characters have charm'          *Books Magazine*
'. . . captures the imagination'          *Best*
'It's an enthralling tale obviously well researched . . . I look forward to the next two sections of this highly absorbing tale'          *Shropshire Star*

Reviews for *Black Cameo*:

'A good family storyline, lots of atmosphere and strong love all add up to make a book of substance'          *Woman's World*
'Those who liked the first book will like the second'          *Books Magazine*
'[Donna Baker] has certainly done her research into the industrial history of the Black Country . . . [and] her characters are strongly coloured'          *Bristol Evening Post*

# Black Cameo

## The Glassmakers Saga

Donna Baker

Riverside Books
Fairview Farm
Littley Green
Essex CM3 1BU

ISBN 1 904154 48 4

Printed and bound in the United Kingdom

To Jane Morpeth

# Acknowledgements

As well as the books and people who helped with information in the writing of *Crystal*, I would like to include the following:

Baccarat, of Paris, who showed me their museum and gave me much information; the Musée de la Poste, Montparnasse; Gerard Ingold's book *Saint-Louis – From Glass to Crystal*; *John Northwood* by his son John Northwood; the library of the *Illustrated London News*; and the British Museum, where you can still see the Portland Vase.

# Chapter One

On this fine July morning in 1856, barely four months after the end of the war in the Crimea, the people of the villages around the fast-expanding market town of Stourbridge were making ready for a holiday. Picnics and parades were rare events in their lives, and this one was especially enjoyed, for almost every glassmaker in the area would walk in procession today behind a brass band, carrying a glittering sample of his trade. Each year there was some new novelty to be admired, and perhaps bought to take home, by those who had money to spare for such things. And after the procession, there was the picnic itself, held in the park surrounding Prestwood House, with all the sideshows and fairground attractions that invariably accompanied such events. It would be a long day and for most a happy one, a bright memory to carry through the rest of the year.

Only for ten-year-old Emily and for Paul would it end in confusion; but they had no idea, when they woke that morning in their bedrooms at Henzel Court, that today's picnic was to be any different from any other.

Nor had Christina Compson as she opened her eyes and found her husband leaning over her, his dark brown eyes intent, his black hair, still untouched by any grey, curling over his head.

'Joe . . .' Sleepily, she reached up and wound her arms around his neck, drawing him down for the first kiss of the morning; and then, remembering, 'Oh! It's picnic day – and the sun's shining. Oh, I'm so glad.'

'Aye, it's going to be a scorcher, too.' Joe Compson's voice was as rich as it had ever been, still coloured by the accents of his native Black Country dialect. 'There's a mist over Wordsley – when that clears it'll be as hot as a furnace. You'll have to tell Jane to give an eye to the

1

children, make sure they all keep their hats on or they'll be getting sunstroke.'

Christina smiled affectionately at him. 'You're like a mother hen with the children, Joe. I wonder how many other fathers are so loving. Even though they –'

'They're all our family,' Joe interrupted with a slight frown. 'Why shouldn't I love them? You forget, Christina, I didn't grow up as you did, in a nursery where I hardly ever set eyes on my parents. We all lived together, close, and did things for each other. And I think that's a better way – poor we may have been, but we grew up close and happy because that was the only way to be. Look at your sister Alice's children, they come down to the drawing room for half an hour at teatime, and that's the only time they see their ma and pa. They think more of their nursemaid than of their mother!'

'My father loved me,' Christina protested. 'And took me with him too, wherever he went. You know that, Joe.'

'Aye, I do.' His face softened. 'I remember you coming into the glasshouse that day, all togged out in your brother's clothes, set on seeing everything. And after that your dad brought you in with him as often as maybe. But he was a different sort of man, old Joshua Henzel. There aren't many made in his mould. And not many in yours, come to that. Not many young girls would have taken on a glasshouse as you did when you were barely twenty years old and made a success of it too. Especially with the other Henzels all breathing down your neck, waiting to get their foot in the door.'

'I just wanted Henzel's to go on running as Papa would have wished,' Christina said. 'Cousin Samuel and Harold would have taken it over and changed it for their own ends – they would never have gone into lead crystal and fine tableware as we did. And whatever success had come, they would have taken all the credit for it, for all the work that Papa had done to build it up. I couldn't allow that. And he knew that I wouldn't – why else should he have left it to me?' She gave Joe one of the sudden, impish smiles that turned her into a young girl again, impulsive and eager, ready to take her father's glasshouse into new and exciting realms, ready to try new ventures and determined to make them succeed. 'He knew what I could do, and he trusted me. I always felt he was there, encouraging me, even when the cousins pressed me hardest.'

'And even when Jeremy was at his most persuasive?' Joe said quietly, and Christina sighed.

'I nearly made a bad mistake there,' she acknowledged. 'Things could have been very different . . . but luckily I saw sense just in time.' She shivered. 'I sometimes wonder what my life would have been like . . . but it's not hard to imagine. And when I do, I give thanks for you, Joe. When I think how nearly we lost each other –' She sat up and reached forward into his arms. 'Joe, we'll be together always now, won't we? Nothing will ever happen to part us.'

Joe clasped her tightly, feeling the softness of her small body wrapped in his powerful arms, held against the hard muscles of his great chest. Christina was an odd mixture, and still, after eight years of marriage, capable of surprising him. But he was accustomed now to her occasional moments of doubt, her fears that Fate might yet tear them apart, and he understood them. She had been through a great deal of unhappiness before they had finally destroyed all the barriers between them. Her father's death and the struggle of running the glasshouse, a woman in a man's world, while holding the Henzel cousins at bay; the constant pressures put upon her by Jeremy, who had eventually lost all control and been thrown out by a Joe who had come close that night to murder; Jean-Paul – and Joe could still feel a pang of jealousy when he thought of Jean-Paul; and, last of all, the children, Paul and Emily. None of it had been easy, even for a girl like Christina, filled with a courageous determination to go her own way, and she had enjoyed little support for her actions at home, her Aunt Susan having been in a perpetual state of flutter over Christina's 'unladylike' ways. Only her brother Harry had stood firmly beside her, but he had been several years younger besides being absorbed in his own ambitions to become an engineer.

'Nothing will ever come between us, my love,' he said quietly, resting his dark face against her bright hair. 'We're safe, aren't we? Bringing up our family, working together in the business. The other Henzels – well, they know better than to try to do us now. And Jeremy will never come here again. You've nothing to worry about. Everything's right with us – and it's picnic day and your tea's getting cold!'

Christina laughed and pushed him away. 'Then what are you doing, keeping me chattering here? Pass me the cup, Joe.' She sipped the tea the maid had brought before she woke, and nibbled at the thinly sliced bread and butter that accompanied it. 'I suppose the children are in a fever of excitement. Though I'm still not sure we should allow Sarah to go. She's such a baby still and gets easily tired.'

'She's five years old and you can't leave her behind. And Emily will take care of her.'

'Emily is not a nursemaid, Joe. She's your daughter.'

'And must take her share of responsibility. I've told you before, Christina, I mean our children to grow up knowing they have to earn their place in the world. I had to and you had to. They're to be no different.'

'Of course not. But sometimes I feel that Emily . . .' Christina stopped. It was an old contention, and today was no time for drawing out old arguments. 'She's the eldest, of course, and the eldest often seem to assume more responsibility. I remember Alice when we were in the nursery –'

'Your sister loves convention, just like your Aunt Susan – and not like you!' Joe said with a twitch of his lips. 'And Emily is a natural gaffer, like her father. She *enjoys* being in charge, Christina. You might as well put her talents to good use – though we'll have to be careful that she doesn't begin to organise *us* when she's grown. One masterful woman in the family is enough.'

'And for that remark, Joe Compson, you will be sorry,' Christina warned. 'But not now – there's no time. The parade will be starting in less than two hours. I only hope that Jane keeps a close eye on the children when we're not with them.' She got out of bed, reaching for her wrap, and with their arms about each other's waists they strolled to the window, gazing down at the spreading streets, the packed houses and the smoking factories. There were times when you could barely see the village and its neighbours for the heavy pall of smoke that lay over them, a burning, sulphurous blanket that seeped through every crack and laid an encrustation of soot and grime on every surface. On days like those, the windows of Henzel Court were kept securely closed; in the small houses and crowded yards of the town, people were less able to keep the dirt at bay so that cleanliness was a quality as much restricted to the rich as was good food, drink and clothing.

But even in this heavily industrialised area of England the sky could sometimes be clear and bright, and it was impossible to feel gloomy for long. It was the day of the glassmakers' picnic – the day when employer and employee alike joined together to celebrate their craft. Today, differences would be forgotten and master and man would stand together.

'Come along now, Miss Emily – we'll miss the parade if you don't hurry yourself.' Jane's voice sounded sharp and excited above the hubbub of the nursery. 'Have you got Miss Sarah ready yet? Her best boots, mind, you know what your ma said.'

'Mamma said Sarah was too young to go to the picnic,' Roger observed. He had been ready for some time; Jane always said that you could trust Master Roger not to go and get himself dirty the minute her back was turned, so he was always washed and dressed first. He leaned nonchalantly against the door jamb now, watching the

5

preparations of the other children with a supercilious air, just as if he hadn't needed the help of a nurse to fasten boots and buttons. He looked like a bored gentleman of at least thirty, rather than a seven-year-old boy.

'Sarah's not too young,' Emily stated firmly. 'She can walk a long way for a girl of five and she'll like seeing the procession. And if she didn't come, Jane wouldn't be able to come and then *we* wouldn't be able to go, so –'

'Mamma would take me,' Roger said. 'She said so.'

'She meant us all,' Emily said.

'She meant just me.'

'Now then, stop your squabblin'.' Jane gave Paul's brown curls a last smooth with her hand and lined the children up to inspect them. 'Yes, you'll do. Now mind what I say, you're to keep all together by me an' don't go wanderin' off in the crowd. There's a lot of strangers come to these parades an' you don't want the gipsies to get you, now do you?'

The children shook their heads. Emily glanced at Paul. Gipsies! The idea of the wild, strange people her nurse and parents so often warned her about always filled her, not with fear, but with a strange excitement. They took little children away, it was whispered, and stained them brown with the juice of berries so that their white skin wouldn't betray them. What happened to them after that wasn't always clear, but she had once pressed Jane into an admission that the gipsies then sold the children they had stolen. Sold them! What for? But Jane had shaken her head and refused to say more. 'You wouldn't like it,' was all she would say, and with that Emily had to be content.

However, Emily had, by listening to every conversation she could and storing all the snippets of information she gained, built up a picture of gipsies as a wild, romantic people who lived in the open and travelled wherever they pleased, lighting fires on which to cook the rabbits and chickens they had killed as they roamed; singing songs and dancing by the leaping flames late into the night. . .

When she thought of being stolen by such people, of sharing their free existence, she was invariably tormented by a restless yearning that swelled inside her and made her want to stamp about the too-cosy nursery, pushing aside the cluttered furniture, and get out, away from the smoky air of Wordsley, away to the woods and fields where the sky was clear and the streams ran bright and grass was green rather than overlaid with a film of soot. She wanted to strip off the layers of heavy clothing she was forced to wear even in summer, to feel the ground warm under her bare feet . . .

However, this morning there were other things to think about. The glassmakers' parade and picnic was too important an event to be missed and she had no intention of being stolen at least until it was all over. And even then it might be inconvenient for Mamma and Papa, who would have to search for her, and for Jane who certainly needed her help in the nursery with the little ones. Emily often felt that the nursery would collapse without her presence.

The children trooped out of the nursery and down the stairs to where their parents were waiting. Emily led the way as usual, stopping at the curve of the stair to look down at them, and wondering yet again whether any other child in the world had such a handsome Papa or such a beautiful Mamma.

Christina and Joe stood in the hall, looking up.

'Don't they look sweet,' Christina said in a low voice. She laid her small hand on her husband's arm. 'I can hardly believe they're ours, Joe. You must admit, we've brought a fine family into the world.'

Joe glanced down at her, his dark eyes amused. 'Even though we didn't do it the usual way?' he asked, and she gave his arm a little shake.

'Don't tease, Joe! And don't say such things in front of them – little pitchers have long ears, and Emily's are sharper than most.'

Joe shook his head sombrely. 'They'll have to know someday, Christina. You can't keep such things hidden for ever. And there are plenty of others who'll remember. Anyway, this isn't the time to talk about that.

They're young yet and I agree there's no need to speak of it now.' He lifted his dark head and watched his family come down the stairs towards him. 'You're right, my love. They're fine children.'

Christina squeezed his arm. Her eyes, green and gold like those of a tiger in the night, were luminous in the dim light of the hall. Beside the massive figure of her husband, she looked small and fragile – yet all those who knew her were aware of the power she could command, and anyone who had felt the flash of anger from those tiger's eyes was careful to avoid it in the future. Only Joe had the power to subdue her, and he used that power rarely; as strong-minded as each other, they also held each other in respect and seldom tried to wield the power they possessed.

Although this didn't mean, Christina thought with a tremor of amusement, that life was ever dull. They had had their storms in the eight years of their marriage, as well as those which had gone before. But – the amusement was quickly replaced by an involuntary shiver of excitement – their quarrels were always resolved, and in the most satisfactory way imaginable. Neither she nor Joe subscribed to the fashionable view that ladies did not find pleasure in physical love.

The children had reached the foot of the stairs and stood before her: Emily, as dark as Joe, her body too sturdy and her face too square and strong for beauty, her brown eyes direct and challenging, confident of her place at the head of the nursery; Paul, slender and already taller than his sister although she was the elder, his hair curling and nut-brown, his eyes a silvery grey that could still bring a pang to Christina's heart whenever she looked into them; and the two younger ones, Roger and Sarah – Roger already showing the stubborn lift of Christina's chin, his eyes hazel, his hair tinged with red, and Sarah, like him yet still no more than a roly-poly, chuckling baby, certainly too young for such a long and tiring day as this yet impossible to leave behind since her enjoyment would enhance that of everyone else,

8

just as her pleasure brightened even the dullest day.

'Well, are you all ready for the picnic?' Christina asked, looking down at the scrubbed faces. 'They look very nice, Jane.'

The nursemaid bobbed. 'Thank you, madam.'

'Then we had better be going.' Christina felt in the waist pocket of her skirt and took out the little watch Joe had given her. 'The procession is almost due to begin.'

Emily felt a thrill of excitement as they turned to leave the house, waiting a few seconds for Christina to manoeuvre her skirt – one of the new crinolines, made especially for today – through the front door. Emily loved the crinoline; she had been present during the fittings her mother had had with the dressmaker and had watched with wide eyes as the hooped petticoat was fitted around the slender waist and the flounced silk of the skirt arranged over it. Her mother looked like a bell, she thought, her tiny figure like a carved handle above the swelling dome. And the tawny colours, the bronze that Christina loved because it matched her shining hair and lit up her glowing eyes, and the shimmering green, both on a chequered black background, were rich and commanding. Nobody would doubt that Christina was a figure of some importance in the district around Stourbridge.

Emily was glad that they didn't live in bustling Stourbridge itself, but in the outlying village of Wordsley, where most of the glassmakers had their premises. Henzel's, Emily thought proudly, was the most important of all those glasshouses. And it belonged to her mother. Her *mother*. Hadn't Papa said so himself, many times – that although in law a husband owned everything his wife had possessed, Henzel's glasshouse was, for some reason Emily didn't understand, her mother's. That was why it was still called Henzel's and not Compson's. And that was why – she supposed – their family was, in some strange way, different from any other family in Wordsley.

However, there was no time to bother with such things

now. It was more important to get herself and the other children into the carriage without crumpling Mamma's voluminous skirt; more important to get down to the glasshouse, where the procession was to begin, in good time. It wouldn't start without them of course, but they had to be there to see everything first, and then go ahead to find another good vantage point from which to watch the whole parade as their own men called at the various other glasshouses on the way and were joined by more and more glassmakers, some bearing the glittering products of their skill, others with silken banners that proclaimed the name of their employer, all marching in step behind the band that would play lustily all the way to Prestwood Park.

'There it is! The band – I can hear it.' Roger was hanging over the side of the carriage as it clattered down the drive. Beside him, Sarah bounced up and down in her seat, not really knowing what they were to see but prepared to enjoy it, whatever it was. Emily looked across at her parents, so upright in the other seat, and then at Paul who sat opposite her, close against his mother, half swamped by billowing silk. No, she didn't want to be stolen by gipsies. Not on a day like this, with her family so close together and so happily engaged. And certainly not without Paul.

The red-brick cones of the glasshouse were now towering above them, a thin spiral of smoke winding from their open tops into the blue July sky. Jake drew on the reins and the horses came to a halt. Emily and the others gazed about them.

They had been here often enough before. Both Joe and Christina came frequently to the three Henzel cones – indeed, Joe still sometimes took off his coat and blew glass himself, at the chair which he had worked for so many years before he had married Christina – and they believed that their children should see and understand every part of the process which brought them a living. Even little Sarah had been inside to gaze in awe at the sloping, soot-blackened walls and watch the men

10

working steadily in the glow of the furnace. And the older children – Emily, Paul and Roger – were quite accustomed to seeing the process of glassmaking take place before their eyes: the gathering of the red-hot molten 'metal' on long irons, the transformation of it by one man's breath into the graceful shape of a wineglass or jug, the careful shaping of stem and foot or handle as the glass cooled and the fire died out of it to leave it plain and clear. They had watched the cutting and engraving processes too, taking place in the long sheds their mother had built behind the cones, and seen the finished pieces, gleaming now as the light caught their heavily cut and patterned facets, packed in crates for transport to London or one of the other great cities, or even abroad to India, Australia, Russia and America.

Emily craned her neck eagerly. All the glassmakers were gathered here in the yard, jostling each other for position in the parade. Each one carried some glass object – friggers, made in their spare time from surplus metal, and what friggers they were! Not for today the little animals, birds and flip-flap toys that all glassmakers fashioned for amusement during baggin-time, or allowed the apprentices to make to develop their skills. Instead, the whole yard was glittering with an array of glass objects that had even Christina catching her breath. And when she and Joe had spoken to the men, congratulating them on their skills and wishing them all a happy holiday, and the band had struck up and the procession begun to move, the sight was almost too dazzling to behold.

'Oh, *look*, Paul! Look at the banner – it's so beautiful. Our own cones embroidered in scarlet, and the name *Henzel's* underneath.' Emily watched it go by, borne high by two of the tallest servitors, and exclaimed again with delight. 'And the inside of the cone on the other side! Who sewed it, do you suppose?' But Paul did not answer; he was already engrossed in gazing at the sparkling glass that was being carried by the rest of the procession and Emily fell silent and watched with equal fascination.

The first men to follow the banners carried trumpets of

glass. They marched proudly as if they were part of the band that went ahead, and as they passed the carriage they raised the trumpets to their lips and blew. The sound produced was almost lost in the general noise, and unlike any trumpet Emily had ever heard before, yet it had a strange purity that seemed to cut through to something deep inside her; a remote, lonely note that made her think of windswept moors and icy mountains. As she stared at them she felt her heart ache, but almost before she recognised the feeling, the trumpeters had passed and the sensation disappeared, and she was staring instead at a throng of jostling glass wands, held high in the air, their stems twisted and coloured with bands of the ruby and turquoise colours which Henzel's had been making since before Emily was born. Many of them had pennants tied to them, scraps of silk that were as richly embroidered as the banners, with the initial 'H' standing out proudly on each one.

There was almost too much to see now. Some of the glass was, Emily knew, brought out year after year for display on the day of the parade. Pieces like the great cut-glass crown and the orb and sceptre made to celebrate the coronation of Queen Victoria eighteen years earlier; the huge star which her own father had made when he was plain Joe Compson, working as a gaffer in the cone; the magnificent sailing ship made by her grandfather, Joshua Henzel, that stood in the hall at home and was brought down to the cone each year for this occasion and carried with reverential care on a crimson cushion.

Other pieces had been made more recently, and there was always great eagerness to see just what new creations the skill of Henzel's glassmakers had evolved. As well as the pieces made in any glasshouse – the walking sticks which were believed to attract disease and were kept at home and washed each morning to rid the house of whatever scourge might have entered overnight; the glass bellows; the long pipes which nobody dared light; and the axes with their twisted handles and shining blades – there were the new ideas: a glass barrel, filled with beer;

12

a basket heavily cut to look like wicker and filled with fruit; another shaped like a gardening trug, with the heads of flowers on thin stems drooping from its ends; a cage with glass birds inside; a flock of pearl-pink doves that seemed to shimmer freely through the air, carried on slender glass wands that were almost invisible beneath their rosy wings.

And last of all came the glass for which Henzel's was famous: the gleaming rock crystal, so brilliant that it seemed almost alive in the morning sunshine. Wine-glasses, decanters, jugs, goblets, all richly cut and engraved, set out on crimson cushions which were carried high by the men who had made them. In pride of place was the Compson Chalice itself – the great vessel blown by Joe Compson while he was still Christina's best gaffer and before there had ever been any thought of marriage between them. The Chalice had been the first piece of crystal made by Henzel's to the new recipe when the excise had been repealed in 1845, not long after Christina had inherited the family business; it had been intended as a showpiece, a symbol of what Henzel's – and Christina Henzel in particular – could do, and it shone as clear and brilliant as on the day it had been blown. Even at a distance the clarity of the engraving on its sides could be discerned; the exquisite delicacy of the portrayal of the Henzel cones on one side, the entwined initials C and J on the other. There was a story behind the engraving of those initials, Emily knew, but she had never been told it; it was one of those mysterious, grown-up things that she would 'understand when she was older'.

But she was old enough to know that this fine rock crystal was the glass which Henzel's took seriously, the glass which Emily had seen setting out on journeys that would take it all over the world; the glass which had been made here by Henzels since they had first come from France as exiles to set up home in a strange land and begin a tradition which had lasted ever since.

And yet – she laughed aloud as Paul nudged her and

pointed – even the gaffers who bore this glass so proudly carried their own friggers too, for each man wore a hat made of glass, top hats, sailors' hats, even soldiers' tricorns, that shone plain and unadorned, relying on nothing but shape and novelty for their attraction.

The procession passed and Emily drew a sigh and turned to her mother. But there was no time to speak; already Jake was urging the horses on to follow the procession on its way through Wordsley, gathering the men from the other glasshouses as they went, and everyone was eager to see the different displays – 'as much to steal their ideas as to admire them' Christina had observed once, but everyone understood this to be a joke, since only their rivals' own pride kept any design safe from copying once it had been put on general sale.

Riding through the streets in the open carriage was something the children always enjoyed, and never more so than on this day, when everyone came out to cheer the procession on its way. It was a holiday for almost all; the schools closed, shopkeepers came to their doors and servants crowded up from basements to watch the glittering parade, while those who could joined in and followed the lengthening crowd to the park. It was almost worth taking a day off work, some of them said; you got better food at the picnic than you ever did at home, and a full belly was something to consider, so long as you could earn enough the rest of the week to pay the rent. Not that the glassmakers were bothered by such things; with new pots, set in the furnaces the previous Friday, still getting up to heat and deliveries of new materials being made on Mondays, work never began until Tuesday. Glassmakers were an independent sort. They always had been different in their ways and took a pride now in keeping it that way.

By the time the procession reached the park it had been augmented by glassmakers from Brettell Lane, Audenham and even Brierley Hill, each house represented by its own silk banner and array of friggers. Emily gazed at them all, devouring their beauty and longing to possess each item she set her eyes upon. If she had a glasshouse of her own, like Mamma, she wouldn't bother with tableware; she would set all her men to making such entrancing objects as sailing ships, crowns, pipes and trumpets and baskets of flowers. People must want those more than an ordinary glass to drink from, she thought, and when she had enough for herself, then she would make them for sale.

The carriage turned into the park and came to a stop in a grassy corner, where the horses could graze and Jake hob-nob with the other drivers.

Emily was out of the carriage at once. 'Can we go and look at everything, Mamma? I want to see Ben. And Uncle Will. And Jane says there will be men making birds and ships with lamps, and I love to watch those.' Impeded as she was by layers of clothing, she was nevertheless hopping from one foot to another in her excitement. 'Please, Mamma, may we go?'

Christina looked down and laughed. She seemed younger than ever today, her skin glowing like that of a girl, the bright waves of her tawny hair already escaping from the hat she wore. She held out a small hand for Joe to help her down from the carriage, using the other to gather her skirts up out of the way of the wheels, and once on the ground she glanced about her as eagerly as Emily herself.

'Of course you may go, but mind you stay with Jane and help take care of the others. No wandering off alone or with Paul. There are far too many people about today.' She gave the little group an anxious glance. 'I don't know . . . Perhaps we had all better stay together. You may be too much for Jane. It's a great pity that Nurse is poorly today, especially with Ruth away too, she is always such a help . . .'

'Oh, please let's go with Jane.' Emily was in an agony of impatience now. 'I'll help her, truly I will, and so will Paul. You know you'll want to talk to people, Mamma, and we want to *see* things!'

Paul stepped forward, arrow-straight, eyes silver in

15

the sun. 'Don't fear, Mamma, I'll look after the girls and Roger will do as I say. You're always telling me to be the man of the family, after all!' He gave his mother a bright glance and she smiled back at him, her expression relaxing, and glanced at her husband.

'What do you say, Joe?'

Joe laughed. 'The child's right, Christina. You and I'll go far too slowly for these impatient folk. Let them go off with Jane, the maid will take good care of them and Paul's got a sensible head on his shoulders. But we can all go as far as Henzel's stalls together, if Emily wants to see our own men first, for that's where I'm heading. Now, stop jigging about like that, Emily, you make me fair tired to look at you, and Sarah, if you don't close your mouth the flies will walk in. Come up on my shoulder now, there's a brave girl, and you'll be able to see more than any of us.'

He swung the fat little girl up high and she squealed with delight. Emily watched a little jealously. Of course, she knew she was too big now to be carried on Papa's shoulder, but even when she was small she was sure he'd never carried her as often or as willingly as he did her sister. Nor had he taken her on his knee so much, or played with her in the same easy, affectionate way. It was almost as if there were some barrier between them that he could not surmount and she could not understand.

He thinks I'm ugly, she thought wistfully when she compared her square, dark sturdiness with Sarah's roundness and sunny smiles. And I am. I'll never be beautiful like Mamma, or pretty like Aunt Ruth. I'll always be ugly and nobody will ever really love me. Except Mamma, of course. And Paul.

As if he had read her thoughts, Paul came to stand close beside her and she felt his hand close warmly around hers. At once the day brightened again and she turned to give him the joyous smile which she never saw in a mirror and so never knew transformed her face. Already Joe was striding away from them, with Sarah perched high on his shoulder and Christina swaying gracefully at his side.

'Come on, Emily,' Paul said, still clasping her hand as

he urged her to keep up. 'We'll miss everything if you don't hurry. Henzel's stalls are just over there, see – and Papa's stopping to talk to someone already!'

The park had been changed overnight into a vast fairground, with sideshows and donkeys to ride as well as a number of stalls selling hot pies, soup, tea and coffee and a variety of confectionery: toffee, humbugs, gingerbread, Bath buns, finger-biscuits, cheese-cakes – the list seemed almost endless to Emily and she clutched at the little bead purse in her pocket, wondering what to buy with the pennies she had been given.

But first, there was the glass which was the whole purpose of this delightful day. And here they were at the stalls which had been set up and laid out by Henzel's glassmakers – the men who worked for Christina and Joe in the three great cones at the foot of Dob Hill. And already Emily's dark eyes were searching for Ben.

'There he is!' Forgetting her instructions to help take care of the younger children, she pushed through the crowd already collecting around the stall and waved her arm to attract his attention. 'Ben! Ben! It's me, it's me. Show me what you made.'

The tall, thin youth behind the stall turned and saw her, his rather grave face relaxing into a smile at the sight of her eager expression. Ben was in the last year of his apprenticeship and a favourite of Emily, who knew all the glassmakers in Henzel's cones. And Ben was special. He lived with her grandmother, Sal Compson, in the terraced house Joe had grown up in, and was therefore almost a part of the family. He had lived there for some eight years now, in fact – ever since he had come to work in the glasshouse as a twelve-year-old boy. Where he had lived before that, Emily did not know and had only lately begun to wonder about. Someday, she meant to ask him. But there was no time for that now, with so many excitements all about her.

She waited eagerly as he bent and lifted something from the boxes that were strewn about the ground and which held a clutter of glass ornaments. Friggers were a

17

bonus for the men; anything they had been able to make, provided it was not too large, could be sold today and the proceeds put into their own pockets.

All the same, he could spare the frigger which he had fashioned especially for the dark-haired child who hopped so excitedly in front of him now. Emily watched as he unwrapped it carefully, dropping the paper on the ground as the shining glass was revealed. Quite plain, but delicately shaped and even cut a little to give it a more lifelike form. He handed it across the crowded stall and Emily reached out both hands, her eyes shining like the glass itself in her delight.

'An elephant! Oh, Ben . . .' She gazed enraptured at the chubby animal, laughing at the comical expression on the wrinkled forehead, stroking the curving trunk with the tip of one finger. 'He's lovely. *Thank* you. I'll keep him always.' Her eyes darted about the stall. 'What else did you make?'

'The ship. The bird of paradise, with the long tail.' He touched them briefly and Emily admired the delicate structure of the tiny ship, its shimmering sails billowing as if hoisted before a strong gale, and exclaimed with pleasure at the flowing tail of the bird of paradise. 'The swan, and the pipe. And the ponies and pigs and lambs.' He waved his hand over the group of glass figures which he hoped to sell. There was little enough, really. Apprentices weren't allowed much metal for making friggers, nor did they have the time. But Emily was delighted by it all and would have stayed longer, asking questions and admiring. But before she could speak again, Jane had her by the arm. 'Come along now, Miss Emily. You can see Ben's busy an' he needs to sell his work – you don't want him to lose money through your chatter, do you? An' there's all the other stalls to look at too.'

'Yes, come on, Em. I want to see the lamp-blowers.' Roger, never content to wait for others, was already looking bored. He tugged at Emily's arm, urging her towards a nearby stall where there stood a magnificent glass fountain, nearly a foot high, its central column almost hidden by the spray of thin strands of glass that shimmered like the water they represented, curving gracefully out and over as if flung in droplets into the clear air. Around it stood an array of different pieces – birds, flowers, animals, people, all in different hues – and behind these sat a man dressed in a colourful striped jacket, blowing more figures from tubes of glass with the aid of a lamp-flame.

'It's Mr Davis and Mr Johnson,' Jane whispered to the children. 'They're famous – my sister May saw them in Nottingham at the goose fair. They say they're the only glass ship-builders travellin' the country – look.' She pointed at the glass sailing ship beside the fountain and Emily heard the two boys draw in their breath.

'Oh, I *want* it,' Roger said yearningly. 'Look at the rigging – and there are *men* in it, see? Jane, how much would it cost? Have we enough money? Do you think Mamma or Papa –'

'No!' Emily glowered at the beautiful object. 'It's no better than the one Grandfather made, that stands in our hall. *None* of their glass is any better than ours. Henzel's glass is the best in the world, and don't you ever forget that, Roger. And Henzels don't buy other people's glass.'

Roger gave her a mutinous look. 'I don't see why not. If I want it –'

'You *don't* want it,' Emily stated. 'You're a Henzel, just like me. And *I* don't want it because I don't ever want anything that's not Henzel's. So nor do you!'

There was a short pause, while she and Roger glared at one another. And then both were startled by a peal of raucous laughter from somewhere behind them, somewhere close. Emily whipped round, her face already flushed with anger.

Staring down at them were two women. They were half leaning on each other, their own faces reddened from a different cause, and they were the kind of women the Compson children recognised as coming from the poorer parts of the town, the parts that made their mother look sad and their father grim. Their clothes were ragged and dirty, their hair long and unkempt. Their faces were grey beneath the grime that few poor people could afford to wash away, but their eyes were bright and insolent and their expressions lively with scorn.

'Did you hear that, Moll?' one exclaimed in a screaming voice that set Emily's teeth on edge. 'Henzels, she says! An' proud of it, too, for all the world as if it were true. When all the time she's nothing more than a –'

'Stop that!' Jane stepped forward quickly. 'Get off out of here an' leave the children alone. They're naught to do with you.'

'Naught, indeed? That's all you know, Miss Nursemaid.' The woman cackled and Emily shivered. There was something in the voice, in the staring eyes, that gave her a feeling of dread. 'Why, I knew all about this wench afore she were even birthed. I know more about her than any of you. Yes –' she raised her voice, attracting the attention of several of the people around the stall '– I know all about young Emily Haden, more than her own father if truth were told. But truth never is, is it? An' everyone's forgot poor Maggie now.'

'What's she talking about?' Emily demanded. She shook off Paul's restraining hand and thrust herself forward. 'What do you mean? Are you talking about me? Because I'm Emily *Compson*, and my father knows all about me, and I've never heard of this Maggie you speak of.'

'Emily *Compson*, is it?' the woman shrilled, and gave another cackle. 'Oh, my dear, my dearie me!' She affected to lean on her friend for support and wiped her eyes. 'Emily *Compson*, if you'll believe it!'

Emily stared at her, frightened by the ugliness and venom in the grating voice, but before she could speak again Paul had pushed in front of her. His hand was gentle as he set her aside but she could feel the anger quivering through his fingertips and she saw that his eyes were blazing with an anger that was as cold as ice.

20

'How dare you speak like that to my sister?' he demanded, his young voice rapier-sharp. 'Tell me what you mean by it.' He stepped right up to the dishevelled pair and faced them, head flung back and eyes raking them with scorn. 'This is my sister, Emily Compson – how could she be called Haden? We have no kin of that name, nor would it be any business of yours if we had.' He took in the women's dishevelled condition and contempt touched his lips as he added: 'You are here simply to cause mischief and you'd better go at once before I call my father to deal with you. And my father is Joseph Compson,' he said proudly, 'and I don't believe you'd be willing to repeat your lies to him, so take them with you.'

'Lies, is it?' the woman shrieked, but Paul stood his ground.

'Yes, lies, for there's nothing a woman like you would know about us, and I don't suppose you even know what you mean yourself.'

'Oh, I know, all right. Never you fret about that. I know.' The woman's eyes shifted over the little group, and Emily shrank back against Jane, who was vainly trying to push a way out of the crowd which had gathered in the hope of seeing some fun. 'Just you ask your dad when you get home, ask him about Annie that used to be mates with his Mag. Aye, an' ask him about Maggie too while you're at it – Maggie Haden, just in case he can't call her to mind no more now that he's gentry. Ask him where your precious sister was the first two years she were alive an' see if he'll tell you where she really come from.' She laughed shortly, the sound bitter and unpleasant. 'Aye, an' ask him about yourself too, while you're at it –' She fixed him with a stare that was almost evil. 'Joe Compson's son! Brother and sister! Bastards, both of you – bastards! An' poor Maggie allowed to die in her own filth while Christina Henzel carried on with Frenchies an' got away with it. Compsons an' Henzels!' she ended bitterly. 'I wouldn't even *want* to claim kin with they!'

21

Her impassioned words had caused the crowd to fall silent; even Jane was transfixed, her face white with horror, unable to prevent the tirade. But when Annie panted into silence, everyone seemed to move at once. The children, bewildered and already half in tears, turned to their nursemaid for protection and at the same moment she came to life and pushed furiously through the knot of people. And from the neighbouring stall, where the Henzel's workmen had been listening with equal dismay, came Ben, an avenger, his lanky legs propelling his body swiftly into the throng, his long arms swinging to catch Annie and Moll by their scruffy necks and hurry them away. For a few moments, all was confusion; the struggling bodies pushed against the stall which threatened to overturn, and above the tinkling of breaking glass the agonised voices of Mr Davis and Mr Johnson could be heard screaming for care. Emily felt herself caught up, swept almost off her feet in the mêlée; she looked round desperately for Paul, terrified that he had been knocked to the ground and trampled, and then for little Sarah. To Roger, she gave barely a thought – Roger invariably emerged unscathed from almost any escapade. And then, to her relief, she saw above the heads of the people about her the massive figure of her father bearing down upon the confusion, and heard his great voice bellowing above all the noise – and the crowd, hearing it too, fell quiet and stood still as he came amongst them.

'What in Hell's name is going on here?' Joe Compson roared. 'Are those my children in the middle of that shambles? Jane, what's to do? Emily, take hold of young Sarah's hand and bring her to me. Paul, look to Roger.' He waited until his family, somewhat the worse for wear, was gathered around him. 'Right, now get away from here. I'll hear more about it later. Was it young Ben I saw going off with two women? Were they aught to do with this?'

'They started it, Papa,' Emily cried. 'They were talking to us – saying they knew things about us that no one else did. They said I was no Henzel and Paul wasn't my brother, and we should ask you about it. They called us –' her brow wrinkled ' – they called us *bastards*, Papa. What does that mean? What is a *bastard*? Is it something bad?'

She waited anxiously for his answer. But Joe did not speak. He stared down at her, his face as white now as Jane's. And then Emily saw Christina appear behind him, and her face was white also. And she knew that to be a bastard was very bad indeed. And that somehow, without even knowing it, both she and Paul had committed this terrible sin, and must spend the rest of their lives in atonement.

# Chapter Two

*Bastards*. The word rang through Emily's head all the way home from the park. She and Paul were bastards, that was clear enough. But what did it mean? Why would nobody tell her? And why was Jane looking so frightened, and her parents so angry and upset?

What was so dreadful about being a bastard? It must make her different in some way, yet she had never felt different. And Paul looked just the same as ever, only disturbed and worried just as she was herself. She looked at Roger. *He* wasn't one, apparently. What was so different about him? She couldn't see anything. Except the look in his eyes: curious, avid, hopeful that she was about to be accused of some misdemeanour and punished for it. And that was just Roger being Roger. Sometimes, Emily thought bitterly, he was a very mean little boy.

She hoped very much that Mamma and Papa intended to tell her what it all meant as soon as they reached home. Otherwise, why should they have to leave the picnic so early, almost as soon as they had arrived in fact, and before seeing any of the main displays in the big marquees, or the children's races, or even the picnic itself? She stole another glance at her parents' faces and began to feel frightened. Were she and Paul to be punished for this dreadful thing they had done, whatever it was – for being *bastards*? Perhaps Mamma and Papa hadn't even known about it themselves until today and were now taking them home to beat them, or to thrust them into a cupboard in the dark with nothing to eat or drink for hours. These terrible things had never happened to either her or Paul, but she had read about them in stories and knew that they did happen to very bad children. And she and Paul must have been very bad indeed.

If only she *knew* what it was they had done . . .

Tentatively, her hand crept out and found Paul's. She wound her fingers about his and felt his reassuring squeeze.

'Oh, Paul,' she whispered, darting little glances at her parents in case even this was wrong, 'what's going to happen to us? Will we be locked up? Is Papa going to beat us? Will we –' the thought slid suddenly into her mind and now it had lost its thrill and become menacing, something to send cold fear trickling down her spine ' – will we be given away to gipsies?'

'Gipsies? Never!' His fingers were warm around hers. 'Whatever made you think that?'

'I don't know. It was what that – that person said, about us not being Compsons at all. What can she have meant? And Papa looks so angry and Mamma so upset. And it's all our fault, I know, but why? What have we done?' She remembered Annie's venomous look and shivered. 'It must be something very bad.'

Paul's clasp tightened and he too sent a swift glance in their parents' direction. But both were gazing out over the road, almost as if they were too ashamed – or too disgusted – to meet the children's eyes. 'It isn't anything we've done,' he said seriously. 'And I'm sure Mamma and Papa aren't angry with *us*. What that woman said can't have been true – she knows nothing about us.' But his voice wavered very slightly and Emily glanced at him with fresh alarm. 'Anyway,' he went on more stoutly, and the warmth flowed from his hand to hers as if he were giving her his own strength, his own sure confidence, 'you don't have to worry, Emily. I shall look after you.'

And Emily felt comforted; even though it felt strange, for usually it was the other way about.

'I knew it!' Christina paced the floor of her bedroom, her hands clasped in front her. She twisted her fingers together and lifted her huge eyes, their green depths swimming with tears, to Joe. 'I knew it would happen

26

one day. Those poor children, Joe! We should never have let them go to the picnic.'

'Christina, be sensible. We couldn't shelter them for ever. We knew they'd have to be told sometime.' He sighed, his dark brows gathered together. 'I only wish we'd told them before, so that they needn't have found out this way. That Annie! I could kill her – she did it just for spite, you know, spite and from being the worse for drink.'

'If it hadn't been her, it would have been someone else.' Christina crossed to the window and stared down at the massed factories and foundries below. It was a sight that had rarely failed to bring her satisfaction, but it failed her now. Of what use were all these businesses, all these flourishing manufactures, when her family was in turmoil? 'And we still have to decide what to say to them now, Joe. How can we explain it? They're both so young – how can they possibly understand? And Roger – he's barely eight years old but as sharp as a needle. Already he's asking the most embarrassing questions. What are we to tell *him*? Oh –' she covered her face with her hands ' – it's too bad! Just when I supposed that our little family was so comfortable together.'

Joe moved to stand beside her. He took her in his arms and she rested against the breadth of his chest. He was like a rock to lean on and for a moment she felt that everything must come right, simply because Joe was here. But hadn't he assured her, only this morning, that nothing could go wrong for them? She shook her head and straightened up, lifting her eyes to his face.

'Christina, my love,' Joe said quietly, 'this isn't like you. Haven't you always stood by your own actions, no matter what others may think? Didn't you determine to keep Paul when he was born, knowing that everyone in Stourbridge knew what he was? And Emily – did you think of this when you brought her home? And would it have made any difference if you had?'

Christina shook her head. 'I didn't think of it, Joe. I

thought only of her, with no one to care for her and living in that terrible place. I didn't think at all – I simply knew that I had to bring her home, that her place was here with us. And Paul – I could not abandon him. He's my son.'

'And wouldn't you do the same again?' he asked, and she nodded. 'Then why are you worrying so? You're not ashamed of the truth and neither am I. I know I wasn't best pleased about Emily, but that was naught to do with what you did, or who she was. It was Maggie, and she's dead now, and I've had time to feel sorry for the way she ended. No, Christina, we've brought our family into the world for better or worse and we stand by them; that's understood. And we've always agreed that it's better they should know the truth one day, though it's a shame they should have learned this way.'

'And on such a happy day, too,' Christina said sadly. 'Joe . . . how much must we tell them?'

'As much as they ask and as little as we can,' he answered. 'Just that they have different fathers and different mothers, and then let them think it out for themselves as they grow. They're young yet, Christina; they'll soon forget this day and come to accept that our family is different from others. And they have a father and a mother now, they have a home and a brother and sister. It won't be so very bad.' He lifted her chin and smiled. 'You've never been one to concern yourself with what others may think, Christina. Don't tell me you're going to start now.'

'Bastards! Bastards! Emily and Paul are bastards!'

Roger capered around the nursery, waving his hat in the air, while little Sarah watched, wide-eyed, her thumb in her mouth and Emily and Paul stood close together just inside the door.

Jane turned from the press where she had been folding their clothes and made a rush for the excited boy. She grabbed him by the arm and shook him roughly. 'Don't you dare say that, Master Roger! Don't you dare use that word – it's a bad word, that is, not for little boys to use, an' I don't want to hear it again in this nursery, do you hear me? Or I'll be straight down them stairs an' tellin' your ma and pa.'

She finished with a cuff and thrust Roger from her so that he staggered, one hand holding his head, and set up a wail that was as much indignation as pain.

'But it's true! The lady said so. Emily and Paul *are* –' he caught Jane's eye ' – what she said. Anyway, I don't believe it's a bad word; I've never heard Jake or Edward say it.'

'Jake and Edward know better,' Jane said grimly. 'Now, Miss Emily, don't stand there like a stuffed duck, take off your coat an' help Sarah with her boots. There's still plenty to be done, even if we did have to come home early from the picnic.' She stopped, biting her lip.

Emily came forward slowly and knelt to unbutton Sarah's boots.

'Isn't it true, then? Aren't Paul and I – what the lady said? Bas – bast –' She stumbled over the word, afraid to speak it aloud, but she had to know. 'Bastards?'

'Don't say it again!' Jane cried, agonised. 'Oh, that dreadful woman! I wish Nurse was here – she'd know how to manage this. Sayin' such things to children! Look, Miss Emily, let's get out the dissected pictures or the spills an' have a nice game an' forget all this. That's the best thing.'

'But *are* we?' Emily persisted, and now Paul came forward too, his pale face grave, his eyes the dark, smoky grey they always went when he was disturbed. 'Are we?' they asked, and almost involuntarily their hands reached out for each other and clasped as they stood gazing anxiously at the young nursemaid, drawing together as if in facing her they were facing the entire world.

Jane shook her head helplessly. The situation was totally beyond her, and she had no idea what she should do. 'I'm not sayin' another word about it,' she said firmly at last, taking refuge in one of Nurse's own ploys.

29

'An' the next one that does will be in bed afore they can blink, an' no cake for tea. An' that goes for you as well, Master Roger. There's nothin' clever about shoutin' bad words around the nursery, an' if your ma and pa were to hear you they'd –' She was interrupted by the arrival of the parlour maid. 'Oh, hello, Rose.'

Rose looked down her nose. She didn't approve of such familiarity from the little nursemaid, but she could see that there had been 'words' in the nursery and already had a hazy idea as to what they might be about; news travelled fast around Wordsley and there were already rumours in the kitchen. 'Master Paul and Miss Emily are wanted downstairs,' she said coolly. 'Their ma and pa want to talk to them. You're to send them straight down, Jane – no need to tidy them up. At least, that's what they said,' she added, looking disdainfully at Emily's tear-streaked face and Paul's untidy hair. 'If it was me –'

'All right, I'll see to it.' Jane had had almost enough and wasn't, for once, inclined to knuckle under to the haughty Rose. 'Come here, Emily, an' let's wipe your face.' She produced a flannel from the wash-stand and rubbed it hard over Emily's cheeks. 'An' you, Master Paul. My goodness, you're both all over dust – let's give you a brush down. That's better. Now, go down with Rose an' mind you're both good, sensible children – no bad words, you understand? Your ma an' pa don't want to hear such language coming from you, so mind what I say.'

The two children followed Rose from the room and Jane sighed, and then turned to her other charges. 'All right, you two, you can stop starin'. Master Roger, you can read that nice book your Uncle Harry brought you last week. An' Miss Sarah, come here – let's finish gettin' your boots unbuttoned. We might as well pretend every-thin's all right; at least until we know different.'

In the drawing room, Paul and Emily were facing their parents. They were still keeping instinctively close together, still holding hands. Their eyes were wide and anxious: Emily's dark brown like Joe's, Paul's that pewter grey that could, when he was happy, lighten to pure silver.

Joe and Christina stood together in the middle of the room. For a moment, during the brief period of silence before Rose withdrew and closed the door, the two couples looked oddly alike in their stance, the parents appearing to draw together for strength and comfort as much as the children. But Emily, sensing this, found it even more disturbing for it seemed to leave her and Paul isolated, set apart on the far side of a barrier she couldn't begin to understand. The cold fear, begun when she looked up into her parents' faces in the park, grew until it was a heavy stone lying uncomfortably across her chest.

'Joe . . .?' Christina said uncertainly, and Joe Compson stepped forward.

'Let's all sit down, shall we? We can't talk standing up.' He held out both his hands and the children went towards him. With Christina beside them, they moved over to the big stuffed sofa and arranged themselves on it, Christina in the middle with Paul beside her and Joe at one end, taking Emily on his knee.

'There, now, that's better.' He stroked Emily's arm and she wondered why she didn't feel more contented; wasn't it only this morning that she had wished he would do this more often? But now it was different; she felt stiff and awkward, perched here, and she was unable to relax against him as she longed to do. Perhaps it was because she was a bastard, she thought miserably, and wondered if anything would ever be right again.

'Your mother and I have something to tell you,' Joe went on, and Emily's eyes went to Christina. But her eyes were downcast, refusing to meet Emily's pleading gaze; as if Christina herself were ashamed – or Emily too wicked to be acknowledged.

'Papa . . .' she began, but Joe hushed her.

'Quiet, my love. It's not an easy story to tell, and it's not easy for such small folk to understand – though you're not so small as all that, after all. Paul here is nearly as big as I was when I went to work in the foundry, and there are plenty of girls no larger than Emily scrubbing out kitchens or making nails.' He stopped suddenly as Christina's head jerked up, and to her astonishment Emily saw a deep flush spread up his neck and over his face. 'Well, no matter,' he said hastily. 'We're not talking of them but of you. Both of you. Now tell me, what did you understand by what that woman shouted at you in the park today?'

Emily glanced at Paul, who was sitting between his parents and staring at his feet. She wished that she could still hold his hand, still take comfort in that wordless communication between them. He seemed to have gone somewhere else, to some place where she could not reach him. Then he looked up and met her eyes briefly before turning his own gaze on Joe.

'I know what bastard means,' he said clearly, and the word was like a gunshot in the quiet room. 'It means someone who hasn't got a father. But she's wrong, isn't she? We *have* got a father.'

Emily stared at him. Someone who had no father? But that was nonsense! And yet, if it were, why did her mother hide her face in her hands as Paul spoke? Why was her father looking so grave?

'I don't understand,' she said, and her voice was frightened. 'Amy hasn't got a father. He was killed in the war. But nobody calls her a bas –'

'All right, Emily, you needn't say it again. We all know what the word is.' Joe spoke firmly. 'It doesn't mean quite that. It means – well, it means someone who was born with no father. Someone whose mother wasn't wed. Now do you understand?'

Christina spoke then, her voice dry and colourless as if she had been weeping for a very long time. 'Of course they don't understand, Joe. There is so much more to know before you can understand that.' She looked up at Emily for the first time. 'You cannot understand this yet, Emily, but you will have to believe what we say, and believe that we only tell you now because you cannot be hurt by thoughtless or cruel people if you know the truth.

32

And I am afraid there are always such people in the world, even when we least expect them.' She paused and drew a long, difficult breath. 'Emily, your mother was not married to your father. And Paul, your mother and father were not married either. Those are the plain facts. They make no difference to the kind of people you are. You are Emily and Paul and you are part of our family, and you will grow up to be as good and as worthwhile as anyone else. Never forget that.' She lifted her head proudly and her eyes began to flash with some of their old fire. 'What happened before you were born has no effect on who you are now. I honestly believe that and I want you to believe it too. Will you promise me that?'

Wordlessly, the two children nodded. Then Emily's face clouded and her brows drew together. 'Then are you not our mamma and papa? Don't we belong here?' Her voice rose shrilly. 'I won't believe it! It's not true! You *are* my mamma and papa, you are! Look – look at me – everybody says how like Papa I am – I can see it in the mirror.' Frantic now, she twisted and turned on his knee, beating his chest with her fists. 'Tell me you're my papa, tell me,' she screamed, gripping the lapels of his waistcoat with both hands. 'I won't be anyone else's, I won't!'

'Emily, Emily, quietly now, quietly.' With a gentleness that sat oddly in his large frame, Joe calmed the panic-stricken child, his huge hands moving tenderly over her shaking shoulders until she collapsed in a quivering heap against him. 'There now, don't be afraid. Of course I'm your papa. Your mother didn't mean that.' He stopped, a look of confusion on his face. 'At least . . . Listen to me, both of you. You both belong here. You're both part of our family. But between you and the two little ones there are . . . differences.' He sighed and rubbed a hand over his face, then held Emily a little away from him, gazing intently into her eyes. 'Are you listening to me, Emily? Do you understand?' He waited until she nodded her head and then turned to Paul, who nodded too. 'This is the truth, and you don't need to know any more than this, for the time being at least. Paul –' He paused, as if the words were difficult to say ' – I am not your real father. Your father was another man; a man who lived here for a time before you were born. And Emily –' again the pause, while she stared at him with wide eyes and thumping heart ' – I am your papa but your mother was . . . someone else. Someone I knew many years ago, before I married your mamma.' He waited for a moment and then added with a quiet force that struck both the children to their souls: 'And it makes no difference; no difference to any of us. You are all our children, our family, with nothing to set any of you apart, and you must think of us, as you always have, as your mamma and papa. Do you understand this? Do you want me to say it again?'

Slowly, Emily shook her head. The facts were confusing but she could grasp them. She looked at her father, and knew that nothing had changed; she looked at the woman she had always believed to be her mother, and knew that everything had.

'And Roger and Sarah?' she asked. 'Do they belong to someone else too?'

'No. They were both born after your mother and I were married, and they both belong to us. As you do too,' he added hastily, but it was almost too late.

Emily gave him a direct glance; it was as if she were turning away already from her childhood, when fairytales could be spun and believed because it was pleasurable to believe them. She was entering the world of the adult, the world of reality; where nothing was what it seemed and strangers must tread warily. And there was another thought, too, struggling to take shape. It formed at last and her glance sharpened.

'So Paul isn't your boy,' she said slowly. 'And I'm not Mamma's girl. And that means –'

'You are as much our boy and girl as ever,' Christina interrupted, as if to prevent the thought being given expression; as if by so denying it, it would cease to exist. 'Nothing is any different, Emily, you must believe that.

34

We love you both as much as Roger and Sarah. We –'

'That means,' Emily continued, ignoring the interruption, 'that Paul isn't really my brother. And I'm not his sister. We're not related at all. Are we?'

Joe and Christina looked at each other. Their eyes communicated: Christina's questioning; Joe's resigned. We have to tell them the truth, his glance said; there can be no more lies. And Christina bowed her head in acceptance.

'No, Emily,' she said quietly. 'You are not related.'

'You mean you told them? Everything?' Susan Henzel's face paled, only two red spots burning high on her papery cheeks. 'Christina, are you mad? Those poor children – Emily barely ten years old, Paul only nine – how could they be expected to understand such things? How could you?'

'I know, I know.' Christina spoke wearily. How often, she thought ruefully, had she had similar confrontations with her aunt? When she had announced her intention of running the glasshouse herself; when she allowed Joseph Compson, a common workman, to come calling on her in the evenings; when she had brought Jean-Paul over from France to help her set up the new engraving shops; and when she had refused to marry her cousin Jeremy. Each one punctuated by her aunt's raised hands and horrified voice, repeating always the same words: '*Christina, how could you?*'

'I agree with every word you say, Aunt Susan,' she said now, thinking that this in itself was unusual. 'I did not want the children to know the truth – at least, not so soon. But it was quite unavoidable. That dreadful woman Annie – a friend of Maggie Haden's, apparently. Drunk, of course, and only too delighted to humiliate Joseph and myself, and to hurt the children. And when so much had been said, what could we do but tell them? We have told them only what is necessary. No doubt we shall have to tell them more as they grow older,' she added with a sigh. 'And you may be sure,

Aunt, that I wish as heartily as you that it should not be so. But no one can undo the past.'

'No, indeed.' Susan's face took on a sad expression. She had found long ago that nobody could learn by anyone else's mistakes – and the wildfire spirit of Christina Henzel, least of all. Christina had gone her own stubborn way, flouting all convention, determined to take what she considered her own regardless of all consequences. Consequences which were with them still.

'Poor Emily,' Christina said now. 'And Paul. They have a great deal to overcome. But I can't be sorry, Aunt Susan; I can't regret any of it. Would any of us wish that they had never existed – would *you*? Can you honestly say that you would rather I had gone to Italy and borne my son in secret, instead of having him here where everyone would know him for mine? Can you really tell me that I should have left Emily to starve and die of disease as her mother did, in that hovel built of mud?' She shook her head. 'I know there have been those who shunned us because of what I have done; but were they truly our friends? And those who love us behave now as if there were never anything amiss. Even Joe has been accepted. And why not? Weren't our own forefathers working glassmakers, just as he was? Is there really shame in using one's hands to make a living – especially when you are creating something both beautiful and useful?'

Susan Henzel shook her head. 'I don't know, Christina. I seem to know so little these days. So much has changed . . . There is Harry, leaving the glass business altogether and becoming an engineer. And marrying Ruth – nothing but a serving girl! I know she became your friend and companion, Christina, and I know she is Joseph's sister, but all the same! And Samuel and Harold, they visit so little these days. They are still offended over the glasshouse, you know, and I believe Alfred is too, we hear so little from Newcastle now. And Jeremy.' She stopped and her mouth worked a little. 'I still miss Jeremy. What happened, Christina? Why did you quarrel so badly that he never comes? Couldn't you possibly make it up?'

Christina sighed. She had never told her aunt the truth about Jeremy and the attack he had made on her when she had confronted him with her knowledge about Jean-Paul's death. She shuddered still to think of what would surely have happened if Joe had not come in at that moment, to find them, clothes torn half away, rolling furiously together on the floor. But Jeremy had been no match for Joe, either in strength or in fury, and Christina had watched him being thrown unceremoniously from the front door and known that he would never come into Henzel Court again.

'I can't tell you what happened, Aunt Susan,' she said gently. 'But I can't allow Jeremy here again, ever. I'm sorry you miss him, but I can only say that he is not the man you believed him to be.'

'Well, I don't understand it,' Susan grumbled. 'I met him the other day, at your Aunt Lavinia's At Home, and he was most pleasant and delightful, asking after you and the children just as he always does. And he has never married, you know. I believe he still feels in his heart that he was the one who was really meant for you.'

Christina's compassion gave way to exasperation – a condition all too frequent when conversing with her aunt. 'Please don't say such things!' she said sharply. 'You know perfectly well that Joe and I are happily married, a good deal more happily than many other people I am acquainted with. Now: we are to hold a dinner party next week, and I wanted to discuss the menu with you. That new dish Mrs Jenner prepared on Sunday was very good, I thought; it would be ideal for a small dinner party. And one of her special puddings, perhaps with a cream sauce . . .'

Ben left the park with money in his pocket and heaviness in his heart. It had been a good day, as far as the glass-makers were concerned. The sun had shone, there had been plenty of people from Stourbridge itself and its outlying districts, and the glassware had been admired and exclaimed over by people who rarely saw the

37

sparkling beauty that was fashioned on their doorstep, knowing only that it was made in the tall, sooty cones, cut and engraved in the long workshops and then packed away to be sent to the far corners of the earth. Some of them had bought the friggers: young lads had given them to their sweethearts; older men to their wives. The stalls set out that morning were empty now. With the other men, Ben cleared away the scattered debris and counted his takings before setting off for home.

The money was welcome enough. Ben's wage of five shillings a week was barely enough to live on, and he would have found life hard indeed if Christina Compson had not arranged for him to board with Mr Compson's mother Sal, who had firmly refused to move to Henzel Court, even after the death of her husband William, and stayed in the little terraced house to make a home for her younger son. Will Compson was only a few years older than Ben, his own apprenticeship completed and now working as a servitor. The two lads got on well together, working turn and turn about during the week and spending their weekends in common pursuits: tending Will's pigeons and taking long walks into the countryside with Ben's whippet at their heels, to let them loose to fly home. The ability of pigeons to find their way back from anywhere they were released never failed to fascinate the two young men.

Ben had been living at Sal's and working in the Henzel cones for so long now he had almost forgotten the life he had led before Christina Compson had brought him to Wordsley. But those early years had burned too deeply into his soul ever to be truly eradicated, and every now and then he would find himself thinking again of a childhood spent in cold, grinding poverty; of bitter winter nights passed huddled in the doorway of a mud house, or curled in some waterlogged ditch; of hot summer days when his nakedness had gone unremarked as he ran the dusty tracks searching for broken glass to be sold for cullet, nails dropped by hurrying nailmakers, anything which might earn him a farthing or two for bread and a cup of water. If it had not been for old Em, who had taken in Maggie Haden and had thrown him scraps as a wealthy woman might toss food to a straying dog, he must surely have died, as so many motherless, homeless children died. But somehow he had survived, along with a few other ragamuffins; survived to run the errand to Christina Compson that had changed his life.

His thoughts came back to the present and his face lit up. For, coming towards him, her skirts rustling against the long grass, was Florrie, her dark curls tossing in the breeze that had sprung up to cool the heat of the afternoon.

'So there you be!' Brown eyes glowed in the rosy cheeks, and a small, work-roughened hand smoothed the cotton print uniform the girl wore. 'I couldn't get off afore – Cook was that grumpy today, because the master had people to luncheon an' none of us could get out to see the parade.' Florrie worked as kitchen maid in one of the big houses on the road that led out of Stourbridge towards Bridgnorth. Her family lived in the wooded country near Kinver and she went home to see them on every holiday she had and, in spite of her indoor life, still managed to retain the healthy bloom of a girl reared away from the smoke of the town. 'What was it like? Did you sell plenty?'

'Everything I made,' Ben said, and grinned at her pouting face. 'But I saved you a piece, special, Florrie. Here it is, look.' He felt in his pocket and brought out a tiny fat bird made of glass. 'It's a wren, see?'

Florrie took the tiny scrap and held it cupped in her hands, as tenderly as if it were real. 'Oh, Ben, it's lovely. Look at the dear little beak an' that tail, stuck up behind.' She squeezed his arm. 'I'll put it on my washstand. It'll look nice there, with the shell our Jacky brought back from the seaside that time.'

They were standing at the gate of the park and Ben glanced around. There were still plenty of folk around, but none that he knew. He caught at Florrie's hand and gave it a little tug.

'Come an' have a walk in the park, Flo. You don't have to get back yet, do you? I was hoping we could find somewhere nice and quiet an' have a talk, like.'

Florrie gave him a quick, darting look, and then put her head on one side, considering.

'I mustn't be long, Ben. I've only bin given half an hour – there's people to dinner as well tonight an' Cook only let me out to do some shopping.' She indicated the basket swinging from her arm. 'I ought to go straight-away.'

'I'll help you do the shopping.' He pulled a little harder. 'Come on, Florrie, just for a minute or two. We hardly have any time together.'

'Ent you afraid you'll hev to pay foot-ale?' she asked as he pulled her towards a clump of trees. 'If any of the workmen sees you with a girl –'

'Not on picnic day. They all turn a blind eye then. I reckon we could play cards or anything today an' they'd not fine us.' Ben sighed. 'I'll be glad when this apprenticeship's over, though. I want to be a real glassmaker, like Mr Compson. A gaffer with my own chair working under me, blowing the real big pieces – urns an' vases. New kinds of glass. I can do it, Florrie – I know I can do it, if they'd only let me.'

'Not much chance of that, though, is there?' she said shrewdly. 'With you not being out of a glass family, like. There's too many gaffers with their own lads working apprentice – ent that what you told me? If they don't want you to get on, they'll find ways to stop you.'

'Aye, it's true. But Mrs Compson always looks out for me when she comes in. I wouldn't have got a job in the glassworks at all without her say-so. I reckon that'll help.'

The trees were tall and cool. Ben threw himself on the shady grass, pulling Florrie down beside him. He stared up at the sky, a shifting pattern of hazy blue beyond the softly moving leaves.

'They came to the picnic today. All of 'em, even little Sarah. But it were spoiled, Florrie. They couldn't stop.'

'Spoiled? How?'

Ben rolled over, pulling at a blade of glass, shredding it and dropping the scraps back on the ground.

'Some trollop came up an' started cursing them – Miss Emily an' Master Paul. I tried to stop her, but it was too late, an' Mr Compson took 'em all home again. Almost afore they'd got here – hadn't seen nothing, only Henzel's stall an' the lamp-blowers. Right shame, it were, an' Miss Emily looked real upset.'

'Must hev bin summat cruel then,' Florrie observed. 'Our nursemaid knows their Jane an' she says Miss Emily's a dear little soul, helps look after the little 'uns an' hasn't cried since she were a babby. What were it about, Ben?'

Ben avoided her eyes. 'I don't know. Didn't hear. I just heard the shouting an' that.'

'But you must hev some idea,' Florrie persisted. 'If it were about Miss Emily an' Master Paul . . . There's talk about they two, I've heard it in our kitchen. Don't they say Mrs Compson had Master Paul afore she wed Mr Compson, an' she brought Miss Emily home from some-where else – a gipsy girl, so I've heard, sold her to Mrs Compson when she didn't think she could hev any more childer. Our Cook says –'

'Then your Cook's wrong!' Ben sat up, his pale face flushed. 'Gipsy girl! That's all rubbish. Miss Emily's a Compson, through an' through, even if she ent Miss Christina's –' He stopped abruptly and a deeper colour spread up his neck and over his cheeks. 'Well, anyway, it's not true,' he muttered. 'But you needn't tell anyone I said so.'

Florrie's eyes sharpened. 'Why not, Ben? What do you know about it?' She shifted closer, taking his arm and drawing him round to face her. 'You do know summat, don't you – that's why Mrs Compson's allus taken an interest in you. Why else should she make sure you had a job in the glassworks all those years ago, when you were just a boy? Henzel's don't usually take lads from the Lye an' mek a lot of them, like they did with you. An' you lodge with Mr Compson's brother, too, don't you, an' his ma? Why – what's so special about you?'

Ben shook her off angrily. 'Nothing – there's nothing, I tell you. Miss Christina – Mrs Compson – just happened to come across me when I were a boy an' offered me a place, that's all. Sorry for me, I suppose – I didn't hev no one, after all, no ma or pa or anyone to take an eye for me. An' she knew Sal Compson had room for a lodger so she fixed that too. An' that's all there were to it. An' now I'm grateful, see – I've got a place an' Sal's been like my own ma to me – so I keep an eye out for the children when I see them, an' if anyone abuses them like that slut Annie today, I do summat about it.' He glowered for a moment into the brown eyes, and then his expression softened. 'Don't let's quarrel about it, Flo. I didn't bring you here for that. We get little enough time together as 'tis.' He slipped his arms around the soft body and drew her close. 'Give us a kiss, an' then we'll do that shopping of yours.'

He felt Florrie nestle against him, and bent to give her the shy, tentative kiss that was all they had so far shared. His heart was beating strongly, and his hands trembled over her plump roundness. Would they ever share more than this – this tremulous excitement that could only be snatched at in the odd moments when Florrie could escape from the house where she was employed? Even her afternoon off was supposed to be spent in the company of another of the servants, or in church. And their hurried meetings were dangerous. If it became known that she had a 'follower' she would almost certainly be dismissed, and probably without any reference. How could they ever find the time to learn more of each other, to explore the delights of a real courtship?

There was time now, however; just a little. Enough for Ben to gain courage from Florrie's response; enough for him to kiss her again, and then again; to let his lips move from hers, over her cheeks, her eyelids, her ears, the hollow of her neck.

'Oh, Ben . . .' Florrie breathed, and lay acquiescent in

his arms. And then, because they both knew it could not, must not, last, she sat up and drew reluctantly away from him. 'Ben, I do love you.'

'I love you too, Florrie,' he said, and turned to look down from the knoll on which they lay, across the empty park. 'This is our place, Flo,' he said quietly. 'We first saw each other here, remember? At last year's picnic.'

'I remember,' she said with a softness in her voice. 'It'll allus be special to me, Ben. This place, an' this day. Will it to you?'

'Always,' he said. But there was a tinge of regret in his voice. Regret, not for himself or for the girl at his side who was already brushing the grass from her dress and picking up her basket ready to go back to the town, but for two children whose world had that morning been shattered as if it were as fragile as the glass he loved. And especially for the small girl, her dark face alight with excitement, who had hopped from foot to foot as he gave her the frigger he had kept for her.

He had never told anyone about the bond that existed between him and Emily. He had sworn, years ago, that he never would. But it was there, nevertheless.

# Chapter Three

'It's a new year starting today.'

The nursery fire was already burning brightly, lit early by Daisy so that it would be warm for the children to dress by. Outside, an icy fog mingled with the damp, swirling smoke of the factory chimneys. No sky was visible; even the trees that stood tall at the bottom of the garden, a reminder of when Wordsley had been a country village, were little more than shadows in the gloom.

'Well, I don't think much of it,' Roger said crossly, and shrugged Emily away. 'Go *away*. I can manage to dress myself. I'm not a baby!'

Emily shrugged and moved to help Sarah instead. Her sister submitted with a better grace. At seven, she still possessed a good deal of her baby chubbiness and the buttons of her bodice drew the material tightly across her chest. Emily fastened her in, arranged the skirts of her petticoat and then pulled a plaid wool dress over Sarah's head and began to fasten the buttons down the back.

'There, now you'll be cosy all day,' she said as Sarah wriggled herself into comfort.

'Why is it a new year today?' Sarah inquired. 'What was wrong with the old one? I liked it.'

'There's always a new year in January. It starts the months off again: January, February, March –'

'But *why*? What makes it happen?'

'It's to do with the sun.' Paul spoke from the doorway where he had just arrived from his own room. 'It's because we take a year to go round it and when it gets to January we're back to the start. We have winter and then spring and summer, and –'

'But who said it ought to start then?' Sarah glanced at the window and shivered. 'I think it would be better to start a new year in spring, when everything's growing. It's all dead now. There isn't anything new.'

'So why not have a new year, just to cheer us all up?' Emily picked up a hairbrush. 'You've got untidy again already. Come on – you don't want Mamma and Papa to see you looking a fright, do you?'

Sarah succumbed to the brush and then the children, led by Emily, made their way downstairs to the breakfast room where their parents were already waiting. As usual, Emily hung back a little so that Sarah could run straight to their father for her morning kiss; but to her surprise Joe's caress was brief, almost perfunctory, and he put the little girl from him with barely a glance.

Emily felt a stab of fear. She looked quickly at Christina, and saw that her face too was grave. What had happened?

'It's a bad do, my love,' Joe said, as if he had been already speaking when the children entered and barely noticed the interruption. 'And it's going to get worse, mark my words. Feeling's bad between the men and the masters and whatever's decided at this conference today won't make it better. According to Will when he came in last night, they were set for conciliation. And there was even talk of agreeing to go back to the old minimum wage rule. But I don't see it working. The Midland Association's got too strong now – nearly all the glass manufacturers belong to it and they're feeling their muscle. Look at Grazebrook; look at Stevens & Williams. All their men locked out – and three other factories following their example. And that won't be the end of it, mark my words.'

'But the men won't starve,' Christina said as the children, wide-eyed and silent, began to eat the porridge set before them. 'They have their own association. The Flint Glassmakers' Society gives strike pay.'

'And how long will that last?' Joe asked. 'It has to come out of the working men's wages. And when even more of them are locked out –'

'Do you really think it will come to that, Joe? Even if they make these concessions in Birmingham today?'

46

Joe's eyes were dark, his face sombre. Emily watched him and felt her heart sink heavily in her breast. She was always sharply aware of her father's moods, and always affected by them. If he smiled, so did she; if he frowned, Emily's dark, square face took on an identical expression. Even his mannerisms and gestures became hers as well. Now, seeing him more sombre than she had ever known him, other than on that day over two years before, when she and Paul had been so curtly awoken to reality, Emily felt melancholy settle over her like a dark, heavy cloud.

And when Joe spoke, his voice was as grave as his face.

'I don't like to think of what's going to happen, Christina. Those men are my mates – men I've worked with, drunk with in the tavern, played cards with, aye, and fought at times, too. I'm still one of 'em – even though I sit comfortably here at Henzel Court and eat well and wear good clothes and drive in a carriage. None of that makes any difference, Christina. It's all trappings. Joe Compson's still a common workman underneath it all, and I don't like watching my mates walking the streets with no work to do and no food in their bellies while I've got a good fire to sit by and fine wine on my table.'

Emily's eyes turned to Christina, sitting straight and slender at the end of the table. As usual, the tiny figure was immaculate in a plain, dark morning dress, the only concession to fashion being the full, ribboned pagoda sleeves which accentuated the smallness of her wrists and hands. Already, at twelve and a half, Emily was as tall as Christina and felt large and clumsy beside her. Yet she knew that, small though Christina was, nobody could fail to be aware of her personality. Nobody, having glanced once into those flashing tiger's eyes and heard the ring of that clear, commanding voice, could ignore Christina Compson, the mistress of Henzel's. Now she watched as Christina sat up even straighter and looked directly at her husband.

'Let us have two things straight, Joe,' she said with

quiet emphasis. 'First, you are no common workman. You never were. Even in those days when I used to come into the cone with my father, you were different. Not only in the glass that you made – so much finer than any other – but in the way you were with the men. Even then, Joe, they respected you; even then, you could lead them. And later, when I became mistress – wasn't it you I turned to for help, in making our new designs, in bringing Henzel's into the forefront in crystal manufacture? The Chalice that stands in our library, the first great piece you made – wasn't it that which showed everyone what Henzel's could do?' She spoke as if there were no one else in the room, as if she had forgotten the wondering stares of the children. 'The men nearly followed you on the day that Jean-Paul died,' she said quietly and paused. Then her voice once more rang clear through the silent room, as pure as a note struck from her own crystal and as incisive as an engraver's diamond.

'And hear this too, Joseph Compson: whatever happens at today's meeting, and whatever the Midland Association decides, our men will *not* be locked out. They have not struck; they have never struck. And things will be no different now. They won't strike against you, Joe; they think of you still as *their* mate. And they know that we stand together in this, just as we always have done.' She lifted her head proudly, tilting her chin in the way that had been hers ever since she had first stamped her foot in defiance as a baby in the nursery. 'There will be no strike at Henzel's, Joe, and there will be no lockout. We shall continue working; whatever the other manufacturers decide.'

As Joe had foretold, the Flint Glassmakers' conference in Birmingham, with delegates present from as far away as Dublin, Glasgow and Newcastle, modified their rules in an attempt to conciliate the masters. But it was too late; the dispute, which had dragged on ever since October, was now being seen as the last chance for the masters to bring their traditionally independent men to heel.

'Well, 'tis done,' Joe declared, waving a copy of the *Midland Advertiser*. 'More than five hundred men locked out – and some of them not even society men. That's only two factories here still working, and four in Birmingham. Seventeen silent.' He shook his head. 'I can't see the end of it, and that's the truth.'

Christina's eyes filled with tears. 'Oh, Joe. To think that we should come to this! All those cones empty, the furnaces dying, the smoke no longer billowing into the sky.' She went to the window and stared out. Only Henzel's cones were visible from here, with smoke still issuing from their mouths, but even so she could see that the sky was already clearer, a pale frosty blue shimmering through the haze of the other factories – the forges, the ironworks, the chimneys that soared even higher than the cones of the glassmakers. 'That smoke is our lifeblood, Joe. Where there is no smoke, there is no life – no livelihood. What will they all do?'

'Aye, that's the question.' He came beside her, his hand heavy on her shoulder. 'And the manufacturers think they know the answer. They'll starve them – that's the idea. Starve them into submission. They're all together in this, my love, all the employers, and they'll none of them employ a man from another factory, be it here, in Edinburgh, in Rotherham or in York.' His fingers tightened. 'Have you considered your position in this, Christina?'

'*Our* position?' She turned, eyes wide like those of a questioning kitten. 'Why yes. We stay open and working, Joe. We agreed on that.'

'I know that, and I thank you for it. But that's not what I meant. You and I stand differently on this, my love. You've lived alongside these men – the masters – all your life. You grew up seeing them come to the house, you stood up to them when you inherited the glassworks and forced them to accept you –'

'Not easily,' Christina interrupted, her eyes igniting as she thought of those early battles.

'Not easily, no. But eventually. They took you for one

of them. They'll expect you to stand as one of them now. They were your father's friends.'

'My father would have done just the same as I – as *we're* – doing now. He loved his men – he respected them. He valued their loyalty. He would never have locked out a single one of them.' She thought for a moment. 'In any case, how closely are these other manufacturers our friends, Joe? They're our *rivals*. When this dispute is over, which one of them will want to continue with this Midlands' Association they've formed? It will mean nothing – whereas the loyalty of our men will count for everything.'

Joe looked down at her, his eyes grave. He searched her face, seeing there all the fire of the young Christina he had fallen in love with and yearned for, through all the months and years when it had seemed impossible they could ever come together. He lifted one hand and stroked his fingers gently, tenderly, down the smooth cheek.

'So we stand together?' he said quietly, and Christina returned his gaze with steady eyes.

'We stand together.'

Emily never forgot that winter. It seemed that the whole of her life centred around the strike and lock-out. Much of it she did not understand, but Paul was vitally interested and spent many hours talking with Joe, questioning him about the affair. He tried hard to explain to Emily what it was all about.

'Employers don't like trade unions, and they're getting stronger all the time. They started just as friendly societies, you see, with everyone paying in some money every week out of their wages to help when someone got sick or hurt and couldn't work. And then if there was anything wrong in the factory they tried to put it right. And they soon realised that they were strong enough to *make* the employers put it right. By refusing to work.'

'Striking,' Emily said.

'That's right. If enough people refuse to work, the

employer won't make any money. But the men need money too, to live; so they paid in for strike money too. And that's what the manufacturers hate most.'

'That's what the document is about, the one that Papa was reading at breakfast today, isn't it?'

'Yes. The employers want all the men to sign it before they'll let them in to work again.'

They were both silent, remembering their father's outrage as he read the report in the *Advertiser*. 'Slaves! That's all they'll be – slaves. At least the editor has the wit to say so, here – look.' He thrust the paper under Christina's nose, pointing with a finger that quivered with fury. 'And this is the document that your precious cousins wanted you to agree to, Christina.'

'And should have had more sense than even to try,' Christina said scornfully. 'As if I would demand the very souls of my men, as well as their time and strength! They ought to know by now that when I say No I mean it.'

Emily had been in the hall when her uncles, Harold and Samuel – distant cousins really, but called uncles for the sake of simplicity – had come to see her mother, brandishing copies of the 'document'. Wistfully, she had hung about, wishing that she could follow them into the library where Christina and Joe always received visitors who had come on business; but the door had been firmly closed and she could only strain her ears and try to imagine what was actually taking place.

Christina had received her father's cousins alone, standing small but straight before the fire, with the Chalice Joe had made years before gleaming on the shelf above her head.

'You wish to consult me on some matter?' she asked coolly. 'Presumably it is connected with the strike. As you know, Henzel's have not locked the men out and we have no intention of doing so.'

Harold turned his wooden face towards his brother. 'You see – I told you we were wasting our time. The girl is as obstinate as ever and now she has Compson to influence her –'

Samuel Henzel lifted a thin hand. He had aged in the past ten years or so, Christina thought, his sharp, ferrety face lined and haggard. His life had been one of disappointment: his son Jeremy, the bright hope of Henzel Brothers in their bid to gain control of the rival family business, had failed lamentably and now lived alone and unmarried – there were no grandsons to inherit Samuel's share; and Henzel Brothers, with their insistence on producing mainly pressed and window glass, had never captured the market as had Christina with her fine crystal tableware.

All the same, Samuel was as obstinate as any other Henzel. And he had never forgiven Christina for her rejection of his son.

'Nevertheless, she'll listen to us, Harold. She knows that this absurd situation must be resolved. And this document –' he slapped his hand with the rolled paper ' – is the only sensible way in which it can be resolved.'

Christina gave him a cold glance. 'That I doubt, seeing who has written it. But if you'll both sit down I'll read it, at least.'

She took a seat at a table while the two men sank into armchairs, one on either side of the fire. They looked impatient, restless, as if even after all these years they were still uneasy at talking business with a woman; but Christina ignored their sighs and fidgeting and read steadily, her lips tightening with displeasure. At last she raised her eyes and flung the paper down on the table.

'And you expect me to agree to *this*? You expect me to require my men – men who are third and fourth generation glassmakers, whose families have worked with Henzel's ever since the firm began – to sign their souls away? You expect *Joe* to agree?'

Harold's face was as solid as a tree. He shifted in his seat and opened his mouth, but Samuel's quick voice forestalled him.

'I don't think either of us seriously expects Joseph to agree to such a proposal, Christina. After all, he would have been in a similar position to that of the strikers if it had not been . . .' He coughed delicately. 'But you have always seen glassmaking from the manufacturer's point of view. Your father taught you well, after all, we've all seen the truth of that.' He smiled blandly at Christina's suspicious glance. There were times, she thought, when he reminded her strongly of his brother Reuben, whose mild voice said so little while his lizard's eyes saw so much. 'In fact, it matters very little whether or not you sign this document. The Midland Flint Glass Manufacturers' Association is quite strong enough to exist without you. The question is – are *you* strong enough to exist without the Association?'

Christina stared at him. 'What do you mean?'

'Why –' Samuel shrugged and spread his thin hands ' – it's simple enough, surely. For the first time, we have an association of employers. Why it has not been done before, I have no idea; the manufacturers have always been at the mercy of the glassmakers, with their "fictitious wages" and their ridiculously short working week. What other trade is carried on so, with the men taking three full days' holiday a week and able to decide who shall be employed in their workplace? What other manufacturer tolerates such tyranny from his own employees?'

'But all those conditions have sound historical reasons,' Christina said. 'The fictitious wages are the only sensible method of payment – by determining how many pieces *could* be made in an hour and paying accordingly. Any other method would be far too complicated – in one hour, a man may make ten wineglasses, or twenty. It's far better to suppose that he makes fifteen, than to count each hour separately. And of course they cannot work on Saturday, Sunday or Monday. The new pots need time to come to temperature, the metal has to be properly melted. And materials are delivered on Mondays, too – how could a glasshouse operate in any other way?'

'Well, that's as maybe. We could argue along those lines all night.' Samuel's voice was sulky. 'But the

53

document you hold does not refer to those conditions; it merely requires that a man should sign as follows.' He took the paper from Christina and read it aloud: '. . ."*we agree to give up the Glassmakers' Society. We declare that we will not interfere with your management or right to employ labour, nor contribute funds to any society that shall have this effect, as long as we remain in your employment*".' He laid the paper down and looked from Harold to Christina, his eyes flashing with triumph. 'Tell me what is wrong with that! It seems eminently sensible to me.'

'Eminently tyrannical, you mean!' Christina's own eyes were green flames of indignation. 'Why, you are asking a man to sign away his soul! What rights would be left to him after putting his mark to that? He could no longer resist any imposition the employer cared to make. You could reduce his wages to nothing – they would indeed be fictitious then! You could increase his working hours, and they are quite long enough, six hours on and six hours off for four days – I have lived with a man working those hours, and I know! For a woman with several men, husbands and sons, all keeping different shifts, life must be almost intolerable. You would make it completely so. And you could insist on men working together who could never agree or co-operate; men whose ways and ideas are so different as to make glass-working impossible. It is *right* that they should be able to approve a new worker. It is *right* that apprenticeships should go to the sons of glassmakers. Glassmaking is an art, handed down from father to son, not a mere acquired skill that anyone can learn. It must be in a man's blood, in his very bones and his breath. And the glassmakers know better than their masters who should work with them. It's right that they should make the final decisions.'

Samuel stared at her. The blood had drained from his face, and his eyes burned furiously. He turned to his brother.

'You said that Compson had influenced her,

Harold – and by God, you were right.' He turned back to Christina. 'Perhaps that's why you refuse to join the Association, Christina – because you prefer to make your own rules.'

Christina could feel the colour high in her cheeks, but her voice remained calm. She indicated the document with one scornful finger. 'I tell you, here and now, that I utterly refuse to associate myself with that scrap of infamy. And so will Joe. And so will every other glass-maker in Stourbridge and Birmingham. You will never get the men to sign that, Cousin Samuel – never. Glass-makers have never succumbed to such indignity, and never will.'

Samuel's glance slid away from her blazing eyes. His lips creased into a hard, puckered line. He rolled up the document and got to his feet.

'I see that there is no more use in talking to you than there has ever been. Come, Harold. Our time is too valu-able to waste here.' He started towards the door, then stopped and turned back. 'I'll say this, though. You'll regret having stood against the rest of us, Christina. The Midland Association intends to beat the glassmakers, beat them into the ground. And then you'll be glad to join us – if we'll have you. And glad to accept our terms.'

Christina rose from her seat at the table. Above the fire-place, the Chalice gleamed, the engraving Jean-Paul had made of the entwined initials, J and C, sharp and clear in the soft light. She looked at it; thought of all it had meant.

'I have regretted nothing yet,' she said clearly. 'Thank you for coming, Cousin Samuel – Cousin Harold. I am only sorry that you should have *chosen* to . . . waste your time.'

'Wasted our time indeed!' Samuel said furiously as he and his elder son sat over their port that evening with Harold. 'A waste of time it is, and always has been, trying to make that chit see sense. We should have known better than to have gone to her.'

'Aye, we should,' his brother said heavily. 'Not that

she's such a chit now, brother – a married woman, fast approaching middle age . . . It makes one realise just how swiftly the years pass.'

'She'll always seem a chit to me,' Samuel growled. 'And when I think how different things might have been; if only Jeremy –'

Jeremy lifted his head. The bright, corn-gold hair which had almost enslaved Christina over twelve years ago was fading, the blue eyes were bitter and cynical. The classic, aristocratic beauty he had inherited from his mother Lavinia was now blurred. He looked older than his years.

'Don't let's go into that, Father,' he said wearily. 'It's old history now, and to tell you the truth I think I was well out of marriage with that termagant. She has that trained monkey of a glassblower of hers well and truly under her thumb – I shudder to think what *my* life would have been, had she been so gracious as to accept me.'

'A good deal better, I hope,' Samuel said sharply, 'for you'd have known how to deal with her. Well, there's no use in harking back. And I suppose we'll not miss her signature on the document – there are enough manufacturers standing with us on this issue, and Henzel's have always been pleased to go their own way. It's the sight of them snatching all the market and making money out of the rest of us that riles me . . .' His thin mouth hardened. 'Well, there'll be a demand for our kind of glass once all's settled – windows and conservatories will always be required, while Christina's falderals can go out of fashion at the change of the wind, and disappear altogether in hard times. Perhaps you're right, Jeremy – we're well out of tableware and crystal.'

It was not what he had thought at the time, Jeremy reflected, remembering the discussions which had taken place in this very study when his father and uncles had joined forces to urge him on in his courtship of Christina. They'd wanted her glasshouse with its three flourishing cones then, and wanted them badly. But she had slipped from between their fingers.

Since then, his life had taken a downward turn. Never losing his air of sophistication, somewhat better in breeding than other manufacturers, he had nevertheless felt diminished. That last scene with Joe had been more humiliating than he ever would admit, and his hatred for both Joe and Christina had grown with the years. Beneath the surface, his envy and humiliation had burned and festered. One day, he would exact his revenge, and the forms this revenge would take occupied his mind through many a long, sleepless night.

To Christina's delight, and Joe's satisfaction, the manufacturers were forced to reconsider their demands and produced another 'document'. This one, Paul told Emily, was just the same as the first except that it did not forbid the men to belong to a union. But it still prevented any 'interference' in management, and the Flint Glassmakers' Society had ordered their men not to sign.

'But what are they living on?' Emily asked Paul, her face frowning with concern. 'They haven't earned any money since before Christmas – and now it's almost March. Papa said the employers meant to starve them. How long can anyone live with nothing to eat?'

'I don't know,' Paul said. 'I think it's water that's most important. And Aunt Ruth told me once that the people in the poor parts of the town even have to buy that. But it isn't that bad, Emily. There are other unions, formed by men who work in other trades. They've helped them. Papa told me that all the trades in London held a meeting and they've collected money for the locked-out men. That's the other thing about trade unions, you see – they help each other. No wonder the employers are afraid of them!'

'Well, I'm glad they are,' Emily said staunchly. 'Our factory isn't on strike and nobody's been locked out. Because Mamma and Papa aren't unkind to anyone. They look after our men. Why can't the others be like that?'

The thought of what the locked-out glassmakers were

living on continued to haunt Emily. At each meal, she looked with increasing uneasiness at their own plentiful food, an uneasiness which deepened to guilt when she found herself unable to resist the urges of her normal, healthy appetite. She could not keep out of her mind the thought of children less than a mile away who would like to eat what she so casually discarded. She considered the idea of smuggling half her food into a handkerchief and taking it to them. But how to manage that, with Jane or Nurse ever on the watch? And half of her own provisions would not be enough to satisfy even one of those boys and girls outside.

Worried and unhappy, she tried to gain reassurance from her parents. But they were too absorbed in their own worries to listen. Her father, impatient and irritable, gestured her away with a flap of his hand and told her that such things were no concern for little girls. 'We can't feed everyone in Wordsley,' he said, only half attending, and turned back to his newspaper. 'Just you make sure you eat your own dinner and don't worry your mother over such things, she has enough to think about these days.'

Emily pushed out her lip and ignored him. She went straight to Christina, who sighed and said she was afraid Emily was right, many people would go hungry. 'But for no longer than we can help, you may be sure of that. And our men won't suffer, so you needn't be too unhappy, Emily, my dear.'

Our men won't suffer, but others will, Emily thought, and felt no better. She played with her food, seeing children in homes like her grandmother's, sitting at tables where there was none. What would they do? How could they live?

She was still worrying about it when she and Paul accompanied their father to the glasshouse. This was a common occurrence – Christina, remembering her own delight in watching the glass being made, had allowed her children to run in and out of the cones ever since they were old enough to understand the dangers of getting in the men's way. And they had all, in their different ways, shared in her own pleasure. Paul was fascinated by the cutting and engraving, content to watch for hours as the men used all their artistry to trace the delicate patterns on the shining crystal, begging to be allowed to try himself. Roger was more absorbed by the ledgers in the accounts office than by the glass itself, though he would stand by one chair throughout an entire shift if allowed, counting the number of pieces made in an hour and calculating the different profits made by, say, a wineglass or a decanter. And Sarah loved everything, laughing with pleasure as a man quickly made her a shining glass apple or a glittering animal and slipped it into the *lehr* for annealing, so that she could wait for it as it came cool out of the other end.

But for Emily, as for Christina, the real enchantment of glass lay in its blowing. She would stand for as long as Roger beside a chair, watching as the gatherer slid his long iron into the searing heat of the open pot and draw it out again with a bulb of red-hot glass glowing on its tip. She loved to see the bulb enlarge and lengthen as the iron was swung gently like a pendulum before being handed to the blower, who then inserted it into a mould and blew it to the required shape and size. Only a rough shape, she would think, watching as the gaffer sat down in his chair, the iron laid across the broad wooden arms while he used pucellas and pattens to ease the glass into the graceful lines which had been designed, as likely as not, by her own father. The real skill of shaping was done outside the mould, by an eye which had been making such judgements for years and knew exactly when the glass needed reheating in the gloryhole, exactly when to twist the iron to prevent it sagging out of shape, exactly when to smooth the neck and when to hold out the base so that the foot could be attached.

Best of all, she liked to watch the handles being made for jugs and decanters. There was nothing more delightful than to see the thick golden glass, drooping from an iron brought by the servitor, placed just so on the side of the bowl of the decanter, stretched up to the lip and fixed so quickly that she could only just catch the precise moment. And it was always right, she would marvel; never did a handle twist out of line or appear askew. And she would watch with a kind of longing as the completed piece of glass was carried to the *lehr* and wonder whether she would ever be able to make anything half so beautiful.

And, of course, the glassmaker she watched mostly was Ben. Strictly, she was not supposed to talk to the men but Ben was different; she had known him all her life, he lodged with her own uncle and grandmother so was very nearly 'family'. Both she and Paul invariably stopped by his chair, Paul to discuss the latest piece of glass, for he and Ben were firm friends now and planned to work together as soon as Paul was old enough to leave school and come into the glasshouse, and Emily to ply him with all the questions that nobody else would answer for, as Christina frequently remarked, anyone who undertook to answer all Emily's questions would have to work full-time at the task. It was therefore natural that, with a problem on her mind that she had tried in vain to discuss with her mother and father, she should turn to him.

He was just going off shift when Emily and Paul arrived with their father, and it was easy enough for Emily to catch him as they passed each other in the double doors. Joe and Paul had gone ahead and for a moment, hidden by the men brushing past on their way in and out of the cone, she and Ben were unnoticed.

'Ben – stop. I want to ask you something.'

She saw Ben glance around him before pausing. 'What is it, Miss Emily?'

'Why do you never want to talk to me these days?' Emily asked reproachfully. 'I thought we were friends. But you're not even at home when we go to visit my grandmother. Don't you like me any more?'

Ben's pale face coloured. 'Of course I do, Miss Emily. It's not that. I –'

'And you never used to call me that,' she interrupted.

'Miss Emily. You used to call me Emily – or even just Em.'

'Well, mebbe I shouldn't have. People like you an' me – we can't be friends. Look at who you are – who I am. I'm not even a footmaker yet an' –'

Emily felt her chest tighten. 'But whatever has that to do with it? My mamma and papa were just the same. Ben, you're my *friend*. And I want to talk to you.' Impatiently, she watched as Ben threw another uneasy glance about him, but men were still making their way in and out and no one was bothering about them, other than to mutter an apology if they brushed against Emily or a curse if Ben stood in their way.

'Well, now you have, an' I must be going.' He made to move away but Emily caught at his sleeve.

'No! I haven't said what I wanted to yet. Ben, I want to talk to you about the lock-out.'

'About the lock-out?' His brows lifted. 'What do you know about the lock-out?'

'Quite a lot, as a matter of fact. And I want to know more. About the men who are out – what are they living on? How are they managing? It must be terribly hard. You must know – you see them every day. Tell me about it, Ben.'

Her tone was urgent, insistent, and Ben stared at her doubtfully. She could see that he was wishing someone would come – her father, even Paul – and interrupt their conversation, tell her she must come inside and send Ben away with, as Nurse would say, a flea in his ear. But still no one seemed to be bothering and she tightened her grip on his sleeve. '*Tell* me.'

He shrugged helplessly. 'There's nothing to tell, Miss Emily. I suppose some are having a hard time – but then some allus do. Life ent easy for working people, never has been. We don't expect it to be. An' it's harder for some than it is for others. Like it was once for you an' your ma –' He stopped abruptly, his colour now a deep, flaming crimson. 'Look, I got to go.'

Emily barely heard his last words. She turned with him

towards the outer door, her fingers gripping the rough cloth of his jacket. 'Ben, stop. What do you mean, that some are having a hard time? How hard? Are they hungry? Starving?' Her eyes grew large as she stared at him, eyes as dark as her father's yet softened by concern, a concern that might either deepen to real distress or harden into anger. 'And why is it never easy for working people? My grandmother has warmth, food, a cosy house – she's comfortable enough. Why should it be any different for others?'

Ben looked at her in something like astonishment. 'Hev you never looked around you, Em?' he demanded, forgetting now the difference between them. 'When you've bin to see your gran, hev you never looked at the streets down that way – the housen, the folk, shabby an' neglected because there's no money for more'n just enough food to stay alive, an' some sort o' roof to keep the cold out? Ent you ever seen the cellar shops – a few old boots an' shoes on the path, collected up by some poor body desperate to earn a crust? An' the folk who can't even afford they, kids going barefoot in winter, babbies with naught but a rag or two wrapped round their poor shrammed little bodies. Of course life's hard for working folk, allus has bin an' allus will be. An' you ought to remember it, Em, you of all people, considering where you come from.'

He stopped and bit his lip, evidently regretting his hasty words, and Emily stared at him, shocked by his sudden anger, his forthright words. Again, she barely noticed his reference to herself; for the moment, she was too concerned about the people he spoke of with such passion. 'But my grandmother,' she repeated uncertainly, 'she doesn't live like that. And my Uncle Will, and you . . .'

Ben laughed harshly. 'Your gran's Joe Compson's mother, ent she! An' me an' Will, we're the lucky ones. He's got a good wage as a gaffer, an' as for me, how d'you think I'd manage if I didn't lodge there, if your ma an' pa didn't look out for me?' He stopped again, then went on hastily: 'Anyway, I didn't ought to be talking to you like this, Em. You'd best ask your pa anything you wants to know. An' just forget what I –'

But she never heard what he was about to say. The bustle and clatter of the yard, the jingle of harness as horses brought in carts full of fresh materials, the clop and crunch of hooves on the broken ground, all were drowned by the sudden roar of Joe Compson's voice, and everyone paused to turn towards him.

'*Emily*!' he bellowed, and Emily saw Ben's face flush yet again and caught the agonised look he threw her. 'Emily! Where in Hell's name are you, girl? Come here at once, damn you! Ben, is she with you? Bring her here – or I'll give her such a leathering she'll not sit down for a month!'

'He doesn't mean it,' Emily said staunchly. 'He never strikes any of us.' But her heart was thumping as she and Ben hurried across the yard to face the angry man whose bulk almost filled the doorway to the cone. 'It wasn't Ben's fault, Papa,' she declared as soon as they were close enough. 'I followed him – I wanted to ask him something. He did try to make me go back.'

'Did he indeed?' Joe's voice was a growl now as he glared at the two who stood before him. 'And just what did you want to ask him, miss? What can you have to ask Ben that you can't ask me, hey?'

Emily gave Ben a quick glance. She could see that he was afraid, as indeed any man might be afraid of Joe Compson with his awesome personality and massive physique, and she spoke quickly.

'I wanted to ask him about the strike and the lock-out, Papa. I was worried about the men who weren't receiving any money. Mamma said they were to be starved.' Her original distress came back and coloured her voice, cracking it on the last word, and she felt the tears hot in her eyes as she stared up at the dark face so like her own. Behind him, she could see Paul; he made a little sign of comfort and she blinked back the tears. 'They're starving, all those men and their families – little babies, *starving*,' she declared passionately. 'And nobody's doing anything about it. Doesn't anybody care? Don't *you* care? Isn't there anything we can do?'

Joe looked down at her for a long moment, his brow heavy, and she wondered whether he truly intended to take his belt to her for speaking to him so, and in front of his men. Well, let him! she thought and lifted her chin still higher. It would just prove that he didn't care, in spite of all his fine words – prove that he was keeping his own factory open simply to make money by selling glass when there was no other on the market. Fearlessly, she met the glowering glance. And then the dark brow cleared and the grim mouth relaxed, and to her intense surprise she felt his large, powerful hand gentle on her head.

'We're doing all we can, lass,' he said quietly. 'None of us likes the way things are. Everyone's chipping in a bit to help – they won't starve. And your mother and me, and the others who haven't locked their men out – only a few of us, to be sure, but we've got a voice all the same – we're doing our best to bring about some sort of settlement. Does that satisfy you? Not that a lass like you ought to be worrying about such things, and I still don't see why you had to ask Ben here.'

Emily kept her head well back, still meeting his eyes. 'Because he's my friend. And because I hardly have any chance now to speak to him – he's always out when we go to see Grandma, and you won't let him talk to me here. And it's not fair. It was Ben who helped us at the picnic when those horrible women told us –' Her courage failed her. The word *bastard* had never been mentioned by any of them since that dreadful day. Nor had either Joe or Christina volunteered any further explanation of her or Paul's heritage. But it had been increasingly in Emily's mind of late and she tortured herself for hours, wondering just who and where her mother was and how it had come about that she herself now lived with her father, accepted into the Compson family; wondering, too, who could have been Paul's father and why such a thing should have happened to them both. It had brought the two of them even closer, as if the fact that there was no blood relationship between them were a bond rather than otherwise. As indeed it was, for it set them apart – as Roger was never tired of implying – from the two younger Compsons, full children of both Joe and Christina.

Today, however, Emily was thinking only of the suffering to which she had just awoken. But one day she would remember Ben's words, the shadowy hints that did no more than puzzle her now. One day, she would ask him for the truth about herself and her mother. She had, after all, a right to know her heritage. And if no one else would tell her, she would turn again to Ben.

April the fourth. A sunny day, a clear morning, the trees brushed with green; a softness in the air, the gaiety of new life. The new year should begin here, Sarah had said back in the dank, dark days of January, and it seemed that a new year was indeed about to begin. A new age; the age of compromise between master and man, as the two societies met in Dudley and came at last to agreement.

'Had to, more or less,' Joe observed with a touch of cynicism. 'None of them had a brass farthing left in funds . . . But we've beaten them, Christina – beaten those swine who'd take a working man's rights away from him. They've agreed to fourteen shillings a week for footmakers and the men have agreed to an apprentice for every two chairs. Only one concession made to the manufacturers, and that not so bad when you come to look at it. Every extra apprentice is another society man, when all's said and done – another man to swell the ranks. Aye, it's been a hard struggle but it's been a worthwhile one.'

'And it shows the power of unity,' Christina said thoughtfully. 'The unity of the glassmakers, even though it meant hardship, and the unity of the other trade unions who supported them. The Bell Inn Committee of London – how much did they collect altogether?'

'Over four hundred pounds,' Joe said with satisfaction. 'And they even had seventy-five pounds from American glassmakers. Then there was nigh on six hundred from the Districts, and money from the Tin Plate Workers over Wolverhampton and even subscriptions from local shopkeepers. Everyone was behind our men.'

'And now they're all back at work.' Christina smiled. 'Why are we rejoicing, Joe, when our rivals are back in full production, desperate to make up all the money that has been lost? We should have been making the most of these past months, designing and producing new glass, setting our sights so far ahead that nobody would ever be able to catch us. We should have been encouraging the lock-out – not speaking out against it!'

Joe laughed and took her in his arms. 'It's as well I know your sense of humour, my love! Encouraging the lock-out indeed – when I know you've lost as much sleep over it as any glassmaker's wife wondering how to make ends meet. When I know you've been holding open house at the kitchen door for anyone who cared to come asking.' His eyes darkened as he looked down at her upturned face with its dancing smile. 'As you did before – when Maggie came to call.'

Christina's own expression sobered. 'I couldn't refuse them, Joe, any more than I could refuse her. And – you're not sorry that I did, are you? You're not sorry that I helped Maggie – or that I brought Emily home?' She waited a moment and added quietly: 'I've never felt that you accepted her completely, Joe, and I've never really understood why. She was your daughter, after all, and her mother was dead – and in such squalid circumstances. You couldn't have wanted me to leave Emily there – especially knowing how dear she would be.'

Joe shook his head slowly. 'No, I wouldn't have wanted you to leave her there. Of course I wouldn't. I never lived that way myself, Christina – thanks to your father, we always had a good home, though it might be poor by your standards. But I knew plenty who did and I saw enough of it to know what it was like – water only turned on an hour a day, nowhere to sleep bar a pile of sacks and rags, an empty belly and one privy for twenty families. And Maggie lived even worse than that, in that mud hovel down at the Lye. No, you couldn't leave Emily there, and it was right you should bring her home. But –' he sighed, shaking his great head again ' – I could never forget the way Maggie tried to trap me, and the sight of Emily brought all that back. And I suppose I felt guilty too. I didn't treat Maggie the way I should, Christina, and that's the truth.'

'We all make mistakes,' Christina said softly. 'You and I made our share, both of us. But there's no reason why our children should suffer . . . any more than they have to.'

'No. And the way of the world being what it is, they do have to.' He drew a deep breath. 'And there's nothing either you or I can do about that; except give them a good, loving home. And that's something you've done well, my love. You've given me a family to be proud of. And I'll never cease to be thankful you brought that little scrap home, never worrying that she might bring disease, never caring that she was born of another woman.' He drew his wife close, speaking against her hair as he gazed out of the window and over the crowded roofs at the smoke which issued again from the cones of the other glasshouses. 'I was right proud of that little wench, the way she stood up to me in the yard the other day. Never a fear that I might take my belt to her, the way I threatened – no, she was thinking of naught but the men who might be starving because of the lock-out, them and their families. She meant to know the truth of it and if I wouldn't tell her, she'd find someone who would. And she really cared about those folk, Christina. Aye, she's a grand girl, and it's all due to you.'

'And to you,' Christina smiled. 'She's your daughter, Joe, even if you did find it hard to accept in the early days.'

'Aye and I was wrong about that,' Joe acknowledged. 'I was wrong and you were right. But there's one thing I've never been wrong about.' He took her small, vivid face between his palms. 'And that's the way I feel about you.' He kissed her, slowly, tenderly. 'And I reckon that now this strike's over, we ought to have a celebration of some sort, eh? What do you say to that?'

The celebration took the form of a holiday trip to London, by train.

'London!' Emily said. 'We can go and see Buckingham Palace.'

'London!' Roger exclaimed. 'We can go to the Tower. There are dungeons there where they used to torture people.'

'London!' Paul said and his face lit up. 'We can go and see the Portland Vase.'

The others stared at him.

'The Portland Vase?' Roger repeated in tones of disbelief. 'What's *that*?'

'It's a glass vase. It's in the British Museum. It was made by the Romans, centuries ago, and it's carved in a special way. I've got a book –' Paul ran out of the room and they heard his feet pounding up the stairs. Roger turned to his parents.

'We don't really have to go and look at that, do we? We can see glass any day. The Tower will be much more interesting – all that armour. And the ravens – did you know that if the ravens ever leave the Tower of London Britain will fall? And there's the great bridge too, we must see that. And –'

'*I'd* like to see the Portland Vase,' Emily observed quietly, but Roger flung her a glance of scorn.

'That's just because Paul wants to. We all know you two always stick together. You don't really want to see it.'

'I do –' Emily began, but Christina interrupted, saying firmly: 'There'll be time for us all to see something special. And I must say, I'd like to see the Vase as well.

I've heard of it – wasn't it damaged a few years ago? Do you remember, Joe?'

Joe shook his head, but at that moment Paul erupted into the room with a book already open. 'Here it is! The Portland Vase, first heard of in the possession of Cardinal Francesco Maria del Monte in the year 1600. Since then it's been owned by –' He stumbled a little over the unfamiliar names ' – Cardinal Francesco Barberini, James Byres, a Scotsman residing in Rome, Sir William Hamilton and the Duchess of Portland. I suppose that's why it's called the Portland Vase. And it still belongs to the Duke of Portland, but it's on loan to the British Museum now and has been for, oh, forty years or thereabouts.' He read a little further. 'We really ought to see it, Mamma. It's made of cameo glass – two vessels bonded together, the inner one of dark blue and the outer one of white, carved in relief. Imagine that, and it's never been done since Roman times.' His eyes glowed. 'If only we could make such a thing now!'

'Well, surely we could if the Romans could do it all those years ago,' Roger said, sounding bored with the whole thing. 'Mamma, we may go to the Tower, mayn't we? That's old too, after all, and far more interesting . . .'

In the event, they did all that anyone could have wished. They took a boat to Hampton Court and lost themselves in the maze; they picnicked on the banks of the river at Richmond. They wandered amazed around the great shops and stood with their faces pressed against the railings at Buckingham Palace, watching the Changing of the Guard and hoping for a glimpse of Queen Victoria. They spent a whole day at the Tower of London, which all agreed was every bit as interesting as Roger had promised, and, finally, they went to the British Museum and found the case containing the Portland Vase.

'It was smashed by a lunatic in 1845,' Paul observed, gazing intently through the glass at the dark-blue, almost black glass vase with its classical relief carvings in white, and Christina's eyes met Joe's as they both remembered the events that had taken place in their own lives during that same year. 'Look, you can see the cracks. It broke into more than two hundred pieces, yet they managed to put it together again. That would make a fine dissected picture for you to puzzle over, Sarah!'

'I'll wager the man who did it was punished,' Roger remarked a little gloatingly. 'Did they lock him up in the Tower?'

'Of course not!' Paul took out the book he had carried with him. 'He was hardly punished at all, as it happens. Nobody knew how he could be prosecuted. In the end, they prosecuted him for breaking the case and he was fined three pounds. He couldn't pay so they put him in prison, but a friend paid for him after two days and he was set free.'

'Two days in prison for smashing something so unique and priceless as this!' Christina said. 'Well, we must be thankful that it could be repaired. And now let us go and look at those Egyptian antiquities we passed on the way in, for I think they are most interesting.'

The others moved away but Paul remained with his eyes fixed on the Vase and such a strange look on his face that Emily hardly dared to leave him. She turned back and came to stand beside him, staring at the dense blue of the ancient glass, the purity of its white casing. To her mind, the shape had little beauty; it was squat and had none of the elegance of some of Joe's designs. But there was no doubt that the carving was something quite unique.

'Cameo glass,' Paul said softly. 'And it's never been made since Roman times. They had the secret, Emily . . . but it could be done again, you know. We could make glass just as fine now. We could make it at Henzel's.'

'At Henzel's?' Emily stared at him. 'Do you really think so?'

'Oh, yes.' He spoke calmly, as if the statement he had just made was of no more import than a suggestion for a new wineglass. 'It's simply a matter of finding out how to fuse the two glasses, the blue and the white. And of carving it – imagine chipping away all that white to reveal the blue underneath. It would take time and patience, not to mention skill. But it could be done.' He turned to her and his eyes gleamed strangely, so strangely that she started back, half afraid of this new Paul, disturbed by a passion she had never discerned in him before. 'I could do it, Emily. I could carve that kind of glass, one day. And I mean to do it.'

'You?' She looked into his eyes, feeling a thrill as she saw the determination there, the single-minded purpose. 'You really mean to make cameo glass, Paul? Even though it hasn't been made for thousands of years?'

'*Because* it hasn't been made for thousands of years,' he said. 'And because I know I can do it. I'm going to be an engraver, Emily, an engraver such as Stourbridge – England – has never seen before.' His quiet, determined voice robbed the words of any boastfulness. 'And nothing will stand in my way.'

# Chapter Four

Change, Emily realised as she grew up, was something constant. Sometimes it happened so slowly that you barely noticed it until one day when you remembered how things used to be; at other times it was more perceptible, as in the days of the lock-out when she had begun to understand the nature of work and its place in the lives of both her own family and those of others. And sometimes it could take place with a suddenness that, ever since the day of the glassmakers' picnic, had never failed to frighten her; as if some cruel hand was clutching at her heart with tight, bony fingers and scratching claws.

Harry's announcement was such a change, coming abruptly after his idol, Brunel, had died – of a broken heart, some said – after the disastrous explosion on his steamship, the *Great Eastern*. Harry, who had worked with Brunel ever since leaving Oxford, was bereft; he worked for a while at various projects which had already been planned and then declared his intention of emigrating to America.

'America!' Emily heard an echo of her own dismay in the tone with which Christina greeted this news. 'But it's so far away, Harry – we might never see you again.'

'Nonsense – it's just a strip of water. We'll be back for visits. Or you can visit us. It'll be easier all the time, Sis – the steamships will make the journey little more than a trip to France. And it's a new country – a young country. There are opportunities there. Thousands of miles of railway to be built.' He moved restlessly about the drawing room where the family were gathered. 'This country's almost full now, Christina. There's nothing new to be done. No pioneering work. America's only just beginning.' His eyes glowed. 'I can do some real work there. Real engineering.'

73

'And Ruth –' Christina turned to her sister-in-law, the girl who had come to Henzel Court as a shy, timid serving girl and stayed to become Christina's closest friend and Harry's wife. 'Are *you* happy with this new plan?'

Ruth smiled serenely. 'I'm happy to do whatever Harry wants,' she said. 'And please don't look so impatient, Christina! Few women have their own place in a man's world as you do – not all of us even want it. If Harry wants to go to America, then so do I.'

'And the children? You think the opportunities are as good for them too?' Even now, Christina could not keep the edge of annoyance from her voice; annoyance caused, Emily knew, by her distress at the thought of losing them both. 'I suppose the schools are better – the way of life preferable.'

'We'll have to wait and see.' Ruth's voice was calm, but Emily saw tears in the soft eyes and knew that, although she would not admit it, she disliked intensely the idea of going so far away from her family, and knew too that the parting would be doubly hard for her, since she was also Joe's sister. Nevertheless, she would go without complaint, vowing to the last that all she desired was Harry's happiness.

Emily felt a chill, a foreboding of what her own life might be, supposing she should marry. Was this what marriage was, then? A continual submission of yourself to the needs of your husband? Even if you didn't love him as Aunt Ruth did Uncle Harry?

Christina's marriage to Joe was not like that. But as Emily grew older, she slowly understood that the marriage of her father and her stepmother was something very unusual indeed.

Harry and Ruth, with their two young children, left for America, leaving a raw gap behind them that would never quite be filled. There were letters, photographs, parcels; but no longer the companionable evenings around the fire when Harry was at home, no longer the reminiscences to which Emily loved to listen, about the days when Christina had first inherited the glasshouse.

For Christina, losing her brother and his wife was like losing a part of her past.

Nor was this the only change to occupy the growing years of the two children who were not quite Compson, not quite Henzel. There were Christina's two sisters: Alice, the eldest of Joshua Henzel's surviving children, and Adela, the youngest. There were regular summer visits to Alice's Warwickshire estate, visits that Emily half enjoyed because she loved the countryside, and half hated because she loathed Alice's children. But when she and Paul were fifteen or sixteen, the visits ceased. Alice's husband John was advised to live abroad for the sake of his health, and the house was shut up.

'Well, it's of no matter to me whether the children go to Warwickshire in the summer or not,' Joe remarked. 'I'd as soon they were here with us than off getting fancy ideas from Alice's stuck-up brats. Young Roger is over-inclined to be pleased with himself as it is.'

'Oh, come – he's a clever boy, and can't help but be aware of it,' Christina protested. 'Why, you have only to look at his last school report – his masters all say what a fine brain he has. We ought to be considering what he is to do, Joe, for I don't believe he'll be satisfied with the glasshouse.'

'And why not? Isn't the glasshouse good enough for him, then?' Joe's brows, shaggier now and touched with the silver that was beginning to gleam in his hair, came heavily over his eyes. 'It's brought him a comfortable home, hasn't it?'

'Yes, indeed – but everyone can't be happy working with glass, Joe. Harry wouldn't have been, yet he's made a fine engineer and is doing well now in America. He had other talents and my father was enlightened enough to realise it. I believe Roger has, too. He may not be interested in the making of glass, but he certainly enjoys the selling of it. He's been through all our ledgers, Joe, young as he is, yes, and pointed out a market or two we hadn't thought of besides. He'll run the glasshouse very well one day; not as you or I would run it, perhaps, but from behind the scenes. And who's to say that's not a better way?'

Joe scowled. 'A better way? Why, it's nobbut clerking, Christina – sitting on an office stool, or tramping the streets like a tuppenny-ha'penny commercial traveller. That's no job for a Compson, we've always kept our trade in our hands and in our breath, nor is it any work for a Henzel. *Making* the glass is what's important –'

'And marketing it, Joe. We would be nowhere if our customers never heard of us, or saw samples of our glass –'

'– and keeping in touch with the men,' Joe continued as if she had not spoken. 'It'd be a right shame to lose the contact we have with them. You can only keep that by visiting the cone and talking with them as you do, as your old father did – even working with them, like I do.'

'Well, perhaps you're right. But times change, and so do ways. And I do believe that everyone should do the work they most enjoy. Anyway –' Christina smiled, coming to wind her arms around his waist '– it will be a very long time before Roger's in charge. Neither of us is likely to retire and hand over for a good many years, Joe. And it may not be to Roger even then. There is Paul to think about too.'

Paul. The only Henzel left, for Christina had never changed his name to Compson as she had Emily's. Paul, who was half French, the son of an artist in engraving; and who showed every sign of having inherited his father's talent.

Gradually the two, whose very lack of blood relationship had become a bond, learned more about their parentage. They learned that Paul's father had come to England in 1846 to help set up the long cutting and engraving shops that were now a part of Henzel's; that he and Christina had fallen in love and planned to marry, and that he had died in a glasshouse accident only days before he was due to return to France to make arrangements for leaving his own family glass business and settling in England.

They had learned too that Emily's mother had been a

certain Maggie Haden, living in Amblecote; a packer with Richardson's glasshouse and Joe's companion in the days when he was a gaffer. What had happened between them had never been explained, and Emily was still haunted by the feeling that Ben knew more than he would say. But somehow there was never time to press him for an answer; a working gaffer now, with his own chair in the cone, he was absorbed in glass-blowing and, when she visited her grandmother, Paul as often as not went with her and monopolised both Ben and Will, for the three of them were now fast friends and talked of nothing but glass together.

It came as no surprise to Emily, therefore, when Paul reiterated his intention of becoming an engraver, this time to the whole family. Joe, however, was less well-prepared.

'An engraver?' he repeated, staring up at Paul from his chair. 'But Henzels and Compsons have always been blowers. If you go into the glasshouse at all –'

'As I want to, Papa.' Paul's voice was firm. 'I want to be an engraver. Look, I've drawn these designs. I like drawing – I always have, you know that. But I want to make them on *glass*. I know that's the only way I can make them come to life – to be real.' He paused. 'My father was an engraver. I've seen his work. And I want to continue it.'

Joe's face darkened and Paul held his breath. Although Joe had insisted that Paul and Emily should be told the truth, they were both aware that it was an uncomfortable truth, and not simply because of the stigma of illegitimacy. It brought back memories, painful memories, to both their parents.

'Your father –' Joe began heavily, and stopped; the silence of the room was broken only by the soft spluttering of the fire. He stared into the heart of the flames for a moment, as if thinking deeply, and when he spoke again his tone had altered. 'Your father was a fine engraver. Do you think you can be as good?'

Paul met the dark eyes, his own a bright, gleaming

silver. Standing straight and tall, for he had grown rapidly in the few months since his sixteenth birthday, he could not know how much he resembled his father, how forcibly Joe was reminded of the only man ever to have caused him to feel real jealousy.

'I can only try,' he said quietly. 'And hope that I shall be given more time.' And then he forgot his caution and took a step forward, unable to prevent the deep desire throbbing through his voice. 'Papa, please allow me to do this. Glass engraving is the only thing that interests me. I *know* I can do it well – why, I've already tried once or twice, when a man has let me use his wheel, and it feels *right* for me. It's in my blood, as blowing is in yours. And we need something new – you and Mamma have often said so. I believe that there are new forms to be discovered – if only you'll allow me to learn the old ones first.'

Joe stared at him and Paul wondered if he could sense the quick sweep of excitement brushing rapidly across his skin, the excitement which he felt whenever he watched the smooth, shimmering crystal of a newly made jug or bowl being brought carefully, almost tenderly, against the spinning wheel of the engraver. Would Joe believe that he could create a new kind of beauty – engraved glass that would stand as proudly as a symbol for Henzel's future as the Compson Chalice did today?

Joe sighed and shifted in his chair. 'I don't know . . . Engraving, I've never been altogether happy about it. We have to do it, I know, the market demands it, but shape is what I've always worked for, shape and form. Cutting it about, engraving pretty pictures – it's all very well, but who looks at the shape then? It's lost, as like as not, lost under a bush of prickles that would look better up on Dob Hill, with leaves on.'

'But I wouldn't do that, Papa. I agree with you – shape is vitally important. And my engraving would be . . . delicate, elegant. It would enhance the shape – not destroy it.'

They had gone on for a long time, arguing and discussing, with Joe now veering towards Paul's point of view, now turning away from it. But slowly, almost imperceptibly, the balance of the argument changed. They were arguing now, not as father and son seeing different futures ahead, but as men, each from a secure standpoint. Paul had, subtly, gently, won his day. He began to learn to be an engraver as soon as he finished school.

From the beginning, it was clear that he possessed more than an ordinary talent. In an impossibly short time, he was producing work which matched that of the best craftsman in the workshop; his touch, the other men declared, was akin to magic. He could engrave the most delicate tracery, the most robust of patterns. His work was unique and soon began to be recognised. His future, and that of Henzel's, was assured before his twentieth birthday.

'But it's not enough,' he told Emily as he paced restlessly about the schoolroom, his eyes burning with the feverish glitter that she saw so often these days. 'I can do more – I *must* do more.'

He persuaded Christina to allow him to experiment on cameo glass in the workshops, and he spent many hours poring over pictures of the Portland Vase. The nearest he could get to it was the 'cased glass' which had been made since the beginning of the century; vessels made of two layers of glass of different colours, with the outer layer carefully cut so that the contrast of the inner would be revealed.

'It's lovely,' Emily said when he brought a piece to show them all. 'Can't you be satisfied with this?'

He shook his head. 'It's not cameo,' he insisted, looking with dissatisfaction at the vase, the patterned ruby casing subtly etched to let the plain glass below shine through. 'Cameo is different. Look at the Portland Vase – the background dark blue and the outer layer, the white glass, having the pattern actually carved on it as well as being cut away to reveal the blue. Entirely in relief, and cut so thinly in places that the blue shines through the white like shadows. *That's* cameo.'

'I see,' Emily said and looked again, sighing a little, at the ruby vase. Why was Paul so obsessed with the idea of cameo? she wondered. He seemed to think of nothing else these days. 'Will we ever be able to manage it again, I wonder?' she said wistfully, wishing that it could be done and forgotten, so that they could go on with a more normal life.

'We will,' Paul said confidently, taking the vase from her and gazing at it, his brows furrowed. 'This is no more than a beginning.' He turned to his parents. 'I mean to make cameo glass as fine as the Portland Vase itself – perhaps even finer. Blue and white, yes – but in other colours too: ruby, a dark crimson; perhaps even black. Can you not imagine it? Black cameo glass, with red or gold relief. And none making it but Henzel's. That will make them stare!'

But time went on and still he was no nearer his dream. The fusing of the two glasses for such robust carving as cameo relief seemed to present many problems. And there was little time to be given to it, for orders were pouring in, for both Joe's designs and Paul's engraving. It seemed at times that the cameo must remain a dream.

'We shall have to do something about it,' Christina declared one day. 'We are not the only glasshouse to be talking of this, Paul. And it has already been attempted at least once – we both saw the vase from Munich exhibited in London a few years ago. Not as fine as the Portland Vase itself, but an indication that others are working on the idea. And there's the vase that John Northwood is said to be making, here in Stourbridge – not a copy of the Portland, and executed in clear glass, but very nearly true cameo nonetheless.' She moved to the fireplace and looked up at the shelf above the mantelpiece. 'I do so want our own cameo vase to stand beside the Chalice, Paul.'

'And it shall. I will set it there myself.' Almost heartbreakingly like his natural father, Paul came across to stand with her. 'But the carving is only half the story, Mamma. We need the blank first. The two layers must be perfectly fused, with no stresses that could give way when carving begins. And I believe I know who could make such a blank, if he is permitted to work upon it.'

'And who is that? Your father, of course.'

Paul looked down at her gravely and shook his head.

'No. I think this needs to be blown by a younger man. A man who will hold his reputation for many years to come. Papa is of the past – respected, yes, and with good reason. He could certainly blow such a piece. But we need to show our rivals and our customers that Henzel's will not end with you and Papa – that fine glass will continue to be made even when you both retire. If I am to attempt a copy of the Portland Vase, or even any other piece of cameo that will bring us fame – as such a piece certainly would – then it ought to be blown by one of my contemporaries. Do you see what I mean?'

Christina's brows drew together as she stared at her son. She hesitated, biting back the indignant words that came spontaneously to her lips. Joe too old to blow the blank? What nonsense! How dared Paul even suggest such a thing? He must be suffering from a swollen head – overwhelmed with his own talent. A talent by which she and Joe had been first surprised and then amazed, for Paul had taken to the art as naturally as to eating and drinking, and had hardly seemed to need teaching at all.

But now – to imply that Joe, one of the greatest glass-blowers the industry had ever known, was not capable of making a blank good enough for him to carve . . .

'And have you someone in mind for this important task?' she inquired coldly. 'Some unsung genius in our own cones – someone whose skill has gone unrecognised? I shall be most interested to know.'

Paul sighed, but his expression remained determined, his mouth firm and his grey eyes unwavering. 'Yes, Mamma,' he said quietly, 'I do have someone in mind.

Someone who I believe will become as fine a blower as Papa – given the chance.' And as Christina opened her mouth he lifted a hand to forestall her. 'You have already given him all the chances he has ever had. Give him this one too. He will repay you a hundredfold, I know it.'

Christina stared at him. 'Ben,' she whispered. 'You're talking of Ben Taylor.'

'Ben,' Paul agreed. But he could not know what the name meant to her, what memories it brought to her mind, what was the strand that bound them together.

She turned away from her son, silent, fighting her emotions. For Ben to take what was rightfully Joe's – how could she allow it? She felt Paul come to her, felt his hands on her shoulders.

'Please, Mamma,' Paul said, turning her to face him, 'don't be upset by what I say. Papa *could* make the blank – we both know that. But for the publicity, for the good it would do to the future of Henzel's, I believe it would be better to use a younger man. We would make a team then, you see, the blower and the engraver. A team that could last forty years or more.'

Christina was silent for a moment, frowning and biting her lip. Paul's voice was persuasive and his argument sound. Yet would Joe think it so – or would he feel rejected, cast aside as an 'old man' even though he was barely fifty and as powerful as when they had first married? She sighed and moved away. It would be less difficult if Paul were Joe's true son; if his resemblance to Jean-Paul were not so striking.

'Well, there's no need to decide now,' Paul said diplomatically. 'I have a lot to learn before I'm ready to attempt such a difficult task as the Portland Vase. And I'm not sure I can learn it all in Stourbridge.'

'Not learn it here? But where else could you go?' Startled, Christina turned quickly to stare at him. 'We have the best glassmakers in the world in Stourbridge. What could you learn anywhere else that you can't learn here?'

'Engraving techniques.' He smiled at her a little rue-fully. 'We've advanced a lot since you brought my father to teach the local engravers – but not as much as we could, I feel. The Bohemians – the French – they're all developing new techniques. We can't afford to let them overtake us. I could learn from them, Mamma, and I could put that learning to good use. I ought to, Mamma, for the future of Henzel's. I ought to go to France.' He paused, then added quietly: 'I have connections there, after all.'

Christina bowed her head. 'I'm sorry, Paul. I still find this difficult to speak of. But – yes, your grandfather Thietry would certainly find great pleasure in meeting you at last.' She felt her throat tighten as she thought of what that might mean. Suppose the Thietrys, headed by old Marc, should claim him as their own – press him to stay, never to return to Stourbridge. And, more than that, she had a superstitious feeling about the journey to France. When Thietrys had come to England, Jean-Paul twenty years ago and Marc thirty-five years before that, each visit had resulted in pain and tragedy. Her Aunt Susan's life, embittered and wasted; Jean-Paul's, lost. Who was to say what might happen if Paul were to go in his turn?

'Have you talked with Emily about this?' she asked, clinging to straws.

'Of course I have,' he answered, his tone surprised as if it were unthinkable that he should not discuss his plans with Emily. 'But she thinks too highly of my skills – she doesn't believe I have anything to learn from anyone!' He smiled.

Christina regarded him thoughtfully. It was plain that Emily had not taken his suggestion seriously; when she realised that he meant it, her reply might be very differ-ent. She might still be an ally, should Christina ever need one.

But there was no reason why it should ever come to that. Christina had ruled both her family and the entire glasshouse for too long to be able to imagine defeat now.

She had only to speak in a certain tone, a tone in which everyone could hear the iron, and she would be obeyed.

'You can learn all you need to here,' she said. 'You may have all the French and Bohemian glass you need to study, and you can study it here, in the place where you belong. There is no need for you to go to France; ever.'

Like Christina, Emily reached the age of twenty-one without ever considering marriage; and this, naturally, was not at all pleasing to her great-aunt, Susan Henzel.

'Nobody will think of her in a year or two,' she observed acidly. 'Any girl still unmarried at nineteen is on the shelf. And here is Emily, into her twenties and not even thinking of the future, as far as I can see. There was that pleasant young Mr Richardson, only last month, turned away with barely a glance. And the widower from Dudley, a good enough match for any young girl. Does she intend to remain a spinster, interested in nothing but good works? Because I can assure her, it is a life that leads much to be desired.'

'As does an unhappy marriage,' Christina retorted sharply. 'I have never encouraged Emily to think that marriage must be the only goal in a young woman's life. I truly believe that she doesn't even think of it yet. Doesn't *want* it. And there has certainly been no young man whom I would have considered good enough for her. She is an unusual young woman, Aunt. She needs a very special kind of husband, if husband she is to have at all.'

It was a matter she had discussed more than once with Joe, for Christina was more concerned than she cared to admit about the future of her stepdaughter.

'I don't know what sort of man she needs, and that's the truth,' Joe said thoughtfully. 'She's a self-willed wench and likes her own way – and she's had it, too, what with Paul being so quiet and the others a good bit younger. She'll have a shock when she's wed, there's no doubt about that.'

'But she isn't spoilt, Joe. She always helped Nurse and Jane when they were all in the nursery together, and acted quite the little mother. She has never been a child who enjoyed being waited upon. And look how hard she works now, caring for the families of men who are ill or unable to work, and on the Poor Relief Committee she has helped set up.'

'That's her working-class instincts,' Joe said with a grin. 'All the same, she can be a little madam when she's a mind – I've seen her when one of the servants behaves a bit slack. Trouble with Emily, she needs something to do – like you had at her age. And since neither you nor I intend to pop off and leave her a glasshouse to play with, this committee is her answer, where most girls would think of marriage.'

'A glasshouse wouldn't be the answer anyway. Emily isn't as vitally interested in glass as I am – she loves it, yes; but not to the extent that she'd give her life to it. She is more interested in people, people who need help in some way.' Christina rose and paced the floor, her skirts rustling. 'As for marriage – I believe I understand Emily's needs there. She may not be my daughter, but she is like me in many ways. She is strong-willed, passionate; she needs a man who is at least as strong as she. It would be bad for her to marry a man she could dominate.' Christina looked gravely at her husband. 'I fear sometimes that she is becoming too attached to Paul.'

'Paul? But they're brother and sis –' He stopped, then went on, 'Well, any road, they *think* of themselves as brother and sister.'

'I am not so sure. It was the first thing Emily said when we told them on the day of the picnic, remember? *"Then Paul isn't really my brother . . ."* Have you forgotten that, Joe?'

'Why, no, I haven't forgotten. But it's never been mentioned since. They've grown up together like any other brother and sister. They're close, yes, but –'

'Too close. Joe, they're never out of each other's sight! Except for Paul's hours in the glasshouse and engraving shop, they're always together. And Emily finds excuses enough to spend much of her time there – to talk to the men, she says, to inquire after their families. But have you not noticed how often her eyes stray to Paul, how much time she spends at his elbow, watching him work? And when they're at home together –' she waved her hands helplessly ' – she's always with him, always at his side. She behaves like – like a wife. It's as if she were so sure of him that she's never thought of anything else.'

'Well, as I see it there's nowt to worry about,' Joe said comfortably. 'From what you say, it's all on Emily's side. Paul's never thought of it – too bound up in his engraving – and like as not, he never will think of it. Emily'll find herself a husband and get wed, and Paul will do the same.'

'No.' Christina shook her head. 'While Paul is there, Emily will never notice another man. No suitor would ever have a chance with her. Even though she may not realise it, Paul is in her eyes and, I fear, in her heart. That, I'm sure, is why she has never thought of marrying any of the other young men who have paid court to her.' She paused and added: 'And I am afraid that one day she will turn to Paul and see him, not as her brother but as – as –'

'As a lover,' Joe said quietly, and she nodded. 'Christina, you don't really think so?'

'Yes.' She sank down on the chaise longue beside him. 'Yes, I do. And if he doesn't feel the same about her, she is going to be terribly hurt. And if he does – it would be wrong, Joe. There may be no blood relationship between them, it's true, but they *have* been brought up as brother and sister. Can you imagine what people would say?' She shook her head. 'There has been enough scandal in this family, Joe. A marriage between Paul and Emily, who have always been treated as children of the same family, would outrage everyone and stir up old tales, tales that are best forgotten.'

'You've never feared other folks' tongues before,' Joe observed, but she shook her head again.

'For myself, I would not fear them now. But for our

children . . . They have enough to contend with, Joe. The stigma of illegitimacy may not have touched them too harshly yet, but it's always there and will never leave them. Add the taint of what many people would regard as incest – or as close to it as one may come – and their lives could become insupportable.'

Joe's face still betrayed his doubt, but he thought again before asking, 'And what can we do about it, my love? I've never seen my way to interfering in our children's lives, once they're grown.'

'We should have parted them long ago. We should have sent Paul away to school. But since it is too late for that –' Christina brushed back the chestnut hair which insisted on escaping from its ribbons '– we must part them now. It is the only way to give Emily a chance to think of other men, to consider whether marriage is right for her.' She sighed and knew that the solution lay in the proposal Paul had made to her some time ago; the proposal she had found so difficult to accept.

Even though it meant parting with Paul, her firstborn, her only legacy from the first man to love her. Even though, once in France amongst a family he had never known, Paul might find himself as much at home as he was in Stourbridge. Even though he might never come back.

'Paul wants to go to France,' she said, and stood up, turning to face Joe; the leaden weight of misery already settled on her heart. 'He wants to learn more of the art of engraving. And I think – I think we should permit him.'

'*Paris*?'

Emily turned and stared at her stepmother, her eyes widening. 'We're to go to Paris? All of us?'

'Your father and I, you and Paul.' Christina smiled. 'We decided it would be a good opportunity to see something of France – to widen your own experience. And they say the Paris Exhibition will be the most marvellous yet – even more wonderful than our own Crystal Palace.'

'That I find difficult to believe,' Emily replied, thinking of the pictures of the great glass edifice that had been constructed in Hyde Park. She had been considered too young to be taken to that but had spent hours poring over the pictures in the *Illustrated London News* which arrived each week and were kept in carefully bound volumes, and had asked her parents to describe their own visit so many times that she could almost believe herself to have been present.

And now she was to go to Paris – for the great International Exhibition which was to be held that very year! She should be filled with excitement, tingling with anticipation, glowing with delight as Paul so clearly was. So why did she feel so apprehensive? Why couldn't she share his pleasure?

'A journey to Paris, Emily,' he said, gripping her hand. 'Just you and I and Mamma and Papa! Think of it! To see all those great new boulevards, and the superb buildings. It's a city like no other – new, modern, all the dreadful slums and narrow streets swept away and fresh air and light allowed to pour in. And they say the Bois de Boulogne is like a fairytale now – the forest cleared, lakes created with islands in them and wide lawns to walk on . . . and no smoke! Can you imagine what it must be like to walk under a clear sky?' His face was alight and he was holding both her hands in his now, swinging them back and forth in his enthusiasm. 'And the Exhibition – don't you long to see that? There will be exhibits there from all the countries of the world. And glass – there will be more glass there than we have ever seen at one time in our lives.'

'Yes, I'd like to see the Exhibition,' she acknowledged. 'But other than that . . .' She turned to Christina. 'Will we be staying long?'

'Oh, not long, I daresay,' she answered casually. 'A few visits, perhaps, nothing elaborate.'

'Visits?' Emily said quickly. 'You mean to the Thietry family? Paul's grandparents?'

Christina raised her brows at the sudden sharpness of

Emily's tone. 'But of course,' she said gently. 'It would be most impolite not to make visits.'

Emily turned to Paul. 'But that's all? It will be just a visit? You won't be staying longer? We are just going for the Exhibition?'

To her dismay, Paul turned away, avoiding her eyes. She stared at him, then at Joe and Christina.

'You do mean to stay,' she said in a flat voice, and he made a quick movement, turning back to her.

'Not for ever, don't think that! I'd come back, of course I would, and bring greater skills with me when I do. But I must stay, Emily. There are things I can learn there, I know it – things I need to learn. I couldn't go for a short visit and turn my back on them.'

Emily turned again to her parents. Surely they must be against his staying in France. Paul had told her of Christina's reaction when he had first proposed it. But even as she opened her mouth, Christina forestalled her.

'It's quite true, Emily. Paul is to stay in Paris. Everything has been arranged.' She looked pityingly at the white-faced girl. 'Believe me,' she said gently, 'it is for the best.'

'Oh, how *lucky* they are,' Sarah said longingly as she lay stretched on the rug in front of the schoolroom fire with a book open in front of her, its illustrations full of glittering luxury, masked balls, wide tree-lined boulevards and opulent new buildings. 'I wish I could go to Paris. But Mamma says she may take me later. It would interfere with my studies now, she says, though goodness knows what use they'll ever be to me. And I expect she'll take you, too. We'll go together, just like Emily and Paul.'

'And with better reason,' Roger grunted. He was sitting at one of the old desks, his schoolbooks scattered around him, for this was where he preferred to do his work and sometimes helped Sarah with hers. 'Perhaps she hopes to leave them both there.'

'Roger! How can you speak so?' Sarah looked up at

him, her eyes half shocked, half laughing. 'As if Mamma would do any such thing – you know how much she thinks of Paul, and of Emily too. She'd be lost without them both in the house.'

Roger frowned. Sarah, of course, could never take such an idea seriously. Yet it was one that he played with increasingly; the thought of both Emily and Paul leaving Henzel Court, leaving the family which had sheltered them. Leaving him as the elder son, the only son, as he had every right to be.

'Don't you think it is time she accustomed herself to the idea?' he asked, and Sarah looked up again from her book, her own smooth forehead creased.

'You mean because Emily might get married? Well, I suppose so – she's twenty-one, after all. But she wouldn't go far away, would she? Not as far as France, anyway!' Her laughter was the same infectious chuckle that had been a part of her ever since babyhood. 'And Paul won't marry for years yet.'

'I didn't mean that.' Roger looked thoughtfully at his sister. Barely a year younger than he, she had always seemed a baby to him – naive, open-hearted, distributing her affection carelessly to all who came within her small sphere. It was something he had never been able to understand, this apparent liking of hers for the whole world. Nor the desire to be liked. Roger had never cared particularly whether or not he was liked, so long as life went his way. Nothing – and nobody – should stand in the way of his getting what he wanted.

In the past two or three years, he had become more sure of just what it was he wanted. And knew that there was no certainty at all that he would get it; not in the present circumstances. But now, it looked as if they might change.

'What did you mean, then? Why else should Emily or Paul leave home? Where would they go?'

Roger drew a pattern of sharp, pointed lines on the sheet of paper that lay before him.

'Well, Paul could stay in France. His family is there, after all, and –'

'*We're* his family! He's never even seen the Thietrys.'

'No, but they're just as much his family as we are. More than Emily is, for instance – she's not related to him at all. Why shouldn't he stay there? We've had him for twenty years, after all.'

Sarah's mouth puckered. 'Roger, that's a horrid thing to say! As if we didn't *want* Paul here – as if he's a parcel, to be passed around like that game we used to play, pushed from one family to the other as if he didn't really belong anywhere.'

'Well, and isn't that rather what it is like? After all, he's not Papa's son and many men would have turned him out years ago – never allowed him to stay. He's not a Compson, he doesn't even use our name. As for Emily –'

'He's Mamma's son. And Emily is Papa's daughter. Of *course* we want them here. They're part of our family.'

'Part of what family?' Roger sat forward, his elbows resting on the desk, one finger jabbing towards Sarah who flinched as if he were actually poking it into her eyes. 'Sarah, what is "our family"? The Compsons. Our father's name is Compson, Joseph Compson. Only those whose names are really Compson are proper members of our family. *And Paul isn't a Compson.* There's no Compson in him at all. And Emily isn't either – not really. Her name ought to be Haden, just as that woman said in the park – you don't really remember it, but I do and that's what she said. And it's true. Neither of them are Compsons. *We* are.'

'I don't care about any of that,' Sarah said, her voice quivering. 'Paul is my brother and Emily is my sister. They are related to us, Roger. They're part of us.' She lifted her chin defiantly, looking unexpectedly like her mother. 'And Paul has more right than any of us to live here, in Henzel Court. His name is Henzel. And he was the first.'

Roger drew a few more spikes, his pencil stabbing viciously at the paper. 'He has not. He has no legal rights at all. I've asked my friend Henry Scannell at school. His father's a lawyer and he found out all about it for me. Illegitimate children can't inherit a thing. Henzel Court will never be Paul's, and neither will the glasshouse. When Papa and Mamma die, they'll be mine. *Mine.*' He threw her a glance that was pure triumph. 'And then there will be changes made. For one thing, Henzel's will become Compson's. As it should have been right from the time of Mamma's marriage.'

Sarah's eyes were wide, the green flecks shivering like tiny flames of dismay in their hazel depths. A dusting of freckles stood out against the white skin of her cheeks and her soft lips trembled. When she spoke, her voice was little more than a whisper.

'Roger, how can you speak so? Paul has always been a good brother to you, and Emily a kind sister. We've been a happy family – Mamma and Papa have always tried to make us so. And now you speak as if – as if you hate them.'

Roger's pencil was calmer now. He drew a large frame around his patterns and then, slowly, a straight, cool line through them all. He regarded the page with a degree of grim satisfaction, and then glanced again at his sister.

'I don't hate them, Sarah. I don't hate anyone. And I don't wallow in sentimentality, either. There's too much else to think about. But I can tell you this, and I mean it. If Paul goes to France and stays there, as I believe he will, then the road will be left open for me. *I* shall be the son, then, the true son of Joe and Christina Compson. They'll begin to listen to me, to take notice of me.' He smiled, but it was not a smile that required response and Sarah shrank back, her expression betraying her distress. 'Paul's a fool! Engraving – yes, he may be a fine engraver, but so may a hundred other common workmen. He may bring fame to Henzel's, but he'll never bring fortune. Whereas I . . . I shall use my talents in a much more productive way. By the end of this century,

Sarah, *Compson's* will be the best-known name in glass-ware, and then we shall see who knows best!'

'You'll see all them French glasshouses,' Ben said longingly as he and Paul discussed the journey in the kitchen of Sal Compson's little terraced house, with Sal bustling about preparing a meal for Will's return from shift. 'Baccarat – St Louis – outlandish names; but what do it matter when they turn out the glass they do? I've seen pictures of some of it, an' Mrs Compson brought in a paperweight to show us once. It had a lizard inside it – not real, o' course, but you could swear it was. Well, you'll hev seen it yourself.'

'Yes, I have.' The paperweight, from the St Louis glasshouse in Lorraine, stood on Christina's desk now. Sarah, feeling sorry for the very lifelike lizard, disliked it, but for Roger it seemed to hold a peculiar fascination; Paul had often seen him holding it cupped in his hands, turning it this way and that so that the lizard's eyes seemed to move and wink like jewels in the frozen head.

'Not many lizards around Wordsley these days,' Ben said with a grin. 'They likes the sun too much. I reckon he'll see more of them in France, don't you, Ma?'

'It wouldn't surprise me what they has in France,' Sal said tartly. At almost seventy, she was still as spry as ever, darting about the small room like a bird in a cage, her eyes as sharp as her tongue. 'Put a few more coals on that range, Ben, or the stew will never cook. An' you watch what you eat while you're there, Master Paul – I've heard they eats frogs an' snails an' all sorts of nastiness. You'll be as likely to find a lizard in your stew as in a paperweight there, an' that's looking on t'bright side!'

Paul laughed and grimaced. 'I shan't touch stew until I'm back in Stourbridge! Nobody else's is as good as yours anyway, Gran.' Although Sal was always, exasperatingly, determined to remember her 'place' where Christina's family were concerned, Paul and the other children had been brought up to accord her the respect that was due to their grandmother.

'It'll be interesting to see the glasshouses over there,' Ben said thoughtfully. 'They still use wood, don't they? Or did I hear talk of them going over to gas?'

'The Siemens furnace, yes. I don't think any of them have actually converted to it yet – it's a very new invention. And I don't think we'll be going to Lorraine – it's a long way away. But we'll go to all the showrooms – Baccarat have a very fine one – and talk with the manufacturers.' He hesitated. 'We have . . . family connections with one of them. In fact, we're going to stay with them.'

'Aye, I'd heard.' Ben gave him a swift glance and Paul knew that while the exact nature of his 'connections' might not be entirely clear, most of Wordsley, and the bigger area of Stourbridge too, must be aware of them. And Ben more than most, having lodged for so many years with Sal. So there was little or no point in concealing it.

'We'll be staying with my grandfather,' Paul said firmly. 'And I shall be staying on for a while – to learn more about engraving.'

'Now that is news! French engraving is – well, I don't want to belittle the work our men do – it's my belief Stourbridge glass is the finest in the world – but there's always summat we can learn, an' I reckon engraving might be it.'

'So do I. And I, especially, have a lot to learn.' Paul leaned forward eagerly in the armchair old William, Joe's father, had sat in after every shift and finally died in, one evening after a particularly good blowing at the glasshouse. 'Ben, you know that I have been trying to make cameo glass. I want to bring something new into glassmaking – or, rather, something so old that we have lost the secret long ago.' He paused, his face bright with eagerness, yet half shy as he added quietly: 'I want to copy the Portland Vase.'

'The Portland Vase? Ent that the one in that big museum in London? The one that got smashed by some loony?'

'Yes, that's the one. Dark blue, with white relief

carvings. They mended it – there were copies already made in pottery, by Wedgwood, and they used them as a guide. And it's been back in the museum for a long time now. I've seen it myself. And just lately glassmakers have been beginning to wonder if we could do such fine work again. After all, if the Romans could make it, surely we can. We *must* have progressed since then! We have coal to give us a more reliable melting, we have fine furnaces, the best of everything. I mean to try anyway – and succeed.'

'Then you surely will,' Ben declared. 'But it'd mean a deal of work – that cameo glass int just etched, it's carved. What sort of tools will you use for that? One slip, an' the whole thing's ruined. An' the two colours, bonded together – that int easy. Take master blowing, that will.'

'Exactly. And you're the man I want to blow it.' Paul leaned forward again. 'Ben, I want us to work as a team. You to blow the vases – the blanks – and me to carve them. Do you think you can do it?'

'Blow cameo blanks?' Ben stared at him. 'But why not your dad – Joe Compson? He's the best blower in the cone. He ought to do that.'

Paul smiled. 'That's what my mother thought. We've had some long discussions about it. But my father – Mr Compson – he took a quite different line.' Paul remembered his own surprise at Joe's reaction to the suggestion that Christina had found so disturbing. Yet why should he have been surprised, after all? Joe Compson had always been ready to give credit for fine workmanship. 'He could make the blanks, it goes without saying. But he agrees with me that this is a new enterprise and it should be undertaken by a new team. Two men who are of an age, who can work together for many years to come.' Paul paused. 'It means a lot of work, Ben, work which may not seem productive. You may have to make many blanks before you get the fusing of the glasses absolutely right. And I'll almost certainly need a lot of perfect blanks, just to practise carving. It's a long job, Ben, and I need to feel sure that you're willing to see it through to the end.'

'Oh, I'd see it through all right. I just wonder why you

chose me? There's Mr Compson's brother Will – he's a good blower –'

'But not as good as you. My father and I have agreed on this, Ben. You're the best young blower the glass-house has. You're the man we want for the job. The man I want to work with.'

Ben pulled at his lip. In the black, polished range a coal shifted and sparked. 'An' you want me to work on this while you're away in France?'

'I do. Even though I may be gone some time. You'll need that time anyway, for your own experiments. This will be different from the cased glass we've made before, Ben. The two layers will be thicker. They have to fuse as nearly perfectly as can be achieved. No bubbles between them, as few defects as possible. The carving will place a great strain on the blank and it's got to be strong. And, of course, we can't afford to lose you on your own chair – the work you're doing now will still need to be done.'

'Sounds like I'm going to be on permanent shift,' Ben said and Paul laughed.

'Not quite as bad as that, Ben! We'll have to reduce the time you spend on your normal work, of course. And . . .' he frowned a little as he thought of Emily's continuing anger at the idea of his staying in Paris . . . 'I do hope to be in France for some time. Long enough to learn all they have to teach me. You'll have time.'

'Sounds as though you're set to be someone important at Henzel's, Ben,' Sal remarked, giving the stew a stir, and Ben immediately looked up at her, his face anxious.

'Do *you* think I'm stepping in over Will, Ma? An' Mr Compson, too? I don't want to cause trouble –'

Sal turned, a wooden spoon dripping with thick gravy in her hand. 'Trouble? An' just what trouble do you think you'll cause here? Ent we allus got on well together, you an' me an' our Will? Aye, an' young Florrie too – you know you could hev stayed in here together if you'd a mind, not that I don't respect her for wanting her own place, two women in a kitchen never did do . . . But you'd hev bin welcome, all the same. An' why? Because you've bin like another son to me, Ben, an' don't you ever think otherwise. Another son . . . An' Joe Compson's my son too, for all he's a fine gentleman now with a grand house an' fancy weskits. An' he knows well enough what's good for Henzel's, him an' Miss Christina both. If they say you're to do this blowing, whatever it is – cameo or summat fancy – then you do it. They know better than you. An' when our Will hears of it, he'll say just the same, see if he don't.'

'Well, are you satisfied?' Paul asked with a grin as Sal dipped the spoon back in the stew and stirred with a vigour that almost killed it. 'I know I wouldn't dare argue with my gran when she speaks in that tone of voice!'

'Nor me,' Ben acknowledged ruefully. 'All right, Ma, you can tek that fierce look off your face – I'll do whatever they want. Aye, an' do it well too,' he added with sudden energy. 'Henzel's shall hev a new team – all right, Master Paul?'

'All right, Ben,' Paul said, and held out his hand. Ben took it in his and they gave each other a brief, firm shake. And then they heard the door open and Will's voice calling down the narrow passage that led past the parlour to the kitchen.

'You in, Ma? Summat smells good – my supper, is it? By, I'm that hungry, I could eat a horse, so I could.'

'Or even,' Paul said dryly, 'a lizard.' And the three of them burst into laughter while Will, big, broad and grimy from his day's work, stood in the doorway and stared at them.

The rival Henzels, who had harassed Christina so much during the early days of her inheritance and again during the great lock-out, discussed the news with the sourness which they inevitably, now, brought to any mention of Christina and her affairs.

'France! Some new, fancy idea of hers no doubt,' Samuel grumbled. 'And what good will it do the business, all this gadding about? I suppose they'll be showing their glass at this Exhibition and expecting a flurry of new orders. Well, good luck to them, we're doing well enough ourselves. We don't need to go jaunting about all over the Continent.'

Jeremy, who with Harold had come to dinner and to discuss glasshouse matters, as they did at least once a week, glanced up from his newspaper. 'The chance wouldn't come amiss. I'd like such a holiday myself. At least it would be a change from the smoke and grime of Stourbridge.'

'I daresay the smoke and grime of Paris are not very much different,' Samuel said sharply. 'And I can see no cause at all for any of us to go gadding over there, simply because Christina chooses to do so. Our products are of no interest to such an Exhibition and we're better off here.'

Jeremy shrugged. 'I quite agree. All the same, I'd like a trip to Paris. It might be useful; instructive . . .'

'And we know just what kind of instruction you'd be seeking!' Samuel snapped. 'No, Jeremy, let those who think they have time go jaunting about the world. We have work to do here. And it will be a pleasure to be able to ride the streets of Stourbridge for a few weeks without the danger of running into Compson, lording it in a carriage that should belong to a Henzel.' He shook his head. Nearly twenty years might have gone by, but the bitterness of Christina's marriage had never lessened. 'Well, enough of that. Harold, have you seen Reuben lately?'

'I called in last week with some newspapers he might not have seen.' Harold shook his big head. 'Not that he seemed particularly interested. He's going downhill fast, Samuel. Thin as a wisp, lying there in that great bed, he makes barely a hump beneath the blankets. And they keep the room so hot! I could scarcely breathe. He seemed interested only in gossip – like some old maid. A kitchen girl would have been better company for him than I.' He turned to his nephew. 'He asked after you, Jeremy. I believe he'd like you to visit him.'

'Why do you never go there, Jeremy?' Samuel asked. 'You and Reuben used to be so friendly. Yet of late you've hardly seemed to care whether he lived or died.'

'And does it truly matter much either way?' Jeremy demanded bluntly. 'He's an old man, ill, useless. He keeps that great house for himself like some mouldering mausoleum, when others could bring it to life again. Life can mean little or nothing to him now – wouldn't it be better if he died?'

There was a short silence. Samuel looked shocked and angry. Harold's face was stiff with displeasure. At last he said, heavily, 'Let us hope that others think more kindly of you, Jeremy, when your turn comes to be old and ill. Although I cannot believe that they will – what cause do you give them, after all? You grow more callous with each year, and when your family has gone you will have no friends at all; no one to care for you.'

'Then I shall know what to do,' Jeremy retorted, and stood up. 'Excuse me, please. I feel the need for fresh air.' He strode quickly from the room, closing the door with firm, angry precision behind him.

The two older men glanced at each other and sighed.

'Perhaps I shouldn't have spoken so,' Harold said. 'He's your son, this is his home. But when he talked like that of poor Reuben . . . Whatever his faults, he is old now and needs comfort. A short visit would not have cost Jeremy much.'

'I don't know what it would have cost him.' Samuel leaned forward to poke at the dying fire. 'Ring the bell, Harold, we need more coals. I confess I don't understand Jeremy at all now. I have to remind myself that he's my son. And as for his friendship with Reuben – that died long ago. I never knew why. It was almost as if Jeremy were afraid of him – and yet that's impossible. What could there be to fear?'

'What indeed?' Harold agreed; and a heavy silence fell on the room until the maid came in with more coals and brought the fire to life with a rattle and crash that drove silence far away.

Jeremy, striding down the street with quick, angry steps, could have answered their question; but he never would. He would never speak to anyone of what had passed between him and his Uncle Reuben, nor of what Reuben had driven him to do. It was a memory he had tried to bury deeply in his mind, but he could never quite clear its flavour. A flavour whose bitterness would never fade.

The argument between Paul and Emily raged between them for days. It went on whenever they were together, following them around the house, to the drawing room, the library, the old schoolroom where Emily stood at last, gazing from the window, her dark hair untidy, her square face almost ugly in the distress which she had made no attempt to hide. Her brown eyes were dull with misery, almost hidden by the unfashionably heavy brows which she refused to pluck. She shook her head in despair.

'I can see what they're trying to do! I know just what they mean to happen.' She came across the room, holding out her hands, palms upwards. 'Don't you see it too, Paul? They mean to part us. You'll stay in Paris and I'll be brought home to be a young lady. We shan't see each other for – oh, for months, even years.' She clenched her hands into fists, pulling them up against her breast. 'I couldn't bear it, Paul.'

'But why? You've always been so strong. You've always taken charge – looked after us all, ever since we were tiny. You used to decide what games we would play, you always took the leading part. We all depended on you; we still do.'

'No. Roger and Sarah don't depend on me. Not now. Roger's almost a man, and he's never forgotten what you and I are. He's never considered us full members of the family – just waifs, taken in out of the storm, with something shameful about us. He may not say so, but it's

100

there; and one day, when it suits him, he'll use it against us.' She spoke without bitterness, knowing that Roger was not the only one to look askance at the position she and Paul held in the Compson family. Stourbridge society had never forgotten their origins and, although Christina and Joe were sufficiently respected in the district to have ridden above censure, the two who bore the stigma of illegitimacy would be lucky to do so as well. 'And Sarah – she doesn't need anybody. Everybody loves her. I can't stay here without you,' she said miserably. 'You'll forget me. You'll stay in France for ever. And then I'll be alone, completely alone. Paul –'

'You won't be alone. Mamma will be here – Papa –'

'Mamma's not my mother – she's yours.'

'Emily, she loves you! She loves you as well as any of the rest of us, you know that.'

'She didn't bear me. She didn't carry me, she didn't give me life. Another woman did that, and she lived in a slum. I know Mamma loves me – but she can't feel for me as she does for you and Roger and Sarah. How could she?'

Paul gazed at her helplessly. 'Emily – I never realised you felt like that.' He fell silent and she saw that he had no answer for her. Her heart sank heavily. She had never uttered these thoughts before, never dared to hear them spoken aloud although she had always longed to hear them refuted. But Paul said nothing.

She bent her head, fighting the tears that she had never allowed to fall. Her hands were clenched now on the back of a chair, the knuckles gleaming like marble through the stretched skin. She felt Paul come close to her, his hands laid gently on her shoulders, and with a sudden movement she twisted into his arms, laying her face against his breast while he held her and stroked the dark hair and whispered into her ear.

'You don't mean any of that,' he said softly. 'And you don't believe it. Of course Mamma loves you just as much as the rest of us. And of course I won't forget you, you goose.' He held her away from him, tracing the glinting tears with one finger. 'We'll go to Paris together. We'll see the Exhibition. And then you'll feel better, you'll see. And I shall be home again before you've missed me. But let's forget about that. Let's enjoy our holiday.'

Emily sighed. Clearly, the prospect of months, perhaps even years, apart, did not bring such pain to Paul's heart as it did to hers. She could feel the eagerness in him, the desire to travel to the country that was part of him, to absorb new knowledge, perfect new skills. And she knew that she was powerless against the need which drove him on, the seeking for perfection which made him the artist he was.

'Yes,' she said quietly, her tone a little dull. 'Let's enjoy Paris.'

# Chapter Five

In the aftermath of a bitter winter, Paris did not at first extend to the Compsons the welcome that they had expected from the world's most frivolous city. The streets were dark under a sullen sky, the fine new buildings alien as they towered forbiddingly above. But even though, in that first chilling moment, it seemed to turn its back upon the visitors, Emily still felt a thrill of excitement at being on foreign soil. And the reception given them by Marc Thietry, who had come to the Gare du Nord to meet them, was warm enough to make up for the scouring wind and the drifting, icy sleet.

As they rode through the streets in the Thietry carriage, Emily craned her neck to stare past Paul at the sights they were passing so rapidly, gazing up at the high buildings with their flat, disapproving faces, tall windows and frowning shutters. Their roofs were like jumbled hats, quaintly angled or turreted, tiled with shiny dark blue slate. Some wore a more friendly air, with flower boxes on tiny wrought-iron balconies, but there was no colour yet in the boxes; it was as if the bulbs planted in them had poked out their small green noses, taken one look at the bitter weather and dived back under cover.

Along the pavements there was a throng of people, and as the carriage turned away from the wide boulevard into a narrow side street, leading steeply up the hill of Montmartre, its progress was slowed by the numbers strolling unconcernedly about in the road. The driver shouted and, Emily supposed, swore and flicked his whip, but they took little notice. And considering the knobbly surface of the road, Emily could only feel relieved; to have gone at any speed over these large cobbles would surely have shaken their bones from their bodies.

'How strange,' she observed out loud, staring at the

women who poked and prodded at the fruit and vegetables on the stalls that lined the street. 'I imagined that everyone would be dressed in the height of fashion.'

Marc Thietry laughed. 'Not in these streets, I fear. You must go to the places where people of fashion gather if you want to see beautiful clothes. The theatres and the great restaurants, or to the Bois de Boulogne. Here are only the poor, or the housekeepers doing their marketing.' He nodded out of the window, where Emily could see stout women clad in vast and shapeless cloaks, their arms looped with baskets of cabbages and fish. The stalls and shops which opened on to the street were attended by equally shapeless women in shawls, or by men in shabby jackets and caps, with greasy-looking scarves knotted loosely about their necks. She gazed at the goods which were displayed on every side: great baskets filled with live crabs and oysters; broad counters spread with cold-eyed fish; heaps of big green cabbages; mounds of carrots; turnips and potatoes; strings of shining bronze onions. In the windows of the butchers hung sides of lamb and pork, even a deer with its soft roan skin still on its body, and two small antlers protruding from its head.

Emily felt her heart leap, just as it had when the ship had entered the harbour at Calais and she had known she was about to step on the soil of another country. It had skipped again when the train pulled in at Gare du Nord and Paul, clasping her hand closely in his, had begun to point out the sights of Paris. Now they were really here, in Paris – she, Paul, Joe and Christina. And her doubts had been dispelled by the thrill of the different sights she saw, the strangeness of hearing a foreign language spoken on all sides, the knowledge that she was actually in France.

Paul was talking to Marc Thietry, diffidently trying the French that Christina had insisted all the children should learn, and Emily turned back to give them her attention, tightening her hand on his. It had been a strange moment, watching Paul meet his grandfather for the first time, and she had been sharply aware of the difference between him and herself. She could not forget that he belonged here in a way that she never could; that the tall, somewhat stooped old man with the silver hair and the eyes that were so startlingly familiar, was his grandfather, related to him by a blood tie she did not share.

It had needed a deliberate effort of will to thrust the unwelcome thoughts from her mind and think only of the excitement of coming to the world's gayest and liveliest city.

'We've read about the rebuilding that's taken place over the past ten years or so,' Paul was saying. 'It's a tremendous project. Baron Haussmann must be an exceptional man, to be able to plan such changes.'

'Exceptional indeed.' Marc Thietry bowed his silver head. 'A giant among men, in fact. Willing to drive himself with hard work, and ruthless with others. Yet he did not draw up the original plans – that was done by the Emperor himself. Napoleon wanted the great monuments for which Paris is famous – the Hôtel de Ville, the Louvre, our great church of Notre Dame – released from the mess of smaller, insignificant buildings which cluttered around them. He wanted to give them light, air and space so that their admirers could stand back and see them as they should be seen. Broad, spacious boulevards, fine new railway stations which would bring people into the very heart of the city. He was determined to rid Paris of its slums, its narrow, hidden alleyways where vice and crime held court, and make it clean and bright and welcoming, not only to the people who lived here but to the many visitors who come to see and admire.'

'It is beautiful,' Christina said. She had been strangely silent since they had stepped down from the train and passed its snorting engine to be welcomed by Marc Thietry, as if the meeting had brought her pain; as if sad memories had been stirred by the resemblance between the old man and her son – the same slender figure, the same silver-grey eyes. And although Marc Thietry's hair was now white, it still retained the springing curls that Paul had inherited.

A small movement in the seat opposite attracted Emily's

attention and she saw her father's hand close comfortingly over Christina's. A brief glance passed between them. Christina smiled, and the smile brought Emily an odd comfort. Neither France nor the Thietrys had possessed the power to separate Joe and Christina; neither could they part herself and Paul.

The streets were still wet with slush, the mud flying up from the horses' hooves and the wheels of the carriage as they progressed. The Thietry house was high on the hill of Montmartre, enclosed in its own peaceful garden. Here the family descended and Marc led them through the tall gate with its lacework of wrought iron that stood in the high wall.

As she looked around the garden, Emily gave a cry of delight. It was as hilly as the street up which the horses had just laboured, but she could almost have believed herself in another world – a miniature countryside of tumbled hillocks, flower-strewn shrubs and tiny, gnarled trees that bent tenderly over shimmering pools. It was shadowed now as the evening closed in, but as she watched a boy came out of the house with a long taper and, reaching up, set it to several gas lamps that stood high beside the smooth paving which wound between the foliage. They flared into life and the garden became a fairyland of glowing colour, reflected and magnified in the pools and casting mysterious shadows under the dwarf trees and spreading bushes.

They did not linger in the garden. Everyone was too tired to want anything more than a wash, a rest and perhaps a hot, comforting drink. Only Emily dawdled, attracted by the quiet peace after the bustle of the journey, but as she hung behind her father looked back from the top of the steps and called to her.

'Come on, Em – we're letting the cold in. And Madame Thietry is waiting to meet us all. You can look at the garden tomorrow.'

Emily followed him reluctantly and they stood together for a moment at the door. 'I know, Papa. But it's so beautiful, and we'll never see it again quite like this. By tomorrow evening we'll know it and the shadows will be just shadows.' She glanced doubtfully at him wondering whether he understood. Then she turned away and gave an exclamation. 'And look! The lights are coming on all over the city!'

Joe followed her gaze and she heard him give a small grunt, and knew that he did understand what this strange, exciting city was already beginning to mean to her. Without speaking, he slipped a heavy arm around her shoulders and drew her close, and they stood looking down at the glittering lights that stretched below.

Shops, houses, streets, all were alive with the gas that lit the new, brave city of Paris. Emily watched in awe, comparing the sight with the smoke-laden fogs and swirling flames that set their sullen glow over the area around Stourbridge. Her pulses tingled. Down there was the glamour she had heard so much about, the gaiety, the laughter, song, dancing and all the fervent delight of the Second Empire.

She looked up at her father with shining eyes and then turned quickly away to go inside, in search of Paul.

Joe remained outside for a moment, staring at the city as his daughter had stared. But neither she nor anyone else knew that he was comparing it with his own memories; of dark nights on Dob Hill, looking down through the glow of the furnaces at the ink-dark streets that teemed below as he made love to Maggie Haden; where, on one unforgettable night, Emily herself had been conceived.

After a few days, Emily felt as if she had been in Paris for ever.

Marc Thietry and his wife Cécile had been kindness itself. Monsieur Thietry, having assured himself that they had recovered from their long journey, had taken them out every day to see the sights. Madame rarely accompanied them on these outings; short, plump and dark, her interests lay almost entirely with her home. Her English was almost non-existent and although all except

107

Joe spoke good enough French, she talked very little and her manner towards Christina, in particular, had been reserved at first, until the two women had spent an hour together privately and shared their memories of Jean-Paul. After that, she had thawed and her motherly nature asserted itself. Paul, her grandson, she took to her heart immediately and she was a pleasant and considerate hostess to Emily and Joe.

The last member of the Thietry family had come as a surprise. Nobody had known much about her; Christina, who had corresponded on a regular, though infrequent, basis with Marc ever since the accident that had killed his son, had been aware that a niece had come recently to stay with the Thietrys, but had gained the impression that she must be a middle-aged spinster with no other family to take her in. It was only as they sat around the dinner table on that first evening that they had heard the truth about Véronique: that her father, one of Marc Thietry's brothers, had taken a young bride, little more than a child, after his own widowhood and that both he and his wife had died in a cholera epidemic only three years before, leaving the twelve-year-old Véronique alone in the world.

'Of course we went at once to bring her home,' Madame Thietry said. 'She was living in Lorraine, you understand, where the glassworks is – Pierre managed it for the family. But she could not stay there, Marc's other brother is too old to take charge of a young girl, and Gabriel has his own family to concern himself with. And besides, we have always considered *chère* Véronique our own special niece.'

Véronique smiled at her aunt, and Emily saw Paul looking at her. He seemed fascinated by the child, as if Véronique were some fairy creature – as, indeed, she looked – and might disappear at any moment.

Since then, they had been always together – she, Paul and Véronique; sitting close together in the carriage as they rattled through the steep narrow streets of Montmartre or along the airy boulevards of the centre of the city, gazing up at the great façade of the Cathédrale of Notre Dame, watching the flowing waters of the Seine, alive with river traffic, or simply sitting in the boudoir at home, with Véronique playing the piano-forte and singing French songs in the soft, pretty voice that went so well with her effervescent personality.

Paul might well be fascinated by the child – for child she was, as Emily reminded herself – but there could be no more than the ordinary interest anyone might feel for something new and unusual. Surely no more than that?

And the sightseeing was in itself interesting enough to take Emily's mind off anything more disturbing. It seemed that there was something new around every corner, and the whole family was enthralled by everything they saw. But nothing – not even the great cathedral itself – could compare with their visit to the Thietry showrooms.

'This, I suspect,' Christina declared, giving Joe one hand and lifting her skirts with the other as she stepped into the carriage, 'will be an even better treat than the Exhibition itself. You could not have devised a more delightful way to pass the afternoon, monsieur. And on the way, I know that Paul and Emily would like to hear the history of your glass factory.' She paused and added, 'Jean-Paul told me, of course, many years ago. But I would like them to hear it from you.'

'Ah yes.' The grey eyes were momentarily sombre, clouded as if by a brush of wintry chill, turning to Paul as if seeing back into the past, when another young man rode in this carriage through the streets of Paris. 'Yes, I should like to tell you our history,' he said quietly. 'After all, it is your history too, and one you should know.'

Emily stared at him, feeling the chill touch her too. Suddenly, she was swept by a sense of isolation, of not belonging – as if Paul had already, in some indefinable way, begun to retreat from her. She reached for his hand, but he seemed unaware of her. He was watching his grandfather, his face intent, and on his other side Véronique was equally absorbed. She stared at them both, then quickly shook the feeling away.

Marc Thietry gave the order for the coachman to take them to the showrooms, and then settled back. His eyes were hooded, as if he were still in the past, and when he spoke the thinness of his voice was accentuated; like a wisp of sound, coming down the centuries.

'You must know,' he began as the coach made its way through the busy streets, 'that after the religious persecutions of the sixteenth century, when so many glass-makers fled to England and began your own industry in Surrey and then Stourbridge, there was very little artistic glassmaking in France. Just a few small forest houses producing bottles and such glass as was needed for every-day use. All other glass was imported from Bohemia, and some of it from England too. And so it continued until a century ago, when the king – Louis the Fifteenth – agreed that glass should once again be made in Lorraine.'

'Where our own ancestors came from,' Christina said softly. 'The Hennezels, and the Thietrys who are now Tittery in England, and the Thisacs who are now Tyzacks.'

'Just so. It was in Lorraine that glassmaking was perfected. It was fitting that it should become famous there again. As it has.'

'Baccarat began at that time, didn't they?' Paul asked.

'Indeed yes. Baccarat and Thietry Cristal were set up at about the same time, and in the same area. And there were many advantages for France. Imagine, at a time when we had only just endured the terrible rigours of the Seven Years' War, large amounts of money which we needed for our own recovery were instead going out of the country, to Bohemia. Making our own glass would keep that money in the country, paying our own people, giving them work. Not only those who made the glass, but the woodcutters too, who had been suffering extreme poverty, having been unemployed for several years. And what better use for those huge forests than to be used in glassmaking?'

110

'No better use!' Joe declared vigorously, making them all laugh. 'And what's so funny about that? Glass is the best thing on earth. I'm proud to be making it.'

'And so are we all,' Christina said, taking his arm. 'It was just the way you said it . . . Please go on, monsieur.'

'Well, it took time to set up the factory. First of all, a suitable site must be found – close to the river, for the wood could only be transported to the factory by floating it there. It must also be near to a good-sized village, for the recruiting of young men who could be trained as glassmakers. And when the site was chosen, the factory must be built, as well as homes for sixty or seventy families, and a canal dug to run the length of the factory, to take the wood from the river to the furnaces.'

'I don't understand,' Emily said. 'If the factory was to be built near a village, why did you need to build houses? Surely the glassmakers could have lived in their own homes, just as they do at home.'

'Ah, the answer to that lies in the fact that we use wood whereas you use coal for your furnaces,' Marc Thietry replied. 'Coal is predictable. The coal furnace can be stoked and tended so that one knows just when the elements in your glass mixture – the metal – will fuse and become workable. With wood, this is not so. The condition of each tree, each load, will vary, and the weather too has its effect. Nobody can tell just when a wood furnace will bring the metal to the correct temperature, so the workers must be at hand, ready to come to work as soon as that point is reached, and a bell is rung to summon them. That is why French forest glasshouses are always built as a community – the château, the courtyard, the chapel, the houses and the glasshouse itself.' He smiled, half regretfully. 'But there is change on the way, even in our traditions. Soon we are to begin using the new gas furnace and they say that this will produce an even more beautiful crystal.'

'And that's how Thietry Cristal began,' Paul said, his eyes glowing.

'That is how we began.'

The carriage was now passing along the rue de Rivoli with its colonnades, and Véronique began to point out the people promenading along the pavements. Emily stared at them. Now indeed she was seeing the elegance of Paris; here, going in and out of the exclusive shops, were ladies and gentlemen who clearly had nothing more to do than spend money. She gazed in awe at the brilliant silks, the glowing velvets and rich, deep furs. Jewels glittered everywhere; on wrists, on ears, around necks that were white and slender and necks that were short and fat. And the opulence was reflected in the windows of the shops: lengths of sumptuous fabric, draped like the swatched curtains of a grand theatre; fashionable gowns arrayed on haughty mannequins, sparkling displays of diamonds; and, in one window, the gleam of crystal. Thietry crystal, Véronique declared proudly.

'Yes, we sell some of our wares here,' Marc said. 'And in many of the other shops and *grands magasins* of the city. But our main showroom is that which we are going to see now, in the rue de Paradis.'

'And there are other glass and porcelain showrooms there too, aren't there?' Christina asked.

'Indeed. We ourselves have a fine position, immediately next door to our greatest rival, Baccarat, at bis 30. The building itself is exceptionally fine – constructed thirty-five years ago, so considered by the Baron modern enough to continue to stand! And the showrooms of St Louis are there too, so we are in excellent company. But all along the street, from rue du Faubourg St Denis to Poissonière, you will find the showrooms of all our best glass manufacturers, and those of porcelain too. The Parisian, when he shops, likes to have plenty of choice, you see, and without walking too far!'

They fell silent, gazing at the sights which they were passing: the imposing buildings of the Louvre, the Palais Royal, the churches and gateways and the vistas which had been built during the past dozen years or so. Even Véronique, sitting on the other side of Paul, was quiet, her bubbling chatter silenced by the grandeur.

'It's very beautiful,' Christina remarked at length. 'Paris must be proud of the Baron.'

'Not all of them, by all accounts,' Joe said quickly. 'From what I've read, there are quite a few who didn't like what he was doing, isn't that right, monsieur? Liked the old Paris better, dark and dirty though it might be. And it hasn't done everyone good, whatever they might say. Turned quite a few out of their homes.'

'Indeed, I'm afraid that is true. Many narrow streets had to be demolished to make way for the fine boulevards you see today. And that meant a great many homes lost. Of course, many more were built; most Parisians now have apartments in the tall houses you see around you –'

'But what did they do while the houses were being built?' Emily asked, suddenly disturbed by a vision of a darker Paris. 'Where did they go?'

'Who knows? They had to fend for themselves. There were many sour jokes about it at the time – cartoons which showed a man going out in the morning and giving his keys to the concierge while saying: "And give my respects to the Baron and tell him I would like to sleep here again tonight, if he has no objection!" It was almost true in some of the poorer quarters that one hardly dared leave one's home for fear it would be demolished before one's return. And not everyone saw the new buildings as an improvement; many people regretted such things as the destruction of the old church of St Benoît in the Latin Quarter. Such monuments cannot be replaced.'

Emily looked again at the tall, many-windowed buildings that lined the wide streets – streets that were wide, Paul had told her, not so much for the spacious look and feel which she found so attractive, but more so that troops could march easily along them and quell the riots which had been such a feature of life in the city. She thought of the people who lived there, the people who had once dwelt in small, crowded hovels. Were they really any better off now, perched halfway between heaven and earth? Did they eat better, dress more warmly, lie more comfortably in their beds – or were they still grindingly poor; trying pathetically to cook a little gruel for their families over guttering fires? And those who had not found homes after Baron Haussmann's transformation – what did they think of the spacious new boulevards and the elegant shops?

'And here we are at last,' Marc Thietry declared as the carriage turned into a narrow street off the rue du Faubourg St Denis. 'Rue de Paradis – a fitting name for a street of glass, *n'est ce pas*? And here you see our own showrooms, of which, I think, we deserve to be proud.'

Emily looked up as the carriage passed under the arches of the façade that led into the courtyard. To the left and right, she saw long buildings, built of a mellow stone; ahead was a mansion, approached by a flight of wide, shallow steps.

It was more like a château than the city office of a manufacturer. But this, she knew, was the centre of Marc Thietry's life. This was the heartbeat of Thietry Cristal.

She turned to Paul, and her heart tripped and stumbled. It was as if he was transformed; enraptured. His cheeks had blanched to the pallor of ivory, his eyes darkened to the steely grey of a gun-barrel, blazing like stars on a cold winter's night. And once again, Emily saw the passion that lay deep inside him, the passion that she had glimpsed before as she watched him bend over an engraving or saw him carefully, almost religiously, handle a piece of glass.

Her heart stumbled again. She reached out to touch him, blindly, her fingers needing no guidance to know the familiar warmth of his arm, his body. But there was no response; it was as if she was not there; as if he were already lost to her.

The Thietry showroom was more than a collection of glass. Like the Compson Chalice that stood on the mantelpiece at home, it was a symbol of something enduring, the symbol of a family. In all its different pieces, it displayed the different aspects of the Thietry history. And, regarded in even the simplest light, it was not far short of a palace.

Nobody could enter the showroom and not be overwhelmed by it. Emily, climbing the wide oak staircase, had been impressed already by the chandelier that hung in the square hall below, and by the great cut crystal bowl, supported by the bronze figure of a Greek god, which stood as a centre-piece on a round polished table. But as she reached the top of the stairs and stood looking down the length of the gallery, she could not repress a gasp. And she could sense her own awed reaction reproduced in every other member of her family as they gathered around her on the wide landing.

'This is truly magnificent,' Christina said at last, and moved forwards. 'Joe, we have nothing like this.'

'No, and maybe we should,' he agreed, and Emily saw that even his reservations about France and French glassmaking were evaporating in the glory of the dazzling glass that shone on every side of them. 'Why, a showroom like this would bring in more custom than any of Roger's fancy catalogues. And you've some fine blowers working for you, monsieur,' he added, turning to Marc Thietry. 'Look at these vases, Christina, my love. And these cups and bowls and decanters. Aye, there's craftsmen in these shops, as fine as any we've got at home.'

It was a considerable concession for Joe to make, but Emily knew that her father was never one to withhold praise when it was deserved, and she felt her cheeks grow warm with pride. Content again, she followed her parents round the showcases, listening as they discussed the different methods displayed by glass that dated from nearly fifty years before up to the present day. She looked at the shapes Joe so admired, the delicacy of the engraving that Christina loved, and thought of the men who shaped the glass with the skill that had been handed down through generations until it was perfect; fit to stand on the table of a king, an emperor, even a czar.

115

'Our best pieces, of course, are at the Exhibition,' Marc Thietry observed as they gazed. 'You will see those tomorrow. And the pieces displayed by our rivals, of course – Baccarat have entered a giant fountain and several vases. I have seen them myself – the two vases engraved by Jean-Baptiste Simon, standing seventy-three centimetres high, made of clear crystal cased with ruby red and engraved by wheel to represent the themes of Earth and Sea. One shows the forest, with animals such as deer and dragons and Ceres, the goddess of agriculture; the other depicts the ocean, with fishes, sea-horses and animals such as otters, water-snakes, frogs and shrimps, all among the reeds and plants of the sea. They are extremely fine, and have taken Simon several years to complete.'

'Several years!' Christina said. 'Do you hear that, Paul? Do you think you could spend several years in engraving just one vase?'

'He's not here,' Emily said, turning to find herself alone, and her heart missed a beat. Then she saw him, standing by a showcase on the other side of the room with Véronique. Their heads were close together; one nut-brown, the other so fair that it was almost silver.

'Paul!' There was an edge to her voice that startled her. 'Come and hear what Monsieur Thietry is telling us.'

Reluctantly, Paul glanced up and came towards them. His face was alight, his eyes glowing. He listened with impatience to Marc Thietry's description of the Simon vases and when his grandfather finished speaking he broke in almost rudely.

'Mamma, the engraving here is far superior to anything we are doing! I must see the men at work – I want to visit the workshops. You have workshops here in Paris, don't you, *Grandpère*? If not, I must go to the Lorraine. There are techniques – methods – I must see them. I must learn them. You understand that, don't you, Mamma? Papa?'

Marc Thietry was watching his grandson, a little smile

on his finely chiselled lips that reached the tiny wrinkles around his light grey eyes; it was a smile of delight, a smile of possessive pride.

Marc Thietry had accepted Paul as his own.

And, after all, the sun did shine for the opening of the Exhibition, just as every optimistic Parisian had declared it must.

Emily woke to find dawn already at the window. Almost as soon as her eyes were open she was out of bed and skipping to the window. She pulled aside the muslin curtains, unfastened the shutters and flung the windows wide, leaning out into the sharp, cool air.

Paris lay below her, spread out in smiling glory under the apricot glow of the rising sun. From her window high on the hill Emily could see across the tumbled roofs to the wide boulevards, almost to the gleam of the river Seine itself. And just beyond that, although she could not discern them, were the crystal domes of the glass pavilion that housed the Exhibition – the statues, the paintings, the machines and the fabrics that had been sent from all over the world to display man's highest attainments in civilisation.

Emily hugged herself, thinking of the excitements that she had already experienced in this city, so different from her provincial English home. The narrow, hilly streets of Montmartre, filled with gossiping Frenchwomen, the flights of steps that led from one street to another; the tree-lined boulevards with their grand buildings; the shining river with its islands and especially the Île de la Cité, where stood the magnificent cathedral of Notre Dame. The music issuing from cafés; the flower sellers, the vegetables piled high on market stalls.

If only she did not have this uneasy feeling about Paul, that they had lost the closeness she had always cherished; that he had begun to grow away from her, to a place where she could not follow.

At that moment, there was a tap on the door and Véronique entered.

'Oh, you're awake! I'm so glad. Isn't it a wonderful morning? Everything shines, just like my uncle's glass. And this afternoon we shall see the Emperor and the Empress themselves! Are you not excited, *chère* Emily?'

She danced across the room and sprang on to Emily's bed, landing as lightly as thistledown, her shimmering, silvery-blond hair floating like a halo of curls around her small face, her blue eyes alight with laughter and joy.

'Say you're as excited as I am,' she commanded, reaching over to possess Emily's square hands in her own delicate fingers. 'Say it!'

'Of course I'm excited.' But Emily's pleasure, which had lifted and thrilled her as she gazed from the window, seemed dim and heavy in comparison with Véronique's ethereal delight. She felt suddenly large and clumsy with that featherlight body so close to hers, and she could not convince herself that her feeling was due entirely to the contrast between her own rather heavy cotton nightgown and Véronique's gossamer silk peignoir. Everything about Véronique was light and airy; a bubble of gaiety seemed to float about her slender person as she danced through the days. To Emily, Véronique was Paris itself; while Emily represented nothing but the oppressive gloom of industrial Stourbridge.

'But you are so solemn!' The slim fingers shook hers, the laughing eyes frowned in playful disapproval. 'Don't you ever laugh and sing and skip about, Emily? Are you always so serious?'

'Indeed I'm not! Why, only just before you came in I was –' But already Véronique's attention had strayed. She slipped off the bed, wandered about the room picking up Emily's hairbrush, her silver-handled mirror, the little glass elephant that Ben had made and which went everywhere with her; and finally ran to the window and leant out, her fair curls fluttering softly in the breeze.

'It's going to be a beautiful day! I knew it would be – I said a prayer at Mass yesterday. And lit a candle.' She turned from the window. 'You must hurry, Emily, or we shall surely miss the fun.' And with a silvery laugh, she left Emily to dress.

The sun shone down as the Thietry party made its way to watch the Emperor and Empress arrive for the opening of the Exhibition. Spring seemed to have arrived overnight; the trees that lined the pavements and stood grouped in the little squares were brushed with green, the window-boxes high on the face of the buildings were spotted with yellow as daffodils and narcissi opened tentative faces to the sudden heat. And now the streets were full of flowers too; great masses of them, spilling from the baskets of the flower girls and the old women who sat in doorways and held out bunches of violets, primroses and jasmine to passers-by. Marc Thietry leaned down as they passed one wrinkled crone and tossed her some coins; in return, she filled the carriage with flowers which the women, laughing and exclaiming, pinned on to their dresses and, when they had enough, tossed the rest to girls in the crowd who caught them and threaded their stems into shabby shawls and rusty black cloaks.

'This is the route the Emperor will take,' Marc said as the carriage passed the palace and crossed the broad space of the Place de la Concorde. 'See, there is the Seine herself on our left, all dressed up for Their Majesties, glittering as if she wears an evening gown of sequins and pearls.'

Emily gazed out at the crowds, clustering and pressing behind the troops of the line which were ranged two deep along both sides of the road, swords and bayonets held high and gleaming in the sun. Swiftly, following others, the carriage moved along the Cours de la Reine and the Quai de Billy. On the north side of the river, facing the Exhibition building, the slope of the Trocadero was a solid mass of people and all around the Pont d'Iena, where they crossed the river, were the several thousand workmen who had slaved so hard to have the Exhibition ready for today; proudly, they carried their picks and shovels, ready to hoist them into the air as soon as the royal coach came into view, and some of them held huge tricolour flags surmounted with golden eagles which would make a grand display in the gentle April breeze. And all around the boundary of the Champs de Mars, where the Exhibition had been set up, was a deep crowd of excited sightseers.

As she followed the Thietrys out of the carriage and found a spot from where she could see, Emily thought of the glassmakers' picnics at home; there was not so much difference really. Here were the men who had done the real work, who had set to and used strength and muscle and sheer hardworking skill to build the Exhibition; inside, it would be filled with the fruits of the labours of yet more men, men the world over, who had similarly worked and striven, who had learned their crafts and perfected them, just as the glassmakers did. And people like the Emperor and Empress, the rulers of the world, came to admire and venerate. Did they ever pause to think how much better it was to be one of the creators – one of those who worked?

Or was it? Emily looked again at the thousands of workmen with their picks and shovels. None of them was well-dressed; their clothes were shiny with wear, or green with mould and rust, their boots shabby, their faces thin and lined. They had toiled night and day to make this afternoon possible; yet, proud though they appeared, they contrasted sadly with the ladies and gentlemen of society whose places had been saved near the great entrance, and who were dressed in the finest silks and satins, their hair carefully dressed, their faces painted and their bodies well-nourished and sleek.

She turned to Paul, wanting to share her thoughts with him, but although his hand was in hers his head was bent towards the animated face of Véronique, who was busily pointing out all the sights.

'See, Paul, *la Grande Porte* – the great golden eagles on each side, with their wings spread so wide – are they not *magnifique*? And the canopy, such a beautiful green, with the lovely golden bees and golden cords, stretching to the very doorways of the palace – for it is a palace, *n'est ce pas*? Just as your own Crystal Palace was which Emily talks of so much, even though she could not have seen it.'

'I have!' Emily broke in indignantly. 'It's been moved, but you can still see it and both Paul and I have.'

'Ah yes, but not as the Great Exhibition. And that was – how many years ago? Fifteen, sixteen? The marvels you will see here today will greatly surpass those, I am convinced.'

Emily said no more. Véronique was right, of course – that was why she and Paul had come here, why Joe and Christina had brought them, because this Exhibition was to be the greatest ever seen. All the same, she couldn't help feeling a twinge of disloyalty to her own country in admitting this. Nor, although Véronique had shown her nothing but friendliness and affection, could she suppress that uncomfortable twinge of something very like jealousy, whenever she saw Paul glancing at the French girl with that strange absorption in his eyes. But that was ridiculous – Véronique was no more than a child.

The brightness of the afternoon was suddenly dimmed and a shiver goosed across the bare skin of her neck and arms. She looked up, thinking that a cloud must have passed across the sun, but it was as bright and clear as before.

'There they are! The Emperor and Empress!' '*Ici Leurs Majestés*!' The cry was taken up and sounded on all sides. ' *Vive la France! Vive l'Empire*!' The crowd was waving and shouting, its enthusiasm rising as throats opened and voices lifted to the sky, the sound mingling with the music of the military bands which lined the route behind the glittering troops.

'See! See, Paul, see, Emily!' Véronique was bouncing excitedly on her toes, gripping Paul's sleeve as she pointed at the coach that had now come into view across the bridge, drawn by four stately black horses, each ridden by a cavalryman, flanked and followed by others equally magnificent. The coach was open so that the royal couple were easily seen by the cheering crowds, the Emperor lifting his tall silk hat in regal acknowledgement, the Empress inclining her head graciously. 'Now they will drive to the pavilion, where the Princess Mathilde will receive them. Oh, they are so *magnifiques*, are they not? So *impressionnants*.'

Emily stretched up on tip-toe, straining her eyes to see. Eagerly, knowing that those at home – Aunt Susan and Sarah especially – would expect a full report, she took in and memorised every detail.

On the side of the coach nearest her, sat the Empress Eugénie whose beauty was legendary; a majestic figure in a vast gown of glowing, plum-coloured silk trimmed with black velvet, she looked as radiant as a bride and as costly as an exotic jewel.

Beside her, the Emperor was a contrast. Clad entirely in black, only his head could be seen as he lifted the top hat in answer to the cheers of the crowd, and there was nothing particularly handsome about it. To Emily, he looked pale, almost sallow, though much of his face was hidden behind the heavy, waxed moustache and the goatee beard which had, in his honour, been renamed the 'imperial'. But in spite of his unprepossessing looks, she knew at once that there was something different about him, some charisma that could only come from being royal, from being a Bonaparte. And when he lifted the drooping lids and appeared to look straight at her, she felt her breath catch at the burning expression, the blazing pride that shone out from them.

The coach disappeared through the great portal and a collective sigh went up from the crowd. Emily listened to the babble of the Parisians around her, straining to understand their comments. 'Didn't she look exquisite?' 'You thought so? I thought her gown was hideous – that dreadful colour, and the black – they do nothing at all for her complexion!' 'He looked ill, didn't you think?' 'They say the Prince Imperial is at death's door, that is why he was not in the coach.' 'Nonsense – it is an abscess of the knee, nothing more than that. He will be here as soon as he can walk with comfort.'

'There,' Véronique said, as if she had arranged the whole display herself. 'Was that not *magnifique*? And now what are we to do? For there is no use trying to go into the Exhibition today, the Emperor and Empress will be shown everything first. Where shall we go to spend the rest of the afternoon?'

Her question was asked directly of Paul, as if he were the only person whose opinion mattered. And perhaps, Emily thought, it was. For she was always ready to do whatever Paul wanted and so, since they had left Stourbridge, it seemed that Christina and Joe were as well. As if everyone recognised that they would be losing him soon; as if they were preparing for their loss.

She looked at Paul and her heart kicked as she caught the expression in his eyes as he gazed down at Véronique: they were dark, as dark as the Seine. And in that moment of intense jealousy, Emily knew what Christina had recognised months ago: that she was herself in love with him, as deeply in love as any girl could be. No longer, she acknowledged, could she think of him as she had been taught to do, as a brother. No longer could she deny the yearnings of her own heart.

He was the only man she would ever love. And she was losing him.

# Chapter Six

Without Christina and Joe, Henzel Court seemed too empty, too quiet. A force seemed to have gone out of it, a powerful, dominant force made up from Christina's fire and energy, personified in the quick, light sound of her footsteps, the music of her voice, and from Joe's great roaring laugh, his giant bulk that filled the rooms, the thunder of his voice which echoed through the house when he was angered. Without this force, Henzel Court seemed only half alive.

At first, Susan Henzel revelled in the unaccustomed peace, the sensation of being in control. And even though it was for only a few weeks – or perhaps because the time was to be so short – she let it go to her head.

Her friends came daily to sample Mrs Jenner's tea and cakes. Adela, with her two daughters, was invited to come and stay. But none of that was enough. And Susan conceived the idea of a dinner party; a family dinner party but, nonetheless, a dinner party that Christina would never have countenanced.

When Roger heard of it, he smiled sardonically.

'Well,' he remarked to Sarah, 'while the cat's away, the mice will play.'

Sarah looked up, startled. 'Why, what do you mean? We're doing nothing that Mamma and Papa would disapprove of, are we?'

Roger leaned back from his desk, tilting his chair, his long legs stretched out in front of him, his arms lazily reaching above his head. He was supposed to be studying for his entry to Oxford in the autumn, but he knew that his work was well up to standard. He glanced at his younger sister. She was the only member of the family who really looked up to him – Paul and Emily still treated him rather as a child, which he resented all the more when he considered their relationship. He decided to relax a little and laughed. '*We're* not, no. But what of Aunt Susan?'

'Aunt Susan? Whatever do you mean?'

He glinted a look at her. 'Why, her famous dinner party, of course. The one she's planned for Friday night.'

Sarah stared at him, still uncomprehending. 'The dinner party? What's so strange about that? It's only family – Uncle Harold and Aunt Ada, Uncle Samuel and Aunt Lavinia and Cousin Rupert and –' She stopped again and her eyes widened.

'Exactly,' Roger said, and his smile showed all his fine, white teeth. 'And Jeremy.'

'Cousin Jeremy,' Sarah said faintly. 'How strange. He's never been to see us, in all the time I can remember. And now, when Mother and Father are away –'

'He comes. Now, why do you suppose that should be?'

'I don't know. I've always supposed that he didn't like our family much. After all, we're business rivals.'

'Stuff! We're no more Jeremy's rivals than we are Uncle Samuel's, and he comes often enough – though I know there's not much love lost between him and Mother, or Father. And Uncle Harold comes too, and Aunt Ada and Aunt Lavinia, if only for the sake of appearances. They visit us and we visit them, even though we've all heard how the cousins tried to make Mother hand the business over to them before she and Father got married. Why should it be any different for Jeremy? Why should he be the one to stay away? There must be something more.'

'Mamma never even speaks of him, it's true,' Sarah acknowledged. 'Nor Papa. I suppose they just don't like him much.'

'But why not? There's something more there, Sarah. We've never even been allowed to meet him. Even when we've seen him in the street, we've never been permitted to do more than nod or bow, and Mamma and Papa never even do that. And if we're invited to Aunt Lavinia's house, Mamma always makes sure to ask if Jeremy will be there before accepting. There must be some reason. And why should Aunt Susan invite him now, the moment they're away? I tell you, I mean to find out.' He let his chair tip forward again, his face determined.

'How? Will you ask Aunt Susan?'

'No. I don't think she'd tell me. She might even withdraw the invitation if she thought I was especially interested. Or find some way to prevent me being there, so that I still won't meet him. Aunt Susan may be prepared to annoy Mother and Father by inviting Jeremy here while they're away, but she won't risk making them really angry. Perhaps she wants to make up the feud, whatever it is – but she won't tell either me or you the truth of it all. If she even knows it herself,' he added thoughtfully. 'And I want to meet our cousin, Sarah. Perhaps he might tell me.'

Sarah looked doubtful. 'Do you really think you should meddle, Roger? Whatever it is, it's none of our business. It can't do any good to know.'

'Don't you think so? I disagree! I think it could be very useful to know. Whatever it is,' he said slowly, 'it's because of something that happened before we were born. Everything interesting in this family, Sarah, everything that makes it different, happened before we were born. Mother inheriting the glassworks; the cousins trying to take it from her; Paul and Emily being born – it all happened within those few years. And whatever reason it is that keeps Cousin Jeremy away from Henzel Court – that happened then too. It *is* our business, Sarah – because you and I are the only true, legitimate Compsons. It's important. And if Cousin Jeremy knows anything about it that we don't – anything we *should* know – well, I mean to find it out.'

'But why?' Sarah asked at last. 'Why does it matter so much? Why do you want to dig up all these old things? If Mamma and Papa wanted us to know, they'd tell us.'

'And they wouldn't be half so interesting,' Roger grinned. 'Don't you realise, it's the secrets, the things people try to hide, that are most worth knowing . . . If there's a secret in this family, I mean to ferret it out. And Cousin Jeremy is as likely to know as anyone.'

'Well, I wish you wouldn't ask. It's only going to make everyone unhappy, bringing up the past. I'm sure neither Mamma nor Papa want to talk about it now, or even think about it. And there's Emily and Paul, too – you must think of them.'

'Oh, I do,' Roger said with an odd note in his voice. 'I think about them a lot.'

'Then you surely don't want to upset them, reminding them of –' Sarah paused. 'Why not let things be, Roger?' she asked pleadingly.

'Let things be! When they're just beginning to be interesting? No, Sarah! As I said – when the cat's away, the mice will play. Aunt Susan may think she's being very daring in asking Cousin Jeremy to her dinner party, but she doesn't really expect it to lead to anything else. She has no idea just what tricks mice can get up to when there's no cat about to watch them – no idea at all.'

'Go to dinner at Henzel Court?' Jeremy laughed, a sound that was hard and abrupt and held little mirth or pleasure. 'This has to be a jest.'

Lavinia shook her head. Never for a moment forgetting her aristocratic birth, she had aged as elegantly as she had done everything else, and was now a thin, fine-boned woman with an iron-straight back, immaculately dressed grey hair and blue eyes that had not faded so much that they could not still, when necessary, turn to ice.

'No jest, Jeremy. Susan most particularly asked that you should go too. You know she has always been fond of you – I believe she even hoped at one time that you might marry Christina.' Lavinia's tone showed that she had managed to forget that Susan had not been alone in this hope; Lavinia herself had never liked Christina, nor

128

believed her good enough to be Jeremy's wife, but she had been furiously indignant when he was rejected. 'And it is time that silly feud was made up,' she added.

'I hardly think that Cousin Susan's dinner party, held in Christina's absence and certainly without her knowledge, counts as "making it up",' Jeremy returned dryly. With a languid movement, he rose and moved over to the ornate, gilded mirror that hung above the mantelpiece, his long fingers smoothing back the fair hair that was fading now to the grey of a wintry sky. 'Still, I must confess I'm tempted . . . if only because I know just how angry Christina would be if she knew.' He smiled thinly.

Lavinia looked at him, her eyes thoughtful. 'So you'll come with us? I believe Adela will be there too – she's brought her daughters to stay for a while, to keep Sarah company. It's a long time since we've seen Adela, poor child. I understand she's quite altered. Such a pretty little thing, she used to be. Now, if it had been *she* –'

'Well, it wasn't. And just as well, for I've become convinced I'm not the marrying type.' Jeremy took out his snuffbox. 'May I, Mamma? Yes, very well, I'll come with you to Cousin Susan's clandestine party and enjoy savouring the thought of what Christina and that labouring husband of hers would say if they knew . . . When are they expected back from Paris, by the way? What a tremendous joke if they were to arrive back while the party's in full swing! But I suppose Cousin Susan will have made quite sure that's not likely to happen.'

His mother gave him a quelling glance. 'I imagine she has. I cannot myself see anything at all humorous in such a situation. Your sense of the ridiculous sometimes baffles me, Jeremy. However, I believe that Christina has written to say they've decided to stay on for two or three weeks longer, but that after that they will certainly be coming home. I should think they'd be glad to, as well. I cannot imagine how Joseph comports himself in such company – the Parisians are so sophisticated, so particular about manners. And as for Emily . . . she seems so *gauche* at times. Awkward in some odd way – as if she doesn't fit in; or isn't even sure that she should.' Lavinia lifted one narrow shoulder. 'Well, I suppose that's not surprising, in the circumstances . . .' Delicacy forbade her to go on; she paused a moment. 'She's really a very fortunate girl.'

Neither of them spoke of why Emily was so fortunate, but the knowledge hung in the air between them. They sat silent for a moment; then Jeremy closed his snuffbox with a snap.

'Well, it will be interesting to see if Paris makes any difference. And meanwhile, I'll accompany you to Henzel Court on Friday. It will be intriguing; yes, intriguing.'

His eyes took on a faraway, musing look, and Lavinia glanced at him again, this time with curiosity. But Jeremy was evidently not in confiding mood. He gave her an enigmatic smile and then rose to his feet.

'Until Friday then, Mamma. And let's hope for a pleasant and instructive evening.'

Pleasant, yes. But – instructive? Lavinia watched as he made his way from the room, and her blue eyes, so like his, were puzzled.

But then, she had never really known Jeremy.


'. . . and when I come down from Oxford, I hope to take over all that side of the business,' Roger concluded with something of a flourish. 'There isn't really anyone here who has sufficient knowledge, you see. Father and Mother do their best, of course, but . . .' He let the sentence drift away, silence conveying his meaning more accurately than words.

Jeremy took his cigar from his mouth and smiled. Since the ladies had retired to the drawing room, the talk had become easier. Harold and Samuel, at the other end of the table, were deep in conference with Rupert on some matter concerning the glasshouse. None of them was listening to the conversation between Jeremy and the young cousin he had never before been allowed to meet.

'It's so silly, this family feuding,' Susan had said as she introduced them. 'And I know what it is! A silly quarrel that both you and Christina are too proud to make up. Well, all you need is a third party to do it for you, and I've decided that I should act. And I've no doubt Christina will be as happy to see you here, when she comes home, as I am tonight.'

Jeremy's glance had been quizzical, but he took Roger's hand and shook it, his eyes moving over the boy's face with some interest. He was like Christina all right, with that tawny hair, though his eyes were not quite so green – a touch of Compson's darkness there. And something else – something that didn't remind him of Christina, but of someone else, some other member of the family – the resemblance escaped him and was lost. He smiled slowly, letting the old charm show through, and saw Roger respond.

Jeremy turned to smile again at Sarah, standing close beside her brother. Here again he saw Christina's colouring, but softened now to a gentle warmth, the fieriness of the hair quietened to the russet of sun-dried bracken, the tiger's eyes transmuted to those of a timorous kitten. How much did these two know? Very little, probably. Christina would hardly have told them the whole story of what had happened that night. And she clearly had not told Cousin Susan, or he would not be here now. And these two children – the only two Christina and Joe Compson had managed to produce between them – seemed pleasant enough. Impressionable – they were both regarding him with liking in their eyes.

It might be amusing to play with them a little. Just while their parents were away. See just how much he could charm them – win them over. Just for the pleasure of knowing how much Christina would dislike it. And to see what happened when Christina and Joe returned. He felt a lifting of his jaded spirits. Perhaps, after all, it had not been such a bad idea to come tonight.

From that moment, Jeremy exerted all his charm. He set out to capture the heart and interest of his young

131

cousin Sarah, and to impress Roger with his business sense and experience of the world. With acute sensitivity, he had seen exactly what aspect of his nature – or what he chose to display as his nature – would most please each member of his new coterie. By the end of the meal, he was well on the way to achieving his object; and what was more, his performance had been watched with approval by his parents and uncle, and with complacent delight by his Cousin Susan, who was now confirmed in her long-held belief that Jeremy was a thoroughly charming man and would have made an exceptionally suitable husband for her obstinate niece Christina.

'Now, you won't linger too long over your port, will you,' she admonished the men as she rose to lead the ladies out. 'We'll be expecting you in the drawing room for coffee – now, mind!'

The men watched them go. Samuel stroked the straggling grey whiskers that had once been brown and luxuriant, and gave his brother a quizzical glance.

'Susan's revelling in her position as mistress of the house once more. I wonder just how much she'll tell Christina about this evening.'

Harold laughed. 'Precious little, I guess! She's like a child playing house. Well, I hope she's enjoyed her little party. Pity Reuben couldn't have been here to make it complete.'

'Aye, she'd have liked that. Not that they were ever close – Reuben's never been close to anyone, family or no. Have you heard how he is, Hal?'

'Poorly.' Harold shook his big head gravely. He had worn better than Samuel, keeping his thick hair although it was now white. 'I doubt he'll last much longer.' His eyes turned to Jeremy, sitting at the end of the table with Roger. 'You ought to visit him, Jeremy. You won't have much more time. And he was good enough to you once. He took a lot of interest in you, if I remember.'

'Yes, he did,' Samuel agreed. 'Go and see him, Jeremy. It'd please your aunt, too.'

Jeremy hesitated. The thought of visiting his dying

uncle was abhorrent to him, yet there was no reason that he could give for refusing. How could he say that the thought of visiting Uncle Reuben, talking to him, looking once more into those lizard's eyes, perhaps even touching the reptilian skin, was a thought that sickened him? How could he tell them of the memories it would stir – memories that he had spent over twenty years in trying to suppress? He wanted to say no: a plain statement of a callousness that would come as no surprise to his father and uncle.

But as he glanced up, he caught Roger's eyes on him, and paused. He had spent much of the meal talking to his young cousin and observing him. He saw the boy as an empty slate on which he could draw anything he chose, and the idea excited him. Jeremy hoped very much that he would prove to be as cold-hearted and self-seeking as Jeremy himself. But he might equally be as soft-natured and compassionate as that kitten of a younger sister of his, and shocked by Jeremy's attitude towards a dying man.

And then, looking more intently into the hazel eyes, Jeremy knew suddenly of whom Roger reminded him. Why, the boy must be the image of Reuben himself as a young man! That sandy hair, the eyes that were not quite brown, not quite green, sliding away if you looked too deeply, as if their owner were somewhat shy – or perhaps wanted to conceal his thoughts . . .

Suddenly, surprisingly, Jeremy found himself wanting to see his uncle again after all. He wanted to see if there might be gestures, expressions, mannerisms he had forgotten, which would tie this unformed youth even more tightly to the old man. He wanted to see if Roger might, with careful guidance, become equally devious; even more dangerous . . .

His idea of using Roger as an instrument of revenge against Christina sharpened.

He turned his eyes away from Roger and smiled charmingly at his father and uncle.

'Very well,' he said, as if there had never been any

question in the matter. 'I'll go and see Uncle Reuben. You're right – he did take a great deal of interest in me once. I ought at least to wish him goodbye.'

'Well,' Samuel said, in obvious surprise, 'that's very good. I'm sure he'll be most grateful.' He turned to his brother. 'And now, Harold – about that new order for window-glass . . .'

They drew together, with Jeremy's brother Rupert shifting his chair to join them. Jeremy glanced at Roger.

'So your Aunt Susan is being a little naughty,' he murmured. 'Well, when the cat's away . . .'

Roger laughed aloud. 'That's exactly what I said! Sarah didn't understand at first, but . . .' He paused. 'It's good to meet you at last, Cousin Jeremy.'

'And I'm glad to have the chance to meet you too, Roger. Let's drop the "cousining" shall we?' He held out his hand with a friendly smile, and Roger took it. 'Now – tell me, what are your plans for the future – your future? You surely don't,' his smile flattered Roger and invited him to laugh a little, 'intend to follow your father into glassmaking, do you?'

Roger gave the laugh expected of him. 'Good God, no! At least, not as a glassmaker – well, that goes without saying, doesn't it.' His own smile, faintly deprecating and modest, nevertheless suggested that he was clearly made for higher things; and, moreover, that Jeremy himself would naturally recognise this. 'But I can see that there's potential there. Potential that Father and Mother don't even begin to realise.'

'Indeed?' Jeremy murmured, and waited for Roger to say more.

'Oh yes, without doubt. I've been through the books. And I've looked at what other glass manufacturers are doing.' Roger leaned closer. 'Paul sent me some of the catalogues from this Exhibition they've gone to see in Paris. Now, you should see some of the glass the French are selling to countries like Russia! Huge candelabra. Chandeliers such as have never been seen before. Great vases made of cased glass and bordered with gold. I tell

134

you, we've never even dreamed of some of the glass they're making there – and the prices they must command. Why, we've never even gone into paperweight production on any scale, yet look how popular such trinkets are. Sulphides, made to commemorate special occasions, with a cameo head encased inside – why aren't we making those? For civic occasions – presentations to retiring mayors, for instance. Small, yet they demand high prices. And *millefiori* – ideal for a gift to a wife, or a favourite mistress.' He gave Jeremy a quick, sidelong glance as if to assure himself that this worldly reference had not been lost. 'But it's the large, elaborate pieces I want to see being made here. They're our showpieces. The Orientals love them – and they'll order more for their palaces. And when they have those, they'll buy table services, elaborately cut and engraved, and gilded or figured with bronze. That's the way the market's going, but you have to have a wider outlook to appreciate that, and that's what I fear Mother and Father just don't have.'

He stopped at last and took a drink of port. Jeremy gazed at him speculatively. In Roger's impassioned speech, there had been more than a hint of Christina's fire. Given the chance, the boy could go a long way. But would Christina and Joe, each still in their prime and clearly intending to continue to run the glasshouse for many years yet, give him that chance? Would they listen to his ideas, or would they shrug them aside and tell Roger he must wait?

Jeremy knew that Joe Compson had never been a lover of decorated glass. He had always believed that form was of prime importance – the shape of the glass, as fashioned by the breath, the hands and the skill of the man who blew and marvered it. Glass, he said, was seen at its best when it was plain, its smoothly polished or gently curving sides reflecting the light without interruption. It had been a bone of contention between him and Christina when she had first set up the cutting and engraving shops, and it was only the clear demand of the market that had forced him to change his mind.

Jeremy knew the kind of glass Roger was talking of, and he felt sure that Joe would object to it with every fibre of his glassmaker's body.

'It all sounds most reasonable to me,' he said smoothly. 'But of course, it takes a younger eye to see these things, to begin with. That's the way of the world, I'm afraid. Older people cling to the ideas of their youth; they're afraid to give way in case they find themselves no longer useful. Naturally,' he added, 'you'll be overseeing things at the glasshouse yourself while they're away. An excellent opportunity to try out some of these ideas of yours. And when they come back and see how successful you've been . . .'

Roger hesitated. The thought of actually interfering in the glasshouse was one he had occasionally played with but had never quite dared to carry out. Yet – why not? He had left school, had little to do but study until he went to Oxford. At the same age, Paul had already been at work in the glasshouse, not only learning his craft but making suggestions, introducing new designs. Why should Roger not have an equal say?

He recovered himself quickly. He did not want Jeremy to think that he had not seen and taken every opportunity offered him.

'Oh, yes,' he answered casually, 'but you know what these labourers are . . . it takes time to get new ideas into their heads. They're worse than Mamma and Papa, in fact!' He laughed. 'But you're not like that, Jeremy.'

Jeremy smiled and made a small movement with his hand. 'Well, perhaps that's because I've always refused to become hidebound . . . and because I've never married. Domesticity has never caught me in its toils, so I've been able to keep a more detached view of life.'

Roger gave him a cautious glance. 'I did hear that you wanted to marry my mother once,' he ventured, and Jeremy laughed.

'Oh, that was years ago, when we were all a good deal younger than we are now! Passions run high when we're young, Roger – take note of that, and take warning. Any passion, given time, will cool. And meanwhile, there are other ways . . .' His eyes narrowed a little as he surveyed the boy. 'I think perhaps you need a little education in these matters,' he murmured thoughtfully. 'Clearly, your father would not be able to undertake it – I have no prejudice against him and his background, you understand, but it does have its deficiencies when it comes to introducing a personable son to the world . . . When did you say you go to Oxford?'

'In the autumn,' Roger said proudly, and Jeremy nodded.

'Something should certainly be done before then. Come to see me at home one afternoon next week. You know where I live?' Roger nodded. 'Then let's make it – shall we say, Tuesday? And – we'll keep it between ourselves, hm? A private discussion between men of the world.'

A silence fell at the other end of the table. Harold drew out his heavy gold watch and gave an exclamation.

'Half an hour! We ought to rejoin the ladies, I think.' He pushed his chair back and stood up. 'That all seems very satisfactory, Samuel. I'm glad we've had this opportunity to sort the matter out. Rupert – Jeremy?'

'Just coming, Uncle.' Jeremy smiled blandly, and turned back to Roger and said quietly, 'Tuesday, then?'

And, under his breath, Roger replied, 'I'll be there.'

He would tell nobody, Jeremy knew. And not merely because he had been asked to keep their meeting quiet; but because he was of a naturally secretive nature and would have done so anyway.

Jeremy stood back to allow the others to precede him. He was smiling. Who would have thought that, after all these years, the weapon for revenge would be handed to him so readily?

'. . . so I've decided we should experiment with new colours,' Roger ended. 'The true ruby that has eluded everyone . . . new blues and greens. Even black.' His eyes gleamed. 'Yes, a dense, jet black would do very well.'

The small group of men stirred uneasily, glancing at each other for support, and it was left for Ben to voice their objections.

'New colours?' he said doubtfully. 'Mr Joe never said naught to me about new colours afore he went away. Nor Mrs Compson, neither.'

'And why should they?' Roger said sharply. 'Presumably they can run their own glasshouse as they wish without consulting you at every turn! It should be enough for you that I'm giving these orders. I take it you're capable of carrying them out?' he added in a scathing tone, glancing round at the uncertain faces.

Bob Pritchard, the overseer, spoke up next. His voice was reproachful rather than indignant at this slur on the men's abilities, as if he had decided that Master Roger was only a boy, when all was said and done, and not so handy with words as his mother, nor as likely to understand the men's point of view as his father. 'Of course the lads can do it,' he said mollifyingly. 'It's just that we hadn't got no orders about it, see – didn't know there was any plans to go into new colours.'

'Well, you know now, and I'm giving you your orders,' Rogers said tersely. 'Ruby and black, they are what we're aiming at. Not the wishy-washy pink that passes for ruby – a real, deep, glowing colour. And the black –'

'Nobody's managed a true black so far,' Ben said quickly. 'It allus turns purple in the daylight. We'd hev to try different recipes – buy in different oxides and such.'

'Then do so.' Roger turned on his heel and surveyed the interior of the cone. The tall, smoke-blackened sides tapered above him to the round disc of sky that showed above the open top. In the centre of the floor, the dome of the furnace rose, the open mouths of the pots that were set around it glowing orange and red like the gaping jaws of fire-breathing dragons. The men worked around them in a steady rhythm, each chair a team of wordless efficiency; the gatherer drawing out the long iron tipped with its glowing bulb of metal, the blower breathing life into the swelling vessel, the gaffer sitting in his chair to shape and fashion the design on which he worked, a design that, as likely as not, had been first scrawled in an old schoolbook by Joe Compson himself. Occasionally, a man would pause as he swung his iron or passed it like a javelin to his mate, and glance in Roger's direction as if wondering what the younger son was doing here, giving orders, and the sight angered Roger; why should he *not* be here, why should he not be taking his part in the running of the family business? He had told Sarah that one day he would inherit everything: it was time he began to make his presence felt.

He turned back to the group of men he had summoned to hear his orders and looked them over. Bob Pritchard, uneasy but with little choice but to obey; Will Compson, his own uncle, interested more in his own chair than in any new-fangled ideas his nephew might dream up, and confident that Roger could do little harm before Joe came back and set everything to rights. And Ben Taylor.

Ben was Paul's friend. The two of them worked together, evolving new designs for Ben to blow and Paul to engrave. They spent a good deal of their spare time together. And it was Ben whom Roger most needed on his side, if his experiments were to be successful.

'I want you to take charge of this,' he said in as friendly a manner as he could manage. 'Ask in the office for all the old recipes you need, and order whatever materials you think may be necessary. I'll see that you're given every assistance.' He smiled. 'I want to have something to show my father and mother when they return – something that will surprise and please them, and I think you are the man to achieve just that.'

Ben's expression did not change. He looked at Roger unsmilingly.

'An' the cameo blanks?' he said. 'I'm supposed to be working on they for Master Paul. He's expecting me to hev summat for him to work on, time he comes back.'

The cameo – Roger had forgotten that. He swore softly to himself, but kept the smile fixed on his face. 'Oh, that's all right,' he said easily, 'Paul's written to me about those. You're to forget them for the time being – concentrate on the new colours. After all, he's not going to be back for quite a while.' Never, if luck should go my way, Roger said to himself, before continuing. 'And he might well decide to try the new colours for the cameo glass anyway. A vase in deep ruby might be even more effective than the dark blue of the Portland Vase. Or black – think of that. Black cameo. It could be extremely dramatic.' He gave Ben a friendly nod. 'Anyway, let me know if you have any problems. And I'll come in as often as I can to see how things are progressing.' He walked swiftly away before Ben could raise any more questions and slipped out through the double doors.

Outside, he leaned against the red-brick wall and took a deep breath. Well, he'd really done it now! Interference in the glasshouse was something neither Joe nor Christina would ever be likely to brook with equanimity. He just hoped that Ben Taylor would not let him down – would be able to produce a glass of both deep, stable colour and fine quality before they returned from Paris.

If he did – well, it would show that Roger was something more than the schoolboy they all took him for. It would give him some standing in the business. And it would set him on the first step of the road towards his rightful inheritance.

Reuben Henzel was lying in his bed at the house which looked over the main street of Stourbridge and the Talbot Hotel. He had had the bed moved, during the early stages of his illness, so that he could see out of the window and continue his favourite occupation of watching what went on in the street below. But now, so thin and frail that he made barely a ripple in the bedclothes that covered him, and so pale that he could scarcely be discerned amongst the pillows, he had lost interest in the street. He had lost interest in almost everything.

Interest struggled to revive, however, when his nephew Jeremy was announced.

'Jeremy . . .' The old voice was little more than a thread of sound. 'Jeremy, what brings you here? After all these years . . .'

'They told me you were ill, Uncle,' Jeremy said cheerfully, depositing a basket of fruit on the bedside table. Having come, he had determined to make the best of it; what could the old man do to him now, after all? 'I decided it was time to pay you a visit.'

'Time? Time doesn't mean much to me these days. Time's been no friend to me, Jeremy. Nor to you either, from the look of you.' The faded, lizard's eyes slid over him. 'You've aged, Jeremy. Yet you're still a young man – what are you, now? Forty-five, fifty?'

'Just past fifty, Uncle.' There was a hint of resentment in Jeremy's tone; he disliked being reminded of his age. He was too sharply aware of how wasted his life had been, how empty it was now.

'And never married, just like me.' Reuben wheezed a little and lay silent for a moment. Jeremy wondered if he were asleep. Then the voice fluttered through the room again. 'We had some good times together, though, didn't we? Made some plans.'

'Did we?' Jeremy said coldly; but Reuben was back in the past, haven of the old, and would not be deflected.

'Oh aye, we made some good plans. That Christina – what a hussy she was! Led us all a pretty dance, and you especially. First she would, and then she wouldn't – you never did manage to tame her, did you, nephew? Took a rough, raw glassmaker to do that . . . No, you were never a match for either of those two.'

Jeremy sat down beside the great bed. His body was stiff with the effort of curbing his tongue, restraining the anger that trembled through his lips. After a moment, he thrust down his temper and said coolly, 'Christina would have been no wife for me, Uncle. Too headstrong by far. Compson was welcome to her – still is.'

'Indeed?' Weak and exhausted though the voice was, there was still energy for a thread of mockery. 'Well, I'm glad you have no regrets, nephew. And still a beautiful woman, so they tell me.' The old eyes watched him, unblinking as a snake's.

'She may be. I never see her now.' Jeremy's indifferent tone barely concealed the vexation that seethed within him. Reuben was silent for a while, as if gathering together the few tattered wisps of strength that remained to him. A sullen fire burned in the grate, creating a fitful draught that did little to freshen the stuffy and over-furnished room with its dark crimson wallpaper almost blackened with age, and its plush upholstery that was thick with dust. From outside, muffled by thick curtains, came the sound of horses' hooves, the rattle of carts and carriages, the voice of people in the street.

The voice wheezed again from the depths of the bed.

'Yes, those were good times. Interesting times. Joshua dying untimely, leaving everything to that chit . . . all of us, pulling this way and that to wrest it from her . . . I admired her, you know. She had more to her than any of the rest of you. She deserved to win.' He chuckled, a rattling travesty of mirth. 'And you, growing more desperate with each day as she eluded you – almost any man better in her eyes, it seemed . . .' The eyes watched Jeremy's increasing anger and a thin cackle shook the scrawny frame and ended in a cough. 'Aye, but she didn't get the other one, did she? The Frenchman. She didn't have it all her own way. Aye, you did well there.'

'What do you mean?' Jeremy came half to his feet, his voice harsh in the stuffy room. 'What are you saying, Uncle Reuben? The Frenchman's death was –'

'An accident. I know. But a very *opportune* accident, wouldn't you agree?' The thin voice held all the old insinuating cadences, the old eyes were bright in the parchment face, the only signs of life in the wasted body. 'I'm surprised that nobody else realised just how opportune it was – how convenient. Or did they?'

Jeremy took a step towards him, his fist raised. Whether he would really have struck the old man, he never knew, but he paused in the act and saw Reuben's eyes watching him almost with pleasure.

Slowly, Jeremy lowered his hand. He turned away. It had been a mistake to come. He had always known it would be a mistake ever to encounter his uncle again. For a while, over twenty years ago, he had fallen under that malevolent spell and it had ruined his life. Everything he had done since then, every degrading act he had committed, had been done and committed in an effort to forget.

'Maybe Christina did suspect,' Reuben said with a faint cackle. 'Was that why she wouldn't have you – eh?'

Jeremy turned back to the bed. He stared down at the frail shell of his uncle with loathing. He wanted nothing but to get out of the room, as quickly as possible. But there was a feverishness lighting the pale eyes, a desperation that looked out from the empty soul within. There was fear; fear of dying, of what might lie ahead. It was as if Reuben were afraid to be left alone, as if he would do anything to keep Jeremy with him, to hold his terrors at bay.

And well may you fear, you old devil, Jeremy thought bitterly. And well may I fear, too, for what you drove me to do. But I've had to suffer the memory of that all these years. Why should you escape?

'Very well,' he said quietly. 'I'll tell you the truth about what happened that day. I've only ever told one other person, and that was in temper and caused me more trouble than I care to think about. But I shall tell you, too, tell you all the horror of it, because you deserve to know. It was half your doing, after all.' He paused and the old eyes stared up at him, unwinking, afraid. Reuben lifted a skeletal hand, clawing feebly at the air as if to stop him, but Jeremy ignored the mute plea that he saw in the crumpled face. He spoke again, ruthlessly, sparing nothing. 'Yes, I killed Jean-Paul Thietry. I pushed him into a pot of molten metal, searing, white-hot glass. I pushed him so hard that there could be no question of his surviving. Nobody could survive that, Uncle. His face – his head –' In spite of himself, Jeremy's voice shook at the memory '– went straight down into the pot. Can you imagine the effect, Uncle? Can you picture the result, what we saw when they dragged him away? It was like thrusting a piece of meat into a furnace. He came out *cooked*, Uncle. Roasted, like the pig he was.' His eyes burned into the old man's face. 'He just screamed the once,' he said quietly. 'It sounded like a soul in torment and I have heard it ever since.'

Reuben was moving his head slowly from side to side. His face was working, his mouth shaping words that would not come, his eyes terrified. He tried to whisper something but his voice had gone and he mouthed the word over and over again. 'No, no . . .'

'Yes, Uncle,' Jeremy said, and his voice was hard, implacable. 'Yes. I killed Jean-Paul Thietry, and precious little good it did me. And it was at your instigation. Do you realise what that means? You are as much to blame as I. You are as much a murderer as I am. And for that you will suffer in Hell. As I will.'

The old man's face twisted and distorted. A gurgling sound came from his throat, harshened to a rattle. He half lifted himself in the bed, body arched in a spasm of agony. His eyes begged, pleaded, implored for mercy, for absolution.

Jeremy looked down at him without pity. He watched as the expression froze and stiffened, leaving a look of pure terror, as if with their last glance the eyes had looked on unnamed horrors, on punishment that could not be borne. His uncle was dead. And Jeremy was glad.

But Reuben had left a terrible legacy; all the evil and the guilt clung like a miasma to everything in the room. And to Jeremy most of all.

# Chapter Seven

The Exhibition was a magnet; in the week in which it opened, the Compson family went four times – and the glass displays drew them all. Henzel's had, of course, sent its own glass, a stand of fine tableware that glittered under the soaring arches of the glass roof, and they spent hours studying the exhibits so proudly contributed by such firms as Baccarat, St Louis and Clichy, as well as Thietry. But they were also attracted by the many exotic stalls and kiosks from countries like Turkey, Egypt, Mexico and Arabia. It was, Emily said as she wandered around with Paul, like walking into a fairytale. She almost expected to step on to a magic carpet and be wafted away to some strange and mythical land where great birds flew and talked, and genies spiralled smokily out of lamps.

There was no magic carpet. But there was, almost as unbelievable, a hot-air balloon – a vast yellow and green globe that soared overhead, tethered by a long rope, with a huge two-tiered gondola that swung beneath it and carried people like toys to view the Exhibition from the air. It was called *Céleste* and it was flown, Véronique told them, by the famous French photographer Nadar, who took photographs from the balloon itself, showing the Exhibition laid out like a child's elaborate toy, a bird's-eye view of pavilions and tents, with the great glass dome that the Emperor had called the 'greatest gasometer in the world' gleaming and reflecting the glittering sunlight like a giant bubble in the midst of it all.

'Oh, I should like to go up in the balloon,' Paul said longingly, and Emily clasped his arm and begged to go too. But Véronique shuddered and covered her mouth with her hands and declared that nothing, but *nothing*, would compel her to fly in the air like a bird. 'For I am *not* a bird,' she insisted, 'and not a butterfly, nor anything that has wings, so how could I fly?'

Emily glanced at her with irritation. She was growing tired of Véronique's kittenish, little-girl ways and she was exasperated by the way the French girl clung to Paul, following him everywhere, constantly demanding his attention, behaving more each day as if she owned him.

Worse still, he seemed to enjoy it! Emily had expected that he would quickly tire of the charms of his little cousin. But the fascination Emily had noticed on the first day seemed to have increased; he barely took his eyes off her now and scarely noticed Emily herself. Hurt and distressed, she withdrew into herself, trying to tell herself that it was no more than a passing fancy, that the closeness between Paul and herself would reassert itself soon enough. Surely, she thought, surely he must feel for her as she felt for him; surely such love could not have grown in her heart alone. But more and more, she was gripped by the cold fear that he was already lost to her.

Véronique was gazing at him now with huge blue eyes, limpid and comically imploring, and he laughed indulgently. 'But you are the nearest thing to a bird that I have ever seen,' he teased her. 'A little jenny-wren, perhaps, or – no – you're a humming-bird, tiny and bright as a jewel and never still for a moment. And always singing and laughing. Of course you could go in the balloon, Véronique. People are doing it every day – Nadar takes a dozen at a time to look at the Exhibition. Do say you'll come with me – it would be such fun. We might even be able to see the house from up there.'

But Véronique shook her head and refused again and Emily, chilled to the heart by a tone and expression he had never used towards her, cut in brusquely and asked how the balloons worked. 'What makes them fly? Why do they stay up – and why do they come down again?'

Paul turned back to her. 'They're filled with gas. The gas that comes from coal and is used for lighting and cooking – see the long tube, leading from the gas supply to the balloon?' They watched as the brilliantly coloured envelope, laid flat on the ground, swelled and began to rise as if already anxious to be aloft. It was held down by ropes, with men struggling with the basket to keep it weighed down, while those at the crown leaned back on the straining cable, paying it out slowly so that the balloon rose steadily with the gas that was filling it. Emily clasped her hands excitedly together as she watched the giant sphere rise slowly into the air until it swayed above the basket, almost vertical, a mass of silken fabric transformed into something live that pulled at its bonds in a vain effort to escape.

Nadar himself was in charge of the operation. He marched importantly around the space that had been cleared, clearly conscious of the crowd that watched so admiringly but affecting not to notice them. He examined the ropes, the anchor that hung from the lower part of the basket; he shaded his eyes and stared up at the billowing silk. And then, at last, he turned and waved his arm. There was a sigh from the crowd, and those who had paid for their voyage into the sky walked self-consciously out into the arena and climbed into the great basket.

'It's like a house, that basket,' Véronique murmured as they watched the aeronauts scramble aboard and peer out of the windows like so many rabbits going to market. 'No, I would not go in that for a million francs.'

'I would,' Emily said. 'I'd go with you, Paul.' But again, she had the feeling that he had not heard her.

Nadar climbed aboard. He went straight to the top of the basket, from where he could operate the valves that released the gas when he wanted the balloon to descend. He leaned out and shouted to the men below, and they began to cast off the ropes that moored the vessel to the ground.

'Aah!' Again they heard the collective sigh from the crowd. The balloon lifted a little; hesitated; then, slowly, rose into the air, tethered now by only one long rope. It began to drift away as it rose and there were a few tiny screams from people on the ground. But those in the basket made no sound; their faces were awed as they rose, and then became little more than spots of pink. Emily could see them turning to each other, pointing out things on the ground. She longed, passionately, to be with them. And then, as the balloon reached its maximum height, they were too high to be more than pinpricks, tiny silhouettes against the sky, and the globe hung above them like an exotic and mysterious visitor from another world.

'Tomorrow,' Paul said. 'Tomorrow I'll go up. After we've been to the showrooms again. And perhaps then you'll come with me – yes, Véronique?'

But Véronique shook her blond curls. And Emily, watching them laugh into each other's eyes, turned away her head. Her heart felt sick.

'It's been a wonderful evening. Simply wonderful.' Véronique smiled gaily around the table. 'And to think that it isn't over, even yet. Here we are in the Café Anglais. We have been to the Conservatoire and seen the new actress Sarah Bernhardt – although I had much rather have gone to hear Theresa sing. But no matter! We have our supper to choose, wine to drink. And who knows what famous people might come in for us to see! They all come here, you know – George Sand, Madame Rimsky-Korsakoff – '

'And none of them more beautiful or enchanting than you,' Paul said, lifting his glass to her. 'Is that dress made by the famous Mr Worth?'

Véronique laughed. 'Of course not! Have you any idea what he charges for his clothes? One would imagine it should be less now that he has discarded the crinoline and does not need so many yards of material – but no, they are more expensive than ever. The new fabrics, the trimmings – lace, jet, Lyons silk and brocade – all cost a great deal of money.'

'Too much for a young girl,' Marc said, watching her with an indulgent eye. 'Perhaps when she grows up a little . . .'

'Oh . . .' Véronique pouted. 'I am quite grown up now, *mon oncle*. Am I not, Paul?'

She gave him a quick, fluttering, upward glance and Emily saw the colour come into his cheeks. Swiftly, she held her own menu in front of him. 'Help me to choose what to eat, Paul. There's so much, I'm completely bewildered.'

The menu was like a book, ornately decorated, its parchment covers opening to pages that were made of fine tissue with the choice of dishes written on them in delicate copperplate. Paul and Emily stared at them, trying to decipher the elaborate lettering, and Véronique leaned over, her silvery curls brushing Paul's cheek.

'Caviare for *hors-d'oeuvre*, of course. And carp next – or would you prefer this: *mouton à l'Anglaise*! Imagine, an English dish in the fashionable Café Anglais! And then I shall have the *poulardes à la Mazarin* and the ortolans, and all the vegetables, and perhaps the peaches. And after that –'

'After that,' Cécile said firmly, 'you will be ill. Give me the menu, child, and I will choose something more suitable for a young digestion.'

'Oh, yes,' Emily said in relief. 'Choose for me too, please, madame.'

It was difficult not to be overawed by the restaurant. The golden walls were lit by sparkling crystal chandeliers, their glitter reflected in a dozen or more mirrors that encircled the domed ceiling. All around them, seated at round tables covered with long white cloths made of satin, sat the other diners: whiskered men in tail coats and tight breeches, with white waistcoats and frilled shirts; women with bare shoulders and flowing gowns of rich velvet or sumptuous tulle, lavishly trimmed with ribbons and laces and sparkling jewellery that were echoed in their elaborate *coiffures*.

Emily glanced round at her family. Christina, of course, would look at home anywhere; dressed tonight in her favourite bronze, gold and green, her rich tawny colouring needed no further embellishment. Only a necklace of heavy gold, sparkling with emeralds, and a pair of matching earrings decorated her flawless skin, and Emily remembered her exclamation of delight when Joe had presented her with the jewels only a few months ago, on their wedding anniversary. 'But when shall I wear them?' she had cried then, holding them against her. 'They're far too showy for Stourbridge.' But here, in Paris, they looked restrained, even modest, amidst all the opulence that surrounded them.

Paul, too, looked completely at ease. He was talking to Véronique again, half turned away from Emily as he gave the younger girl his full attention, and Emily looked at his slender body in the new evening clothes and felt a chill of loneliness. Here in Paris, he seemed to slip easily into Parisian ways, and there were moments when he became almost a stranger. He seemed more commanding, more in control. He ordered the waiters about with ease, even in such ornate surroundings as these. He was cool, as nonchalant as any other young Parisian in the restaurant, quite unabashed by the patronising air of the haughty waiters, and Emily wondered how he had managed to learn such manners in such a short time. Or were they simply a part of his nature; part of his French ancestry?

She saw that Christina was watching him with pride, a pride that was mixed with a wistful sadness. And suddenly she felt herself to be on the outside of some charmed circle, a hungry, ragged child with her nose pressed against a window, gazing longingly at the warmth and affection within.

The only place on earth where she really wanted to be at that moment was in Wordsley – in Henzel Court, in the old schoolroom, with the fire blazing and the fog coming down outside, and Nellie running in from the street, breathless, with an old shawl thrown round her shoulders and a dish of fresh, hot muffins in her hand.

Christina reached her bedroom later with a sigh of relief. She kicked off her shoes and stretched her arms wearily.

'Thank you, Nellie. I'll just take off this gown and you

can hang it up. You needn't wait any longer. Mr Compson will help me.'

Together they struggled to get her out of the dress, its tight-fitting bodice fastened with a score of tiny buttons up the back, its skirt voluminous with its layers of lace petticoats and yards of flounced silk. At last she stood breathless in chemise and stays, and Nellie gathered the mass of brilliant material together and disappeared.

Joe came to help, his big fingers moving as delicately as butterflies over her back as he unfastened the stays that Christina's slender waist still hardly needed. He dropped the restricting whalebone and gently turned her round to face him.

'You were the best-looking woman in the place, my love. And I'll wager not one of them looks as fine as you do this minute.'

Christina laughed. 'And you're a bigger charmer than any Frenchman, Joe. Did you enjoy it?'

'Enjoy it? I'd as soon have a drink with the lads in the tavern any day of the week! Well –' he caught her expression and grinned a little '– almost any day, anyway! It was an experience, I'll give you that. Something to remember when we're back at home. But – I don't feel easy in those places, do you? I mean, it's all so – so overdone. Too much money, and when you look behind it, it's shabby somehow. Those dresses – they look so fine, all that lace and trimming, but if you look close you can see they're not properly clean, half of them. And most of the women proper sluts, no better than they should be, as my ma would say. And they're all so open about it all; talking about courtesans and lovers and such in front of a chit like Véronique – it all seems a bit queer to me.'

'Yet the Thietrys are respectable people, and extremely careful of Véronique – they watch her every moment and she is never allowed to go out alone.' Christina moved over to the mirror and began to brush her hair thoughtfully. 'You're right, Joe, they have a different attitude from us. And it's beginning to worry me.'

'Worry you? Why should it?' He came behind her,

151

slipping his hands round to cup her breasts, his dark eyes meeting hers in the mirror. 'We'll be going home soon, and thankful enough I'll be too.'

'Yes, Joe. *We* shall be going home.' She turned in his arms and looked up into his face, the brush still caught in the thick, rippling curls of her tawny hair. 'But we promised that Paul could stay. And now – I'm not so sure.'

'You think it'd be bad for him?'

'I'm sure of it. He's so impressionable, Joe. So volatile. Already I can see the idea that he's half French going to his head. He is beginning to feel that he belongs here – that this is his true home. He is developing an arrogance that I don't like.' She moved away from Joe's encircling arms. 'Marc Thietry is kindness itself, he means nothing but good, I'm sure. But he doesn't realise the difference between the French and the English. His sophistication, the manners of the Parisians, their whole attitude towards life, towards work and wealth – it's not like ours, Joe. They think too much of pleasure – of frivolity. The restaurant tonight, it was full of people who live like that all the time. And they know nothing of what is happening outside – the poverty that still exists in the back streets, the threat of war that they choose to shrug aside. It's decadent.'

'I think so too,' Joe said soberly. 'There's things here I don't like at all . . . But you don't think our Paul would be affected by these things, do you? He's a decent lad, we've both seen to that.'

'I know.' Christina sighed. 'I'm probably worrying over nothing, Joe. All I know is, I'd be happier if Paul were coming home with us.'

'And Emily? You haven't forgotten why we thought it might be best for them to be parted for a while?'

'I haven't forgotten,' she answered seriously. 'But I think somehow that the risk is now less great. Paul has grown away from Emily while he's been here, and she knows it. I think perhaps I worried overmuch about that, too.'

She stood beside the big bed, looking down absently at the coverlet. And Joe came to her again and this time when he drew her into his arms she did not move away.

'Then stop worrying now, my love, about all of it,' he said softly. 'Come to bed.' And he bent his head and laid his mouth on hers with a tenderness that increased, with the ease of long years of loving, to passion. And Christina felt the fire rise within her, as it always did, to meet the burning need that spoke silently in his lips. She arched herself against him and let her hands move slowly up, over the muscular back and the wide shoulders, to tangle luxuriously in his thick, curling hair.

'I wish everyone could be as well-matched as we are, Joe,' she whispered as he lifted her and laid her gently on the bed, and Joe laughed deep in his throat.

'That would be asking for paradise. And paradise . . .' he let one hand run lightly down her body from shoulder to thigh, causing her to draw in a quick breath and move suddenly with urgent desire '. . . paradise belongs to us.'

' "A mirror to mankind",' Christina read. 'What a wonderful description that is.' She folded the newspaper she was reading and looked around the room. 'That is exactly what the Paris Exhibition does, don't you agree? It holds up a mirror to mankind.'

Joe grunted. He was deep in his own paper; copies of the English newspapers were available in the city only two or three days after being printed, and he buried himself in them as soon as they appeared, reading both the home and the international news.

'How do you mean, madame?' Cécile asked. 'How is it a mirror?'

They were all gathered in the salon for the after-dinner hour; Véronique was seated at the piano, her slender fingers wandering idly over the keys to provide a background of rippling notes as dainty and featherlight as herself. Marc Thietry, like Joe, had immersed himself in a newspaper. Cécile had taken up her usual seat, almost hidden in a corner, where she sat sewing by the light of a gas lamp, and Paul and Emily were together on the sofa, looking at one of the Thietry glass catalogues.

Christina laid her paper down.

'A mirror to mankind,' she repeated thoughtfully. 'Why, I suppose because it reflects so much of the world today. Not just because of all the wonderful exhibits, but because the whole world seems to have come to see it. Look at our visit today. We saw and mingled with people of almost every nationality – not only from all over Europe, but from Russia, Japan, even China. Why, I believe that that part of it – simply promenading the walks and sitting in the various restaurants and cafés, trying each other's style of food – all that is even more important than the Exhibition itself, impressive though that is. It must take us all a step nearer to world peace.'

'And sharing in each other's achievements too,' Paul agreed. 'All the marvellous machinery, displayed there for all to see and for every country to take back home. I agree, Mamma. Exhibitions such as this one make the world a better place.'

Joe grunted again. But his tone was cynical, and Christina turned quickly.

'Are you going to tell us we're wrong, Joe?'

'Are you going to tell me you're right?' He jabbed a finger at the page before him. 'Oh, I know the exhibits are all very fine. The machines, the engines, the paintings and fabrics – aye, if you believed all that *they* tell you, you'd think the world was a right comfortable place. But there's plenty that still live hard, even in this city they're all so proud of.' He glanced at Marc Thietry. 'I'm sorry, monsieur, if that offends you, but it's true enough and I don't think you'll deny it. I've been out a bit on my own, just walking about, and I've seen a few things in those warrens behind the boulevards that I reckon a lot of Parisians would rather forget. People living in one room, no windows but a hole in the tiles that lets in air right enough and all else too – cold, wind, rain, snow, flies, vermin – aye, and naught but an old animal skin or a bit of rag to block it up with. People with no furniture, nothing but a few sacks and a rickety iron stove they've found when the houses were being demolished, and clung to all the time they were homeless. Those are the things you don't show in your fine Exhibition.' He paused. 'Like I said, I don't mean to cause offence, especially since we're guests here, but I'm a blunt sort of a man and I speak as I find.'

Marc Thietry stirred uncomfortably and cleared his throat. He glanced around the room. Emily found her eyes fixed upon him; she was unable to tear her gaze away. Her heart beat with admiration for her father and indignation that people should still be living so, when she herself was warm and comfortable and well-fed. Was every city like this, then? Were there always to be those who had nothing, while others possessed so much?

'Well, you are right, of course,' Marc said at last. 'I cannot deny that even now there are parts of our beautiful city which are not at all lovely – like blemishes on the face of an exquisite woman. But like those blemishes, these eyesores will gradually disappear. It is not possible to do all at once.'

'I understand that. But does there have to be such a contrast between the – what do you call 'em – the *bourgeois*, and the poor? There's money being made here, all right. Every man has his carriage and his horses, his coachman and his lackey. Every lady has her lady's maid and her cook. Well, that's the way it is at home, I'm not denying that. But the people who keep the whole thing going – the men who do the *work* – why, they live in poverty. If there's enough money to pay for carriages and fine clothes, there's enough to put bread and meat into the mouths of those who work for it – that's what I say.'

His voice did not rise; it remained at the same level, only growing more intense. Christina laid her hand on his arm, but Marc Thietry shook his head and gave a small laugh.

'Don't concern yourself, madame. Your husband is a

man of strong opinion. Why should he not say what he feels to be right? And I agree with him. Not enough is done for the man who does the work, the labouring.' His grey eyes gleamed a little as he added, 'And am I not right in thinking that one could find the same situation in your own cities? You are not going to tell me that there are no poor in England, no inequalities? And in our own industry, at least, we are making efforts to redress the balance. Look – I will show you.' He rose and went to the large bureau that stood in the corner of the room. 'Here I have some of the papers of our own factory. See.' He brought a sheaf of documents and dropped them in Joe's lap. 'This is how we care for our own people.'

Joe began to leaf through the papers, Christina moving closer so that she could translate. For a few moments there was silence save for the soft murmuring of her voice, and then she glanced up, her green eyes sparkling.

'This is excellent, monsieur! See, Joe – since the early thirties there has been a doctor living in the glasshouse community, and a school operated for the children.' She read further, her finger moving slowly along the lines, her lips whispering the translation. 'And you have your own savings bank too, and even a scheme to give a pension to the men who can no longer work.' Her eyes danced at Joe. 'Well, you can't complain about that! It's as good as anything our unions have done, and all organised by the employers.'

Marc smiled. 'It is not so bad, is it? What do you think, Joseph? Does it redeem us a little?'

Joe shrugged. 'I can't say that's not good, because it is. It's just a pity more don't follow your example. And that goes for English manufacturers as well as French. You're right, monsieur – we have just as much poverty in our streets. It's just the way Paris tries to pretend it's not there and goes all out for show that sticks in my craw. How long have you been working this scheme?'

Marc laughed and threw out his hands in a disclaimer. 'Alas, I cannot claim that it was our own idea. The firm of Baccarat began such a plan before we did. But it was so clearly successful that we very quickly copied them. As our closest rivals, we watch them carefully, just as they watch us, and we do not allow them to keep anything successful to themselves, you understand.'

'Successful?' Paul asked from the sofa. 'In what way? I mean, how do you measure success – in terms of production, I imagine.'

'Indeed. That is what we are all here for, *n'est-ce pas*? But such success can be derived in many ways. For example, a healthy worker is also an efficient worker, you will agree there? So, *naturellement,* we wanted our men to be healthy and prosperous – and in Lorraine they are our family too. And we also saw that a workman who is well cared for by his employers will have a greater loyalty. Do you not find that yourselves?'

'Yes, we do,' Christina said. 'There was a great strike and lock-out in the glass factories nearly ten years ago. We refused to sign the document other employers wanted to enforce, and we refused to lock out our own men. And they didn't strike – we kept working all the way through.'

'Aye, and helped those who were locked out, too,' Joe said. 'And you're right, monsieur. Men who've been well treated don't forget.'

Thietry nodded. 'It has been proved here too. In 1848, not long after my son died, we went through a great crisis here in France. Times were as hard as during the Revolution over fifty years before, and our production ceased altogether for a while. We were forced in the end to make our own bread to give to the workers who had nothing. And perhaps it is for that reason, and because of our medical and pension schemes, and the schools we have established, that we, too, have never had a strike.' He paused and smiled. 'You may say, as some have done, that we have bought the loyalty of our workers. We prefer to think that we have earned it.'

'Aye, and so you have.' Joe shuffled the papers together and handed them back. 'Thanks for showing us these, monsieur. I can see you're not one of those that believes in keeping all the profits for your own comfort and forgetting who helped to earn it. I reckon there's food for thought there for us too, don't you, my love?' he added to Christina. 'All the same –' he tapped the newspaper that still lay on his knee '– I don't think we ought to be too pleased with ourselves over the way the world's going. Your Exhibition is all very fine, I'll grant you that, but there's things there that make me feel uneasy and I don't mind admitting it.'

'Uneasy?' Christina stared at her husband. 'How do you mean, Joe?'

'Why, look at that great gun we saw yesterday. The one sent by – what was his name? The Prussian.'

'Herr Krupp,' Paul said.

'That's it. Krupp. Great black monster of a gun, weighs fifty tons they say – and it's not the only one, either. I was having a look at all those exhibits while the rest of you were off admiring that so-called Peace statue the Emperor put in. Peace! You take a look at the things men are thinking up now to kill each other with, and you'll agree with me – peace seems to be a thing of the past, more than the future.'

There was an uneasy silence, broken only by the tiny snap of cotton as Cécile broke off another length. Then Marc laughed and said, 'Oh, but men will always put on a show of strength. It means nothing. In fact, it helps to keep the peace – who will go to war with a country which can manufacture such weapons? And if we make them too, who will attack us? No, the Exhibition is a force for good, it must be. We are all beginning to see now that nobody can win a game of mutual destruction. And it is by witnessing each other's skill in both art and industry that we learn to appreciate our neighbours and the peace that is between us.'

Joe shook his head. 'I'm sorry, monsieur, but the news don't agree with you. Look here, in the very next column to the one that reports on the Exhibition – an article all about the Luxembourg question. Rumours that France has issued an ultimatum to Prussia and might even go to war over it. Stories that the French government has been buying horses for the army. It doesn't look good to me.'

'Rumours! Stories! You know these newspapers, they'll print anything to cause a sensation.' Marc shook his silver head and went over to the cabinet. 'You are depressed, Joseph. You need a brandy to lift your spirits.'

'Well, maybe you're right. Though I don't know why I should be down. You've given us a good enough time here.' Joe accepted the glass that was handed him and warmed the bowl in his palms. 'Truth is, I reckon I've been away from home long enough. I need to get back to my cones. I've been missing the feel of a blowing iron in my hands, that's about the top and bottom of it.' He turned to Christina. 'Time we went home, I reckon, don't you, my love?'

Christina smiled and took his hand. 'Perhaps you're right, Joe. I keep finding myself thinking of home too. Roger and Sarah – I've never been away so long from them. And the cones, and the engraving and cutting shops – I keep wondering if all's well. And we've seen so much here – there are so many new ideas in my head, ideas I want to try out for myself.' She looked over at the Thietrys. 'You've been so hospitable, I wonder how I can possibly bring myself to leave. But, well –'

'One's home is always the best place,' Cécile said gently. 'I know I could never bring myself to leave mine.'

Home. Emily felt the word strike like a knife into her heart. Like Christina and Joe, she had found her thoughts turning to her home, to the smoky town with its dour mills and forges, its long factory roofs and tall chimneys, its clattering machinery and gritty roads. Life there, she thought, was real, it was down to earth, honest and genuine.

But, in leaving Paris behind her, she would also be leaving Paul. Slowly, as if it gave her pain, she turned her head to look at him, hoping a last, faint, desperate hope that he might have changed his mind, might even now announce that he would be going home with them.

But immediately, her hope was dashed. Paul was sitting upright in his chair. She could see that every muscle was tense, every nerve alert. His face was bright with eagerness, his eyes glinting as silver as stars on a frosty night.

And, as she might have known, they were fixed on Véronique, beautiful as an exotic butterfly on the far side of the room.

Véronique, the kitten, the little girl, the enchantress. Véronique, who would soon, all too soon, be a woman.

'Paul. Please, Paul, don't look like that. Don't you want to go home at all?' Emily's voice was thick with tears she could not shed. 'Don't you have any wish to see the others again: Sarah and Roger and Aunt Susan? Don't you even want to begin work again, engraving –'

'Engraving? Engraving the same glass as before we came away? When I could be working here, on new glass, using different techniques?' He whipped round on her, his eyes blazing with that same strange, fanatical light that had so frightened her before. 'I thought *you* might understand, Emily.'

'I do – I do!' Panic was in her voice now, she dared not let him see that she cared nothing for his desires, only that he should come home again and be her gentle, loving Paul once more. 'But it's not just the engraving, Paul – it's everything. How can you want to be left here, alone in a strange city, a strange country? I don't –'

'It's not strange. It's *my* city, Emily, my country. The Thietrys are my family as much as you and Roger and Sarah are. It's time I learned about that part of myself. Their blood runs in my veins – how can I come for just a few weeks and then turn my back on them? I'm their only grandchild – I'm *important* to them.'

'You're important to us – to Mamma and to me.' She caught at his arm. 'Paul, I told you before we left England, I couldn't bear to be without you. And since we came here . . . well, I've felt that I've lost you a little more each day. If you stay here without us, I'm afraid you'll never come home.' She turned away, the tears flowing at last, her hands up to her face. Paul stared uneasily at her, and then turned abruptly away.

'You're talking nonsense, Emily. Of course I'll come back. In any case, what should it matter to you if I don't? Families do part, you know that. Look at Uncle Harry and Aunt Ruth. They've gone to America, but did Mamma make a fuss about that?'

'She didn't like it. She was very unhappy when they left.'

'But she didn't make a *fuss* about it. Emily, I'm a grown man now, I can't be tied to Mamma's apron strings for ever. Nor to yours. I am staying in Paris, and I shall stay as long as I like. Nobody will stop me.'

Emily took her hands from her face. The dark rosiness of her cheeks was streaked with tears, and wisps of black hair were plastered against the wet skin. She shook her head slowly.

'It isn't just the glass, is it? It's her – Véronique. I've seen you looking at each other. You spend as much time as possible with her. You forget me for hours at a time, but you're always thinking of Véronique. I've seen it in your eyes.'

'And what if I am?' he demanded. 'What is it to do with you?'

'It's everything to do with me!' she cried desperately. 'Haven't I lived with you, shared everything with you since we were both babies?' She shook her head blindly, unable to go on, and he cut in quickly.

'That doesn't make it any of your business, Emily. We're not babies now, we're not in the nursery. You can't rule me as you did then. I'm a man now and I have to order my own life. I don't run to you for help or advice.' His eyes were cold, his voice unfriendly. 'You can't run my life for me now, Emily. You'll have to find some other man to play tyrant with.'

'*Tyrant*?' she gasped, and he shrugged.

'Isn't that what you like to be? Emily the big sister,

running the nursery, dominating the rest of the family? Emily, always ready to play nursemaid, keep the little ones under control, order everyone about. Well, you can't order *me* about any longer, Emily. You'll have to find some other man to dominate.'

Emily stared at him, shaken and unbelieving. How could Paul speak to her like this – so cruelly, so angrily, as if she had done something to hurt and injure him? 'Paul, I've never tried to dominate you,' she began tremblingly. 'I want to help you. I want you to be happy, that's –'

'No! *You* want to be happy, Emily. If you wanted me to be happy you'd be encouraging me to stay here, *wanting* me to stay. But you're not thinking of me at all – you're thinking of yourself. You just can't bear to think of me here without you, doing what I choose without reference to you. You can't bear the thought that I might even be happy without you. Well, I shall! Very happy indeed, without you always breathing down my neck, wanting to know where I've been, what I've been doing, who I've been talking to.'

'Paul, that's not fair! I don't breathe down your neck. And if I'm interested in you, what is so strange about that? Haven't we always been interested in each other? Haven't we always shared things?' She approached him, hands held out, palms upwards. 'Paul, what has happened to you? Since we came to Paris you've become a stranger. You seem to have turned away from us – from the whole family. It's as if you no longer care.' Her breath caught on a sob. 'Paul, don't let's part in anger. Don't you see –' she raised her eyes to his, great dark pools of anguish in her ashen face '– don't you see I love you? And I thought you loved me too. I can't bear to quarrel with you like this. I can't bear you to look at me like that – to speak to me so coldly.'

He looked away, discomfited for the first time. 'Well, of course I love you,' he muttered. 'You're my sister, aren't you? Naturally we love each other. But that doesn't mean we –'

'No,' she interrupted, her voice breaking. 'I don't mean that kind of love, Paul. I don't mean a sister's love.' She came close, laid her hands on his arms and looked into his face. 'Have you forgotten – I am not your sister? There is no blood relationship between us at all. I am not even related to you as much as Véronique.' She took a deep breath. 'It is not as a sister that I love you, Paul; it is as a woman.'

He stared at her, appalled, then looked down at the hands that lay on his arms. They were square, capable hands, hands that spoke of commonsense and reliability – hands inherited from Joe Compson, the master glass-blower. They were quite unlike his own long, tapering fingers.

'Emily, you don't mean this. You're just upset . . .' But his voice was wavering, uncertain. 'You can't possibly feel that you – that we . . .' Again, he gave up and turned away, brushing her hands from his arms. She sensed his withdrawal, knew that he could not accept her words, that he would take refuge in outrage. 'Why, it's indecent!' He was on safer ground now and his voice strengthened. 'Whether or not we're brother and sister, it's how we've been brought up, how we've been taught to regard each other. Anything else between us would be – would be immoral . . . I wonder you are not ashamed to say such things, Emily. I wonder you can look me in the face.'

She looked at him sadly. 'You're not being honest with me, Paul. You feel it too – I know you do. You began to feel it before we left Stourbridge. Oh, I wish we had never come here! If we had stayed at home, never come to Paris, you would have –'

'No! Don't say it!' He wheeled round, his face pale now with anger. 'Don't ever say it! It's not true, Emily, it's not true – it's your imagination, you're overheated, overstrung – you're hysterical. Yes, perhaps you're right – *you* should never have come to Paris, it's been bad for you, given you strange ideas. But I – I belong here. It's part of me.' His eyes blazed again with an almost fanatical gleam. 'In Paris, I can do great work – I know I can. And no silly schoolgirl hysterics are going to stop me.'

'Schoolgirl hysterics?' Emily had recovered herself now. She looked at him, seeing a young man in danger of being spoilt by a newly discovered family who made too much of him, seeing an artist who believed himself to be a genius. 'And you say *I'm* thinking only of my own happiness! How many other people are you thinking of, Paul? Just one, I should say, and she no more than a flibberty-gibbet child. And you'll toss her aside too, discard her just as you've discarded me if she doesn't happen to fit in with your plans. Oh, you pretend to be so moral – we mustn't love each other because we've shared a nursery, because we were children together – but you forget about kindness. You forget about love.' She stepped close to him again, but there was no yearning in her eyes now, and the anguish had been supplanted by an anger that was like ice in her blood. 'I offered you my heart, Paul,' she said in a low, throbbing voice, 'and you rejected it. You rejected it as if it were worthless – as if it were an *insult*. I shan't forget that. I shall never forget that.'

She turned away from him and walked to the door. Her back was straight, her head proud on the slim neck. As she laid her hand on the doorknob she turned. Her face was as white as marble, and as cold; her eyes were like stones.

'Stay in Paris, Paul. But when you do return to Stourbridge – if you ever do – don't look to find me waiting for you. I have more useful ways in which to spend my life.'

# Chapter Eight

Nothing anyone could do would bring him back.

It was as if he had died, Emily thought, sitting as she so often did these days at her bedroom window and staring sightlessly out over the hot, dusty garden and down at the rumbling chimneys and roofs of Stourbridge. All the glory and excitement of the trip to Paris was wiped out by that one cruel blow and now life for her had lost its purpose, become meaningless, empty. She spent her time endlessly reliving those days in Paris; seeing again the Exhibition, the Thietry showrooms, the narrow, hilly streets, the airy boulevards; seeing Paul absorbed in the glass his grandfather was showing him; seeing Paul with Véronique, his eyes on her fairy princess beauty, admiring, entranced.

And always, with a pain in her heart that was sharper, more agonising than anything she could have imagined, living again that last quarrel, stabbed by the brutality of his angry rejection.

What are you doing now, Paul? she wondered, as she wondered so often during each long, tedious day and each endless night. And she thought of him living in the house on Montmartre with his grandparents who would make much of him, and with Véronique who adored him.

'He came here? Jeremy came *here*? You invited that man to this house?'

It was the first time Christina's voice had been heard raised since their arrival home, and everyone seated at the dinner table jumped and looked towards her. Joe, at the other end, half rose to his feet, his brows coming together in a dangerous black bar.

'What's that? What did I hear you say?' He looked at

Christina, whose eyes were like dark green wells in the pallor of her face. Two spots of colour flew angry flags high in her cheeks and her breath came quickly, her breasts rising and falling with the force of it. She was staring at her aunt, who was sitting halfway along the table. Between Susan and Christina, Roger sat in his usual lounging position, a small smile on his face and his eyes bright as he watched the sudden interchange. Neither Susan nor Christina seemed for a moment able to speak, but as Christina opened her mouth at last, Susan came quickly to life.

'It was nothing, Christina. Nothing. You weren't even here. I thought –'

'You thought what? That with me out of the way, you were mistress here? That you could do whatever you liked, without reference to my expressed wishes? I *told* you, Aunt Susan, I told you over and over again, that Jeremy Henzel was never to be allowed across my doorstep again. Never!'

'But that was twenty years ago,' Susan said with the impatience of bravado. 'Surely after all this –'

'I said *never*.' Christina's voice was hard with an anger Emily had never seen in her before. Her face had whitened still further and her whole body was rigid. She was on her feet now, glaring at her aunt with an expression that amounted almost to hatred. '*Never*. Don't you understand?'

Susan shrugged. 'I understand that you've borne a grudge against Jeremy for almost half your lifetime, Christina, and for no very good reason that I can see. Certainly no reason that you're willing to explain. I simply felt that it was time you came to your senses and made up whatever silly quarrel it was that caused this feud. Jeremy's quite willing, he's told me so. And if you've any –'

'Jeremy's told you so? You mean you've discussed me with Jeremy?' Christina's fingers whitened on the edge of the table. 'You brought him here – you discussed me with him? How dare you do such a thing? How *dare* you?' Her anger could be seen in every inch of her body, bringing a dark flush to the skin that had been marble-pale and fire to her eyes. 'This is *my* house, Aunt Susan, and I left you in charge because I trusted you. You've betrayed that trust. You've allowed in a man who I swore would never come here again. You've allowed him to come into contact with my children.' Her gaze swept over Roger and Sarah, taking in Roger's lifted brows and Sarah's trembling lips. 'God knows what damage you've done,' she said in a voice that shook in her throat. 'God knows what results your meddling will have.'

Susan stared at her. Her fingers were fluttering at her quivering mouth, her eyes were watering. She tried to speak, failed and tried again. Her voice was weak, high with self-justification.

'I didn't mean any harm. You didn't say I wasn't to have dinner parties. It was so quiet here without you . . . I simply wanted to do a little entertaining, to see my family.' Self-pity crept in and gave her added strength. 'Why shouldn't I, after all? You've always said this was my home. I've spent my whole life looking after your mother, you and your brothers and sisters, I've kept house for you and taken all the burdens off your shoulders so that you could please yourself . . . And now I can't even have my own family come to see me when you're not here. Oh, I know I'm getting old and useless, I'm just a poor relation, but I do think it's a little hard . . .' The voice melted into sobs and she fumbled for a handkerchief and buried her face in it.

Emily could feel the embarrassment that coiled about them all. She glanced at her father, who had slowly resumed his seat though keeping his eyes all the while on Christina in case she should need his support. She looked at Roger, who was leaning back in his chair, still with that maddening smile on his lips – what could he possibly find so amusing in this situation, for Heaven's sake? And she saw Sarah leave her seat to go and soothe her aunt, gently stroking her bent head and making little crooning sounds of comfort.

Christina looked down at the grey hair, at the shaking shoulders, and her mouth softened for an instant, but the anger was still there. 'Please!' she said sharply, 'stop crying. Sarah, help your aunt up to her room. I will speak to her again later.' She waited until the sobbing old woman had been led away and then sat down again and turned to her son. 'And now, Roger, tell me what happened.'

Roger shrugged and lifted his hands. 'Why, nothing, Mother. Aunt Susan simply decided to have a dinner party, and invited all the family. I suppose Aunt Susan thought – well, she said she'd always liked Jeremy and it was a good opportunity to invite him here. I'm sure she meant no harm.'

'No harm! There's always harm where that man is.' Christina brought her hand down sharply on the polished mahogany of the dining table. 'Well, it's done now and I suppose there's nothing to be done about it.' She hesitated, her eyes on Roger's face. 'And so you met your cousin, as I suppose we must call him. You didn't have much conversation with him, I imagine.'

'Oh yes,' Roger said lightly. 'We talked quite a lot.'

Christina's eyes sharpened. 'But you didn't take to him – you didn't like him. After all, he's a good deal older than you, you'd have nothing in common.'

'On the contrary, we got along very well indeed,' Roger said smoothly, his eyes bright. 'I thought it was rather a pity we hadn't met before.'

'Met before!' Christina's hand slapped down again on the table. 'If I'd had my way, you would *never* have met. Roger, listen to me. Jeremy may seem very pleasant, very charming, the kind of man anyone could take to, the kind of man you could trust – but you must never believe it. He is – unreliable. You must not see him again.'

'Oh, come, Mother,' Roger said, discovering some wine still in his glass and lifting it to his lips, 'you can't expect me to agree to that. I'm not a child any longer, to have my friends chosen for me. Jeremy seemed perfectly civilised to me.'

'Civilised! The man's a barbarian!' Joe, at the other

end of the table, had kept silent, believing that Christina would prefer to deal with this in her own way. Now his voice burst from him like a dammed river, held back for too long. 'You'll do as your mother tells you in this matter, Roger, do you hear? Jeremy Henzel should never have been allowed into this house, you should never have met him and wouldn't have if we hadn't made that damned trip to Paris. You'll not see him again, either here or anywhere else, and that's the last word on the subject.'

He glowered down the long table at his son, and Roger stared back, giving him glance for glance, his own eyes calm and unafraid. Emily watched, her hands clasped tightly under the table. For the first time, she realised how unlike Joe's son Roger was. There was nothing of their father in him – none of his giant build, his dark colouring, none of the forceful power of his personality. Neither was he more than a diffused version of his mother, the copper hair reduced almost to sandiness, the green eyes to light hazel, the fire to a subtle smouldering. Yet there was a core of strength running through him like a strand of steel, and he displayed a sense of languid hostility; as if Roger considered himself superior to the man who had begotten him, as if he thought his origins were a source of shame.

You to have shame! she thought bitterly. At least you are legitimate.

'The last word?' Roger said eventually, his voice cool. 'Oh, come, Father, you can't expect me to agree to *that*. Not without a reason. And apparently there *is* no reason why you and Mother have never welcomed Jeremy here. Or if there is, it's one you're not willing to divulge.'

Their glances met again. Joe was clearly controlling himself with difficulty. Emily saw the big hands open and close on the table and shivered, imagining Roger's neck between the massive fingers. Was this what was in her father's mind as well?

'You're right,' Joe said at last. 'The reason is one we're not willing to divulge. Perhaps your cousin would tell you – but it's my guess that even he would be too ashamed to tell the truth of what happened between us. Just take this from me, Roger – the reason's a good one, but it's none of your business. All the same, it's *my* business to see that you aren't contaminated by scum like Jeremy Henzel, and I mean to do it. I don't know if you've seen him since your aunt saw fit to invite him here, and I don't think I want to know. The idea of it sickens me. But *you're not to see him again*. Do you understand that? Is that clear?' He glared at his son. 'I'll not brook any defiance in this, my lad,' he growled. 'So make sure you know just what I say.'

Roger met his eyes for a few more seconds and then dropped his own gaze to the table. He hesitated for a moment, then shrugged again and lifted his glass. There was almost nothing left in it now, but he tipped it up as if he were draining it and then set it down. He glanced at Christina and lifted his brows.

'Well, that seems to be that, then,' he said with a not entirely successful attempt at nonchalance. 'I'm not to see Cousin Jeremy again. And now, if you'll excuse me, I'd like to leave the table – I've work to do. For Oxford,' he added with a glance at his father.

Christina inclined her head and Roger stood up and left the room, swaggering slightly. There was a long pause.

'I think we may be going to have problems with that lad,' Joe said at length.

Christina lifted her eyes. For a moment, she looked blank; as if her thoughts had been many miles, or perhaps many years, away from them. She focused on Joe and a slight frown creased her brow.

'Problems? Oh, no, I don't think so. After all, it wasn't Roger's fault that Aunt Susan invited Jeremy here. And you know he's always liked to argue a little, just to make sure we know he has opinions too. But he's a good boy – he always sees reason, and he never sulks.' She sighed. 'Obviously, Jeremy charmed him. But Roger won't defy us. He won't see Jeremy again. And I don't suppose he intended to anyway, if the truth were known. Jeremy's a middle-aged man – why should he be interested in making friends with our son?'

'Why indeed?' But Joe did not sound convinced. He stared moodily at the table. 'All the same, Christina, I think we should watch him. He's getting a damned sight too independent for my liking. Look at the way he took it on himself to go into the glasshouse and give Ben orders while we were away. Black crystal! The ruby, yes – the trade's been searching for years for the way to make a real deep ruby, and maybe we should have been doing something about it ourselves. But who wants black glass? It's meant getting in all kinds of new materials – arsenic, platinum, iridium and God knows what else. And selenium for the ruby, and antimony for them both . . . He should never have started up such experiments without consulting us. And not a thing we can do about it now. Putting a stop to it all would waste more money than we'd spent.' He shook his head, but his tone was tinged with admiration, try as he might to hide it. 'I just hope we can find some buyers for this black crystal, should we ever make it.'

'I'm sure we will,' Christina said absently, 'And I don't think we ought to be too angry with Roger for wanting a say in the glasshouse. It's a good sign, after all – if he's already got an interest in it, he's less likely to have his head turned in some other direction when he's at Oxford. Perhaps we ought to have brought him into the business before – given him some responsibility. And at least it might keep him occupied, so that he's less likely to renew acquaintance with Jeremy before he goes away.'

Joe grunted. 'Aye, mayhap. All the same, he thinks too much of himself already, and Oxford's not going to help – he's already starting to get conceited about going there, you can see it in his eyes. Looks on me as naught but an ignorant old fogey, fit for nothing but blowing a bit of glass now and then, I know that.'

'Joe, he doesn't! He doesn't think anything of the sort.' Distress now plain on her face, Christina leapt to

171

her feet and came quickly round the table to lay her hands on her husband's shoulders. 'You're not even to let such ideas into your head – is he, Emily?' she added as if noticing Emily for the first time. 'It simply isn't true.'

'Well?' Joe glimmered a look at his daughter and she saw in his dark eyes, so like hers, a reflection of her own doubts and fears, her own sense of isolation. Was it to compensate for such a sense that they both had such strong personalities, developed to withstand the scorn that others might show for them? But Emily did not feel that she had been at all strong recently. Paul's sudden emergence as a man, with a steely determination of his own, had further shaken the confidence whose roots had already been loosened, like a tree in a series of storms.

And her father, surely, could never have doubted himself and his skills. He was known throughout the Black Country, throughout the world of glassmaking, as the finest blower who had ever taken iron in hand. He still blew all Henzel's finest pieces, still designed the shapes that others could only copy.

'It doesn't matter what Roger thinks,' she said staunchly. 'What he thinks tomorrow will be quite different from what he thinks today. It's what other people think of you that matters, Papa – and I know what that is, and so do you. Everyone respects you; and the men in the glasshouse love you.'

He stared at her and gave a short laugh. 'Love! That's an odd word to use.' And indeed it was, when she thought of the rough, inarticulate men who worked in the cones, the coarse jokes and songs, the laughter and the swearing that she wasn't supposed to hear.

'All the same, they do,' she said stubbornly, and saw Christina give her an approving look.

'It's true, Joe. They do. And the whole district respects you. What does Roger's opinion count against that – even if you're right about him? And as Emily says, he'll change; he's young yet, after all.'

'Aye, and that's just why we must watch him,' Joe

insisted. 'He's too volatile, too impressionable. And he has too little respect for his elders. That's dangerous, Christina. He could rebel. He could go against us, and a man like Jeremy could have a lot of influence over him.'

'Rebel? Go against his elders – too little respect?' Christina was half smiling. 'Joe, this all sounds strangely familiar! Didn't my aunt once say those things about me?'

'Aye, happen she did.' Joe's face relaxed into a reluctant grin. 'And she was right, too! And if Roger's inherited half your obstinate nature, my love –'

'And half of yours,' she cut in quickly, 'there's not going to be very much we can do about him is there, Joe! Except hope that his upbringing and his own intelligence will serve to guide him. After all, we can't always be at hand. He has to learn to judge for himself.'

'Aye, he does.' Joe sighed. 'Maybe you're right, sweetheart. Maybe I've been wanting to keep him too much on a tether – and even more since we came back from Paris. One lad going astray is enough. But I always find Roger hard to get close to, somehow. I wish he could let up a bit at times – make it easier to talk to him.'

'Yes,' Christina said thoughtfully. 'I know what you mean. He can be very reserved. But his new interest in glass should help there. At least you can discuss that together.' She shook her head slowly, her hand still resting on Joe's shoulder. 'And I wish very much that Aunt Susan had not held that dinner party. I would be much happier if Roger and Jeremy had never met.'

Ben was working in the cone when Emily went in for the first time since her return from Paris. He had his own chair now, a team of four men – the gatherer who brought the globules of molten, red-hot metal from the pots that were set into the furnace, the servitor and foot-maker who assisted in the making of each piece, and Ben himself, the gaffer. He did all the most difficult blowing and shaping and saw that each piece, whether it be wine-glass, jug or bowl, went to the *lehr* in perfect condition,

173

to start its journey down the cooling tunnel and be removed at the other end, ready for decorating.

There had been few changes in the cone since Christina had first entered it as a young girl, defying her own father's ruling. The furnace still rose like a dome in the middle of the sloping, soot-blackened sides, the smoke that poured from it still drawn up to the open top by the draught that the cone itself created. The glow, the smoke, the clatter, all were the same, and all held the same fascination for those who loved the brilliant, fragile material that could be shattered by the lightest of blows, yet endure for a thousand years.

Emily waited by Ben's chair until he had finished the piece he was working on and turned to take up the tankard of ale that stood ready for him to slake the perpetual thirst that affected all glassmakers.

'Good morning, Ben. It's good to see you again.'

'Miss Emily! I didn't see you standing there. So you're back from Paris, then.' He hesitated. 'I'm sorry Mr Paul didn't come back too.'

'Yes, so are we all.' She wondered how much he knew and decided that it was probably a good deal. Christina had visited Sal Compson and told her, and no doubt Sal would have passed it on to both Ben and Will. 'He thought he would benefit by staying on. He wanted to learn more about engraving.'

'Aye, so he said afore he went. Mind, I think he were right. There's allus something to learn in this job, an' Henzel's don't want to slip behind. Anyways, I daresay he'll be back soon. Time goes by quick enough these days. Did you see a lot of glass over there, then?'

'Oh yes, and some of it very beautiful.' Emily smiled at him, feeling comfortable and at ease with this man she had known ever since she could remember. There was never a time when there hadn't been Ben, first as a thin little boy who had been in and out of her grandmother's house with her Uncle Will, later as the lanky youth who had come to her defence at the glassmakers' picnic, and now as a tall young man with straight brown hair and a smile that lit up his even features. 'The glass made for the Exhibition was most impressive. And not only the Thietry glass – we saw two huge vases in particular, cased with ruby glass and engraved by a man called Jean-Baptiste Simon. They took several years to complete, and they were the finest pieces I've ever seen.'

'Ruby glass, eh? You'll hev heard about Master Roger's experiments here – not satisfied with the ruby us hev been making, it seems, wants summat finer. Put the cameo blanks Paul wanted right in the shade, though it looks as if it'll be a time afore he wants them now.' He paused and added dryly: 'An' did anyone mention the name of the chap that blew these great vases?'

Emily laughed and shook her head. 'No, no one. As usual, the man who blew the glass has gone quite unremarked.'

'Ah, well, we should be used to that by now.' Ben watched as his gatherer thrust the long iron into the searing maw of the pot and drew out a shimmering orange globe of molten glass. He lifted it high, keeping the rod twirling to prevent the glowing mass from sagging, and handed it to the servitor, the iron leaving his grasp just before the servitor caught it, so that for a brief second it hung in the air, almost motionless, between the two men. The servitor inserted the golden bulb carefully into the wooden mould and began to blow, the shape of the glass forming under his breath. After a few moments he removed the swollen globe from the mould and passed the iron to Ben, who began to shape the stem and foot from small lumps of glass brought by the gatherer, rolling the iron back and forth across the arms of the chair to prevent any loss of shape.

Emily watched in silence. She looked at Ben's hands, the long fingers, the bony knuckles, so sure and competent in their work. She watched as he shaped the foot and attached the short punty iron to its base, shifting his grip to this so that the top of the glass could be sheared away from the blowing iron. The young gatherer was standing at his elbow, ready to snatch the iron away the moment it came free, breaking off the tattered, cooling fringe of glass and returning the iron to the gloryhole, where it could be reheated, ready to use again. With steady hands, Ben picked up his wooden pallet and began to smooth and shape the glass, easing out its curves so that at last it gleamed before his eyes, the wineglass designed by Joe Compson years ago and still the most popular line Henzel's produced. Satisfied, he snapped off the punty iron and the taker-in, using wooden tongs, carried the hot glass to the *lehr* for cooling.

'An' when that's cut an' decorated, its own mother won't know it,' Ben remarked, coming back to Emily. 'Aye well, 'tis all a matter of what the customer wants, I know that. Your old dad's never really accepted that though, has he? He still likes the shape best – don't go for all this cutting about.'

'No, he doesn't. He admired the vases I told you about, but there were other pieces he preferred – pieces that had a simple, elegant shape and not too much decoration, like a very tall decanter with engraving like feathers, he quite liked that. If Paul comes back doing that kind of work, he'll be pleased enough. If he comes back at all,' she added in a low voice.

'Don't you think he will, then?'

'Oh yes. Of course he will.' But she could find no conviction for her words. She felt his eyes on her and said quickly, hoping to change the subject, 'And how is Florrie? She's expecting, my grandmother tells me?'

'Aye, that's so.' His grin was sheepish. 'Next month sometime. An' Florrie's keeping well enough, thank you. Gets main tired, but no more than that.'

'I'll call in to see her sometime.'

Ben turned away as the gatherer approached with a fresh iron. 'That's good of you, Miss Emily.' He took the iron and sat down to shape the new stem.

Emily watched him work for a few more minutes and then moved away. For the sake of courtesy, she walked on round the cone, stopping at each chair for a word with the gaffer and his mates. But, having spoken to Ben, she felt she had achieved whatever quest had brought her into the cone. The heavy, leaden misery which had been settled on her breast ever since her return from Paris had eased slightly. She was no less unhappy, felt no less rejected and abandoned; but with his simple, natural talk Ben had dispelled at least a little of her depression.

Emily had circled the cone now and come round again to the double doors. She paused for a moment at the inner one, looking back into the billowing dimness, lit now by a few gas lamps as well as by the glow of the furnace. It was here that her father and Christina had met, here that they had stood and talked and occasionally quarrelled. Here he had once defied her, threatening to lead the men into a strike; and here Paul's father, unwelcome and unwanted, had met his death. And then Joe and Christina had married and started their strange, mixed family, bringing Paul and herself together as brother and sister although everyone knew that they were not; letting the two of them grow up close, dependent, sharing their lives.

And now she stood here alone, and Paul was in France. And she was bereft, as if someone had torn away a limb; and she knew that somehow she had to begin her life again, learn to exist without the man she had come to love. She had told him in those last, angry moments that she had more useful things to do with her life than to wait for him. That had to be true. Somehow, she had to make it true.


'So your mother knows I've been to Henzel Court, does she? And am I to take it she was not amused?'

Jeremy's voice came lazily from the depths of a large, leather armchair where he sprawled with the smoke of a cigar wreathing idly towards the ceiling. He pulled himself up a little, reached out for the brandy at his side and cocked an inquiring eye at Roger, who occupied a similar chair on the other side of the fireplace.

'Amused?' Roger echoed. 'No, I'd hardly say she was amused. In fact, her reaction was rather interesting.'

'Interesting?'

'Much angrier than I'd expected. I'd thought that Aunt

Susan was right, you see – that it was just an old feud, so old that everyone would have more or less forgotten what it was all about, but no one wanted to make the first move to end. Once the ice had been broken, I thought Mother and Father would simply accept it. But –'

'But your mother was angry. And your father too. Well, my dear boy, I could have told you that. Christina swore I'd never darken her doorstep again and naturally that oaf of a husb – I beg your pardon, your father – would agree with that. He never liked me anyway, and with good reason.'

'Why? What reasons?' In his interest, Roger let the unfortunate reference to his father slip by. 'Jeremy, I wish you'd tell me what happened between you all. Mother and Father never will, I know. Please, Jeremy.'

His older cousin stretched thoughtfully and cast him a quizzical glance. 'Tell you? Shall I? Would you really want to know, I wonder . . . ? No, I think not. At least, not just now. You haven't the experience, Roger; you don't know enough of the world. When you do, perhaps . . . and perhaps not. We shall have to see.'

'And when am I ever going to get this "experience"?' Roger muttered. 'It's months before Oxford. And you promised –'

'Yes, I did, didn't I?' Jeremy sat up, his eyes bright. 'Where do your parents think you are tonight?'

'With my friend, Oliver. I often spend the evening with him. He's going to Oxford too so we work together in his room.'

'Good, good. And when would you normally go home after an evening with this friend?'

'At about ten. Father likes us all to be in when he locks up.'

'Ten! That's no good, my boy. Nothing can be done about your education if you have to be at home by ten. No, you'll have to make other arrangements. Can't you say that Oliver has invited you to stay the night?'

'I could,' Roger said doubtfully. 'But suppose Mother

asks? She knows his people, you see; she might easily mention it.'

'Then we shall have to think of something else. After ten – when your father has locked up and presumably gone to bed – couldn't you slip out then?'

'*After* ten?' Roger stared at him and Jeremy snapped his fingers impatiently.

'Of course! You don't imagine that the entire population goes chastely to bed at nine-thirty, do you? We're talking about education, Roger – not schooling. Or do I have to give you lessons first in the difference between those two things?'

'No – no, I understand you,' Roger stammered, afraid that Jeremy was about to lose patience – and interest – in the whole idea. 'Yes, I could come out after Father has gone to bed. But it often isn't until after eleven. He locks up early and then sits in the library, reading, until quite late.'

'And would have no idea that his son was at that moment stealing down the back stairs and letting himself quietly out of the kitchen door,' Jeremy said. 'The kitchen staff will have gone to bed too by then, won't they? The cook, the butler – they all have to be up early in the morning, I imagine.'

'Yes. Parker goes at ten, unless Father wants anything else, and he never does. The house is quite quiet by then.'

'What a thrilling household it must be,' Jeremy murmured. 'Well, then, you can slip out any night at about ten-thirty, just to be safe. And we can visit a little club I know, play a game or two of cards. I don't suppose you've ever played for money, have you? I thought not . . . And I'll arrange a supper party or two, with some young ladies I know. I daresay you haven't had much experience of such affairs, but that won't matter. They're very helpful.' He smiled and Roger stared at him, his heart beating hard, a curious heat spreading itself through his body. He stirred uncomfortably in his chair and Jeremy's smile widened. 'I see you understand me.' He eased his body out of the chair and stretched his arms. 'And now you'd better be going home. It's already nine and you've a long walk back to Wordsley, where no doubt your father will be waiting with his watch in one hand and the key in the other.' He waited as Roger came to his feet and shrugged into his jacket. 'Just as if he'd never sown any wild oats of his own,' he murmured. 'Or perhaps because of that; after all, he did harvest a quite unexpected crop, didn't he?'

He refused to say more, and Roger was left to surmise that he meant Emily. So Jeremy knew something about that too; more than the young Compsons had been told. Something else it would be interesting to find out – one day.


Paul did not cut himself off completely from his family. Letters arrived regularly, telling of the glass he was beginning to study, the engravers who worked in his grandfather's Paris studios and who were teaching him their art. He had even met Jean-Baptiste Simon and watched him at work, and there was talk of a summer visit to the family glassworks and château in Lorraine.

Christina wrote back, giving him messages from the family. 'Tell him he's welcome to come home whenever he's a mind,' Joe ordered, 'and I must admit I'd be pleased if he should – I've missed the lad about the place, and that's the truth. And there's no denying he's the makings of a fine engraver. I don't see why the French should have the benefit of him.'

Sarah wrote too, her letters filled with gay chatter just as if she were speaking to him, the margins scattered with tiny sketches and added comments. But Roger did not write; if anyone suggested that he might, he laughed and said that the women could tell Paul all he needed to know.

And Emily did not write. She tried once or twice, taking pen and paper with a reluctant sense of duty. But her mind turned blank, she could think of nothing to say and she gave up, feeling the rift between her and Paul as a deep, yawning abyss. And Christina, noticing that there were never any letters from Emily amongst the pile put ready for the post, watched her stepdaughter anxiously and finally spoke to Joe.

'Joe, we must think about Emily. She seems so sad and lost since we came home. Obviously, she felt even more deeply about Paul than we realised. She needs something to take her mind off it, something here that will interest her. I'm worried about her, Joe.'

'She needs a husband,' Joe said, and Christina sighed.

'And that's the last solution she would accept just now. And even if she did . . . Emily does have – well, disadvantages that may be difficult to overcome.'

'You mean because she's a bastard,' Joe said bluntly, and she flinched.

'Joe, I hate that word! But . . . yes, it's true. The stigma does follow the children, even more than it does the parents. Emily and Paul are both likely to suffer for our mistakes, Joe – and yet I can't ever regret them, can you? Mistakes that bring people like those two into the world can't be wholly bad.' She paused. 'What will she do? If she never marries . . . Emily is like me, Joe. She needs a purpose. We must help her in some way.'

He shrugged. 'I don't see how. What *do* women do? She wouldn't want to teach in school, I know that – she could hardly wait to leave the place. And what else is there? There's that nursing college, opened a few years back, what was it called, some bird's name –'

'The Nightingale School,' Christina said.

'Aye, that's it. Well, she wouldn't want to do that, would she, work in a dirty hospital full of diseases? And I don't know what else there is. Women aren't made to work, Christina, their place is in the home.'

'Mine wasn't. Mine was in the glasshouse.'

'Aye, but you were different, my love. There's not many women like you. And you were brought up to it. Your father took you about with him, treated you the same as a boy. Emily's not been raised that way.'

'No. Perhaps she should have been.'

'And that's just foolish talk!' Joe declared. 'How else

could we have brought her up? We did the same for her as the others – she went to school, which is more than you or I ever did, unless you count that dame's school I went to for a while, and the Mechanics' Institute. She's had all the lessons you tell me young ladies should have, and she's been taken to the cones and told what happens there along with the rest. What else could we have done?'

'I don't know. Nothing.'

'Nothing. And there's nothing to worry about now. She's upset over Paul, and I agree with you she needs something to take her mind off him, but in a few weeks, you mark my words, she'll be right as rain. And then – why, I reckon she'll do what any other girl in her position does: look around her for a husband. And while she's looking, she'll probably find some good works of some kind to do, and good luck to her.' He gave Christina a hug. 'Don't worry about Emily, my love. She's a Compson, she'll not let things get her down for long. And now you go off and write to your son. And tell him from me he's to come back with a few new ideas for the glasshouse!'

Christina reached up to kiss him and they held each other close for a moment. 'You're a good husband to me, Joe,' she whispered. 'And a good father to all our children.'

She whisked away. And Joe stood looking after her. And knew that he loved her now as much as he had loved her when she came into the cone as a young girl, fresh and challenging and unattainable.

Christina was right in divining that Emily needed a purpose in her life, something to fill her days; what Emily found difficult to understand was that no one had seen this before. It was two years now since she had left school; she had spent some time in going on with some of her studies – in learning French more thoroughly, which Christina had insisted on for all the children; in the sketching and painting for which she had some talent; and in accompanying both Christina and Joe to the glasshouse as they went about their own work. But none of these things were enough to bring true satisfaction, none were enough to fill a lifetime – and, since Paul's rejection, she knew that there was a lifetime to be filled.

And Emily drifted around the house as helpless as a ship without a rudder, without direction, looking aimlessly for something, some sign, that would tell her what to do next.

She found herself going to the cone more and more often. She would come through the double doors, out of the bright sunlight, peering into the umber shadows, circling the cone slowly and talking with every gaffer there. She visited the long engraving sheds, watching the men with their spinning copper wheels trace the familiar patterns on the shimmering glass. But it was never enough. The cones seemed empty, and Paul's chair in the engraving shed, occupied now by another man, gave her a cold, lonely pain.

Keeping her promise, she went several times to visit Ben's wife Florrie, large with the child she was soon to bear, keeping house in a cottage even smaller than Sal Compson's, yet as happy as if she were a queen in a castle.

'An' here I am all over flour!' Florrie exclaimed, letting her in. 'You don't mind the kitchen, do you, Miss Emily? Only Ben'll be back any time, an' I must get his tea on.'

'Of course I don't mind. I love your kitchen, Florrie. It's so warm and homely.'

'Too warm in this weather.' Florrie brushed the damp hair back from her forehead and left a floury mark. She was almost at her time now, her swollen body awkward and cumbersome as she moved slowly around the tiny room. 'I'll be right glad when this is all over, I don't mind telling you, Miss Emily. Though I suppose I shouldn't be mentioning such things to you, you not being a married lady, like.'

'I can hardly pretend I don't know,' Emily said with a smile, although she was still only half aware of what must have happened between Ben and Florrie for her to be in what Aunt Susan called an 'interesting condition'. Christina had told her that she believed girls ought to be told the 'facts of life' before marriage, contrary to the fashionable thinking which held that they should remain ignorant. But her explanation had sounded so bizarre that Emily could hardly believe she had heard aright, and she had been too embarrassed to ask again.

'When do you expect your baby to be born?' she asked, and Florrie sighed.

'I can't believe it's ever going to be born, to tell you the truth. Sometimes I think I'll go on like this for ever, just getting bigger an' bigger all the time. But they allus comes in the end, an' old Jinny Roberts, down the street, that's promised to come in an' help when the time comes, she reckons it can't be far off now. In the next week or so, she thinks. Can't be too soon for me!'

'But you are feeling well?'

'Oh, well enough, I reckon. Actually, I've felt better today than I hev for a long time. That's why I bin making these pies for Ben, an' this morning I turned out three cupboards – seems like I'm fed up with sitting around, an' wants to get summat done. But you don't want to hear all that, Miss Emily. You sit down in Ben's armchair an' I'll mek you a nice cup of tea.'

Emily did as she was told, thinking that she ought to be the one to be making tea for Florrie; there was an odd look about the other girl's face, a strange sort of shine, and Emily didn't believe she felt as well as she declared. And once, while she was lifting the heavy iron kettle, she caught her breath and put her hand to her back, as if she were in pain.

'Please sit down and rest,' Emily said anxiously. 'I'm sure you shouldn't be lifting things. Let me do it.'

'No, no, it's only a bit of gyp. It's bin catching me all morning – reckon I moved a bit awkward when I was doing those cupboards. Anyway, it's made now. Just let it brew for a minute.' She turned back to the table. 'I'll get these pies in the oven, if you don't mind, an' then we can be easy.'

'I brought some things for the baby,' Emily said when they were settled with their tea. 'A little jacket I knitted, and a shawl Sarah's been making. There.'

'Ooh, it's lovely!' Florrie spread the fine, lacy material out on her knee and gazed at it with delight. 'Miss Sarah shouldn't hev done all this for me. It's much too good for the likes of us.'

'Nonsense,' Emily said brusquely, feeling embarrassed. 'Of course it's not too good. Your baby is as important as anyone else's . . . Sarah wants to come and see it when it's born. She wanted to come before but . . . well, I enjoy coming to see you, Florrie. I didn't really want her to come just yet – not until we were friends.'

'Friends?' Florrie blushed. 'I don't know what you mean, Miss Emily. How can the likes of you be friends with such as me? I mean, it's lovely for me to hev you come an' chat an' bring such beautiful things for the baby – but you can't want to be my *friend*.'

Emily looked at her. She felt a mixture of sadness and anger stirring in her breast. What, after all, was so different about the two of them? Only money separated them; the fact that her family was wealthy, and Florrie's poor.

'Of course I can want to be your friend,' she said stoutly. 'And just what do you think I am anyway? My father was a gaffer, just like Ben – my grandmother still lives in a house like this, you know she does. And my mother –' She stopped abruptly. It had been a long time since she had wondered about her mother, but she was suddenly shaken by a need to know more, a need that had been hidden for a long time but now surfaced, so powerful that it almost filled the vacuum left by the loss of Paul. All at once, and without any doubt, she knew that this was important to her, and especially important at this time; as if it were the sign she had been waiting for.

At that moment they both heard Ben's tread coming up the yard outside and Emily remembered the feeling that she had always had, that Ben could tell her the truth, perhaps more of the truth than even her father knew. Long ago, she had been told that her mother was Maggie

Haden, a packer at the Richardson factory, but no amount of questioning had brought more information. 'That's all you need to know,' Joe had told her angrily the last time she had asked. 'Christina's your mother now, and there's no sense in moithering over it any more. You know all I'm telling, so forget it.' But if Ben knew . . . Her heart thumped.

'I don't even know where my mother lived. Or where I was born,' she said clearly as he opened the door. And she spoke the words straight at him, looking directly into his eyes.

Ben halted on the step. He stared at Emily, sitting in his chair by the range. She watched as the colour left his face, leaving it white under the soot and grime left by his day's work. And suddenly she found herself filled with an energy that she had not experienced since she was in Paris, an energy that was composed of a desire to drive away once and for all the shadows that had haunted her life. The mystery of her birth, of the woman who became her mother; the link that she had always known she shared with Ben, which had something to do with that time before she could remember, when Christina had found her and brought her to Henzel Court. She looked at Ben, standing rigid in the doorway, and knew that he could indeed tell her the answers.

Florrie turned to lift the teapot and the spell was broken. Ben threw his jacket on to a chair and ducked out of the doorway again, muttering something about a wash; a moment or two later, Emily heard the sound of the pump being cranked out in the yard and the swoosh of water. And Florrie poured the tea, handed her a cup and then made a little sound as once again she clasped her back.

'That's more than a pulled muscle,' Emily said with concern. 'Are you sure everything's all right, Florrie?' She wished she knew more about babies and how they were born. Aunt Adela had told her once that it hurt: was this how it began?

'I don't know – it seems worse than before.' Florrie looked at her with wide eyes. 'Oh God – I beg your pardon, Miss Emily – but oh, it do feel bad!'

'I'll call Ben.' Emily was on her feet, but as she moved Florrie caught at her hand and held it, squeezing the fingers in a grip that seemed to grind the bones together.

'Don't leave me, Miss Emily. Please. I don't want to be on my own, not with this . . .' Her eyes were frightened, dark with pain. 'It's the baby, it's coming – oh, my *God* . . .' She let go of Emily's hand suddenly and doubled up, her arms crossed over her stomach. 'Shout for Ben,' she whispered through lips that were suddenly white. 'Tell him to go for Jinny – oh, God, *hurry* . . .'

Emily threw her a terrified glance and ran to the open door. She stared anxiously this way and that, up and down the yard, but she could see no sign of Ben. Then she spotted him, talking to a little knot of men on the corner, and she shouted his name loudly, once, twice, three times.

'Ben! Ben Taylor! *Ben*!' The men turned, startled, and she saw one of them grin and say something which made the rest of them laugh. She heard Florrie groan and cry out in the room behind her, and her temper flared. How dared Ben stand on street corners, laughing and talking, when his wife suffered indoors? 'Ben!' she screamed. 'Come in at once – Florrie's ill, she needs you.'

Without waiting to see whether he obeyed her summons, she turned back into the house and found Florrie half kneeling, half lying on the floor, her arms clutching at the back of the chair, her bulging stomach supported on the seat. She was groaning incessantly now and her thin cotton dress was strained tight over the swelling. Emily could see the movements of the child, small protuberances that showed as it wriggled inside the stomach. The bulge was much lower now in the body and as Florrie twisted and strained she plucked desperately at the clothes that hampered her.

'It's going to be born,' she panted, and Emily supported her shoulders as she slid completely to the floor. 'God, they never told me it'd be like this . . . Where's Ben? Where is he?'

'Here.' And he was at Emily's side, his hands gentle as

187

he cradled Florrie's misshapen body in his arms. 'Is it time, my love? Shall I fetch Jinny?'

'Aye, an' go quick – it's all happening much too fast.' Another pain racked the heaving body and Emily quickly caught at Florrie's blindly seeking hand and held it tightly. She looked up at Ben and jerked her head towards the door.

'You heard what she said – be as quick as you can. I'll stay here. But please hurry – I don't know what to do . . .' Her words were lost as Florrie began to scream and Ben, with a last wild look at her, threw himself out through the door. Emily heard his footsteps racing away along the cobbled yard. She looked down at the suffering woman again and her heart twisted in pity. Was it always like this for women? Did everyone suffer so? But Florrie, after a brief respite, was in the grip of a fresh wave of pain, her body twisting against it and then thrusting with a strength Emily had never dreamed a woman could possess, and screaming with each thrust as if even though the pain were intolerable she could not fight the body's instinctive desire.

'My clothes,' Florrie panted when the pain subsided and she lay panting again. 'You'll hev to get 'em off – they're in the way . . .'

With her free hand, Emily began to pull the skirt up around Florrie's body. She jerked and tugged at the thin underclothes, thankful that at least the weather was too hot for Florrie to be wearing much. They began to tear and she pulled ruthlessly, exposing the broad thighs and the thick, dark hair. Shocked, she saw that the hair was not all Florrie's . . . there was something else. A hard, round head.

'I can see the baby!' she exclaimed, and tugged at Florrie's hand, filled with a sudden excitement. 'I can see its head. Oh, push again, Florrie, push hard – it's coming, it's coming. Your baby's being born!'

Instinctively, she braced Florrie's flailing feet against her shoulders, kneeling firm and solid on the floor as the next pain came with the thrusting that made Florrie cry and groan, the thrusting that was bringing her child into the world. The head inched a little further out. She could see a patch of bare skin that must be its forehead, two tiny, slitted eyes. She waited, breathless, knowing that the next few seconds must be crucial. And then Florrie seemed to gather all her strength. The head receded, very slightly, and then responded dramatically as the last vicious pain engulfed its mother's body. Florrie's scream was the wildest and loudest yet; it echoed through the room and down the yard where the neighbours, realising what was happening, were beginning to appear at their doors. The baby's head seemed to surge out of Florrie's gaping body, to be followed by a pair of shoulders that looked already broad and then a slithering, slippery body smothered in mucus and slime which fell into Emily's waiting hands and, almost before she had touched it, set up a wail of protest, of fury and indignation.

'She's birthed it!' Suddenly, the room was full of women, the neighbours who had begun to run as soon as they heard Florrie's screams. One of them dealt with the purple, rubbery cord and another produced a cloth to wrap the baby in. The floor was a mess of blood and mucus and urine which Florrie must have passed, although Emily could not recall it, but the women took no notice of that. Their concern was with the child and its mother. Emily, thankful to be relieved of the responsibility, stepped back, wiping her face and feeling suddenly shaky.

And then Ben was in the room with Jinny Roberts and the rest of the women were shooed out. Suddenly, the noise and bustle ceased and Emily sank down into a chair.

'There's the afterbirth to come yet,' Jinny said, and placed her hand on Florrie's stomach. 'Don't you worry, my girl, it's only one more pain an' then 'tis all done. An' your babby's as strong an' healthy a lad as I ever saw.'

'A boy?' Florrie asked faintly. 'Is it a boy?'

'Aye it is. Didn't she say?' The old woman's eyes turned to Emily, who shook her head.

'I didn't even look – I've never seen a baby

189

born before. I was afraid I'd do the wrong thing.'

'No, you did well. Florrie an' Ben hev got a lot to thank you for. Babbies don't usually come that quick, especially first ones. An' when they do, if there's no one there to keep a cool head, they can die. This one won't, though; not now. Ah – here it comes.' She bent over Florrie and gave a grunt of satisfaction, and Emily rose to her feet.

'I'll go now, Ben. You've a lot to do and I'll only be in the way.' She went to the door and he came with her. 'I'll call tomorrow to see how Florrie is – and your son.' She smiled at him. 'I haven't congratulated you yet.'

'An' I hevn't thanked you – not proper, like.' He stared down at her as she stood at the door in the sunlight. 'I don't know what I can say, Miss Emily. If you hadn't bin here this afternoon – well, I reckon I could've lost the boy, aye, an' Florrie as well, maybe. If there's anything I can ever do for you, Miss Emily, you've only got to say the word.'

Emily looked up at him, at the face still shining from the scrubbing he had given it at the pump, at the eyes she had known ever since she was a child. She remembered why she had come, why she had been seeking him out.

'There is something you can do for me, Ben,' she said quietly. 'But this isn't the time to talk about it. I'll ask you one day, though . . . if I need to.'

She walked away down the narrow, cobbled street. It was still important to her to know about her mother, Maggie Haden. But even more important was what had just taken place and the feelings she had experienced while it was happening. Terror, yes – but excitement too – the excitement of helping Florrie through her brief yet dangerous labour, of helping a brand-new person, a new soul, into the world.

Somewhere in the dim fog that had been surrounding Emily through these unhappy days, she could perceive a shaft of light. And as she walked slowly home to Henzel Court, she kept her eyes fixed on that light, as if it were her salvation.

190

# Chapter Nine

During his first few weeks in Paris, Paul immersed himself in the business of Thietry Cristal. He went with his grandfather each day to the showroom, where he studied the engraving that was being carried out now, both in the Paris engraving rooms and the larger ones attached to the foundry in Lorraine. He also paid a number of visits to the Exhibition, which was to remain open until November, and spent hours examining the exhibits there, especially the cased glass vases engraved by Simon. He looked at the crystal opalines, the perfume bottles in pearly, translucent white or blue the colour of eggshells, with their delicate flower-shaped stoppers. He looked at the lacy filigree work begun by Georges Bontemps of the glasshouse at Choisy-le-Roi, who had been in England since 1848. He looked for a long time at the enamel overlays in blue and red, and thought how like cameo glass they were, yet how much more effective the real thing would be.

Nobody in France, it seemed, had thought of making cameo glass in the style of the Romans, even though they used cameo incrustations in their sulphide paperweights. And Paul found that he did not want, at this stage, to mention it. The French were too clever; someone else might decide to try before he was ready. And he still meant to be the first man to make it since the Romans had produced their exquisitely carved vases, just as Christina had asked him to do.

But that could not be done until he was back in England, and at the moment Paul had no intention of returning. He meant to stay in France for as long as possible, for as long as it took to learn all that the French could teach him.

'Much of our decorated glass is done by acid etching,

of course,' Marc Thietry remarked. 'The kind of engraving that Simon does, for example, is too costly for the average customer, even of such glassmakers as ourselves and Baccarat. Not all our glass is bought by kings and czars! But for them, there is always a need for the truly exquisite workmanship that will be treasured down the centuries. And the man who can accomplish such work is a rarity.' He glanced at Paul, who was handling a newly annealed vase, his fingers moving slowly, almost sensually, over the smooth polished sides. 'It would be a great pleasure to me to discover that you are such an *artiste*.'

'I hope I am,' Paul said, his voice distant as if he were concentrating more on the vase than on his grandfather's words. And then, more forcibly, he said, 'I intend to be, *Grandpère*. And if I cannot be better than Simon – and I doubt if anyone could surpass the work he has done – I will at least be as good.' He laid the vase down, almost with regret, and turned to look full into Marc's face. 'I will give you my promise on that.'

The two men looked at each other for a long moment, the one white-haired and old, the other young and straight. Yet the eyes that stared into each other's were identical: so pale a grey as to be almost silver, softening to the gentle pearliness of a dove's wing when moved, darkening to pewter and smoke when a more powerful emotion imposed itself.

'I believe you,' Marc said at last, quietly. 'And I hope that you will carry out your finest work in the name of Thietry.' His eyes were steady, intent.

Paul moved uneasily. Already, he was aware of the bonds that drew him, both to his French family and to his English. Dimly, he began to see that his loyalties might, at some time in the future, become divided; that it could become difficult – perhaps even impossible – to decide between them. But as soon as the thought occurred to him, he shrugged it away. It was all arranged, everyone knew that he was to stay here for a year, maybe even two or three, to learn as much as he could before returning home. In that time, he would become as fine an engraver as he was ever likely to be. And of course he would be working solely for Thietry Cristal while he was in France.

'I'll do the best I can,' he said, smiling, and Marc looked at him intently, and then nodded.

They continued through the engraving rooms. These had been set up by Marc's father when the business in Lorraine had expanded so much that a Paris showroom became essential. Very soon, it had been seen that the finest engraving would have to be done in the city, since there were so many special orders to be carried out to customers' specific wishes. The most elegant and graceful shapes were retained for this special work: wineglasses, bowls, vases and decanters designed for the most complex engravings. These were brought direct to Paris from the factory in Lorraine and a customer would choose which he wanted, before the engraving itself was designed for him. Thus only unique work was carried out in Paris, for once a design had been allotted to a particular customer it was never used for anyone else.

'Glass which will be sold on the open market is still engraved at the factory,' Marc observed as they came into the showrooms themselves and looked at the long room, lined with mirrors and filled with an array of sparkling glass. 'It is still costly, *naturellement* – Thietry do not make common glass – but you may see such wineglasses on a dozen tables in Paris.' He paused, smiling. 'They are still only the *best* tables, you understand!'

Paul smiled back and moved slowly along the tables. Women were constantly cleaning in the showrooms, polishing each glass so that there was never a speck of dust to be seen on the shimmering surfaces. He picked up a wineglass, its delicately cut bowl held on a stem of deep ruby. It was priced at a figure that would keep an average family in comfort for a month. Certainly, only a wealthy man would be able to afford a set of these, together with the decanters, water tumblers and jugs that must accompany them. He set the glass down again, and wondered if

English glassmakers had any idea of the prices that could be commanded by such exquisite workmanship. Even Henzel's, with their reputation for fine crystal, produced nothing as costly as this.

He lifted one of the paperweights for which the company was famous. They were not new to him; the *millefiori* style had been developed over twenty years earlier, at just about the time he was born, and he had spent many hours as a small boy, gazing at the one his mother had on her desk in the library at Henzel Court. The impression of a cluster of tiny flowers, given by looking directly on to the ends of bundles of fine canes of coloured glass, had fascinated many people and accounted for the popularity of this kind of glassware. It was delicate work, arranging the bundles in the precise pattern required for such an effect before cutting them, but the art had been perfected to such a degree that even the snippets of glass cut from the canes were now used in 'end of day' pieces – bowls or vases made of massed clusters fused together at random and emerging as a surprisingly attractive novelty.

The *millefiori* were not the only paperweights that Thietry made. They also produced sulphides, paperweights of one colour which contained a cameo silhouette, usually of the head of a significant personage – the mayor of a provincial town, perhaps, a monarch at some important point in his life, a notable military figure after a successful campaign. Paul studied these with interest, but he knew that the cameo itself was not of glass but more usually of enamel or porcelain, set on a coloured background and enclosed within the solid glass dome of the paperweight.

'We are experimenting now on photo-engraving,' Marc continued as they proceeded with their tour. 'We are not so foolish as to ignore the considerable market for less costly goods. But you, of course, my dear Paul, will be working with my best engravers. Glass that is hand crafted will always find a market. And we have customers now all over the world – from New York to St

Petersburg, from Java to Mexico. We have agencies in all those cities and in many others: Madrid, Havana, Buenos Aires. We are even –' he smiled '– finding our way into the great palaces of India, which the English had supposed to be their own!'

Paul smiled too, though he was aware that Henzel's themselves had lost orders through what they and other English glassmakers regarded as a poaching of their preserves. But the story must always be the same – the customer had the right to choose, and would invariably choose the best. What Henzel's and the others must do was produce that best. And there was no reason at all why Henzel's should not compete in all the markets as successfully as Thietry Cristal. Once again, he felt the slight tug of loyalties – but was there any real reason why that should worry him, since he belonged equally to both?

Paul looked ahead towards a future that was as dazzling as the glass that surrounded him. From France, he would take back all that was best in what his grandfather could teach him. But he would leave something behind him too – work that surpassed any that had been done before for Thietry. Work that would earn its place in this showroom, to be admired and treasured through the years to come.

'We shall be going to Lorraine in a week or two,' Marc Thietry observed one night at dinner. 'You will accompany us, of course, Paul; I'm sure you must be interested to see our factory.'

'Yes, of course,' Paul said eagerly, though with a quick glance at Véronique. At once, she gave him a smile and a nod.

'I shall be going too. It is my home, you remember. I have many friends there.'

Friends? he thought jealously, and then scolded himself. Of course she would have friends there! And, as Emily had said, she was little more than a child. None of them would mean any more to her than that.

195

But she isn't a child, a voice argued inside his head. She may be young – just sixteen – but she is a woman. French girls grow up quickly, hadn't you noticed that? And Véronique is more worldly-wise than Sarah, who is a year or two older. More, even, than Emily.

'You'll see the château,' Véronique was saying now. 'I'm glad about that. I want you to see where I grew up. And you can meet my Oncle Gabriel, and Tante Annette, and Geneviève, and René. You ought to meet them all, after all, for they are your relatives too. I wonder if you will like them? Geneviève can be a little stiff sometimes, and my uncle does not speak much. But Tante Annette and René, everyone likes them. And then there's –'

'Véronique, you are talking too much,' Cécile reproved her. 'Eat your dinner, child, and do not chatter.'

'She is right, though,' Marc observed. 'Paul should meet his relatives. And it will be interesting for him to see our methods and compare them with the way glass is made in England. There are some differences, I think. So, Paul, if there is anything else you wish to see at the Exhibition, you should go soon, for when we return it will be closed.'

'I meant to go in the balloon,' Paul said, thinking of the great coloured sphere that still floated over the Champs de Mars every day. But somehow, the urge he had experienced to fly in it, looking down at the city, had disappeared. He remembered Emily's excitement; she had wanted to go in it, begged him to take her when all he could think of was persuading the reluctant Véronique. And she had never flown either. He had a feeling that it would be disloyal of him to take the opportunity now, when it was too late for her to enjoy it too. 'But I don't think I'll bother, after all,' he said.

'And a good thing too,' his grandmother remarked. 'I would not like to have had to write to your mother to say you had fallen on to the giant fountain and been cut into a thousand ribbons. Now, Véronique, if you would just ring the bell for Marie . . .'

196

Paul relinquished his ambition with a sigh. It would have been good to have boarded that giant basket, to have been wafted up into the heavens. But he would never have been able to tell Emily about it; and it was exactly the kind of thing he would have wanted to share with her.

There were a number of things like that, things that he wanted to tell Emily and couldn't. He was surprised by how much he missed her.

It was a long journey from Paris to Lorraine. The trains were hot and dusty, steaming slowly through country-side that seemed unendingly flat at first, becoming hilly only as they reached Lorraine itself with its great river valleys of the Meurthe and Moselle, and the mountains of the Vosges rising in the distance. But at last they had arrived at the village and Paul had seen for the first time the glassworks laid out across the river: the factory at one end with smoke and steam rising from its chimneys; the workers' houses in neat rows with trees between them to provide shade and greenness and, holding pride of position at the other end of the large complex, the château.

As they rattled across the bridge that led to the château Paul felt a sudden apprehension. What was he doing here, so far away from home? He didn't belong here, he never could. And already the château seemed hostile, its many windows seeming to frown at him as the carriage halted at the foot of the steps which led up to a wide terrace and to the great oak door of the house itself.

'Don't worry. They will all love you, just as we do,' Véronique whispered, and he felt her small hand steal over his and give it a squeeze. He turned to smile at her.

'Are you sure? They may consider me an intruder. An interloper.'

'Nonsense. And if they do, they will have *me* to deal with!' Véronique lifted her chin and her blue eyes flashed. 'Look, there is Oncle Gabriel already on the steps to greet us – and Tante Annette, see, and Tante

Geneviève. Tante Geneviève is the sister of my uncle Gabriel and René is the nephew of my aunt, so he is not really related to me at all, only by marriage.'

'Your family is as complicated as ours is,' Paul observed and Véronique giggled.

'Then we are well matched!'

The carriage came to a halt and she tumbled out and ran up the steps to fling herself into her uncle's arms. Paul watched a little wistfully as she was greeted with similar warmth by her two aunts. He stepped down more slowly, turning to assist Marc and Cécile from the carriage, and hung back as they too began to mount the wide stone steps to the terrace.

Marc Thietry turned his head. 'Come, Paul, don't be *timide*. Come and meet some more of your relations.' He slipped his hand under Paul's elbow and guided him forward. 'Gabriel, this is your cousin, Paul, from England. Annette, Geneviève – here is the son of Jean-Paul, come to visit us at last.'

Paul held out his hand and found it gripped firmly by the older man. They looked into each other's eyes and, for a moment, Paul thought that he was looking at Joe. The same dark colouring was there, the same thick black hair, the same deep brown eyes. But in another moment he knew that this man was not in the least like Joe. Joe Compson had been reared in the back streets of a crowded English industrial town; he knew about hardship; he knew poverty; he knew that life was frequently unfair, even cruel. Both by falling in love with Christina and by his own skills in designing and blowing fine glass, he had raised himself out of the class in which he had originated and become wealthy. He had never held any pretensions; had always allowed Christina to maintain what he firmly believed to be her rights, and had still retained his own stalwart masculinity. His stature in Stourbridge, in the whole of the Black Country and the world of glassmaking had grown until he stood, not merely physically but in all other respects, head and shoulders above his fellows.

Gabriel Thietry was a big man too, broad as Joe was broad, dark as he was dark; but the largeness of Joe's personality, the power that glinted from his eyes, were lacking in the Frenchman. His eyes were small, like buttons in the florid face, and his mouth, almost obscured by a beard that was too bushy, was small and thin-lipped. He looked at Paul with suspicion, and his grip seemed too tight, as if he were deliberately creating an illusion of friendliness.

But his jaw was tight, jutting with hostility. His dark eyes were hard, narrowed almost to slits; his mouth a hard, compressed line.

'So you are Paul,' Gabriel said and his voice was harsh and guttural. 'My uncle has written much about you. I am glad you have felt able to make the time to visit us.'

Was he being sarcastic? Paul could not be sure. He smiled and bowed a little, and answered pleasantly, 'Thank you, monsieur. I am glad that you took the trouble to invite me.'

He knew that Gabriel had not invited him; the visit had been organised by Marc Thietry. He caught the flicker in Gabriel's eyes and knew that his French cousin was equally unsure of whether there might be any hidden meaning in his words. He turned to Annette and received her kiss on the cheek. 'I am happy to be here, madame,' he said.

'And we are happy to have you.' She, at least, seemed sincere. He smiled at her, taking in the dark ringlets that hung by each cheek, the plump, pretty shoulders revealed by her low-cut gown, the swelling of the full breasts above her tiny waist. Her face was vivid, with sparkling dark brown eyes and rosy, pouting lips that seemed to be formed ready for kissing. Slightly startled by his own thoughts, Paul looked at her in admiration, remembering what Marc had told him about Gabriel's wife. Annette was younger than Gabriel and had recently – unbelievably, Paul now thought – given birth to twin girls. 'They already have three sons, so they are very happy about this,' Marc had said. 'And Cécile, of

course, is most anxious to meet her two new great-nieces.'
But it was impossible to believe that Annette could be the
mother of five children, and Paul took his eyes off her
almost with reluctance as he turned last of all to Geneviève.

Geneviève reminded him instantly of Aunt Susan. Perhaps all spinster aunts became like this, all over the world.
She was tall, thin, bony, her dull brown hair scraped back
flat against her head, her eyes the colour of dried mud and
almost hidden behind a pair of *pince-nez*. Her clothes were
dull too, a dress of brown print that hung loosely on her
gaunt body, a shawl of fraying wool. She was evidently a
good deal older than Gabriel; the skin of her neck was like
crepe and there were down-drawn lines around her nose
and mouth.

'Paul is most anxious to see the *cristallerie*,' Marc said as
they went inside the château. 'You will have no objection,
of course, Gabriel? And he wishes to study our methods of
engraving. I have told him that he can join the engravers
while we are here.'

'You are the *propriétaire*,' Gabriel responded coolly,
and Paul's heart sank. Clearly he was not welcome here;
not by Gabriel, at any rate, and probably not by his dried-
up sister. He caught Véronique's eye and saw her grimace
and then giggle into her handkerchief, and then he turned
to find Annette watching him with a smile on her full
mouth.

'Take no notice of my husband,' she whispered softly.
'He is jealous of any man who comes to this house. Now,
come into the salon and drink a glass of wine and tell me
what you think of France.'

Her hand lay lightly on his arm as she drew him away
from the others and into the large room that ran almost the
length of the terrace, its wide windows looking away from
the cottages and the factory which formed the Thietry
community and across open, rolling countryside towards
the mountains. Paul stood hesitantly, but she urged him
to be seated and handed him a glass filled with wine the
colour of rubies before she settled herself beside him.

'So you have been in Paris for several months now,' she

said, spreading skirts of rustling crimson taffeta around her. 'And you have seen the Exhibition. Tell me what it is like. I wanted to go myself, but Gabriel would not allow it, he said that it was too soon after the birth of my babies. You have heard that I have twin daughters, just five months old?'

'My grandfather told me.' Paul was aware that Véronique had followed them into the salon. 'You are to be congratulated, madame. I would never have thought that you could be a mother.'

She laughed and tapped him with pointed fingernails. 'So - already you are a Frenchman! Has little Véronique been giving you lessons in *l'amourette flirtation*? And please, do not call me madame. I am your cousin, am I not? Annette.'

'Not really his cousin,' Véronique interrupted. 'Gabriel is his cousin. You aren't really any relation, just as René is not my relation. Where *is* René?' she added petulantly. 'I thought he would be here to meet me.'

'No, you are right,' Annette said and gave Paul an appraising glance that made him blush. 'We are not related at all. But you will still call me Annette. And René will be here soon, Véronique. He had to go to the glasshouse - a problem with a new colour they are trying. In fact, I don't see why you should not run down to meet him. It is tedious for you to be here, listening to grown-up conversation.'

Véronique looked at her uncertainly, a small frown drawing her finely marked brows together. She gave Paul a glance that he could not define and drew a pattern on the carpet with the toe of her shoe.

'Oh, if you say he will be here soon, I need not go,' she said at last in a nonchalant tone. 'And I don't find grown-up conversation at all boring, Tante Annette. After all, I am sixteen now. I could be married myself, just like you and my Oncle Gabriel, and start to have my own babies.'

Annette raised her own brows and laughed. 'Such an outspoken little minx! You do not change, Véronique. I am afraid you still have much to learn . . .' And she turned away from her. 'Paul, you have not answered my question yet. How do you like France?'

'I like it very much. Paris was exciting, completely different from any city I have known before. And the Exhibition is spectacular. There is so much to see – I have still seen barely half of it. I hope to see the rest when we return, and –'

'Return! But you have only just arrived, and already you speak of leaving us again.' The fingernails dug into his arm, through the cloth of his sleeve. 'I shall not allow you to leave,' she declared. 'Not for a very long time, anyway. We have much to talk about, you and I.' The dark eyes smiled into his.

'Paul talks to me most of the time,' Véronique put in jealously, and Annette's red lips parted in a smile. She had very small, very white teeth, Paul thought, and wondered if they were as sharp as her nails. And her cheeks were more like roses than the cheeks of any other woman he had ever seen; flushed with a bloom that was as vivid as it was delicate. Beside her, Véronique's blond prettiness faded, became almost insipid.

'Then it is now my turn to have the pleasure of his company,' Annette said coolly. 'And I intend to, you know!' she added with another little squeeze. 'I see little enough of Gabriel, or even of René, and I shall not allow you to spend all your time in the *cristallerie*, as they do. No, I shall demand some attention while you are here.'

Her eyes widened very slightly and held his glance. And Paul, gazing into depths that were like forest pools, come upon unexpectedly in the sudden brightness of a clearing, felt the hairs rise slowly on the back of his neck. The wine, he thought, and set the glass down carefully on the low table before him. It must have a strength belied by its taste. He looked down at the small hand that lay still upon his sleeve, and his heart thudded against his ribs.

Marc Thietry's voice cut across his whirling mind.

Paul looked up, startled, realising for the first time that the others had also come into the salon and were drinking wine and talking. He half stumbled to his feet and his grandfather turned to extend an arm towards a tall young man who had just come in.

'And this is the other member of our family here,' he said proudly. 'René, who is learning the management of the *cristallerie*. René, this is my grandson Paul.'

René stood quite still, looking at him. He matched Paul in height and in breadth, but was much darker and was four or five years older.

'Well, shake hands, then!' came the imperious voice of Véronique. 'And then give me a kiss, René. Don't you know how long you've kept me waiting?'

Paul could never recall in any detail the rest of that first evening at the château. Exhausted by the journey, bewildered by his first meeting with this new branch of his family, he was glad to get to bed early. His room, he found, was at the front of the house, overlooking the small formal garden which separated the château from the workers' houses and the factory itself. He could see the lights still on under the long roof where there must be men still working, teasers tending the furnace, perhaps glassmakers themselves wielding their long irons and engravers bent over copper wheels. Tomorrow he would be taken to see it for himself; but tonight he was too tired to care. He washed quickly in the water left for him, fell into bed and went straight to sleep.

In the morning, he woke early. The light was filtering through the thick curtains. He lay for a moment adjusting himself to his surroundings, and then sprang out of bed and went to the window.

The gardens lay before him, a geometric arrangement of narrow paths between beds of roses. Beyond was the factory, and then the silver ribbon of the river, the soft, wooded hills of Lorraine and, in the far distance, the mountains of the Vosges.

The whole scene was bathed in an apricot mist, the

heavy dew of summer lit softly with the diffuse glow of the rising sun. It was like a great orb of newly gathered glass on the horizon, its brilliance muted by drifting shreds of vapour that were like pearly grey chiffon thrown carelessly down by a woman after a ball.

Paul stared down from his window, entranced. And then a movement caught his eye. The summer mist was rising from the roses and a slender figure, dressed all in blue, hair gleaming with the gold of dawn, was walking slowly along the paths.

Paul dressed quickly and ran quietly down the stairs and out of the silent house to the terrace. He looked eagerly around him and saw Véronique disappearing round the corner of the house. In a few moments he had caught up with her and was laughing at the delight on her face.

'I saw you from my window,' he said breathlessly, and she nodded.

'I always wake early here. It is such a beautiful time of day in the country, *n'est-ce pas*? Look at the silk the baby spiders have woven all over the grass and the flowers. And the dew on the roses – see, like a jewel in the heart.'

She cupped her fingers under a full-blown rose and held it towards him. Deep in the crimson bowl he saw a single dewdrop, clear as a diamond, smooth as a pearl.

Paul stared at it. The dewdrop had the perfection of fine crystal, the rose the exquisiteness of a delicate engraving. If it had been produced by man, that man would have been acclaimed as a genius. It was unique; although there were other roses all around them, each with its own shimmering cargo, no two were exactly alike. Each one was a single, unrepeatable work of art.

Paul had been brought up in an industrial town, heavy with smoke, where even the grass was dulled by soot and garden flowers looked weary before they were fully open. He had seen the countryside on outings to nearby Kinver, on holidays in Warwickshire, but never like this; never in the glow of a summer dawn, in the company of a girl so slender, so delicate, that she seemed as insubstantial as the gossamer itself. He had never, he realised now, really looked at anything.

Véronique took her hand away from the rose and turned to smile at him, and now she was all child again, making that rapid transition from mysterious, ethereal beauty to mischievous *gamine* that so fascinated him. She caught his hand, swinging it in hers.

'Let's go to the forest! See, it comes right to the garden at the back of the house.' She led him quickly away from the roses, out of sight of the factory, to the larger, more private garden behind the château. Paul looked with interest at the dark mass of trees; trees that were tall and old. The forest.

Véronique drew closer and Paul felt her shiver a little.

'Are you frightened?'

'Only a little.' She laughed, a little tremulously. 'It is so mysterious, is it not? So big and dark. Anything could happen in there . . .' She looked at him, her eyes large, the pupils widening. 'Shall we go into the forest, Paul? Shall we explore – and see what happens?'

Paul stared at her and felt a strange excitement, an excitement that was disturbing yet pleasant.

Child or woman? He could not make up his mind. He lifted one hand to brush away a tendril of silvery fair hair from her small, ivory face. His finger touched her skin and his heart leapt. 'Véronique . . .'

'So there you are, the two of you!' René's voice cut harshly across the lawns. 'Don't you know that breakfast has begun and Tante Cécile is almost frantic with worry?' He came across to them, his rapid stride leaving dark footmarks in the dewy grass, his eyes dark with suspicion. 'I suggest that if you wish to explore you ask me or Oncle Gabriel to escort you until you know your way,' he said coldly to Paul. 'It is easy to stray into the forest, and it is not always safe there. We do not like Véronique to be put at risk.'

Paul opened his mouth indignantly, but Véronique's quick voice spoke first. 'Don't be ridiculous, René! We were nowhere near the forest. And we were just about to come back for breakfast, so there is no need for anyone at all to worry.' She left Paul's side and moved closer to the Frenchman, slipping her hand into his. 'Now, don't be cross,' she murmured coaxingly. 'You're just jealous, that's what's the matter with you. As jealous as an old dog when his master makes a fuss of a new puppy.'

René looked down at her. Paul, watching, saw his expression soften a little, though he was clearly still aggrieved. 'Jealous! And why should I be jealous?' he demanded, and slipped an arm around Véronique's shoulders to draw her against his side. 'And who are you calling an old dog, hey?' He pulled gently at the silvery hair and Véronique squealed and twisted away from him. Her face alight with mischief, she aimed a sharp kick at his shin, missed and then turned to run before he could grasp her again. The music of her laughter rippled across the garden as she sped away, and René turned to Paul.

'I am sorry I spoke harshly,' he said formally, 'but you will understand that Véronique is precious to us. And she is still very much a child.'

'Of course. And I shall take as much care of her as you do yourself.'

Paul's voice was equally stiff, but he had not missed the note of warning in René's voice. He felt a sudden relief that they had been interrupted. For a moment, he had been in danger of seeing Véronique as a woman, fully mature, and of treating her as one. And it was too soon; much too soon.

Too soon for Véronique, at any rate. But for himself . . .? As he walked back across the grass with René, talking politely of this and that, he was aware that the moment his finger had touched Véronique's skin had been a moment of awakening. In this summer dawn, far away from home, he had been made sharply aware of desires and hungers that hitherto, absorbed in his glass, he had suppressed. But which would remain quiescent no longer.

\*　　\*　　\*

Paul stood at the door of the glasshouse and for a moment almost believed himself to be back at home.

This French foundry, deep in the heart of Lorraine, bore a strong resemblance to the glasshouses in England. Men moved about in the same rhythmic fashion, gathering glass at the pots that were set into the furnace, passing to each other the long irons with their tips a mass of glowing metal. Others stood on small wooden stools, blowing the glass into a mould at their feet and withdrawing it shaped as a wineglass, a jug or decanter. Gaffers sat in chairs very similar to those in the Henzel cones, marvering the stem, shaping the foot with hinged wooden palettes. Boys ran here and there carrying jugs of ale and cider, bringing cloths to wipe perspiring faces, clearing the floor of broken glass that would be used again as cullet.

And yet there were differences. There was no cone here, no towering red-brick building with sloping sides and open top. The domed furnace was, instead, built in the middle of a great square room, and it had no chimney, merely a narrow flue, for this furnace was powered by gas only recently installed. Around it was built a raised wooden platform on which the gatherers mounted with their spear-like rods, and the glassmakers themselves were dispersed around the platform. Here and there were wooden troughs containing cold water, and on the fringes of the room were women in coarse aprons: some of them with scarves tied over their heads; some acted as takers-in, carrying the hot, newly made glass to the annealing tunnel; others sat with baskets and wooden trays in front of them filled with glasses which they were checking minutely for imperfections – any found flawed were discarded, the rest went on to the engraving shops for decoration.

'It is always interesting to see another glasshouse, *non*?' Marc Thietry murmured in his ear, and Paul turned quickly.

'Yes, it is. Do you find the gas furnace more reliable?'

'Indeed. As I've told you before, wood is notoriously

difficult – one can never be sure when the metal will be ready to work. That is why we had to build the dwellings for the workers so close to the factory, and why they must be ready always to answer the summons of the bell. But now, with our Siemens furnace, we can organise regular working hours, just as you do in England, and it is better, I think. Although –' he shrugged '– I think we also lose a little of the spirit of the family which we enjoyed before. But one cannot have everything.'

'You are very advanced,' Paul said, and his grandfather smiled, pleased.

'Yes, and we intend to make another change soon – to the new Boetius furnace. I have heard others speak well of it and my grand-nephew René is even now investigating its possibilities. The better the furnace is, you know, the better the crystal that can be produced. And that has always been our aim – to produce the finest crystal possible, with the highest degree of brilliance and the fewest flaws. A search, in effect, for perfection.'

'And in engraving too,' Paul observed as they began to walk around the vast room.

'But of course! There would be little purpose in producing a perfect crystal if the engraving were to be indifferent. We use all methods here – we take our power from the canal to work the hydraulic wheels for cold working, and we also use the American method of pressing glass mechanically for the richly moulded crystal that is so popular there – we export in considerable quantities, you understand. And we use hydrofluoric acid etching as well as arab engraving.' He paused by a tray of finished wineglasses that were being checked, and picked up one, turning it this way and that so that the elegant tulip shape caught the light. 'But our best work is done with the wheel. Simon, whose vases you saw in Paris, has perfected the art of wheel engraving and naturally we cannot allow Baccarat, or any other manufacturer, to outstrip us in this way.'

He smiled and they moved on. Paul gazed about him, deeply impressed. The size and efficiency of the big workshop contrasted sharply with the cramped, sooty cones of Stourbridge. Nevertheless, there were aspects he didn't approve so much: the fact that there were women in the foundry, for instance, and the youth of some of the boys running about. The Factory Acts and Children's Commissions in England had banned such practices and Paul thought it a good thing. Glasshouses were no place for women, and although Henzel's employed them as checkers they were segregated from the foundry itself.

Marc was indicating that they should proceed on into the engraving shop but, eager though he was to see the aspect of glassmaking that attracted him the most, Paul paused for a moment on the threshold. The atmosphere of the glasshouse – the flickering shadows, the clatter of the irons, the hot, metallic smell – had brought his home very close for a moment and he needed a few minutes to recover from the unexpected rush of nostalgia. How were they all faring? he wondered. His mother and Joe, Roger and Sarah – and Emily? He had begun to receive letters from them just before leaving Paris, his mother's and Sarah's filled with love and longing. He had read them with tears in his eyes, missing his family deeply yet still convinced that he had been right to stay in France; knowing that they would welcome him back when he chose to return.

Emily's letter had been different. She had written only once, a cool, stiff little note that might have been addressed to a stranger. It was impossible to tell whether she were angry, upset or merely indifferent. She had not written again.

Roger had not written at all.

The lack of interest on his brother's part didn't worry Paul. He and the younger boy had never been close, and Paul had never forgotten Roger's glee as he chanted the word 'bastard' so many years ago. He had been a child then, ignorant of the full meaning of the word, but somehow that same glee had always seemed to be lurking there, somewhere behind his eyes.

But Emily . . . The thought of Emily was an uncomfortable one. Her declaration of love had come as an unwelcome shock. Absorbed by his new life, he had wanted no ties with the old, particularly ties as complicated as that. His instinctive reaction had been wholly defensive, brushing her off almost in fright, as he might a spider or a venomous insect. But deep down, he knew that he had been over-harsh and the memory persisted in his mind with a sense of shame and of loss; sensations which he disliked so much that he learned quickly to push the memory away.

As he stood in the doorway of the engraving shop and stared out over the plain towards the château, he glimpsed, at the top of the steps, dancing along the terrace that ran right round the house, the figure of a girl, slender and fairylike, dressed all in blue and with her hair a soft pale halo around her head.

He smiled and turned away, following his grandfather into the engraving shop. And as he covered his ears momentarily against the screaming of the wheels, his thoughts now were of Véronique – and Annette.

The vase weighed a good eight pounds. Paul held it carefully by the rim, his elbows resting on the wooden bench. The wheel before him, standing vertical on its axle, began to rotate and he lifted the vase and brought it down against the edge; gently, gently, until the two surfaces made contact and he heard the thin scream of copper biting into glass.

It was the first large piece with which he had been entrusted and he was conscious of his grandfather standing close by, watching him. His heart was thudding, but he had no time to be nervous; with each rapid rotation the wheel was biting deeper into the glass and he was forced to give all his attention to the pattern he was engraving, to holding the glass steady while slowly moving it against the wheel in order to make the pattern. His arms began to ache with the first unaccustomed stress exerted on them by their position, but that would wear off; his muscles stood out under the bare skin and he kept his eyes fixed on the glass, his whole mind concentrated on the effort of perfecting a complicated design on the heavy object.

'Bravo!' Marc said when he sat back at last, holding the vase on his lap between fingers that shook slightly with the release of tension. 'But you are not yet finished. There is the fine work to be done now.'

Paul nodded and stood up, surprised to find that his legs also were shaking. What was the matter with him? He had done plenty of engraving before, at home. But this wasn't home – this was Lorraine, the home of Thietry Cristal. He knew he was being tested, and there were those who would be pleased to see him fail.

He bent to his work again; now beginning the fine engraving, the delicate tracery which wove amongst the larger pattern. Every line must be perfect; mistakes could not be hidden as they sometimes could with the heavier cuts, and even a minute slip would be spotted by these eagle-eyed men. For this work, he was using the smallest wheel of all, with a cutting edge as fine as a razor. He turned the vase slowly, almost infinitesimally, with a concentrated precision that left him unaware of the ache in his arms, the tension in his body. The curling pattern came full circle and was at last complete.

Paul, leaning back exhausted and raising a shaking hand to wipe his forehead, discovered that the whole of the Thietry family had gathered round to watch these final stages: Gabriel, René, Annette, Véronique, even Cécile. Even the eldest of Annette's children, eight-year-old Pierre, was there, watching with large, dark eyes.

'Well done,' Marc said quietly, and Véronique leapt up and down, clapping her hands.

'It's wonderful, Paul! You're an artist – the best engraver we have. Oh, may I have the vase, Oncle? May I have it to keep, to remind me of today?'

'That is for Paul to say. It is his vase. Perhaps he wishes to keep it himself,' Marc said, smiling. 'And you know quite well, Véronique, that it isn't yet complete – it must go to be polished, to give all Paul's engravings their sharp, reflecting edge. Then we shall see its true beauty.'

Paul looked at their faces – the proud expressions of his grandparents, the admiration in Véronique's eyes. He turned his glance to the others and saw dark hostility in the faces of the two men.

Marc followed his glance.

'What do you think of it, Gabriel? A fine piece of work, *non*?'

Gabriel reached out and took it.

'Fine enough,' he said grudgingly. 'But no better than anything our own engravers can produce. Why, Henri's work –'

'But Henri has many years of experience,' Marc pointed out. 'He is fifty years old and started to learn engraving when he was a boy of only sixteen. Was he doing such fine work when he was Paul's age – only in his twenties?' He tapped the vase with his fingernails. 'This is as fine as anything Henri does *now*,' he said quietly. 'Does that not tell you anything?'

Gabriel stared at his uncle, his face dark. He gave Paul a quick look from under lowering brows, and Paul flinched at the dislike he saw there. Was Gabriel jealous of his skill? he wondered uneasily. Or did he fear some greater usurpment?

But that was nonsense! Paul was here on a visit only. Surely they all understood that?

Marc was speaking again. His silver eyes looked directly into Gabriel's truculent brown gaze. His tone was measured, as if to make sure that every word was heard and understood.

'I want Paul to have every facility here,' he said calmly. 'He is to be given the freedom of the engraving shops, just as he has had in Paris. He is to be allowed to watch all our processes, all our best men, and to learn whatever he may from them. And René –' he swung round on the younger man '– I want him also to understand the business side of Thietry. Show him your offices, the ledgers, explain our marketing, the foreign agencies – everything he wants to know. And Paul, if there is anything you do not understand, you will come to me at once.' He paused, and when he spoke again his voice had a heaviness in it. 'If life had gone as it should you would have been here as a child, learning the business as Gabriel and René have done, absorbing it through your skin itself. It is only justice that you should know it now.'

He turned away. The little group was silent. At last Paul raised his eyes and let them travel around the ring of faces.

Gabriel's mouth was tight beneath the bushiness of his beard. His dark eyes were fixed on the vase with a kind of intensity, as if he wanted to smash it and by doing so would smash Paul too. René's face was shuttered, his glance on Véronique, unreadable. Cécile's plump cheeks were pale, her expression sad as she turned to follow her husband. Véronique was looking from one to the other, clearly a little bewildered by undercurrents she did not fully understand.

Annette was watching him with eyes that burned. He met them for an instant only and then looked away, startled and disturbed. There was a message in them, a message that went with those sharp little nails that she had dug into his arm on the first evening at the château. Since then, they had had little time alone together, had had no opportunity to talk, but the message had still been there, in her eyes, in the full, pouting mouth.

One day soon, it would have to answered. It was a day that Paul feared and dreaded; yet he knew that when it came, he would not refuse to answer the summons. He would not be able to.

It was as if she wielded some dark power over him and he, like a rabbit fascinated by a stoat, could only wait for her to make her move.

# Chapter Ten

There was an angry restlessness about Emily. She roamed about the house and garden; took to going for long walks alone; climbing Dob Hill and standing amongst the stunted hawthorns to stare hungrily over the smoky landscape, her eyes fixed on some unknown, distant view that lay beyond the rows of narrow roofs, the tall chimneys, the towering cones – away from the claustrophobic streets of Stourbridge to a place where the boulevards were wide and lined with trees, where great new buildings gleamed white in April sunshine and the air was filled with music and laughter in place of the clashing of machinery and the roar of the furnace.

'You seem to have no idea how to spend your time these days,' Christina would say to her in despair. 'Is there nothing you can find to interest you? You used to enjoy painting – why don't you take it up again? Or needlepoint . . .' But she spoke without conviction, knowing what her own reaction would have been to such suggestions made to her at Emily's age; and she was not really surprised when Emily gave her a withering glance.

'Painting! Sewing! They're just ways to pass the time – ways to fill in a life that's already useless. Things like that are a waste of time.'

Christina shrugged helplessly. 'But there must be something you'd enjoy doing – I never had any difficulty in filling my days when I was a girl –'

'Of course you didn't! You had the glasshouse, didn't you? There's nothing like that for me. And there never will be, because you wouldn't allow it, would you?' Emily stared at her stepmother with hostility in her eyes. 'You'll never give it up. And neither would your father have given it up if he'd lived. You know you were fortunate to inherit it so early.'

'Fortunate! To lose my father at twenty!' Christina's eyes flashed, but she calmed herself immediately. 'No, you are right. He would not have handed over the administration of the glasshouse to me, any more than your father and I will hand it to you.'

'It wouldn't be me anyway,' Emily said. 'It would be Roger.'

'Roger – or Paul,' Christina agreed. 'Or, more probably, the two of them jointly. They have different talents, after all, and could run it well together.'

Emily raised her eyes, dark now with misery. 'Paul? You think he will come back?'

Joe, who had been reading his newspaper, lifted his head. 'Of course he'll come back,' he said irritably. 'Why should you suppose otherwise? This is his home, isn't it?'

'Not everyone stays at home.' Emily gazed at him unhappily. 'And you only have to read his letters to tell how happy he is there. The Thietrys obviously mean to do all they can to make him stay. And now he's gone to Lorraine, and you can see he thinks their glassworks is better than ours – more modern, more efficient, producing finer crystal. Why shouldn't he stay? Monsieur Thietry is almost sure to make him his heir – who else is there?' She turned away, her figure drooping. 'We shall never see Paul in Stourbridge again,' she said bleakly. 'I know it.'

'That's nonsense!' Joe said robustly. 'Paul's got too much sense to be taken in by any French fripperies. He might be dazzled by 'em at first, but that won't last. He's got his head screwed on too tight. He'll be back, mark my words. And by that time you'll likely be wed to some fine young man and too busy with your own family to give much thought to your brother.'

'But he *isn't* my brother.' Emily's voice was low and tense. Why did everyone persist in this fable? She turned and faced them both, her hands clasped tightly before her. 'And I'll never wed anyone else . . . Can't you see what you've done to me?' She saw Christina half rise from her chair, caught Joe's sudden tension. 'I *love* Paul – not as a brother but as a *man*. And what have you done? You've taken him away. You've given him back to the Thietrys. Why should he ever come back? You saw how much they made of him. Monsieur Thietry has no true heir – only a nephew. Why should he ever let Paul leave him? Why should Paul *want* to leave him?' Slowly, she moved away, her voice breaking as she uttered the last few words. On a sob, burying her face in her hands, she whispered: 'He'll never come back to me – never . . .'

She sank into a chair, her shoulders shaking, the dark hair falling around her face. Christina, her eyes filled with pity, got up and came over to her, laying one hand tenderly on the vulnerable slenderness of her neck.

'I know, dear. I know just how you feel. But don't you see, it's all for the best. It could never have worked for you and Paul. We saw what you were beginning to feel for him. We felt it would be a bad thing. We never intended that you should be hurt –'

'*Never intended that I should be hurt!*' Emily looked up swiftly, the tears wet on her face, her voice edged with bitterness. 'How can you say such a thing? How could I *not* be hurt? You've taken him away – deliberately parted us, when we were just beginning to know the truth about ourselves – caused me the greatest pain I've ever known, and you say you never intended me to be hurt!' Her voice broke and she turned away again, covering her face once more with her hands. Christina glanced helplessly at Joe and took an uncertain step forward. But before she could touch Emily again, the girl flung up her head and sprang to her feet, wheeling to face them, her eyes blazing with an anger that even Joe might have found it difficult to match, and Christina stepped back involuntarily before the onslaught of her sudden fury.

'You never gave a thought to my feelings!' Emily accused her. 'You don't even care – all you've been thinking about, all this time, is Paul. Paul Henzel – the only one to carry on your family name. And you wouldn't want that sullied, any more than it already has been, by his marrying a slut from the gutter, a by-blow taken in just to impress other people with your goodness. Oh –' she lifted her voice above their protests, and they fell silent before her impassioned words '– I loved you for it. I was grateful that you found me, wherever I was, that you took me in when my mother died and brought me up as one of your own family. I even believed that you loved me. But it was never real, was it? You did it only as a duty. You never forgot that I was a bastard, the child of some woman of the streets.' She lifted her head, flicking a scathing glance at her father through the glitter of her tears, and then turned back to Christina. 'And that's why you didn't want Paul to love me. I'm not good enough for your son, even though he's a bastard too, because he does at least bear the name of Henzel. That's why you wanted to part us. That's why he's in Paris now.'

There was a silence in the room. Christina lifted one hand, reached out towards Emily and then let it drop as Joe rose to his feet. He looked huge, menacing, powerful enough to snap Emily's body between his two great hands. He took a step towards her and paused, as if expecting Emily to back away. But she stood her ground, looking up at him fearlessly, and he was reminded of the day when she had taxed him about the striking glass-makers, when she was only a child.

'You hate any reference to my birth, don't you?' she said clearly, before he could speak. 'You hate my asking you about those first two years, before I came here. You've told me about Maggie Haden, in the days before you were married to Mamma – but nothing about myself. But now you've got to tell me. I must know.'

Joe's thunder filled the room.

'*Must* know? *Got* to tell you?' he roared. 'What's got into you, for God's sake, making demands, accusing us of God knows what? And you'll apologise to your mother before you say another word, miss, or I'll take a strap to you, big as you are!'

'Stop calling her my mother!' Emily exclaimed furiously. 'She isn't – Maggie Haden was my mother. And you've never told me the truth about her – only half of it. Why? Why shouldn't I know? Paul knows about his father – he has a family and they love him. I have no one!'

'Emily, how can you say that?' Christina came to the girl's side and laid a hand on her sleeve. 'We're your family; we love you. Why else do you suppose I brought you here? Why should –'

'But you couldn't have loved me then – you didn't even know me. You brought me here as a *duty*. You're not my *mother*. You didn't bear me or suckle me – Maggie Haden did that, and I must know more about her.'

'But why?' Christina lifted her hands helplessly, let them fall again. 'Emily, believe me, your truth is different from Paul's. His father and I – we loved each other. And his family – Paul is as precious to them as he is to us. The situation is *different*, don't you see?'

'You mean because Paul's family has wealth and my mother came from the gutter,' Emily said flatly, and saw Christina turn in despair to Joe.

Joe came slowly towards his daughter, his face contorted now with rage.

'You little fool!' he growled. 'Do you have to remind us of that? Do you have to bring it all back? By God, it's been hard enough all these years, seeing you about the place, knowing what you meant. A trap, that's what you were meant to be, a trap to bring me to heel. Well, it didn't work – it was *her* responsibility and I told her so. And then to find you here anyway, forever looking at me with *her* look, never letting me forget . . . You have your mother to thank for the love and care you've had in this house, Emily, and don't you ever forget it. And I call her your mother because that's what she *is*.' He reached out an arm and drew Christina against his side. 'More your mother than that other one ever was. Carrying and suckling aren't the important things, my girl – any slut can do that. It's going into danger as *she* did, bringing you home and bringing you up, giving you the same love as the other children had, aye, and all the attention too, and knowing all the time that you came from another woman's flesh – that's what makes Christina fit to be called your mother, and while you live here in this house you'll not forget that. Now you'll apologise,' he said, and his voice sounded through the room like the low, throbbing notes of a great bass instrument. 'And we'll hear no more about it.'

Emily stared at them. They were united against her, Joe's arm thrown protectively around his wife's slender shoulders. They seemed to form an impervious wall, a force that she could never penetrate. She knew then that they would never tell her any more.

She looked straight into her father's eyes, and her own eyes glowered with the same strength, the same implacable obstinacy. Her mouth was tight and angry and her body rigid. She would not rest now until she had discovered the truth, all of it.

'You've never loved me,' she said now, speaking directly to her father. 'You've always seen me as an intruder. I've known it since I was a baby. It was always the others with you – Sarah and Roger, even Paul who isn't your child at all.' Her eyes and voice filled with contempt. 'You say I have to thank Mamma for everything that has happened to me here. I do. I know there is nothing for which to thank you.'

She turned on her heel and stalked out of the door. Behind her there was silence; as if Joe were too taken aback for speech, too astounded to utter a word. It was only when she was halfway up the stairs that she heard his voice at last, roaring out her name. And then it was in a tone that was a mixture of fury and grief, an amalgam of bitter frustration and regret.

Emily paused momentarily on the stairs and then continued on her way. Her heart cried out inside her, urging her to go back; but her mind refused. The scars of a childhood could not be healed by a momentary remorse.

220

And the thought of her mother's sufferings far outweighed any regrets Joe Compson might feel.

Emily was waiting for Ben outside the cone when he came off shift. He paused in surprise when he saw her, then hurried forward. 'Miss Emily – there's naught wrong, is there? Florrie –'

'Florrie's quite well, as far as I know. I haven't been there. I wanted to see you alone.' She faced him, the dark hair drawn back from her pale cheeks, her leaf-brown eyes wide and direct. 'I told you there was something you could do for me. I want you to do it now.'

'Now? But what is it? What's wrong? You know I'd do aught I could, Miss Emily, but –'

'Then do this: take me to the place where I used to live; the place I came from.' She paused and drew a breath. 'Tell me about my mother.'

Immediately, Ben flinched and his eyes shifted away from hers. Before he could speak, Emily went on, her tone relentless, brooking no refusal. 'I mean to know, Ben. It's my right to know. And my father won't tell me.'

'Then I don't know as I should either,' he stammered. 'It's your dad's right, not mine. If he won't say . . . an' it's not just that. I promised, years ago, promised I never would –'

'Then you shouldn't have!' All Emily's desperate need to know, pent up for all the years, came driving to the surface. 'Ben, *I* am the one who has rights in this matter! What right does my father have to say that I shall never know the truth about my own birth? He didn't even want me – he never wanted me. No, *don't* interrupt, don't try to tell me it's not true – I know he has never really loved me, and it's because of who I am, who my mother was. Are those things my fault?' She ignored Ben's frantic pleas to be quiet, ignored the men hurrying by, the curious glances and the muttered remarks. 'Is it my fault that I was born who I was, how I was? Is it my fault I was born at all? Yet I have to suffer for it. Very well. I shall,

221

if that's to be my lot. But at least I can know *why*. I can know who I am. And you can tell me.' She fastened her eyes on his, compelling, burning, a gaze that could not be denied. 'Tell me now. Take me there. Please.'

Her voice broke on that last word, the only word of supplication she had used, and all Ben's resolve crumbled before her vulnerability. He hesitated no longer. Forgetting their positions, his own as an employee, hers as his master's daughter, he took her by the arm and they were just Ben and Emily again, children in a harsh, cruel world. He led her from the cone to a quiet corner, away from the jostling crowds, and there he looked down into her eyes and she knew that by Ben, at least, she would be given the truth.

'All right,' he said gravely. 'I'll tek you there. An' I'll tell you all I can about her. But it's a fair walk from here, mind; and it ent no Sunday School outing, Miss Emily, not even now, though it's better than it were when your poor ma first went there. You're sure you want to see it?'

'I'm sure.' Emily looked at him and felt the tug of the bond that had always connected her with Ben. 'Tell me where it is, Ben.'

'It's the Lye,' he said slowly, and Emily felt a dull thrill of horror as he spoke the name of the most notorious village in the Stourbridge area. 'Lye Waste. Mud City, as they calls it. That's where you was born, Miss Emily, an' that's where I were born too. An' it's the place where your ma died, an' where Mrs Compson come an' took you away to live at Henzel's.'

She wore her plainest clothes; a dark brown skirt with no flounces, a jacket of the same colour and a hat that hid her face. She slipped out alone, telling no one, and she took the horse-drawn omnibus to the place where she had arranged to meet Ben. And from there they walked down the hill together into Mud City.

The Lye Waste had been called by someone the 'last place God ever made', and someone else had added that it was a pity He had bothered. For many years it had been a black spot of poverty even compared with the poorest slums of Stourbridge. There was nothing there that was of any use – the ground was sour and infertile, the area depressing and ill-favoured. And when gipsies had settled there, a century or two before, nobody had bothered to drive them on. If they found the Waste a good spot to live, well, that said a good deal about the manner of their living. And the fact that they were often so poor that men and women alike walked virtually naked about the narrow streets was a matter for disdain rather than compassion.

The streets were formed by the erection of the mud houses that gave the straggling village its name. None of the inhabitants could afford ordinary house-building materials; instead, they scrabbled in the clay and built their houses of a mixture of mud and straw. They lived on their wits, poaching and stealing, so that the area became a byword for thieving and brutality, and no respectable person would venture near.

Emily had learned all this as she grew up, and although conditions in the Lye were now a good deal better – the first church, a Unitarian chapel, had been built over sixty years earlier – she knew that there was still a considerable amount of poverty. And would have been more when her mother had gone there, twenty years or so before.

No wonder her father had been reluctant to tell her the truth, she thought as she went with Ben into the village where she had been born. He was ashamed – ashamed that he had allowed his woman to sink so low, ashamed that his daughter had spent even so much as a day in the squalor of Mud City.

'Are *all* the houses built of mud?' she asked, staring aghast about her at the crowded streets, the roughly thatched cottages.

Ben nodded. 'Best part of 'em. An' it weren't easy, neither; took time to find enough straw an' dry grasses to mix with the mud an' then each course had to dry afore the next could be put on top. They're warm enough, though. Any holes can soon be blocked out, to keep out the draughts.'

Emily shivered. 'They don't look very comfortable to me. So small – and those tiny windows. They must be dark inside, and cold too, with only earth floors. What do people do here, Ben?'

'All sorts. Chain making, puddling, anvils for forges, all that kind of thing.' He hesitated before adding, 'An' nailmaking, of course.'

'And was that what my mother did?'

'Aye. Maggie were a nailmaker.'

'Show me,' Emily said quietly, and Ben took her past one of the cottages to a tiny shed at the back. From inside, she could hear the sound of women's voices, a child whining, the crackle of a fire. And over it all, like the continual rattle of distant thunder, the hammering of metal.

They looked inside. She saw a dim shadowy cave, with figures huddled round a rough table. A fire burned in the chimney, throwing out a ferocious heat. In one corner was stacked a bundle of iron rods, and, as Emily watched, a woman took one and thrust it into the fire, withdrawing it to lay it on a crude anvil, and hammer the end into the shape of a nailhead; she then sliced off the length required, dropping it into a box on the floor, and thrust the rod back into the fire again, working so quickly that Emily barely saw what she did. Beside the fire a child worked constantly with bellows to keep the flame high. There were two more women in the shed, both working in the same way as the first, each moving in a kind of frenzy, as if it were necessary to make as many nails as humanly possible in the shortest available time. Over them all hung a haze of heat and smoke and ash; they were all wearing thin, tattered rags of shawls, pinned and tied around their bodies in a travesty of clothing, and their eyes gleamed white in the dust and grime of their faces.

Emily withdrew quickly. She walked on for a moment, shaking. Then she turned to Ben.

'And that's what my mother did? How she lived?'

He nodded. 'Aye. An' you went with her, Miss Emily. It were in a place like that where you spent the first two years of your life.'

'And then she died.'

'It were the cholera,' he said simply. 'Your ma sent me to tell Miss Christina – Mrs Compson. She come straightaway – she knew Mag, used to give her money an' food, so they said. An' she was with your ma when she died, an' then she took you away.'

'And my father,' Emily said in a steady voice. 'He never came?'

'Not that I ever heard.'

They reached the river and stared down into its muddy depths. Emily thought of the woman who had come here to give birth, who had stayed because this poverty was the best life could offer, who had died in squalor and been forced to take succour from her lover's wife. What sort of a woman had she been? Had she ever stood here, staring down into these opaque depths and thought of ending the misery of her existence?

And what sort of a man was her father, that he could have allowed her to end in this fashion?

'Someone should do something,' she said aloud, lifting her head to stare about her at the mud cottages, the grimy streets. 'Someone should help these people. Nobody should have to live like this.'

'People try,' Ben said. 'But it's never enough, somehow.'

'Then others should try too.' She faced him and knew that at last her life had come into focus. With the sensations she had discovered while assisting at the birth of Florrie's baby, and the knowledge that there was so much to be done here, she had discovered how to use her life. '*I* shall try.'

Roger was waiting while Jeremy finished dressing. Outwardly, he was trying to act the suave, sophisticated man of the world in his black tail coat and trousers and pleated shirt. Inwardly, he was nervous and uncertain, sensations he disliked and therefore tried to conceal.

After what seemed an eternity, Jeremy was ready, and Roger followed him out to the carriage. His heart was beating fast. The night which he had awaited for so long was at last here, after so many delays that he had begun to fear it would never come. First there had been the trouble over Paul, making Roger himself so much more the focus of his parents' attention that he was scarcely allowed out of their sight. In some ways, this did not displease him; he had always felt a jealous suspicion that they both, and especially Christina, placed more value on the elder boy than on himself. The idea had rooted in his mind with a deep resentment, a resentment he had never fully displayed: why should Paul, the bastard, be so favoured? Why should his talent for engraving be considered so much more valuable than Roger's ability to do accounts, to look at and evaluate the glass market with such accuracy? There were plenty of men who could blow and engrave glass, plenty who, with the opportunities and training Paul had received, could produce work just as fine. There were not so many – and certainly there were no others in the Compson family – who could ensure the continuing success of the family business as Roger would.

No, Paul was favoured simply because he was his mother's firstborn, the child she had carried and borne against all the strictures of society. And society had, after a brief struggle, accepted him.

Paul had been wanted, deeply loved. He was different, special, whereas Roger had been conceived decently within marriage, his birth unremarked upon, his childhood no better and no worse than that of any other legitimate son.

'But my dear boy,' Jeremy said when Roger tried to explain this to him, 'you surely can't wish you were a bastard!'

'No, I don't.' The lips, still soft with boyhood, curled. 'I've no envy of Paul in that. But he's been treated differently because of it. My mother behaves as if she must always compensate, always give him that little bit more attention, the best of everything. And I know she has a special feeling for him – because of his father, I suppose. He looks like him, doesn't he?' Roger glanced at Jeremy, his eyes narrowed. 'You must have known Paul's father! Tell me about him.'

Jeremy lifted one shoulder. 'Little to tell, dear boy. Paul's like him, as you say. And he was French, of course – I always feel the Frenchmen are slightly effeminate, don't you, in spite of their much-vaunted prowess with women. Not that we can deny Jean-Paul's, of course – but I don't wish to speak of that, since it concerns your own mother.'

Roger was silent. It was the aspect of the affair that he found most difficult to accept – the fact that his mother had once had a relationship with a man other than his father. His mind shrank away from it whenever the knowledge came too close. Now he thought of a man, only a few years older than Paul, lying with his mother in the days of her innocence, and he was repelled.

And she dared to command his own behaviour! She, who had fornicated with a foreigner, brought a bastard child into the house and then married a common workman!

Roger wondered why he had never acknowledged these thoughts before he met Jeremy, why he had only been conscious of a vague resentment, a jealousy that was little more than the natural feeling between siblings. It was as if Jeremy had somehow enabled him to crystallise those shadowy feelings, bring them out into the open, examine them and know them for what they were. For although he had always been aware of Joe's background, he had never thought much about it, never seen it as a determining factor in his father's character.

Now he saw it more clearly every day. Joe's massive build, his deep voice and great roar of a laugh, all these belonged to the back streets, to the cones and foundries of industrial Stourbridge. There were men like him

227

everywhere; men who were uneducated and ignorant; making their way to work early in the morning, pushing into the public houses in the evenings, carousing their way home at night. They could be seen at work, slaving in front of blazing furnaces, working iron and steel, hammering out rods for nails and chains, operating huge thundering machines, going below ground to scrape for coal. Or blowing glass: as Joe had blown glass, as he still did.

Joe Compson had been one of these men. He had educated himself, it was true; there had been a period, rarely referred to now, when he had left Stourbridge and gone to work in Newcastle for Alfred Henzel, and he had begun then to haul himself out of the pit of the working class. And he had set himself to read every book in the Henzel library, a task which he was still meticulously carrying out night after night. His speech, though still rich with the accents of the Black Country, was almost as cultured as Jeremy's in that he made few grammatical mistakes, used an extensive vocabulary. He could pass in most places for a reasonably well-born man. But he would never deny his origins; he was proud of them.

Proud of them! Roger could not understand it. Proud to have been born in that tiny house, where Sal Compson still lived and Roger visited as rarely as possible. Proud to have worked six-hour shifts, to have owned a whippet and some pigeons, symbols of the working-class man, proud to have been a prize-fighter on Saturday nights, carrying bruises to prove it and dealing out worse. Proud to have taken doxies on to Dob Hill of a night and lain with them without a thought of marriage.

Proud of his daughter Emily, the fruit of one of those unions?

Roger shook his head. Joe's attitude towards Emily was difficult to fathom. Even before their recent quarrel, since when Emily had gone silently about the house, speaking to neither of her parents more than she could help, there seemed always to be a constraint between them – almost as if he resented her presence, her very existence. And yet it was plain that he loved her, even though he could not express that love as easily and as freely as he could with his other daughter, Sarah.

There ought, Roger mused as he climbed into Jeremy's carriage, to have been a fellow feeling between himself and Emily, the two outsiders. But he was too aware of his own isolation as the observer in the family, the one who stood back in the shadows and watched, noting, learning, gradually understanding. And he was too aware of her illegitimacy.

And, of late, he had developed his own resentments, had turned away from the mother who had betrayed him even before he was conceived, from the father who had come from the wrong street, the wrong family, and given him a name that belonged more to the common workman than the noble glassmaker. Well, since it was his name he would make every endeavour to lift it so that it stood side by side with the illustrious Henzels and Tyzacks and Titterys. And since his parents had flouted the conventions of their times and gone their own way, so he would go his. With whom he chose.

'You're remarkably quiet, Roger,' Jeremy observed as the carriage rattled over the rough-paved roads. 'Not regretting tonight's little adventure, I trust? There's still time to turn back.'

'No – not at all.' Roger turned quickly to the older man, able to see only the gleam of his teeth and the shine of his eyes in the darkness of the carriage. 'I was just thinking . . . I was afraid you'd never find time for me.'

'You mean you doubted me? But I gave you my word.' There was a dryness in Jeremy's voice that Roger didn't wholly understand. 'I'm sorry we haven't been able to arrange it sooner. My Uncle Alfred's illness, necessitating my visit to Newcastle, has interfered with a good many of my plans. I didn't imagine I would have to stay so long.' He fell silent and Roger looked out of the carriage window thinking of what lay ahead with nervous anticipation. His only previous dalliance had been with a young parlour maid, loaned to his mother by a friend while Rose had been ill recently, who had happened to be on the stairs so often when he was passing that he eventually felt obliged to kiss the pouting lips she turned up to his face. He had been rather shaken by her immediate reaction, the greed of her open mouth, the soft flesh pressing against his, and had been obscurely glad when she had left that same day. But he'd missed the maid, all the same, and had lain awake for several nights wondering just how the soft, squirming flesh would have felt in his bed and how easy it would have been to satisfy that greedy mouth.

That had been Roger's only foray into the world of seduction. And tonight, bumping along in his cousin's carriage, he was acutely aware of his ignorance. Suppose he couldn't do it? Suppose he was too quick, too slow? How long *were* you supposed to take, anyway? Suppose the girl laughed at him – suppose she told Jeremy?

He almost asked Jeremy to stop the carriage, almost told him that he would turn back after all, that the adventure was too soon, he needed more time . . . But then he chided himself for panicking, for behaving like a timid bride on her wedding night. He was a man, wasn't he? Nineteen years old and still without experience! It was ridiculous. And any father other than Joe Compson would have seen to it that his education was completed before now. But Joe was not of his class, was he? He was a workman, brought up in the back streets. There was no doubt he had had his first woman before he was nineteen; but he was out of his element now, would not have known where to take or send Roger, would never have dreamed of recommending those same back streets. And Christina would never have thought of such a thing, even if she had been willing to loosen the leash she had kept him on since he was a child.

Well, he was off that leash now. He had met Jeremy, who had been kept away from him for so long. And Jeremy knew how a boy should be brought up.

'I hope you've found me a pretty little doxy,' he remarked, trying to sound nonchalant, and Jeremy gave him a quick, amused glance.

'Oh, pretty enough, pretty enough. But all cats are grey

in the dark, you know.' He laughed and Roger joined in, hoping he'd achieved the same patronising tone of his cousin's voice. 'Still, I agree, it helps in the initial stages if the chit's presentable. And I don't think you'll be displeased with this one. Her name is Jessie.'

'You've met her before, then?' Roger was still trying to speak as casually as if this evening were an everyday occurrence.

'Once or twice.' Again, Jeremy's glance was amused, and Roger felt his cheeks burn. Just how well had Jeremy known this girl? He sought desperately for another subject of conversation, but could find nothing. 'And your girl, what's her name?' he asked at last.

'Oh, a little wench called Violet, and as pretty as one too. Deep blue eyes with smudges round them, a nice little mouth, and the rest of her . . .' He waved his hands descriptively. 'Yes, I think we're both in for a pleasantly satisfying evening. You won't be sorry you came, I'm sure.'

The horse was slowing down now and Roger peered out. They were in a narrow side street, a street something like the one where his grandmother Sal Compson lived. But the houses were larger, three storeys tall, and each one had a railed area leading to a basement, and a short flight of steps going up to the front door. Most of the windows were in darkness and there was nobody about.

He glanced doubtfully at his cousin and Jeremy grinned and nodded to his driver, who had climbed out. The man went up the steps of the nearest house and knocked softly on the shabby door.

Roger watched, fascinated, as it opened and a glow of rosy light spilled on to the pavement. He saw a woman appear, speak to the driver and then look past him at the carriage. Her silhouette was tall and shapely, that of a mature woman with hair piled high on her head and an elegance that came only with a certain number of years. Suddenly self-conscious, he drew back, but Jeremy seized his wrist and laughed.

'No backing out now! We're expected. That's Madam

Charlotte and she won't stand at the door all night, so come along.' He dropped down to the pavement and Roger followed him, his heart thumping again as he looked up at the house. But he was given no time to stare. Jeremy was urging him forward, his hand in the small of Roger's back as he propelled him up the steps. Within moments, he found himself standing at the door, bathed in the rosy light; and then his feet were on thick, soft carpet and the door was closing behind him and Jeremy was taking the woman's hand in his, touching the glittering rings with his lips.

'Charlotte, it's good to see you again. And you see, I've brought my young friend, just as I promised. He needs a little guidance in social matters.' He indicated Roger and she turned to regard him with steady grey eyes, her expression calmly appraising.

'The young ladies are ready, I take it?' Jeremy asked.

'And supper too,' Madam Charlotte confirmed. She smiled at Roger and gave him a small nod with her head. 'You will like Jessie, I know. She's one of my best girls.'

She turned majestically, her skirts rustling as she walked along the short corridor and up the stairs. Jeremy and Roger followed, Roger still bemused by the contrast between the shabby exterior of the house and the street in which it stood, and the ostentation within. Everywhere there were rich draperies, chairs with luxurious upholstery and soft cushions, walls hung with paper that shone with gold, candles in gilded brackets that shed a flickering, shadowy light.

Upstairs, they were shown into a room that was set with a small supper table for four. Beside it, on opposite sides, set into curtained alcoves, were two chaise longues, piled with cushions and rugs of thick fur; and amongst the cushions and rugs lounged two women. Women whose appearance brought the blood rushing to Roger's face and set his heart kicking.

In the dim light, it was difficult to see their features. He was aware only of an opulence, the kind of opulence he had seen in old paintings – a voluptuous excess of

232

flesh that made him want to recoil, yet drew him with a dark fascination, a throbbing desire to know more of the shadows hinted at by cleaving folds, by artfully draped lace and softly clinging silk, by breasts that were exposed almost to the nipple, by limbs that were briefly outlined and then withdrawn.

'Come and sit by me,' said the fairer of the two. She brushed a hand lazily up her slender neck, swept back the golden hair that lay loose on her bare shoulders, displaying as she did so a plump upper arm. 'I'm Jessie. And you must be Mr Roger.'

'That's right.' His voice was hoarse and he glanced quickly at Jeremy. But his cousin was paying him no attention. He was concerned only with the dark-haired woman, raising her hand to his lips, laughing with her, his hands already in her hair.

'I've been waiting to meet you,' Jessie murmured. 'We shall have lots to talk about . . . But first we must eat.'

'I – I'm not hungry,' Roger stammered, and she laughed.

'Of course you are! Men are always hungry – one way or another. And we've taken such trouble to prepare this little supper. You must try one of my pies – see, I'll cut a piece off for you.' Her hand rested lightly on his thigh, the fingers almost burning a pattern on it so that he was quite unable to move. Obediently, he opened his mouth and she popped the pie in. It could have tasted of sawdust. She lifted a glass and held it to his lips, and that was better. He recognised the taste of champagne and relaxed.

'There, that's it,' she cooed. 'I can see we're going to have a lovely time.' Her voice was curious, as if she had tried to overlay her natural Black Country accent with the kind of cultured English that Jeremy spoke. It sounded artificial, yet it suited her, suited this strange, dimly lit room with its cushions and drapes; suited the house.

'You look uncomfortable,' she said now as she set the glass down again. With quick fingers, she undid the tie he had struggled so hard to perfect and began to unfasten some of the buttons of his shirt. Roger fought down the desire to pull her hands away – wasn't this what he had come for? But it was all happening too fast. He glanced desperately across the table at Jeremy, not caring now if the older man saw his confused ignorance, and Jeremy gave him a grin of understanding.

'Just relax, Roger,' he said coolly. 'And don't be in too much of a hurry, Jess – we want to eat first. One piece of your pie and a sip of champagne isn't going to be enough to sustain men like Roger and me through the night. Feed him properly.'

'He says he's not hungry,' Jessie simpered, and Jeremy laughed.

'Oh, he is, he is! Try him with something else – a piece of chicken, a few oysters. He'll soon find his appetite again. And – of course – plenty of champagne!'

Jessie giggled and lifted the glass to Roger's lips again. He swallowed nervously, feeling the tingling liquid touch his tongue and throat. Jessie, keeping her blue eyes fixed on his face, drank from the other side of the glass and then offered it back and Roger took and drained it.

'That's better!' She refilled it and gave him another piece of pie. 'Drink up, Mr Roger. I've never had a gentleman called Roger before,' she confided. 'You're my very first! Am I your first Jessie?'

'Yes,' he stammered, and she giggled again. He felt the warmth of the wine steal through his body, the heat creep up the back of his neck and spread comfortingly through his head. His taut muscles relaxed further and he began to notice the inviting curves of her body, the flesh pink and enticing in the candlelight. He leaned back against the head of the chaise longue and allowed her to feed him. He began to feel in command of the situation, strong and masterful with this woman who was so willing to be his slave. A slow, heady power began to throb through his body and he became aware of sensations that were pleasurable but would soon become demanding, crying out for relief. His heart began to pound.

Vaguely, he was aware of Jeremy somewhere in the background, of his murmuring voice and insinuating laugh. But his cousin was now no more than a dim presence. And then, as Jessie reached behind her and twitched the heavy curtain across the alcove, he was not even that.

He thrust Jessie back against the cushions, his hands fierce on those maddening curves, his fingers relentless, ripping away the insubstantial fabrics that impeded him. There was no finesse in his grappling, no elegance, no thought for the body he needed so urgently to possess; and Jessie's little cries and screams served only to goad him on until at last, still fumbling, still clumsy, he thrust himself into her and strained for his climax before subsiding upon her body as he might sink into a soft, accommodating cushion.

Jessie's hands moved in his hair, almost like those of a mother comforting a hurt child.

'There,' she murmured, 'there. It was good, wasn't it? There . . .'

Good? Roger scarcely knew whether it had been good or bad. He was only conscious of the thundering of his heart, the quickness of his breath, as if he had been running a race; and the enormous sensation of relief that swept over him, as if he had unburdened himself of some heavy load. And then, slowly, he began to realise what had happened. He had possessed a woman. He was a boy no longer. He had proved himself, proved that he too had the power of all men. The relief was followed by a fierce triumph. He thought briefly of his parents, of Christina with the Frenchman, Joe with his wench, and he thought with a savage joy of their reactions if they knew where he was now, and what he was doing. And he could do it again! He was the master, this woman his slave.

He raised himself on his elbows and, looking down at the flushed face, lifted one hand to grasp at the tangled hair and pull her to him.

# Chapter Eleven

There were times when Christina looked back with wistful nostalgia to her life as it had been ten, fifteen years before. When she and Joe had been in the fullness of their vitality, working together in a thriving business and bringing up a family of strong, healthy children who each showed signs of individual gifts and talents, who played and lived together in harmony and never gave any hint that things could ever be otherwise.

But now, somehow, everything seemed to have changed, and it all stemmed from that fateful visit to Paris. Paul was far away and seemed to have settled down alarmingly well with his new family. Emily, at first more shaken by her loss than Christina had dreamt she would be, was now withdrawn and hostile, barely speaking to her and Joe, looking at them both with accusing eyes. She was hardly ever in the house; since the day when she had come home and told them, with a bitter triumph in her voice, that she had been to the Lye Waste, she had spent almost all her time there, doing goodness knows what tasks. Joe was furious, but both he and Christina were helpless. They had encouraged their children to be independent, had given their daughters more freedom than most young ladies were allowed, and were forced to accept the consequences.

Roger, too, was a source of uneasiness to Christina. At Oxford now and apparently doing well in his studies, there was nevertheless an air about him when he came home that she did not quite like. A sophistication, a muted insolence, especially in his dealings with Joe. And he was inclined now to go off in the evenings and return late, without explanation.

'He's just growing up,' Joe said. 'I don't like his manner much either, but that's Roger – he's always been a bit inclined to take himself seriously. He's sensible enough, and you must agree he's useful in the office when he's at home.'

'And there speaks the man who said it was "nobbut clerking",' Christina teased.

'Aye, I did, but I can see he's got a good head on his shoulders, and maybe we do need some new ways of dealing with things, as he says. And he has other ideas too, ideas about glass . . . that black crystal he was so keen on, I don't reckon much to that, but the ruby . . . You know everyone's always looking for a real true ruby, and I wouldn't be surprised if this latest recipe doesn't turn out to be it. And you don't have to be a glassmaker to work it out – it's knowing the science of it, the chemical formula as young Roger calls it, that's important.'

'He's certainly taking a great deal of interest in the business these days,' Christina said. 'And I suppose we should count it a good thing. You realise he expects to take full charge eventually. And with Paul still in France . . .'

'What difference does that make?' Joe demanded. 'He knows well enough that Paul's coming back, and with all the experience he's getting over there he'll expect a big say in matters. And he's a craftsman too – and with all his learning and cleverness, Roger must know that the blower and the engraver make up the most important part of the business.'

'He also knows,' Christina said seriously, 'that Paul is not our legitimate son. I believe he expects to inherit everything – as, under the law, he normally would.'

'And under the law, we can leave our property how we like – and we've already sorted that out with the lawyers, without Master Roger's say-so.' Joe sighed. 'I wish Paul would decide to come back soon. That would settle all this. But he doesn't seem to have any idea of it, living in Paris, visiting Lorraine –'

'He's learning. His letters are full of all the differences between French glass and our own, the new techniques he's learning to apply. He'll come back when he's ready – all this is for the benefit of Henzel's in the end.'

'Seems to me it's more likely to be for the benefit of Thietry's.' Joe hesitated, giving her a dubious glance, then said as if he were making up his mind: 'Christina, we have to face up to this. They're not going to let him go, those grandparents of his. I saw it in their faces when we were there. They wanted him then, and they got him. They're going to hold on to him. Look at what he's done. He's been down to Lorraine, worked there, got to know the folk. He's been all through the engraving shops. He's studied with other engravers. He's been accepted as part of the family. And who else is there to take it all over when Marc goes? Tell me that. And it can't be so long now – he's an old man and getting frail, from what the boy says in his letters.'

'There's Gabriel, and his family. He has sons –'

'Aye, and no more than children yet. And Gabriel's only a nephew. And as for that other fellow, René, he's not even related, except by marriage. There's no Thietry blood in him. No, I reckon it's Paul the old man intends to make his heir, or at least to leave a fair share to. And that means we'll never see him here in Stourbridge again, mark my words.' He caught sight of Christina's stricken face and stopped abruptly. 'God forgive me! I never meant to say those things to you, my love. But I've been thinking 'em for a long time and I suppose they just had to come out.'

'Never see him here again?' she repeated faintly. 'Oh, Joe, do you really think that's possible?'

'I don't know,' he said, clearly still cursing himself for ever having said such a thing. 'I just don't know. Oh, I daresay I'm getting it all wrong – take no notice. I get a bit down sometimes – miss him myself, if you want the truth of it. I'd like to see the boy back here, where he belongs, and that's a fact.'

'Where he belongs,' Christina echoed. 'And that's the whole trouble, isn't it, Joe? Where *does* Paul belong? Here, where he was born and grew up – or in France, the land of his father? It must be as difficult for him as it is for us, Joe, and we can only wait until he finally makes up his mind.'

Emily, too, was torn between two backgrounds. But hers were differences of class rather than of country, although she often felt that the Lye was even further removed from her own home than was Paris. The Thietrys lived at least in similar circumstances to the Compsons, in equal comfort. The people of Emily's other background – the men and women of Mud City – might have been a world away.

Even now, although much improved from what it had been when it was the home of a rootless tribe of gipsies and vagabonds, the Lye was still a place apart, its people insular and suspicious. Although there were more factories now, so that only a few nailmakers still laboured in their own dirty, ill-lit sheds, most of the inhabitants of the crowded cottages were poorly paid. And a good deal of the money they did earn went on beer; for only seven thousand people, there were over fifty beer-shops. Tales were still told of the Reverend Bromley, who had come to the Lye in 1845, who would meet the men from work and take their wages from them before they could be spent, handing them to the wives and mothers to be used more sensibly for food and clothing. But there were still plenty of men who came to the beer-shops straight from the factories where they made nails, fireclay pots for the glasshouses, hollow-ware or chains. And there were plenty of families who went hungry because of it, and children with no shoes for their feet during even the most bitter winter weather.

Emily saw some of this on that first visit, when Ben took her to see her birthplace. She looked at the narrow streets, at the rough footpaths, the unmade roads; she looked at the tiny yards and courts, at the better, newer houses that were built with bricks, some of them with a scullery that was detached from the house, where the women would do the laundry and where some families would wash on Friday or Saturday nights, each taking turns in the galvanised bath that hung for the rest of the week on a nail in the wall.

'It's better now than it were,' Ben said, trying obscurely to defend the isolated community. 'Mind, the old Reverend's made a lot of difference. An' the Methodists, too. People like the sermons they get in chapel – a bit of fire about them, there is. They don't mind talking about Hell, an' that. An' you don't hev to be gentry to be a Methodist. Anyone can be a preacher. It's the first time Lye folk hev had the chance to speak for themselves.'

'But they still seem so suspicious,' Emily said, shrinking back as a big, rough-looking man shouldered his way past them. 'They know you, Ben – you were born here and you've been coming back even though you left when you were still a child. But the way they look at me . . . Can't you tell them I was born here too?'

He gave her a glance of astonishment. 'You want folk to know that?'

'Why not? I feel no shame. Why should I? My mother bore me and cared for me, and when she knew she was dying she sent for someone she knew she could trust – Christina Compson. If I should feel shame, it's for my father, who never even sought to find out what had happened to us. And he's no Lye man.' She stood gazing down the tumbled street, watching some small children who played in and out of the puddles. 'I tell you, Ben, I feel closer to these people than I do to my own family.'

'But you won't want to come again, not now you've seen it.'

'Oh, but I will,' she said and turned dark, sombre eyes upon him. 'I shall come again and again. I mean to do something here, Ben – something worthwhile. I've been restless ever since we returned from Paris, searching for something to do, something to fill the long, lonely days. Now I've found it. I mean to spend my time in the Lye, doing whatever is necessary to help the people who live here.'

'But why? Why should you want to do that?'

241

'Because they are my people,' she replied. 'Because I was born amongst them and if it had not been for Christina Compson I would have been here still. And because of my mother; because I want to show that now, even if it is too late for her, somebody does care. And who should care more than her own daughter?'

She questioned Ben closely about what he could remember of her mother. Unfortunately, it wasn't much. He could not recall Maggie Haden in the Lye before Emily was born, and thought that she must have wandered there from somewhere else. 'She lived with an old woman called Em,' he said, racking his brains for memories. 'Folk said she were a bit of a witch – she allus had a bit of medicine by her if anyone had a cough or a cut, like. An' she were allus on hand to help at a birthing, same as you were with my Florrie, or to lay out anyone who'd died. But I don't remember your Ma living along of her much above two years.'

'So she was homeless,' Emily deduced, 'and came to the Lye when she was near her time with me. And Em – Emily, do you think? – took her in. Ben, do you remember the glassmakers' picnic, when those women told Paul and me that we were bastards? They seemed to know all about my mother – it was from them that I heard the name Maggie Haden. Couldn't we find them?'

He shook his head. 'They're both dead, Miss Emily. I knew 'em by sight – so did a lot of others aroun' the town. They were – well –' He flushed and looked at his feet. 'Anyway, they're both dead these past four years.'

'I see. And there's no one else? No family that you know of?'

'I reckon your ma's family must've cast her out, like. Or she wouldn't hev been wandering down the Lye, would she?'

'No, that's true.' Emily sighed. 'I suppose I shall never know any more. But that won't stop me from doing all I can, Ben. The Lye has never been treated properly; the people are oppressed and deprived. And nothing will ever improve until they have better housing, better living conditions, and better education. Well, I shall do all I can to help. It only needs someone to take an interest.'

'Well, your dad knows a lot of people who *could* do summat,' Ben said dubiously. 'But I reckon you'll hev a hard time persuading them. The Lye ent ever going to be a fashionable place, the sort of place folk campaign about.'

'Campaigns? I'm not talking of campaigns!' Emily turned to him, her eyes burning as they had done when she had first declared her intention, only moments – or was it a lifetime – ago. 'Ben, I intend to *work* here. These people need help *now*. They need someone to go into their houses, nurse their sick, teach their children. *That's* what I shall do.' She moved nearer, looking up into his face. 'That day when little Frank was born – I realised then that it was *practical* help I was best at giving. And now I know who I should be giving that help to. There are people here who knew old Em, who knew my mother and who did *not* cast her out. They are the people I want to help.'

Ben still looked doubtful. 'But that sort o' work ent fit for you now. You've changed, you can't be the same as if you'd been raised here. Nursing – that's rough work. You could open a school, I suppose. But there's already schools – the National, that was the Reverend Hill's school, an' the nurse school that Mr Robertson started up two or three years back.'

'Nurse school? Do you mean they learn nursing?'

'No – it's for girls to tek babbies to. Babbies they're looking after, like, so their mothers can go to work. They tek them all morning, tek them up back to their ma's for dinner, then go back in the afternoon until the factories finish. An' the Reverend sees to it that they get a bit o' schooling while they're there. It's only until they're nine, o' course – they can go into the factories theirselves then.'

'And those are the only schools? For all the children in the Lye?'

'There's dame schools, for 'em as wants 'em. Trouble

is, they all cost money an' most people thinks their kids are better off earning it than spending it.'

'But there's already a move to change that,' Emily said thoughtfully. 'People are beginning to believe that all children should have the right to free education. Everyone ought to be able to read and write. The people of the Lye would begin to understand then how others live, outside, and to see that they too can have better conditions. And proper schools would give them the ability to bring about their own improvements.'

'An' would these grand new schools allow nurse girls?' Ben asked sceptically. 'What will the mothers who hev babbies do with 'em? They can't tek 'em into the factories. An' I can't see chapel folk liking it much. Interfering an' all.'

'Who is the minister, Ben?' Emily asked. 'He must be interested in education. Or the lay preachers, can you take me to them?'

'Mr Corbett? He lives down High Street, just by the village clock,' Ben said. 'But –'

'We'll go and see him straightaway,' she said firmly, then noticed Ben's troubled face. 'What's the matter?'

'It's just –'

'Just what?' she demanded crisply.

'Just that – well, you don't live here, like, an' folk round here, they're funny with strangers, allus hev bin. They might –'

'But I *come* from the Lye,' Emily said tersely. 'I was born here. I could have been one of those children playing in the gutter, one of those girls working in the forge, or one of those women with three or four hungry babies clustered round my knee. I told you, Ben, these are my people. And I shall tell them that, if you won't. Now – are you coming to the minister's house with me or not?'

Ben sighed and gave in. There was no arguing with Miss Emily when she was in this mood. And to tell the truth, he was glad to see her back in her old habits, taking charge, ordering folk around, sure that everything she decided must be right. Since she'd come back from Paris, she'd been too quiet, almost faded, with all her spirit gone. The dark eyes, so full of fire, had seemed dimmed, the determined mouth drooping and the square face pale and listless. If coming down to the Lye was going to make such a difference, he wouldn't say another word against it.

The minister's house was attached to the chapel. Emily raised her hand and rapped sharply with the iron knocker.

'He might be out, visiting,' Ben ventured, but even as he spoke the door swung open and a man stood there.

Ben caught Emily's quick intake of breath. He felt his own eyebrows rise. Not that there was anything especially unusual about the man, apart from his unexpected youth and extremely handsome appearance. But it wasn't Mr Corbett, that was certain. The minister was older, for a start, and everyone knew there was nothing in the least handsome about *him*.

Emily recovered herself so quickly that Ben wondered if he had imagined that quick breath.

'I was looking for the minister. Is he in? If so, I'd like to have a word with him.'

The young man smiled down at her. His eyes were as dark as her own and his black hair curled over a broad, pale forehead. 'My father? No, I'm afraid he's out, but if you'd like to come in and wait I'm sure he'll be pleased to see you. I don't think he'll be long.'

The cultured tones were not those of the Lye, nor could Emily detect any trace of Black Country accent in them. She looked up at the young man consideringly. How tall he was – taller even than Ben, taller than Paul.

'Thank you, we should like to come in,' she said and they followed him into the narrow hall, Ben pulling off his cap and twisting it nervously between his fingers. 'My name is Emily Compson, and this is Ben Taylor who has kindly escorted me here.'

'Ah yes, Ben Taylor. I've heard about you – a son of the Lye, made good as a glassmaker, and a fine one too, so I've heard. And so you must be Joe Compson's daughter.' He led them into a parlour, dominated by a large rolltop desk which was cluttered with papers. 'My father will be so pleased that you've called on him.' He moved easily about the room, clearing more papers from the armchairs that stood on either side of the fireplace. 'Please take a seat, Miss Compson.'

Emily sat down. She felt slightly uncomfortable with this apparently imperturbable young man, who seemed not in the least surprised that Joe Compson's daughter and a glassmaker should be calling on a nonconformist minister in the Lye. She looked at the small, rather dismal fire that burned in the narrow grate and wondered what to say next. For a moment, her ardour had faded and she felt at a loss.

'Is it something urgent you wish to discuss with my father?' the young Mr Corbett was asking now. 'Because if so, I could send a boy to find him.'

'Urgent? No, not in the least,' Emily found herself babbling, then took herself sternly in hand. 'But it *is* important.' She raised her eyes, dark as agate, and looked up into the pale face. 'I wonder if you have noticed the condition in which many of the people of the Lye live?'

His lips could have been the finely moulded lips of a classical statue. They twitched a little, smiled wryly. 'It would be difficult to live here, in their midst, without becoming aware of it.'

Emily felt herself blush. 'Of course. So, you live here all the time?'

'Not all the time. My father has only been here himself for two years or so, you know, and I have been teaching at a boys' school in the north. Unfortunately I have been ill and forced to leave my job to recuperate, but while I am here I've been attempting to help my father in his work. I might even stay as his assistant – we enjoy each other's company, and he's been lonely since my mother passed away.'

'Oh, I'm sorry.' Emily felt a quick sympathy for him. 'Then who looks after you both?'

'Oh, we have an excellent cook-general and a maid, we manage very well. But I haven't even offered you refreshment! What shall it be – a cup of tea, a glass of Mrs Grable's lemonade?'

'A cup of tea would be very welcome.' Emily glanced at Ben, wondering if his presence was an embarrassment to Mr Corbett. If he had accompanied her to a vicarage or rectory, she had no doubt that he would have been shown to the servants' quarters long before now. But the minister's son did not seem at all discomfited and went to the door to call down the hall to Mrs Grable, and when she appeared from the kitchen, asked for tea for three; just as if it were the most natural thing in the world to sit down to drink tea together.

'And now,' he said, returning and closing the door before taking the opposite armchair. 'Please, Mr Taylor, do sit down. Now tell me, Miss Compson, why are you interested in the living conditions in the Lye?'

'Because they are so bad,' Emily answered at once. 'Because I believe that everyone has a right to a better life than that endured by some of the people who live in the poorer areas of the Black Country – yes, and other places too. In London. In Birmingham. In Stourbridge. In the Lye. I know much has been done to improve matters, but there's much, much more to be done yet – and I want to do it. Or at least to share in doing it.'

She came to a halt, her eyes fixed on his, burning now with the same vehement passion that throbbed through her low voice. Mr Corbett sat forward, his hands on his knees, nodding his head; the smile touched his lips again and was gone.

'So you have seen the misery that walks the streets of England. And you want to do something to alleviate it. Admirable, Miss Compson, admirable.' He paused and Emily stared at him, feeling obscurely that he was mocking her, that he did not believe in her sincerity or, if he believed in that, did not place much faith in her ability to follow it up with practicality. 'But why do you turn your attention to the Lye? We are not fashionable here, Miss

247

Compson. We are unimportant, unnoticed, forgotten. Nobody will rush to help you if you set up soup kitchens or help fallen women – of whom we have our fair share – or hold temperance meetings. I doubt if anyone will even notice. We might not even notice ourselves – we are an insular species, here in the Lye, and you are likely to find yourself having to drink your own soup or speak to empty halls at your meetings.'

Emily felt her shoulders stiffen with a quick, hot indignation. 'I'm not looking for "fashion", Mr Corbett, or for a little hobby to pass the time and tell my friends about. I want to do something worthwhile. I have been fortunate in my life – I want to share that good fortune. I don't want to patronise, Mr Corbett. I want to *help*. I want to work with them, show them that there is a better way of life. Nurse them when they're sick, teach them when they're well.' She leaned forward, her body tense. 'You're a teacher yourself, Mr Corbett, you know about the new Education Act. Places like the Lye should be served equally with, say, the centre of Stourbridge or fine towns like Birmingham. But will they? I think they're more likely to be forgotten, overlooked. I don't want to see the Lye neglected when it comes to schooling – or to anything else. The people here are as entitled as any others to whatever is provided. And I believe that if poor working people had a better education, they would then know how to help themselves.'

'And your reason for choosing the Lye?' he repeated with a gentle insistence. 'Why not your own village of Wordsley? Amblecote? Or Stourbridge itself? Please –' He lifted a hand as Emily began to protest '– I know I have no right to question you in this way. If you don't wish to satisfy my curiosity, you have every right to refuse to answer.'

Emily gave him a long, steady look, considering him gravely. There was a depth in those dark brown eyes that appealed to her; a cool gravity in the finely chiselled face that brought an unaccustomed quickness to her heartbeat. The hand he held up was thin, with slender fingers and a narrow palm, the nails short and neat; an artistic hand.

'I don't mind answering you,' she said at last. 'I've already told Ben he may tell anyone who wishes to know. I want to help the people of the Lye because I am one of them, Mr Corbett. I was born here, in a little mud house near the river. I lived here until I was two years old and then Christina Compson found me as my mother lay dying of cholera, and took me back to Henzel's. That's why I say I've been fortunate, and that's why I want to help the Lye.'

Young Mr Corbett stared at her. 'You come from the Lye? Mrs Compson found you here? But I understood . . . So you are *not* Joseph Compson's daughter after all? You were adopted by them.'

'No,' she said quietly. 'I was never adopted. There was no need. Joe Compson is my father, but Christina Compson is not my mother. My real mother lies here, buried in a plague pit. She worked in a nail shop behind a mud house to earn such living as she could for both of us. And it was in her memory that I came.'

During that first talk with Stephen Corbett, Emily saw that here was the man who could help her in what had become a crusade. Quietly, she set about convincing him of her determination.

'You're helping your father here already. Visiting people, listening to their problems, giving them advice. I'll come every morning and accompany you.' There was no questioning note in her voice. With the assumption of authority which would have been recognised by those who knew her in the nursery, she took it for granted that Stephen Corbett and his father would welcome her company. 'You can introduce me to people. I'll soon be able to see how best to help them. And meanwhile, we'll make sure that the Lye gets its school – and anything else it needs.'

Stephen Corbett still looked at her with some doubt. Any minister, and therefore any minister's son, knew that rich young women with time on their hands often ventured into slums to 'help the poor'. Such enterprises usually foundered quite quickly – the young women were shocked by the totally unexpected squalor they found in 'romantic' cottages, they were nauseated by the dirt and the smells, the sheer ugliness of poverty, or they were afraid of disease. If they did persist, they became autocratic and domineering, thrusting their way uninvited into people's homes and making themselves too unpopular to be able to do any further good; finally, they discarded the victims of their charity and disappeared, complaining loudly about ingratitude.

He did not think that Emily Compson would prove to be one of the former. Her face, framed by hair like shining jet, pale but for the brilliance of her dark brown eyes, was too strong, her expression too determined. But she might well turn out to be one of the autocratic kind – even if she had been born here, amongst the people she so passionately desired to help. And he wasn't quite sure how much weight that would carry with the independent people of the Lye. It would be quite clear to even the most unobservant that she had not been brought up amongst them.

'You are welcome to come at any time, of course,' he said politely. 'I know my father would be pleased to make your acquaintance. And any help that you may feel you can give . . .' He left the sentence unfinished, lifting one hand vaguely in the air.

Emily gave him a cold glance.

'I don't think you understand me, Mr Corbett. I do not intend to play at this, making gracious descents from my carriage in between calls on fashionable friends and parties. This is important to me, Mr Corbett. When I said I would come every morning, I meant exactly that. I shall spend all my days here from now on, and if you don't find me real work to do, I shall find it myself.' She stood up, drawing on her gloves. 'And now we have to go. Ben has a wife and child at home and I have kept him away from them for too long already. I shall see you in the morning, if that is convenient – to you.'

She gave a sharp little nod and Stephen Corbett rose quickly, hiding a quiver of amusement. Clearly, Emily Compson was indeed one of the autocratic sort. Yet, in spite of her clear determination, there was something a little lost about her. With a brief flash of insight, he wondered why she was still unmarried – and whether this interest in the Lye were not the result of some unfortunate love affair, a way of filling a vacuum.

Only time would tell. And meanwhile, he looked forward to getting to know Emily Compson better.

Emily returned home to find both her parents taking tea in the drawing room, and told them at once what her plans were. As she had expected, they were horrified: first by the fact that she had gone to such a place, even with Ben as an escort – 'And I'll be having words with Ben Taylor about that first thing in the morning,' Joe had growled, setting down his cup with a bang that almost smashed the saucer – and then by the thought of her going again, day after day, risking her health and her good name in one of the worst slums of the Black Country.

'My good name!' Emily said, and laughed. 'What good name do I have? You know well enough what that woman called me at the picnic. That hasn't changed – it never will. What should going to the Lye do to harm a reputation I don't even possess?'

'That's nonsense!' Christina said sharply, and Joe stood up, his face dark with anger. He moved to the fireplace and stood before it, obviously preparing to deliver some speech about gratitude and what made a real mother. But Emily tossed her head and gave him a glance so scornful that he remained silent with his mouth slightly open, staring at her.

'I don't intend to discuss this with either of you,' she said in a clear, cold voice. 'I've told you what I intend to do. I must have something useful to do with my life, since you have taken away the only thing I really value.

251

As for my good name, you've never worried about your own; why should you concern yourselves with mine? I will be going to the Lye every day, and nothing you can do or say will stop me.' She remembered hearing those words before, or some very like them: when Paul had looked at her with eyes that burned with passion and told her that he meant to be a glass engraver.

Joe found his voice.

'Oh, you will, will you? And what will you do about money? Charity's an expensive hobby, had you thought of that?'

'Not my kind of charity. I shall be giving services, not largess.'

'It still won't come cheap. You'll need transport to get there – you don't expect to take the carriage, I suppose? Or do you imagine I'll buy you one of your own?'

'I wouldn't dream of using a carriage,' Emily said, 'but you have always allowed me to use the little pony cart. If you prevent me from taking that, then of course I shall have to use the omnibus, as I did today.'

'And the fare?'

'My dress allowance,' Emily said, 'unless you mean to stop that too.'

Joe glared at her and Christina, watching them both, thought yet again how alike they were, both in looks and in nature. Each as stubborn as the other. She saw the struggle going on inside Joe: saw the steel in Emily's eye.

'Oh, do what you like!' Joe exclaimed at last, turning away. 'Take the trap, and use your dress allowance for whatever you will. It's true enough, the people down there are in bad case, and if that's how you want to spend your time, I've little enough reason to stop you. Mayhap you'll come to see the rights and wrongs of what happened all those years ago.'

'I don't know about that,' Emily said quietly, 'but at least I may be able to try to put right some of today's wrongs. No, Mamma, I won't have any tea. I had some with Mr Corbett. And I want to go to my room now. I have a great deal to do.'

'She means to do this,' Christina said when she had closed the door. 'And really, is it so very dreadful? I know you've never wanted her to see where she came from – but she's always been determined to find out, and she's such a strong-minded girl, it really was inevitable. And she does mean well.'

Joe flung himself down in his seat again and stared into the fire. 'I know. Well, my love, we always wanted 'em to have minds of their own . . . And I don't reckon it'll last anyway, do you? It's no more than a flash in the pan – she'll tire of it soon enough, and then look around for something else to do.'

Christina inclined her head. It was possible. But – remembering that flash of steel in Emily's eye – she doubted it.

Emily needed all the steel her character possessed in the next few months. Even on that first day, walking through the narrow streets with Ben, she had not fully appreciated the scale of the poverty that still existed in the Lye. But Stephen Corbett and his father Jonathan, neither prepared to waste time on a girl who might faint away at the first touch of squalor, made sure that she soon learned the truth.

Of those men who were actually employed, many worked in the forges, the first of which had been set up at the end of the seventeenth century. But there were many other small industries too – the nailmakers, mostly working in factories now, the spademakers and colliers, and the chainmakers who still worked at home, in sheds behind the houses; men, women and children, slaving together in a kind of frenzy to produce as much chain as possible, knowing that even so their payment would be barely enough to keep them alive.

Emily went with Stephen to visit one of these families soon after she had begun to go to the Lye.

'Don't imagine there's anything unusual about the Smiths,' he said grimly as they walked together down the unpaved street, their boots sinking into a mire that Emily thought it better not to examine too closely. 'What you're going to see now is no different from what's happening in almost every home here.'

'My father came from a working-class home,' Emily said coolly. 'And my grandmother still lives in the same house. I'm no stranger to back streets, Mr Corbett.'

'There are back streets and back streets,' Stephen Corbett said quietly and, looking about her at the paths that were never swept, the dilapidated cottages with their broken doors and windows stuffed with bits of rag and sacking, Emily had to concede that Sal Compson's home was a palace in comparison. And the noise was tremendous – a constant clattering, clanking and thumping coming from every doorway, while the air, even to one accustomed to the smoky atmosphere of the Black Country, seemed to have an extra, more acrid bitterness.

Stephen paused outside one of the cottages. Like all the others in the row, it faced across a narrow alley towards the row of sheds where any work was done. It was from these that the noise and the smoke issued. He pushed open a sagging door and beckoned Emily to stand beside him.

A woman was standing by a brick hearth, with a chainmaking block beside her. On the floor squatted a small child – whether boy or girl, Emily could not tell – who was working steadily at a pair of large bellows. The woman did not glance up as Emily and Stephen entered; she continued working, taking an iron rod from the bundle beside her – each at least three yards long – and cutting it into short lengths. On the floor, strewn with coke dust and ashes, the child also continued to work, pumping at the bellows on which, Emily now saw, a baby was actually lying in a makeshift cradle, being rocked to sleep.

'But you can't keep it there – it'll fall into the fire!' she exclaimed, starting forward. Stephen put a hand on her arm and drew her back.

'I imagine she does this every day. And would you rather it was on the floor?'

Emily looked at the dirt and shuddered. 'Of course not! But –'

'There is nowhere else for her to put it. Look – she's cut the rod and is about to make the links. Have you ever seen chainmaking before?'

Emily shook her head. On her visit with Ben, she had seen only the nailmakers, interested in them because her mother had been one. But, hard though that work had seemed, this looked even worse. The iron rods must have been almost half an inch thick and the drag of the finished links on the woman's arm as she forged the next must have been considerable. Emily watched in silence as the woman heated the lengths in the fire, laid them on the block and hammered them into shapes before forming the links and welding the ends together. She worked with astonishing speed, never glancing up at her visitors, and only when the child at her feet faltered in its blowing did she take her attention from her work, giving him a sharp kick with her foot and using an expression Emily had never heard before.

'Don't treat him like that!' she cried, stepping forward again. 'He's doing his best and he's only a mite – he can't be more than six years old. The work's too much for him, can't you see that? And your baby – it must be terribly bad for him, so close to the fire.'

Liz Smith looked up then and threw her a withering glance. 'An' what business is it of yours, Lady Muck?' she demanded coarsely. 'They're my childer, ent they? Tell me what else I can do with 'em – an' that lazy toad's a wench, an' her's nigh on ten year old an' ought to be shutting her own chain.' To Emily's dismay, she noticed for the first time that the woman was heavily pregnant. 'Come back tomorrow an' you'll see another brat on the bellows,' Liz said with bitter resignation. 'Mebbe you'll hev some good advice for me then, too.'

Emily stepped back, shocked but subdued. The woman's voice, harsh though it was, had struck a chord of memory somewhere deep down. She shook her head.

'No, it's not advice I want to give you. It's help.' She

255

looked at the swollen figure. 'Tomorrow? Do you mean you are in labour now?'

'Reckon I am. I ought to know the signs by now – this is my fifth. Should just hev time to finish off these bundles afore it comes.' There were lines of pain and weariness in the grimy, sweat-streaked face. 'I done two hundred links this morning – another hundred should do it, I reckon.' She had still not paused in her labours, talking as she worked. Emily watched the cracked and filthy hands moving, fascinated by their speed and rhythm.

'But you shouldn't be standing here, doing such heavy work. Surely you ought to be at home – resting –'

'Rest!' Liz Smith said on a cackle. 'There ent no rest for the likes of me. I had my last in the evening after a day's work, an' I reckon this un'll be the same. Folks like us can't afford to rest – us only just earns enough to live on as it is. None of us has got any more than what we stands up in, an' with another babby on the way I've had to wean my Johnny on to sop already. An' my man lost his job last week – reckon he'll be working here with me if he don't find another one.'

Emily listened, aghast. The woman spoke in an almost matter-of-fact tone, as if none of this was out of the ordinary. 'But where are your other children?' she asked. 'Are they working too?'

'Other childer?'

'Yes – you said this was your fifth.'

'Oh – them.' A curious expression flitted across Liz Smith's face. 'They're dead, miss. An' if you asks me, they're the lucky ones.'

Stephen moved forward then, asking if there was anything Liz needed that he could provide, whether she needed help during her labour. She shrugged and answered him, still working though clearly in discomfort and even pain; yes, they could do with food, couldn't they always do with food, and a few things to wrap the babby in when it came; and no, she needed no help, old Mag was ready to come in and give a hand. Not that she needed it, but it was as well to have somebody about and her old man was no good; spend his evening in the public if she knew anything, and not come home till he was sure it was all over.

'Are you sure you wouldn't like me to come and help?' Emily ventured, adding when she saw the woman's raised brows, 'I have helped at a birth before.'

Liz Smith laughed shortly. 'Hev you, then? No, I don't reckon old Mag'd welcome you, thanks all the same. She bin doing it since she were a little 'un, helping her own ma. Look, you're a bit in my way, standing there. Not that it int good of you to look in, Master Stephen, but you see how it is . . .'

'I do indeed, Liz. We'll come back tomorrow. And meanwhile, if you need anything, anything at all, you know where to find me. Just send little Jane along with a message.' He nodded and drew Emily outside into air that was, if not fresh, at least a little easier to breathe than that in the shed. 'And now we'll go into the house.'

They crossed the alley and Stephen pushed open the door that sagged on rusty and broken hinges in the rough wall. He entered and beckoned Emily to follow him.

Inside, it was so dark that it was a few moments before Emily could pick out anything at all. But gradually, she became aware of shapes. A wooden table, knocked together out of pieces of ill-matching wood probably picked up in the streets or dragged from the river. A couple of old boxes of the sort used for packing glass and evidently used now as chairs. A shelf on the wall, which was dark with damp, holding a few plates and cups, mostly cracked or without handles. In the hearth, a few sticks piled up for a fire later. And beside it the one chair that the room possessed, one wooden arm broken, occupied by a man who sat with a bottle halfway to his lips, staring at them.

'Here, what do you –' He blinked and wiped a shaking hand across his unkempt and matted beard. 'Oh, it's the minister's boy, ennit? Young Master Corbett. An' who's this doxy, then?'

'Now, there's no need for language of that kind,

Albert,' Stephen said sharply. 'Miss Compson has come to help us. I understand you've lost your job.'

'Job's lost me, more like,' Albert Smith growled, taking another suck at his bottle. 'I told 'un, they'd be sorry they turned me off, lost a good worker there, they did.'

'And so have a good many others, by all accounts. That's the fourth job you've had this year, isn't it?'

'An' what if it is? I'm a good worker, turn me 'and to anything. Nailing, mining, forge work – done it all in me time. No, there's not much Albert Smith can't tackle, an' so I told him, that old fatface o' a Crackback. Mind, he saw his mistake then – would've begged me to stop on if I'd give him a chance, but I weren't sticking around there to be insulted. Wouldn't go back now if they paid me double, an' that's straight.'

'I very much doubt if you'd get the chance,' Stephen told him. 'And if you're such a good workman, what are you doing in here? Why aren't you out offering your services to some other lucky foundry? There must be quite a queue of employers waiting for you to notice them!'

Albert stared at him blearily, trying to work out what he meant, then shook his head. 'I dunno what you're on about. I ent got time for that, anyway – I got to look for another job. Soon's I'm fit –'

'Fit!' Emily exploded, unable to restrain herself any longer. 'Why, you're as fit as you'll ever be now, and you'd be a great deal fitter if you didn't drink so much – you're half drunk as it is. Don't you realise your poor wife is slaving out there in that dreadful shed at this very moment, when she's actually *in labour* with your baby? Why aren't you out there, making chains and giving her a rest? Don't you realise she could *die* if she isn't properly looked after now, yes, and her baby with her!'

'Die? My Liz?' Smith guffawed. 'Never – she's as tough as old boots, that woman. As for the babby, well, we nivver asked for it to come, did we?' He raised the bottle again and Emily, enraged, started forward and snatched it from his lips. 'Here, you give that back!'

'I'll do no such thing!' She held it behind her back, unmoving as Albert Smith lumbered to his feet and then collapsed back into the chair. 'You'll take no more drink this morning. You'll go straight outside, this very minute, and wash under the pump. Some good cold water might put a little sense into your thick head, and then you'll go into that chainshop and take over from your wife. Send her in here, with that poor child she has to lay on the bellows, and I'll look after her for the rest of the day. And after Mrs Smith's birthed and is regaining her strength you can carry on making chains. And since you're so good at everything, you ought to be able to make more than she can manage, and so earn a little more money for your family. Well?' she added sharply. 'What are you waiting for? Outside, and get your head under that pump, or do I have to drag you there myself?'

She moved towards him and Albert cringed. He stared up at her, his eyes flickering and then, as Emily moved again, threateningly, he scrambled hastily to his feet and scuttled past her, keeping his eyes on her the whole time as if afraid she would attack her. With a swift glance at Stephen, she followed the shambling figure out into the yard and watched him go to the pump. He hesitated and looked at her again and she repeated her threatening move towards him.

'All right, all right!' Albert said in a high, quivering voice. 'I'm doin' it, ent I?' He cranked the handle and the first gush of water shot over his feet. 'Here, that's cold! I ent putting my head under that, I'd catch me death. Hey, now, you get away – I never said – here, let me alone, you termagant –' The rest of his words were lost as Emily lost patience and stepped forward, grasping him firmly by the shoulders and thrusting his head under the pump. With a swift movement, she released one hand to crank the handle; the water poured out again, this time over Albert Smith's head, and his howl of indignation brought people to their doorways all along the street.

'And now,' Emily said loudly, aware of the audience they had collected, 'get into that chainshop and send your wife out. And I don't want to see you stop work until you've finished her quota and done some more besides.'

Muttering and grumbling, Albert did as he was told. Within a few minutes, Liz came out, looking bewildered and carrying the baby. Her face was drawn with pain and at the sight of her several women came forward, clucking with sympathy. One of them took the baby from her and said, 'You're just about at your time, Liz. You oughter hev old Mag here now. I'll send our Billy.'

'Take her indoors,' Emily directed. 'Get the fire lit and a kettle of water on. Find some bedding for her to lie on, and we'll need clean cloths and something to wrap the baby in.' She glanced around and noticed Stephen, who had withdrawn a little and was observing the scene with a strange expression on his face. 'Mr Corbett – is there nothing in your father's house? No blankets ready for emergencies such as this?'

'I believe there are,' Stephen answered, 'and I'll send for them at once. But what are you going to do now?'

'Do?' Emily said sharply. 'Why, I shall stay here, of course, until I'm quite sure that this poor woman is safely delivered and that the baby is properly cared for.'

She turned away, evidently dismissing Stephen. 'And now, if you don't mind . . . there really is a great deal to do here just now.'

Stephen bowed his head and smiled. 'Then I'll leave you to it. And, if you don't mind my saying so, I think you've done very well this morning. I don't believe I've ever seen Albert Smith look so frightened, nor move so fast. The Lye obviously has a few surprises coming to it.'

But Emily had already gone into the cottage with the other women. And Stephen, with a slightly quizzical look, set off to do the errand she had given him.

From the chainshop came the sound of hammering, as Albert Smith began to work on his wife's quota of chains.

* * *

As the winter drew in, Emily became a familiar figure in the Lye. The story of her routing of Albert Smith had spread quickly and the men, in particular, treated her with a certain wariness. But as it became known that she had herself been born in a mud cottage and spent her first two years in the smoke and dust of a nailshop, the people began to accept her as one of themselves – a termagant, as Albert had called her, but no Lady Muck; no job, it seemed, was beneath her. She would roll up her sleeves and tackle anything – from the delivery of babies when old Mag was already occupied to the scrubbing of floors and the cleaning up of old men or women who had become incontinent. She would cook the dinner or mend a shirt, and she seemed to have access to a small but inexhaustible supply of old but good clothes, especially children's.

'I find myself paying more calls than ever before,' she told Stephen and his father as they sat drinking tea together one afternoon. 'My friends lock their clothes presses now, when they see me coming! But they're all so generous – look at these little dresses. Liz Smith's baby will look like a doll in one of these.'

'The children of the Lye will soon be the most fashionably attired in the Black Country,' Jonathan Corbett remarked, smiling. 'You're a great asset to us here, Emily. I don't know quite how I ever managed without you – or Stephen.'

His eyes, Stephen noticed, were anxious as they rested on him. He sighed a little, knowing that soon he must make up his mind about his own future. He had originally only come to the Lye for a short period, while he found a new teaching post. He had stayed on, happy enough to help his father with his difficult flock, but he knew that Jonathan feared that he would soon be getting restless and wish to move on.

Stephen knew that his father would miss him very much if he did decide to leave. Not solely because of the work that he did – Jonathan Corbett also valued his company. Despite the work which brought him into contact with so many people, he was a lonely man. There were few Lye people of any education at all, and certainly none who could share his interests in books and music. With Stephen, he could pass a few pleasant off-duty hours and return to his work refreshed.

Did he really want to go back to schoolmastering? Stephen moved a little restlessly in his seat. He was interested in the subjects he taught, but less enamoured of his pupils. Most boys had to be forced to study, often with results that made him wonder if it were all worthwhile. They were insolent too, treating their masters as if they were some lesser species – when they could get away with it. Seeing that they didn't was a wearisome and brutalising affair and Stephen was tired of beatings and lengthy detentions which wasted what little spare time he had. He was tired of marking essays and listening to the tedious efforts at reciting half-learnt poetry. He was tired of the other masters, the back-biting that went on amongst them, the tyranny of the headmaster.

Whereas here in the Lye, he had begun to feel he was doing something really worthwhile. And here, too, he had met Emily.

He glanced across at Emily's head, now bent over some list that she had drawn up and was showing his father. Jonathan was fond of Emily, he knew. And he, himself? Stephen had never yet allowed himself to feel any strong interest in a woman. Brought up strictly on the Bible, he had developed a moral attitude that forbade any light relationships and he would have been horrified at the suggestion that he might seek relief from the sensations which sometimes caused him discomfort in the way that many other men might. Instead, he firmly repressed all such sensations as sinful, to be ignored until marriage permitted their expression.

As a result, he had developed a way of retreating quickly at the slightest hint of flirtation or possessiveness on the part of any female acquaintances. But more than once lately he had found his dark eyes resting on Emily, and had been conscious of an odd feeling somewhere under his heart.

Would Emily ever consider becoming the wife of a schoolmaster – or a minister? Neither would bring her a life as comfortable as the one she had known. But she seemed careless of her comfort, thriving on the hard work which she shared with him in the Lye. She certainly held all the qualifications such a marriage demanded. Together, they could make a formidable team. Together, they could bring this whole disreputable area back to God.

As if she felt his eyes on her, Emily glanced up suddenly and met his glance. Her own softened and her expression changed – only very slightly, little more than a warming of her skin, a parting of her lips. And then she returned to her list.

Stephen frowned. Marriage was not a question to be taken lightly. His own background was impeccable, of course – but Emily's . . . Could a girl born of a slut, fathered by a man who might be respectable now but certainly had not been in his youth, ever defeat such a heritage? Or did she carry a streak of wantonness in her even now, hidden under that pale, firm brow, behind those warm and – the word sprang unbidden to his mind – *sensual* eyes?

But Stephen continued to watch her. And, slowly, his mind, his emotions, and his body began a secret war.

# Chapter Twelve

Paul was engraving a great covered goblet. It was his most ambitious work so far. Standing over two feet high on a heavy stem, it was clear crystal, layered with ruby. Paul was engaged in making a lithophane, or engraved picture, in the deep red outer layer, so exposing the clarity of the crystal beneath. It was the nearest he had yet approached to the cameo glass that his mother liked so much, and he had taken meticulous care over its execution and written to Ben several times about the making of the goblet itself, so that the glassblower could apply the lessons learned in France to his own work and especially to the making of the blank vases of white and dark blue, for the copy they hoped to make of the Portland Vase.

'It seems that the temperature of the outer glass is critical,' he wrote. 'If it is too hot, it will crack or craze the inner vessel which has already been made. The technique you must use is the reverse, that of cupping. Make the outer vessel first, of opaque white glass and, while still hot, fill it completely with the coloured glass, straight from the pot and still on its blowing iron. Marver the whole then, to weld the two glasses together and give shape. Then reheat, blow and make the final shape before adding the handles. I believe you will find this method efficient.'

Ben had tried this, but he wrote back many times to tell Paul of disappointments and failures. Welding the two glasses together was not easy; time and time again the different temperatures caused stresses within the glass which cracked it, either immediately or much later when one of the engravers was working on it. But the failures gradually became fewer, and Ben's letters spoke more and more of his desire to see Paul back in Stourbridge, where they could work together on their great enterprise.

'They say Mr Northwood is making cameo glass, and hopes to copy the Portland Vase too. Sir Benjamin Stone, as has a house in Birmingham, has made the blank and Mr Northwood works on it whenever he can. And Mr Richardson has offered £1000 for the first copy to be made. So the sooner you can come back home, Mr Paul, the better us shall all be pleased.' He continued with a few lines about the other work the glasshouse was carrying out, the new wineglass Joe had designed, the black and ruby crystal which was slowly coming to perfection. And at the end of the letter, after his signature, he added a note: 'Florrie asks me to send you her good wishes and say the baby's coming along well. Miss Emily was in to see him last Tuesday, but she don't have so much time now. We'll all be pleased to see you back. Ben.'

Paul read the letter thoughtfully. The coloured crystals interested him, especially the news that Roger was taking a hand in the experiments. But he was more concerned with the news about the cameo glass. So Northwood was making cameo! He wondered how Christina felt about that. She would not like to be beaten by a rival glassmaker; she might even grow impatient and ask one of her other engravers to do the work. They were, after all, already working on Ben's blanks. But that's just an experiment, to make sure the blanks are ready for me when I return, he thought indignantly. Mamma knows that I am the best engraver she has – and now that I have the experience of working in France, I can outshine any man in Stourbridge. She *must* wait for me to go back!

But how long would she be prepared to wait? When did he mean to go back? And sometimes, following that

266

thought, would come another, creeping insidiously through his mind: did he mean to go back at all?

Paul looked again at the letter, re-reading the brief mention Ben had made of Emily. There were times when he was conscious of a surprising longing to see Emily again. He thought now of her dark hair, drawn back smoothly over her head to form a mass of curls at the sides, of her eyes that could be as dark and warm as velvet. He thought of the way she had ordered him about during their nursery days, of her unexpected vulnerability as she grew older, her anguish when he had stayed in Paris; the declaration of love with which she had so astounded him. He remembered it now with a pang of regret. He had been unnecessarily cruel to Emily then – more cruel than he had understood at the time, although now the pains of love were as familiar to him as tooth-ache. And he felt a deeper regret too, a regret that was less easy to analyse. Was it her innocence that he regretted? His own?

He thought of the few brief letters she had written to him, letters that had never thawed from their chilly stiffness, never betrayed the slightest warmth of feelings towards him. Had he killed it entirely, the love that she had offered him so passionately? Or had it simply died a natural death, proved to be the passing fancy he had told her it was?

Well, brothers and sisters did part and lead different lives, and Emily was evidently learning this now and turning to other interests. Paul had been surprised to learn of her visits to the Lye and her interest in the people there. 'You know that I believe young women should have the freedom to lead their own lives, just as young men do,' Christina had written. 'And Mr Stephen Corbett, the minister's son, is a worthy young man and promises to take good care of her while she is in those rough areas.'

The minister's son? An earnest, bespectacled young man, no doubt, forever on his knees, preaching poverty and sacrifice through the day and sleeping comfortably in a warm bed at night. Paul dismissed him easily from his thoughts.

He had continued to write home regularly, filling his letters to Emily and Sarah with descriptions of the *soirées* he had attended, the plays and operas he had seen, the restaurants where he had enjoyed exquisite suppers. To Christina and Joe, he had written about glass, the glass of Thietry and Baccarat and St Louis, the glass of Émile Gallé and others who were bringing in innovations. He had described his own work, the engravings he was making, the new pieces being made by his grandfather, by Gabriel. 'The most wonderful pieces are the great chandeliers,' he wrote. 'They grow more magnificent each year; shimmering clusters of crystal, cut like diamonds, that hang overhead and shed a thousand dazzling lights into every corner of the room. And floor chandeliers like the one being conceived even now – it stands twice as high as a man and will hold almost eighty candles. There is great demand for these grand pieces in countries like India and Russia. We ought to be making them in Stourbridge.' He signed the letter with a wry twist of the pen, imagining his mother's reaction to the suggestion that Henzel's should produce chandeliers and candelabra. 'What, glass that has never been blown!' she would exclaim. 'Moulded crystal, when we possess the finest blowers in the land! The boy has lost his senses.'

And sometimes he believed he had. For what sane man would have allowed himself to reach such a state of confusion over two such very different women?

Véronique and Annette. He was still no closer to understanding himself, let alone them. During that first summer at the château, he had felt himself to be no more than a shuttlecock, tossed back and forth in some fitful game. Yet he was sure that Véronique herself was quite unaware of any rivalry between herself and her aunt. Light and pretty in her summer gowns, she flitted about the château like a butterfly, bringing a smile to the face of even the grumpiest glassmaker, her singing outstripping that of the birds. Her attachment to Paul was, he knew, totally innocent. Wasn't that why, although enslaved by her from the very beginning, he had determined to wait, to give her time to grow up; to enjoy her as a child before taking her as a woman?

But Annette . . . with Annette, his relationship was quite different. There was no innocence about Annette.

On that first evening, when she had dug her pointed little fingernails into his arm, Annette had made it quite clear what kind of behaviour she required from Paul. And it had been only his own unbelieving doubts that had kept them apart for so long. After a week, however, Annette had grown tired of waiting. And Paul had awoken one night to find her beside his bed.

'What is it? What's wrong?'

'Ssh!' She laid her fingers across his mouth, lightly, as if he were kissing them. 'Don't make a noise, Paul, *mon cher*. We don't want Gabriel to hear, do we?'

Gabriel? Paul stared up at her, seeing her face clearly in the moonlight that flooded the room. She was wearing a lace wrapper, the pale delicacy of the pattern contrasting with the darkness of her hair and eyes. As she bent over him, it fell open and he felt the softness of her breast brush his cheek, the slight roughness of her nipple against his lips.

'Annette . . .' he murmured, meaning to protest; but the word was lost in a groan. '*Annette . . .*'

'Paul, *mon cher*,' she whispered in a deep husky tone, and slid into the bed beside him. 'Do you know how you have kept me waiting? How I've longed for a sign, a word, a tiny hint that tonight, any night, you would be ready for me, ready to embark on our adventure of love . . . Why are you so cruel to me, Paul, why? Is it that you Englishmen are as they say, so very cold? I cannot believe it.'

She was moving gently against him. He could feel the incredible softness of her body, a softness he had never imagined possible, almost as though she had no bones at all. Yet she was real enough, rounded and generous, offering a richness of flesh that sent the blood thundering through his head and brought a hard, throbbing masculinity to his limbs. Yet even now he could not quite give in, could not quite forget his strict up-bringing, the values his parents had impressed upon him.

'Annette,' he gasped at last. 'What about your husband? Gabriel . . . and your children . . . Annette, we must not forget . . .'

'Forget what? That I am married?' Her voice laughed at him in the darkness. 'Paul, you are an innocent. Have you not heard of a woman who takes lovers? How do you think I would be able to tolerate living here, out in the country, if it were not for the little diversions that make life amusing? And to have such a one as you, an Englishman, and so young and fresh – no, you are not going to deny me the exquisite pleasure of teaching you your business, are you?' She paused and he felt her lips moving softly over his neck while her hand slipped softly, sensuously, down his body. 'I am right, Paul, am I not? You have never possessed a woman before, *n'est-ce pas*?'

He lay flat, his head swimming, quiescent under her caresses. The first wild throbbing of his blood had steadied now to the slow, heavy beat of a great drum. He lay quite still, his mind recording every tiny movement she made, every exquisite touch of her cool fingers on his burning skin, every separate point of contact between them. Hearing, sight, smell and taste were all subjugated to the overriding supremacy of the sense of touch, the sense of feeling, and the sensation of her skin against his was the only reality.

'Am I right?' she insisted in the low, throaty murmur that seemed to thrill through his very pores, and he moved his head slowly, unwillingly because it cost him an effort he didn't want to make, and whispered, 'Yes.'

'I knew it!' There was as much triumph in her tone as if she had shouted it from the château roof. 'And I shall be your first teacher, Paul, the one you will always remember. I shall show you how a woman likes to be loved, what she enjoys and what will make her love you.

270

And you must promise to remember me when you are old, *non*?' She shifted her body across his and he felt the weight of her warmth and softness overflowing his own lean narrowness. 'You must never, never forget.'

Forget! It was impossible that he could ever forget one moment, one delicious, tantalising second of this world into which he had been so unexpectedly and triumphantly swept; this world of silken skin and soft hair, of tangled limbs and seeking mouths.

'Never forget . . .' Annette had said as she left him.

And he hadn't. He had never forgotten that first night, nor any of the wild, dangerous nights that had followed – nights when he had been convinced Gabriel must wake and miss his wife, when he was paralysingly certain that someone must hear, suspect. But Annette had thrived on the risks they took, delighted in the kisses snatched behind the trees in the garden or on the stairs indoors. She had lost no opportunity to touch Paul's quivering body, her fingers finding his thigh beneath the table at dinner, the nails digging in to remind him of their first meeting; her breasts brushing him lingeringly, sensuously, as they passed in the doorway, her scented hair wafting against his cheek as she leaned over him during a game of cards.

She held him in thrall. And he knew it; wanted, sometimes quite desperately, to escape. There could never, he knew, be any true love between himself and Annette. Everything between them was based on the powerful, irresistible desires of the body. There were times when he hated her for the power she could wield over him with no more than a glance; times when he swore that he would put an end to it. But Annette had only to look up at him with that naked sensuality in her glowing eyes, to touch him lightly with those pointed fingernails, to shape her full, curving lips for a kiss, and he was lost, held in fascination, his body responding even while his mind recoiled.

Afterwards, he was almost ashamed to look in the mirror at his own satiated face. Yet before three days had

271

passed, he would be tortured by a feverishness that was almost unbearable and endured with a misery alternating with gratification as Annette used him like a toy, raising him to a pitch of excitement that went beyond toleration before allowing him his release; and then ignoring him completely for days at a time, until he was driven nearly crazy with frustration. Again and again he vowed that when she next came to his room he would reject her, send her cold from his bed; again and again she came, as soft and sweet as an April breeze, and thawed his miserable heart into warm, throbbing passion once more.

She filled his mind with darkness. He watched Véronique dancing about the lawns, playing with the children's pet dogs, riding her pony. He heard her read to Cécile as she sewed, sing to Marc after supper, and felt soiled and weary. And when Véronique looked up at him and fluttered gilded lashes over laughing blue eyes, he wondered what had happened to him since he had come to France, and what would be the end of it all. And Stourbridge – the world of smoke and gloomy skies; of clattering forges and surly red furnaces; of the glitter of glass and the warmth of a coal fire; of muffins for tea and the music of the organ-grinder in the street below the window – had never seemed so far away as it did then.

It was a relief, at the end of the visit, to return to Paris, even though he was attacked at first by a gnawing desire that dominated his senses and almost drove him back again to Lorraine. But the increasing responsibility placed on him by his grandfather, and the absorption which he could still feel for his engraving, helped him.

The ruby goblet with its clear pattern and matching lid was the pinnacle of his achievement so far.

'Superb,' Marc said as they stood in the Paris engraving studio on the morning that it was completed. 'As fine, I almost dare to say, as anything that Simon has made. Do you not agree, Georges?'

The little man, who had been the Thietrys' chief engraver for many years, nodded. He looked at Paul with almost as much pride as Marc. 'You are right, monsieur. He is as fine an engraver as his father before him. It is a thousand pities . . .'

'A thousand pities indeed.' Marc examined the goblet again. 'Not a flaw on it.' His thin white hands, the veins blue and prominent with age, moved slowly over the glass. 'Paul, come with me into my office. I have something that I wish to discuss with you.'

Wondering a little at his grandfather's sudden gravity, Paul followed him into the little room he used as a private office. It was, naturally, filled with glass – examples of patterns used over the years, some now obsolete, others still favoured, pieces that Marc had an attachment to, for some reason, even pieces that had promised to be exceptionally fine and then been damaged in their final stages. They stood on every surface, on the shelves, the windowsill, even the desk where Marc used them as paperweights, and they were all dim with dust.

Marc stood the ruby goblet carefully on the cluttered desk, settled himself behind it and indicated the other chair. 'Sit down, Paul. Now – how long is it you have been with us? Since April last year, isn't it – when you and your parents came for the Exhibition.'

'That's right. Just over eighteen months.' Eighteen months since he had seen Joe and his mother – eighteen months since Emily had told him she loved him. And in that time he had fallen in love with a sprite of one French girl, as delicious and elusive as syllabub, and succumbed to a dark and insatiable desire for another.

And he had learned a great deal about glass, and achieved a standard of engraving that he did not believe he could have aspired to without the experience gained in his grandfather's studios.

'I did not think you would stay so long,' Marc said quietly. 'No – do not misunderstand me – you have certainly not outstayed your welcome! But I had expected that you would wish to return to England before now. The fact that you have not gives me hope.'

'Hope?' Paul said. 'I don't understand.'

273

'I mean,' Marc said, 'the hope that you will never go back – except for visits, of course. Paul –' He leaned forward over the desk and Paul saw that his hands were knotted together '– I want you to consider very carefully what you wish to do with your life. I want you to think what your life would have been if your parents – your true parents – had married. If my son, your father, had not died.'

'Not very much different, perhaps,' Paul said cautiously. 'My mother had inherited Henzel's. She would have wanted to stay in England and run it, just as she did.'

'And my son would have inherited Thietry Cristal. Somehow, they would have had to combine the two. And you – Paul, do you not think it possible that you might have come to France and learned to run the company here? Do you not see that you would have been the natural heir – and that I would like you to have that position now?' He waited a moment while Paul stared at him, and added: 'You are the rightful successor to me, Paul. Thietry Cristal should be yours.'

'But Gabriel –' Paul stammered, and Marc flicked an impatient hand.

'Gabriel is not a direct descendant! He is a good manager, yes, and runs the factory well enough. But he has no imagination, Paul. He has no vision. Now, you – I have seen that you have many ideas which would benefit our business. You are willing to look at new methods. You do not dismiss glassmen like Émile Gallé, for instance, as fools and charlatans. Yes, those are the words I have heard Gabriel use! Paul, if Thietry Cristal is to go into the future – into the twentieth century, which is not so very far off, after all – it needs a man of vision, with the strength to carry out his ideas, to take it there. And you are that man – not Gabriel.' His eyes were shining. 'Paul, I want you to stay in France, to follow me as your father would have done, as you would have followed him. It is here that your future lies – what is there for you in England, after all? A business which must be

274

shared by your brother Roger, who has no feeling for glass and who already believes himself to be your superior.' Paul gasped a little – how did his grandfather know that? 'Yes, it is easy enough to deduce from the remarks made by your mother, even though she may not realise it herself.' Marc lifted the goblet and examined it again. 'You were a good engraver when you came here, Paul, but you could not do work as fine as this. Will you consider whether Stourbridge is indeed your true home – or whether you should remain here, in Paris?'

Nothing, as far as Paul knew, had been said to the rest of the family. But, as if the thoughts themselves had reached out to the château and disturbed the air there, Gabriel arrived less than a fortnight later. He brought Annette and the children with him, saying that it seemed a pity not to celebrate Christmas with the rest of the family. They distributed themselves around the house on Montmartre and settled in as if they owned the place. Perhaps that was their intention, Paul thought, to show him who were the rightful heirs to Marc Thietry's property. But he could not think of that now. Annette was here, and her eyes were on him with as much greed, as much avidity as they had been when she had first seen him.

'I'll come to your room tonight,' she breathed as she passed him in a doorway, and Paul felt his heart leap with a mixture of fear and longing.

'Gabriel –'

'He sleeps soundly. I make sure that he does.' Her eyes moved over him as if she were inspecting a succulent feast. 'Tonight . . .'

He spent the rest of the day in torment. Since leaving the château in September, he had fought the torture of desire and believed he had begun to win. Annette no longer haunted his dreams as she had done at first. And with Véronique present every day, he had been forced to face his shame. If he were ever to be worthy of her, he must end the liaison with Annette. Yet here he was, almost agreeing to her proposal to come to his room on the very first night of the visit! How could he be so weak?

I won't give in. If she comes, I'll tell her it's over. It's too dangerous here, anyway – someone is bound to find out. Gabriel – or someone else. And then what will happen?

He saw himself sent back to England in disgrace. Véronique lost to him for ever. Cut off by his grandfather. And the doors of Thietry Cristal slammed in his face.

But nothing ever happens exactly as it is imagined.

Paul lay awake that night, and the night after, and Annette did not come. He hardly knew whether to be relieved or dismayed. With her presence filling the house, all the old desires were flooding back into his body, turning him hot whenever she was near, creating a discomfort that he could barely tolerate. He sought her eyes but when she did glance his way it was with nothing more than the amiability which she was extending to all the family. Had she changed her mind, decided after all that the affair should end, that it was too dangerous to carry on here in Paris? He woke in the mornings with a feeling of relief that one more night had passed without being sullied; but one glance at Annette, at the full, pouting lips, the luxuriant hair, the curving voluptuousness of the figure that he knew so well, and he was lost again in an agony of desire.

Yet he knew quite clearly that he did not love her. His feeling towards her was more like hate. And even that seemed to add fuel to the fire that smouldered in him whenever she was near.

On the third night, she came.

Paul, just drifting into sleep, was awake instantly. It was after midnight. The house was silent. He heard the soft noise of the door and twisted in his bed. He saw Annette, a ghostly figure in her long white nightgown, come gliding into the room.

She fastened the door and came to the bed.

'Did you think I had forgotten you, *mon* Paul?'

Paul did not answer at once. His throat was dry, his heart thumping. He stared up at her and Annette sat gracefully on the edge of the bed and held out her arms.

'*Cher* Paul, it has been a long time . . .'

'Not so very long,' he said huskily, and stayed where he was. Annette frowned.

'Paul? Is something wrong?'

His voice had gone again. He swallowed and found it. 'Everything. This. You and me.' She understood at once, he was sure of it, but she continued to gaze at him, her arms outstretched. Then, slowly, she lowered her hands and began to unfasten the buttons of her nightgown.

'No!' Paul said, reaching out to stop her and then drawing back quickly. 'No, Annette, don't do that. I . . . I want to talk to you first.'

'Talk to me?' Her eyes were narrowed but she was keeping her tone light. 'Since when have we wished to *talk* together, Paul? Such a waste of time, especially here in Paris, with the moon at the window. But if you must –' She shrugged.

Paul hesitated, searching for the right words. 'Annette, we must stop this. It's too dangerous. It's wrong. We – we don't love each other. There can be nothing for us. And at any moment, someone might find out. Gabriel might suspect already. We must take no more risks.'

There was a silence. The planes of Annette's face, lit by the moonlight, were hard. Her eyes glittered.

'So,' she said, 'you wish to end it – the pleasure we have shared. I presume you have some good, *English* reason for doing so?'

Paul flushed. Annette was adept at humiliating him, usually with some barbed reference to his birth. But he had determined that this time she would not have her way. He knew all of her many weapons now – the seductive manner she could turn on at will; the sweetness that hid a thread of steel; the sneers at his manhood that roused him to a fury of passion so that afterwards he was disgusted by his own behaviour; the storms she could whip up and the calms she could soothe. He knew them all, and believed himself to be armed against each one.

'Do I need any reason?' he asked, attempting to keep his tone light. 'Other than those I have already given you? After all, you would end it without a thought if you wished to do so.'

'Without a thought, indeed,' she agreed with a flash of her eyes. 'But that is different, my Paul. You owe me everything. You had never known a woman until you met me, you were young and *gauche*, you had no finesse, no *subtilité*. I have taught you all. I owe you nothing – nothing, do you hear me?' Her small foot stamped on the floor of Paul's bedroom. 'Yes, I would cast you off without a thought if I cared to, and one day I assuredly shall. But I am not ready to do so yet.' She came close and he could smell the perfume on her hair, the warm, musky odour of her body, and see the voluptuous, inviting curves of her breasts beneath the lace of her wrap. 'We have been apart too long,' she murmured in husky tones. 'You have been thinking too much, my Paul, letting yourself dwell on matters that don't concern us when we are together in this room. Here, there is nothing but us, don't you see that? Outside is a different world. Gabriel, René and the rest of them . . . they have nothing to do with what happens in here.' Her breasts were moving softly against him and he could feel the slow, throbbing heat begin, the desire mount. 'Forget them, my Paul,' she murmured on a thread of sound. 'Forget the worries that you have imagined – they are not real, none of them is real. Only you and I are real . . . only this . . .' Her slim, cool arms wound around his neck, pulling his head down to hers, and he felt her soft lips moving over his mouth, seeking gently, teasing it open, her tongue insinuating itself to play with his, a dancing flame that burned in his mouth like a firefly flickering in the dark.

He groaned against the soft flesh, knowing that there

was no escape. His body had yearned for this and his blood surged, roaring in his ears so that he could barely hear Annette's whispers. He felt the hardness in him and knew that she had won.

His arms went round her almost of their own accord, his hands finding the familiar yet still intoxicating contours of her body, moving over the softly swelling breasts, touching the hardened nipples, sliding down the curving buttocks and into the folds and creases that were already dampened by her own excitement.

Only in his final collapse did Paul acknowledge in that small, overridden part of his mind that he had been powerless against Annette because he had wanted to be. Only then did he feel the familiar swamping disgust; only then did he turn away.

From that moment, he was obsessed by the difference between the two women: Véronique, fresh, flirtatious, still childlike in her innocence; and Annette, sultry and depraved, every look and every gesture studied in its intention to seduce, every word heavy with hidden meaning. He wanted nothing but to be free of her, yet knew that their relationship was still not ended, that she still wielded her sinister power over him. And until he was free, he knew that Véronique was beyond his reach. To go to her still warm from Annette's bed would be to besmirch a frail and lovely blossom with the filth of the midden.

Why did Gabriel never suspect? Annette had said that she would 'make sure he slept' – did she drug him at night? Did he never wake and reach out for her? And if he did, and found her missing, would he search for her?

Paul shivered at the thought. But his days were occupied with other concerns.

'Since I am here,' Gabriel said at breakfast one morning, 'I may as well make myself familiar with the business in Paris. It is foolish to run the château without knowing everything here, don't you agree, *mon oncle*?'

'What do you wish to know, exactly?' Marc Thietry

asked. 'It seems to me that you manage the château and the glasshouse very well. Why bother with what we do here?'

'But it is here that is the nerve centre. How can I know that we are producing the right glass, in the right quantities, if I do not know what is happening here? Our agencies abroad – the marketing – everything is dealt with in Paris. In Lorraine, we simply make the glass to your orders, we do not know what is going on.'

'But you don't need to,' Marc said reasonably. 'Paul and I –'

'Paul? You mean he helps you with the management?' Gabriel asked sharply.

'But of course. He has been learning all the time –'

'I thought,' Gabriel said, 'that he came to France simply to improve his engraving.' He darted a look at Paul, a look of suspicion and dislike.

'But of course,' Marc said easily. 'And I think you will agree that he has done that with great success. But I also felt it a good thing for him to understand how our business is run. And he has been a good pupil. I believe he could take over tomorrow, should there be any need.'

'Indeed?' Gabriel said, a dangerous note in his voice. 'And I?'

'You? My dear Gabriel, you are my right-hand man! There is no question about that. How could we manage here if you were not there in Lorraine? Why, the glasshouse is the essential part! We cannot sell glass if it isn't made.' Marc reached across and laid his thin white hand on Gabriel's square, stubby fingers. 'My dear boy, what are you worrying about? Nothing has changed.'

'No?' The dark eyes stared out of the swarthy face, first at Marc and then at Paul. 'It seems to me that everything has changed.' He paused. 'I have worked all my life for you, *mon oncle*. I have lived in the country, making your glass for you, keeping the factory alive, looking after the men, trying out your new ideas. Everything you have suggested has been carried out, everything done as you wished. And I believed that one day, I would be rewarded.'

'You have been paid well,' Marc said. 'You have had a

comfortable home. Why should you suppose that all that will not continue?'

'But I do not *wish* it to continue!' Gabriel exclaimed. 'All this time, I have looked forward to progressing in my work – to taking on more responsibility, learning the whole of the business. I did not expect to be left to – to moulder away in the country, doing the same thing until I die.'

'You are not mouldering. You are producing excellent glass. It is what you are best at, and what I wish you to continue to do.' Marc began to rise, as if the discussion were over, but Gabriel put out a hand and stopped him. Paul saw that his dark face was suffused with anger.

'And if I do not wish to continue? If I say no – I wish to come to Paris and learn what there is to be learned here? As Paul has done?'

Marc looked at him. His eyes were like pewter, flat and dark. There was no added colour in his face, no flush of rage, but Paul could sense the anger in him. He waited, wishing that he had left the room before all this began but knowing that it concerned him deeply. He remembered the interview he had had with Marc in the office. Had someone overheard, passed it on to Gabriel?

'If you say that,' Marc said quietly, 'I shall simply tell you not to be so foolish. You are needed at the château.'

'And what of René, then?' Gabriel's voice was loud and hectoring. 'What is he doing, learning my job? What of when he marries Véronique?' Paul stared at him, shocked, but Gabriel ignored him. 'Will you not wish to give him a good position, some responsibility? Will you not tell *him* to manage the factory and the château? And with Paul here – what is to be left for me, tell me that!' He leaned forward over the table and stabbed his finger at the old man. 'Just who is to be your heir?' he demanded. 'Who is to inherit all this when you die? Once upon a time, I thought that René and I would share it, run the whole concern together. But now it seems different. Paul has come, and Paul is the new golden boy. Is he to take on the whole of Thietry Cristal? Are we to be left with nothing but the scraps? Tell me, Marc – I have a right to know.'

There was a long silence. Paul watched the two faces, the one so pale and cool, the other so dark and angry. For a moment, although he had never liked Gabriel, he found himself sympathising with him. The man had, after all, worked hard and could not be blamed for expecting some inheritance. And now it looked as if that were to be snatched away from him. And, worse than that, he was being cuckolded by the very man he feared – Paul himself. If he ever suspected . . .

Marc sighed a little. He looked at Gabriel with something very like sadness in his face.

'Very well. You are quite correct in thinking that I wish to make Paul my heir. And why not? He is my grandson – my direct descendant. If Jean-Paul had lived, he would have inherited and none of you would have given any thought to the matter. And Paul would have followed him. Why should it be any different now? And you, Gabriel, would have worked at the château in just the same way and been content to do so. And when we speak of René, let us not forget that he is not even related to me. He is the nephew of your wife. I have no obligation towards him, and he could leave at any time and go to work for another man.'

Gabriel interrupted, furious. 'So I was right. It is the newcomer who is to be favoured – a boy, barely out of the cradle, not even brought up as one of the family. You realise what he will do, don't you? He'll take Thietry Cristal and make it nothing but an – an offshoot of Henzel's. He is an Englishman. He is not one of us, and he never will be. You are throwing away a heritage.'

Marc glanced at Paul, who had sat silent and uncomfortable during the whole of the argument. He raised his fine eyebrows slightly. 'Well, Paul? Is that what you will do?'

Even more now, Paul wished that he was out of the room. He looked wretchedly from one man to the other and shook his head. '*Grandpère*, I've never even thought about inheriting Thietry Cristal. Gabriel's right – I came simply to learn engraving. The idea of staying here for good was never suggested.'

'It is being suggested now,' Marc said quietly. 'Would you do as Gabriel fears? Will he be nothing but the manager of some distant glasshouse belonging to the Henzel family? Or will you stay here and run it as it has always been run? Will you do as I believe you can do, and make Thietry the greatest glass manufacturer that has ever been known – greater than Baccarat, greater than St Louis? It is for you to say.'

Paul stared helplessly at him. He thought of his home in England, the grey, swirling murk of the Black Country, the dust and the soot, the way you could not leave the house without being covered in a film of tiny black specks, the noise and the clatter of machinery issuing from every building. He thought of the cones, rising stalwart amongst the tall chimneys, the narrow streets, the sluggish canal.

He thought of Christina and Joe, working together, producing fine crystal, bringing up their family, continuing what had become a dynasty in the glass industry. He thought of the rest of the family – of Sarah and Roger, Aunt Susan, of Harry and Ruth who were in America and prospering. He thought of Emily.

All these seemed to be ranged at one side of his mind, like the ranks of an army. And facing them, opposing them, were the showrooms and studios in Paris, the château and the glasshouse in Lorraine. His grandfather and grandmother. And Véronique.

Véronique. Of all that had been said in the past half hour, one remark still burned in his mind and overshadowed all the others. It was the remark Gabriel had made about René. *What of when he marries Véronique*?

René – marry Véronique?

What was a mere glasshouse beside that?

He looked again at the two faces watching him. The pallor of his grandfather, the white skin stretched like fine parchment over the bones of his skull; the florid swarthiness of Gabriel with his small, dark eyes and bitter mouth.

'I am sorry,' he said at last, lifting his hands in a gesture that he did not realise was wholly Gallic. 'I can't decide this now. I have never thought of running Thietry Cristal. Even Henzel's . . . It's too soon. And there's plenty of time.'

'Not so much, perhaps,' Marc observed. But he did not look displeased. 'Perhaps you are right, however. These matters should not be decided in a hurry. And your engraving is the most important to you, just yet.'

Was it? Or was Véronique even more important? And was he to see her married to René, to stand by helpless, unable to lift a finger to prevent it?

He thought of Annette, and was sickened. He knew that never must he take her into his bed again.

Early that afternoon, Gabriel announced that he was taking his family back to the château. Cécile was distraught, Annette furious, the children petulant. Only Marc accepted the sudden departure with equanimity, wishing them all goodbye with a calm smile, consoled his wife and then invited Paul into his study.

'Gabriel is angry at the moment,' he observed, 'but he will come round. He realises that I am still the owner of Thietry Cristal, and have full power to do just as I wish. And you, Paul – you will have all the time you need to make up your mind. And if there is anything you want – any change you would like to make – you have only to ask.'

He meant in the glasshouse, of course. But Paul, staring into the silver eyes that were so much like his own, wondered what his grandfather would say if he asked for Véronique.

# Chapter Thirteen

Joe and Christina spent more and more time at the glass-house, as if the frequently empty house had become oppressive to them, a sad reminder of the family in which they had once delighted and which seemed now to have been split asunder.

'I'm sure I don't know why it seems so quiet these days,' sighed Aunt Susan on one of the few occasions when the family took tea together. 'When you were young, Christina, I used to think how pleasant it would be to have a peaceful afternoon now and then. Now they seem to stretch ahead like a desert.' She lifted a thin bone china cup to her lips and then brushed them delicately with a wisp of lace. 'I can't understand why you don't make Emily spend more time at home,' she complained fretfully. 'An unmarried young woman like that, gadding about in unsavoury parts of the town – it isn't at all seemly. She ought to be here, with her mother, helping about the house, arranging flowers and so on.'

Christina smiled faintly. 'Aunt Susan, one doesn't *make* Emily do anything. She is as headstrong as I was at her age; more so. And remember how she was before she began to go to the Lye – listless, bad-tempered, unhappy. At least she feels her life has some purpose now.'

'Purpose! What *purpose* does a young woman need, other than that of finding a husband and bringing up a family?' Susan Henzel's nose gleamed red at the tip. 'Presumably Emily sees herself as a clergyman's wife – well, she may be lucky, I suppose, and it's certain that nobody else is likely to take –'

'Aunt Susan! That's enough!' Christina's eyes flashed. 'Emily will marry if and when she finds the right man, and not at all if she so chooses. Neither Joe nor I

285

believe in arranging marriages for our children – we want them to be happy. And Emily *is* happy now, whatever you may think. She feels she is doing something useful. I shall do nothing to dissuade her, however *unseemly* her activities may seem to you.'

'Useful!' Susan said in a high voice. 'Going down to the Lye day after day, wearing those dreadful clothes and consorting with the most ruffianly people. Certainly I think it unsuitable for a young lady to be allowed to behave so, and I shall continue to say so, whether you like it or not.' She rose shakily to her feet and fumbled for the stick she now used. 'Well, when something dreadful happens, don't say I didn't warn you. I don't know what this family is coming to, I really don't. Paris! Oxford! The Lye Waste!' She pronounced each name as if they were equal in decadence and made her way to the door, muttering to herself. 'I warned them what it would be. I told them. But who ever listens to me? Who ever did? Even Joshua . . .' The door closed behind her and they could hear her voice fade as she shuffled along the passage to her own room.

'Poor Aunt Susan,' Christina said after a pause. 'She's growing old. She sees her life wasted on a family who never appreciated her, never listened. And the pity of it is, she's right. Nobody ever *has* listened to her. Father never did – I didn't. And now here we are, with Paul in Paris and no talk of his coming home yet, Roger at Oxford and answering only to himself, and as for Emily – well, I sometimes fear that Aunt Susan is right and that we're in danger of losing her altogether. Not from her activities in the Lye, but –' She raised troubled green eyes to her husband. 'Joe, there are times when I think she looks at us as though she hates us . . .'

It was true that Emily could no longer see Joe with the adoring, uncritical eyes of a little girl. When she looked at him now, she saw only harsh rejection in that broad body, that dark face with its deep brown eyes; she saw only the picture of her mother, shadowy in the murky depths of the past, huddled in an old shawl as she roamed desperately seeking shelter for herself and her child, or crouching over a guttering fire as she hammered out nail after nail in a pathetic frenzy to stay alive.

For the whole of the winter, Emily kept up her resolve of going to the Lye almost every day. She drove herself there in the trap Joe allowed her to use, disregarding the stares of people who were shocked by her unconventional behaviour. The people of the Lye had, as she had told Ben they would, accepted her as one of themselves; they knew her and none of them would have harmed her. Her odd figure, attired in clothes that might have been more suited to a farmer's daughter than to a young lady from one of the best-known families in the district, was a familiar sight in the alleys that wound between the tumbled houses. Everyone nodded to her as she passed, women bobbing with respect, men doffing tattered caps. Some, more daring than the others, even called her Em. She didn't mind; the name, spoken in rough, uneducated tones, warmed her more than the sound of her own father's voice these days.

With Stephen Corbett and his father, she visited the poorest of the inhabitants, bringing help and comfort wherever she could; knowing even as she did so that it could never be enough, yet driven by her need to do the best she could. The thought of staying at home, like Sarah, or even accompanying her mother to the glasshouse where her presence might be welcome enough but was quite unnecessary, was as shocking to her as her present way of life was to her great-aunt Susan.

'What else would I do?' she asked Stephen as they walked wearily back to the house beside the chapel after visiting some of the families who lived on the banks of the river. 'How could I go back to living at home, the dutiful daughter of the house, arranging flowers and paying calls, after seeing what I've seen here? The Smiths, still no better off than the first day I came. The Barstows . . . Those poor children today – I believe not one of them will grow up. Lying there on damp, filthy rags, coughing so pitifully . . . They haunt me, Stephen.

I know we cannot really help them – nothing we can do will save them. Yet I can't walk away. I have to try.'

'Yes,' he said soberly, 'we have to try. Even though we know that families like the one we've just seen are doomed. They don't even have a mud house to live in – just that tent, made out of old sacks stretched across a few staves. And no money, other than what they can beg or scratch from the ground by selling broken glass as cullet. That man will never find work, you know, Emily.'

'I know. Who would employ him – a nailmaker, still trying to sell handmade nails? There really is an evil in machines, Stephen. The old life for a nailmaker was hard – I should know. But at least he could earn a living of a sort. Now that nails are factory-made, there's less employment than ever.'

'And it's the same in so many trades,' Stephen agreed. 'Yet what can be done about it? You'll never stop manufacturers from using machines, nor from inventing bigger and better ones that need fewer men and women to work them.'

Emily sighed. 'And there are more and more people all the time. Babies being born, children growing up – even though so many die, there are still more coming. Flooding into the towns from the countryside, needing more and more houses. It can't be right, Stephen.'

They came to the chapel and stopped. Emily's trap stood outside the door; the horse had been taken to the stable.

'Do you ever regret giving up your teaching job to stay here and help your father, Stephen?' she asked. 'It all seems so hopeless, like trying to stem a flood. There is so much to be done here, and only a few of us who care enough to do it. Don't you ever feel like giving up?'

He looked down at her, his face grave and calm, the face of a statue chiselled in marble. His lips were firm, unsmiling, his dark eyes serious under the broad forehead. As always, he appeared to give careful consideration to her question and it was a moment or two before he answered in the voice that was so sombre in speech, yet which could lift so passionately in the singing of a hymn.

'Give up?' he repeated thoughtfully. 'No, Emily, I never give up. Once I have set my mind to a certain course I follow it through to the end, whatever that may be.' He spoke with an implacability that brought an odd shiver to her spine, but even as she wondered at it his expression softened a little and he took her hands in his and added quietly: 'There is much to keep me here, Emily. I would not want to leave now.'

For a long moment, they stared at each other. Emily felt herself to be almost drowning in his gaze, drawn into those strange dark wells and held there. Not until he willed it could she finally lower her lashes and break the spell; and then she dropped her glance to the hands that held hers, staring at them with an intensity that recorded every detail in her mind for ever.

'I must go,' she said at last, her voice trembling a little, and drew her hands out of his grasp. She raised her eyes, almost afraid to meet that dark, penetrating gaze again, but his own eyes were veiled now and he merely nodded and turned to call the stable-boy to bring her pony. 'I shall see you again tomorrow?' It was as much a question as a statement, as if she no longer felt certain of the relationship that had developed between them.

Stephen bowed slightly. 'I shall be here, just as usual. You know that I value everything you do.' His eyes were on her again, filled with unspoken secrets, and Emily turned hastily away, busying herself with the harness, climbing into the trap. She felt his hand under her elbow, guiding her steps, and a shiver ran through her body. Quickly, she sat down and took the reins in hands that shook.

'Tomorrow, then.' Thank goodness her voice, at least, was still steady. She flicked the reins, chirruped to the pony and took a breath. 'Goodbye, Stephen.' She could not trust herself to say any more.

He lifted a hand. His eyes were still fixed on her face

and she felt the colour mount. And as she drove away, she wondered just what had happened during those last few minutes, what had changed. On the face of it, nothing. And yet . . . everything had. A few words, a glance, a pressure of hand on hand, and the whole world had shifted slightly on its axis and nothing would ever be quite the same again.

That winter threatened to be hard and cold. There were few jobs to be had at the Lye and many people seemed likely to starve. Stephen and Emily discussed over and over again what was to be done.

'They need work, they need money and they need food,' Stephen said. 'And many of them need shelter – those cottages are in a sad state, leaking, draughty and even falling to pieces. But what can we do about that? One hardly knows where to begin.'

Emily looked at him. Almost all the parish work now rested on Stephen's shoulders. Jonathan, worn out and failing in health, did little more than take the Sunday services in the chapel, and as often as not he would hand over the evening service to his son.

'Food is the most essential requirement,' she said decisively. 'And surely we can provide something there. They need a good hot meal each day – with that inside them, they'll have more heart to look for work or to mend their houses.' She thought for a moment and then looked up eagerly. 'Why not run a soup kitchen? Soup is nourishing and cheap to make – we can beg vegetables and scraps of meat from the shopkeepers, the kind of thing they might throw away – from kitchens, too. I'm sure a great deal of useful food is wasted by some of the big houses around here. Some of the women can help prepare it and we'll serve it at noon every day. It would relieve at least some of the hunger.'

'It certainly would,' Stephen agreed. 'But where could we set up such a kitchen? It would need to be large enough for the serving as well as the preparation – and it would have to have kitchens . . .'

'The old nurse school,' Emily said. 'It's been little enough used since the board school opened. I know the building is poor, but there's a good long room, and there are fireplaces. We could make some of the soup here and get the bakery to heat the rest. And then it can be kept hot there while it's being served. Let's see what we'll need.' She reached out for a piece of paper and a pencil. 'Enough large vessels to make the soup – I daresay that won't be hard, every large kitchen must have more utensils than it needs. Preserving pans would be ideal and they're not wanted at this time of the year . . . Bowls and spoons, the people will have to bring their own. We'll need fuel, of course, for the fires at the school.' She thought again. 'Have I left anything out?'

'You seem to have thought of everything.' Stephen hesitated a moment, then said quietly: 'I don't know how we would manage without you, Emily. It was a fortunate day for us all when you came to the Lye.'

Emily felt herself blush a little. She glanced at Stephen, half smiling, and felt her blush deepen. The dark eyes were fixed on her and at the expression in them she turned her head hastily away.

'Well,' she said quickly, 'so that's decided. We'll arrange a team of women to prepare the vegetables, and we'll find benefactors to supply us. I'll make everyone I know help. It's time more people took an interest in the Lye. I'll visit all my relatives and all Papa's and Mamma's friends.' Her face darkened. 'No doubt they'll all consider me even stranger than they do already, but what matter? At least it means that I can do anything I like with a measure of freedom, since they've almost given up expecting conventional behaviour.'

She saw concern in Stephen's face. 'Emily, I don't like to hear you speak like that. Nothing you have ever done has been unconventional in any but the best sense. And surely in your family . . .'

'Unconventional behaviour is barely noticed?' She gave a little laugh. 'But that depends wholly on attitudes, doesn't it? What you think of as normal. And I didn't really mean Mamma and Papa when I spoke of relatives thinking me odd. I was thinking of – oh, Roger, for one. And my uncles and aunts – Harold and Samuel and Lavinia. They have already despaired of my family, you see, so naturally I am expected to be even more peculiar. Especially when you consider the circumstances in which I joined the family.' The sense of isolation that had oppressed her since childhood returned and she was shaken by a sudden yearning for Paul, the only one who really understood.

'I think you are still bitter about that,' Stephen said after a pause, and Emily shrugged.

'Bitter? Perhaps. Wouldn't you be bitter if you had been born of a mother you never knew, or could not remember – a mother nobody wanted to talk about?'

'Perhaps I would.' He made a movement towards her and checked himself. 'Emily, if there were anything I could do to help . . .' He took her hand and looked earnestly into her face.

She felt him draw near, felt his hands on her shoulders. His touch was gentle yet she could feel the strength in his fingers. It was a hard, masculine strength that she desperately needed and could draw from no other source. She had recoiled from her father, had never been close to Roger; and Paul . . . Paul was far away and might never return to her. Only this man, the minister's son, tall and pale and intellectual yet prepared to work himself to the bone for the poverty-stricken people of the Lye, was close to her now; only he could offer her his strength.

With a tiny cry, she turned into his arms and buried her face against the rough material of his jacket. She felt rather than heard his muffled groan, and found herself being drawn up from the chair, caught against him in a grip that made her gasp out all her breath. One strong, trembling hand rested against her cheek, turning her face up towards him, and then his lips were on hers, crushing her mouth. A fierce maelstrom of emotion shook her; she clung to him, her head forced back painfully on her shoulders, her mind whirling as she found herself responding to his passion. Stephen, Stephen . . . his name thundered through her mind. And yet, as she laced her fingers behind his neck to hold him closer, there was another name too, a name that fought to be heard, a name that it was vitally important not to forget; a name that brought another man's face to her mind, another man's lips to her mouth and throat, another body to press against her own.

She had never known him in this way. But even as Stephen Corbett held her in his arms, it was Paul her heart yearned for, Paul whose love she craved.

'Stephen, no. Please . . .' With an effort, she pushed him away and looked up into his face, trembling. He was breathing hard, his eyes glittering, dazed as he stared at her. She saw the blood rush to his face and the realisation dawn.

'Emily! Oh, my dear . . . Emily, can you ever forgive me? How could I behave so badly . . .' He passed a shaking hand over his brow. 'I don't know what to say . . .' He shook his head and turned away, his shoulders bent. 'I can't tell you how ashamed I feel . . . to behave so. I don't know what came over me. I –'

'Please. Don't apologise.' She reached out to touch his shoulder and then drew back her hand. 'I think we are both overwrought. Stephen, let's forget it. You meant to comfort me, I know. Let's leave it at that.'

'Comfort?' He gave a short, bitter laugh. 'And what comfort is it now, to know that you'll never want to come here again?'

'But of course I'll want to come here again. Why shouldn't I?'

'To be alone with me? Knowing what I am?'

'Stephen, you're my dear friend who has stood by me all these months, helped me, worked with me. I trust you. I know that – that what has just happened between us will never occur again.' She gazed at him, feeling a fresh stirring of the hunger that had driven her into his arms, and shook herself angrily. 'Let's go on as we

293

always have done,' she said softly, and held out her hand, this time not drawing it back. 'As friends.'

Slowly, he reached out. He took her hand in his and looked down at it. Then he raised his eyes to her face.

'We can never do that now, Emily,' he said quietly. 'We can never go on as we were before. We know too much now, about each other.'

She saw that he had recognised and felt the emotion in her, the desire leaping to match his own, and her eyes fell. Was it what she wished, a friendship only? Surely it must be? And yet . . .

Paul was lost to her. He might never return from Paris. Was she to live lonely throughout her life, yearning for a love that could never be?


The first steaming cauldron of soup was served at noon on a bitter Monday in December. The doors of the old nurse school, where girls of eight or nine had taken small babies and even managed to learn to figure a little or to read a few words, were opened to a queue of impatient people and within minutes the room was filled with jostling men and women, each using elbows, fists and even feet to get to the table first.

Emily and the women she had recruited as helpers stood ready to ladle the thick, savoury mixture into the bowls that were held out under her nose. They stared in some dismay at the eager throng and Emily gestured for them to stand back.

'We can't possibly serve you unless you're quiet,' she said, raising her voice to be heard above the babel. 'Make a proper queue and come forward one at a time. *One at a time*, Bill Smith. Have you all brought bowls?' There was an assenting murmur. 'Very well. Now, no pushing, please. We don't want any soup spilled, do we?'

Grumbling a little, the crowd moved slowly along the table, receiving a bowl of soup and a chunk of bread each. Emily watched them carefully. She knew most of them by name now – even by the curious nicknames that

Lye people used in preference to their given names. There was the old rogue they called Wockum, thrusting his way through to get to the front of the queue. There was the red-haired Fire-lock and his two cronies Mow and Latchet, always to be found together and usually in the beer-shop. There were the toothless sisters, Moll and Dolly Dandy, the old midwife Mag Turner, the nail-maker Shagsby who refused to work with machines, Liz Smith and her children – three of them now, since the baby Emily had helped deliver had survived to take its place on the bellows – and a throng of others.

The soup kitchen had been hard work. She had had to find women to prepare the food; to get permission to use the school; to find the things on her list; and to find the food, persuading her friends to donate food from their own kitchens ('Leftover vegetables are exactly what we need for our soup. And if you could spare a little meat or bacon as well . . .'), going from shop to shop in Wordsley, Amblecote and even Stourbridge itself to beg a few turnips, carrots, potatoes, even cabbage leaves. ('You know you would only throw them away.') And she had gone in her own trap to collect everything, returning laden with goods and looking, as Stephen said, like a market woman down on her luck.

'I don't care if I do,' Emily said. 'Look what I've got! We shall make good soup with that, Stephen, and enough to last several days too, I hope.'

'And then?'

'And then I'll go and fetch more,' she said staunchly, and turned quickly away from the look in his eyes.

Watching now as the hungry people of the Lye scrambled for their soup, she thought again of that look. It was an expression she had seen increasingly in his eyes, and it never failed to bring that strange tingling to her stomach – the sensation she had felt when he had touched her hand as she climbed into the trap, when he had so unexpectedly kissed her. Since then, she had managed never to be alone with him, never out of the sight of others' eyes – but the look had come into his face again and

295

again, and she knew that soon something must happen.

Impatiently she shook her head, and stepped forward to pick up a ladle. What was likely to happen, for Heaven's sake? Stephen was a respectable man, a minister. He had been tired, overwrought – they'd both been excited by the idea of the soup kitchen – the control they both exercised as a matter of course had, for a brief moment, been lost. And it was her fault as much as his. She remembered the thrill of excitement she had felt, the surging pleasure she had taken in those kisses . . . And Stephen had been so apologetic, so angry with himself.

Christina had told her that women could feel pleasure in the kind of physical love that was expressed between husband and wife. She had told her that it was something very precious, to be cherished. Was this what she felt for Stephen, then? And if so, what of Paul? What of her feelings for him, the longing that still assailed her, the misery that still on occasions overcame her?

Forget him, she thought, ladling soup out with a savage speed that had it spilling from the bowls. He's gone. By now, he's probably engaged to that little butterfly Véronique. And even if not, he made it clear that he'll never love you. *Forget him*. She spilled some more soup and looked up into the face of the man she was serving to apologise.

'And if you think you're getting a second helping, Bill Smith, you'd better think again!' she exclaimed furiously. 'You were first in the queue as it was. Now go straight outside and don't come in again until tomorrow morning.'

But she could not feel truly angry. The people were genuinely hungry, after all. And the soup really was very good.

'A great success,' Stephen said.

Emily started and looked up from the pan she was scrubbing. It was the last one; she had told her band of helpers to go home to their own families now, since it was already dark. They had each left with a large bowl of soup, payment for their day's work, promising to return first thing tomorrow morning.

'Yes,' Emily said, brushing a curl back from her damp forehead, 'I believe it was a success.'

'I looked in once or twice, to make sure that everything was under control. I thought some of the men might be awkward to handle – like old Wockum, and Fire-lock.'

'No, one or two tried to get second helpings but I think we spotted them in time. There was just enough to go round. We managed very well.'

'You manage everything very well,' Stephen said. He moved closer to her. 'You're good at this kind of work, Emily.'

'Thank you,' she said uncertainly, and felt her heart quicken.

He looked at her, and she felt her colour rise and knew that the moment she had tried to evade had at last arrived. And this time there could be no evasion. Even so, she gestured towards her half-washed pot and made a slight movement in the direction of the low earthenware sink.

'Leave it,' Stephen said. 'Let it wait.' He put out a hand and laid it on her arm, looking down into her eyes. His face was serious. 'Emily, have you ever thought . . . what an excellent wife you would make for a minister?'

'For . . . a minister?' she breathed.

'For me.' He waited, his eyes holding hers, then added urgently: 'Emily, I've been thinking about this for a long time. I need a wife. I need someone to help me, to work with me, to live with me.' His pale face warmed a little with colour. 'Ever since you came to the Lye and told me that you wanted to work here, to help . . . I didn't believe you at first. I thought it would be a passing whim, a fancy. But even so, there was something . . . And it wasn't a passing fancy. You've worked hard here, not caring what task you undertook, not caring what the risks were. You were *made* for this, Emily. We could do so much together. And so much more if we were married.' He stepped closer, slid his hand down to her wrist, took both her hands in his. 'I need you, Emily. Will you marry me?'

Emily stood very still. She looked up into Stephen's eyes and for the second time that day she thought of Paul. And for the second time that day reminded herself that Paul was lost to her, that he didn't want her love anyway. He had thrown it back at her like an unwanted gift; what could she do with it but offer it to someone else?

Stephen had not said he loved her. But he had said he needed her, and the admiration was clear in his eyes, had been for months. And when he had kissed her . . . What was that but love?

If she married Stephen, she could leave home. Leave her father's domain. Leave the constant reminder of her mother and what he had done to her. Start afresh in the place where she had been born, going on with what now seemed to be her life's work.

*You were made for this* . . . Stephen understood. She had worked with him ever since that first day. And now, with her hands in his, she felt a quickening of excitement. Marriage with the young men who had come to Henzel Court to seek her hand had not attracted her. Even though they were mostly the sons of manufacturers, expecting to inherit at least a share in such businesses as ironworks, collieries or glasshouses, she had known that with any one of them her life would have been the same: running a house, bearing children, calling on other women and having them call on her. She would never have found a husband who would have treated her as a partner – as Joe treated Christina.

But with Stephen . . . There would be work to do, work she loved and was good at. A husband who already had the power to send a thrill through her body, even though he was not the man she loved. And she would have her independence.

She looked up and met the dark, questioning eyes.

'You don't have to answer now,' Stephen said. 'Think

298

about it. I know I ought to have asked your father first, anyway.'

'No, indeed you oughtn't,' Emily said warmly. '*I* choose the man I shall marry.' She returned his look gravely, and then smiled. 'And I choose you. Thank you, Stephen.'

She lifted her face for his kiss, her heart already beating a little faster in anticipation of the sensations she had felt before. But Stephen bent his head only a little. He touched her lips with his, briefly, as if he were afraid to bruise her. Then he stepped back quickly, as if he had been stung.

Emily opened her eyes and looked up at him, puzzled. But there was no mistaking the look on his face. It was transformed with joy.

After the wedding, she thought, and found herself hoping that it would not be too long to wait. After the wedding he will love me as I want to be loved . . .

The family, as usual, greeted the news of her engagement with a variety of responses. In accordance with custom, Stephen had gone to see Joe and ask formally for Emily's hand. The request had not come as any surprise to Joe – Emily, having decided to bury her grudge against Christina over Paul, had already confided in her. And Christina, having given the matter some thought and come to the conclusion that Emily could do a great deal worse – and also feeling considerably relieved that the child seemed at last to have got over that unfortunate infatuation for Paul – had told Joe. And without actually saying so, she managed to make it clear that she thought it was quite a good idea.

'You think she'll be happy with him?' Joe asked.

'I don't see why not. They know each other well – they've worked together for eighteen months or more now. I should think they know each other a great deal better than most young couples, who have only met in the drawing room or on picnics. And Emily seems to enjoy the life.'

'Still . . . a minister. He'll never make much, Christina.'

'Does that matter? They'll have enough. And we can see that Emily never wants.'

Joe grunted. 'Aye, there's that. But a man ought to support his own wife . . .' He let his words trail away as he thought of what marriage had brought to him. 'All right, so I'm never one to talk!'

'Don't be silly, Joe. You've supported me – Henzel's couldn't have gone on without you. Didn't I have to go all the way to Newcastle to tell you how much you were needed? Anyway, none of that is the point. All we should concern ourselves with is whether Stephen will make Emily happy. And if you think the answer is yes . . .'

'I don't know. He seems a bit of a cold fish to me. What do *you* think, my love? You're better at summing people up than I am.'

Christina thought for a moment. 'I think he wants to marry her very much. He is certainly in love with her – you have only to watch his eyes following her about to see that. As for Emily – I think she could make a very happy life with him, and a useful one too. But as to whether she loves him or not . . . I'm not sure, Joe. There is something in her eyes, a kind of hunger, but I don't quite know whether it's love.'

'Well, if it's not, I don't doubt it'll grow once they're wed,' Joe declared. 'She wants to marry him, doesn't she? Well, then – the girl must have her reasons. She's always known her own mind, after all. And she's no silly miss straight out of the schoolroom. She'll not do anything foolish.'

'No . . . Then you'll give your consent?' Christina kissed him. 'I think it's just as well – knowing Emily, she would have simply eloped with him if you'd refused!'

'And that'd do his job a lot of good,' Joe grunted. 'Aye, I'll tell the lad he can have her. Maybe that'll make her smile a bit – she's done nothing but scowl at me for months. Tell you the truth, I'll feel easier when she's out of the house – she's been naught but a black cloud about the place ever since we came back from Paris.'

'And we both know why that was,' Christina sighed. 'I hope she really has forgotten that childish passion she had for Paul. I want to see her happily settled, Joe.'

July seared its dry heat over the dusty yellow grass of Dob Hill; the stunted bushes were hung with shrivelled leaves and haws that had formed too soon and did not swell. The 'bread and cheese' of children was tasteless and uninteresting, and even the birds found little nourishment in the small, hard berries.

And one morning, towards the middle of the month, Emily put on her wedding dress and rode in the Henzel carriage with her father to the church of Holy Trinity, on the hill at Wordsley, and married Stephen Corbett. She vowed to love, honour and obey him until death them did part; and he, for his part, promised to worship her with his body.

The words gave her a thrill of excitement and apprehension. Suppose, after all this time, she were to disappoint him? She still did not really understand what was expected of her. When Christina, remembering that awkward little talk a few years ago, had asked if there was anything she needed to know, Emily – also remembering that talk – had said no, nothing. But she hadn't believed what Christina had told her then, hadn't properly taken it in. And she could not ask her to repeat it, in case she was horribly wrong.

Or even, she thought as she slipped into the dress that was the finest garment she had ever owned, in case she was right . . .

There was too much to think about now, anyway. The ride to the church, feeling self-conscious beside her father, who seemed to be struggling with something he wanted to say and could not find the words for. The entry into the church, with the sea of faces turned towards her – Sarah and some small cousins in pretty dresses, waiting to attend her, Roger as an usher, showing people to their seats. Her family and friends, including Harry and Ruth, back from America for a holiday. Stephen's father, looking frailer than ever. Even some of the people she knew at the Lye, dressed in an assortment of 'best' clothes, sitting right at the back of the church and whispering.

The service, soon over. The ride back to the house, with Stephen this time, as awkward and self-conscious as Joe. The wedding breakfast, the speeches and the toasts. And, at last, slipping up to her bedroom – the last time she would use it – to change into another new, but more practical, dress for the drive back to the Lye, to start her new life straightaway.

When she came downstairs, her parents were nowhere to be seen. She found them at last in the library, where Joe was standing reading the newspaper he had not yet had time to glance at.

'Joe,' Christina was saying as Emily came into the room, 'what is it? What's happened?' And Emily caught the look that passed between them and saw Christina's face whiten with terror.

'Papa . . .'

'It's what we've been expecting,' Joe said, ignoring her. 'War. France has declared war on Prussia, and God knows what will happen next.'

Emily reached blindly for a chair, something to cling to. The world had shifted, was swinging about her. She could not see.

'War? In France? And Paul is there . . .'

Christina turned sharply, and in that moment Emily knew a closeness with her stepmother that no blood relationship could transcend. Instinctively, the two women drew together, staring with fear-darkened eyes at Joe, still in all his wedding finery.

'He must come back at once. He must be brought back,' Christina said, but they all knew she was crying in the dark. Paul was a man now; he had been away from home for too long. Stay or return, it would be his decision.

'And it's useless for us to fret about it now,' Joe

declared, throwing down the newspaper. 'There's nothing we can do about it either way. Paul's a sensible lad, he'll not do anything foolish. And you –' his eyes, dark as her own, fixed on Emily's face '– you've a husband to go to now. It's him you should be thinking of.'

A husband! For a moment, Emily had totally forgotten the events of the day, forgotten that she was now a married woman. Mrs Stephen Corbett . . . The name sounded unfamiliar, alien. Yet it was hers now, and her father was right. She had a duty to the husband who waited somewhere in the house. She had made solemn vows to him only a few hours ago, vows that she must, intended to, keep.

Christina came to her and laid her small hands on Emily's arms, looking up into her face. The closeness was still there, a bond that would never break again; and Emily, understanding what was in the other woman's heart, bent to kiss her.

She left them there in the library, preferring to go to Stephen alone; knowing that thoughts of foreign wars must be dismissed from her mind; that what might have been was now no more than a shadow. Her own life had been set in another direction; today it was beginning anew. And as she found her husband and looked up into his pale, handsome face, she felt that disturbing sensation somewhere below her heart, already warring with the shock of the news she had just heard.

Stephen. The man who had held her in his arms just once, when his lips had been harsh with passion, his body hard against hers. With him, she had known the urgency of desire. With him, surely she could forget.

# Chapter Fourteen

News of the war filtered through to the family in Stourbridge by way of newspaper reports.

'The French have gone mad!' Joe declared, flinging down his copy of *The Times*. 'Declaring a frivolous war that they're not even ready for! Look at this – outdated weapons, soldiers being sent hither and thither like lemmings, no tents for them to sleep in when they finally do arrive, gunners with no guns, no food stores in Metz which is the most important depot of them all – what in God's name do they think they're playing at? And this general here – Leboeuf, however you pronounce the outlandish name – claiming that the army is ready down to the last gaiter-button. Who does he imagine will believe that?'

'Almost everyone, I should think, since there are probably no gaiters in store to need buttoning,' Roger observed dryly. 'And it says here that Louis-Napoleon himself has ridden out to begin the advance into Germany. He has already passed through Metz and intends to capture Saarbrucken, and he has the Prince Imperial himself with him.'

'More fool him, then,' Joe grunted. 'He's as likely to lose France the heir to the crown as well as the war . . . He stands alone in this, Roger. No other country will go to his aid. His only hope is the commander, Trochu. But will Napoleon allow him to command? He's a bad ruler, a weak man, letting himself be goaded into war by the rantings of a Parisian mob and that sly adventuress Eugénie. He's bringing ruin on his own country, that's what he's doing.'

'Then let him do so, if he is so foolish,' Christina exclaimed. 'My concern is with Paul. Why doesn't he come home? What is keeping him there, in danger?'

'And that,' Joe said heavily, 'you know as well as I do. It's that girl, my love – Marc's niece, the pretty little fair-haired minx that took his eye the first moment he saw her. She's a woman now, and a beauty too, I'll warrant. I reckon that's why he's staying. That's why he'll never come back to Stourbridge.'

That summer, they said, was one of the hottest anyone could remember. Flowers grew, bloomed early, withered and died. As the droughts grew worse, harvests failed, fruit refused to swell, sheep and cattle thirsted in the fields and farmers and peasants came together to pray for rain. The French army grew short of fodder for their horses and sold them to farmers who had even less chance of feeding the starving animals. The sun shone down relentlessly, day after day, blistering the green hills to a dusty brown, drying the leaves on the trees in a travesty of autumn.

The rumours of war, reaching out into the corners of France throughout that long, hot summer, seemed no more than the faint, faraway rumblings of a distant storm. Much more important to Paul were the complications of his feelings for Véronique and the affair, still not resolved, with Annette. A family some hundreds of miles away, deep in the murkiness of England's most heavily industrialised country, could hardly hope to compete for his attention; indeed, their faces seemed misty, their voices had almost completely faded from his memory and the trust they had placed in him to return was buried under a burden of guilt.

Even the cameo glass to which he had given so much thought, the carving which he had practised so meticulously in his grandfather's workshops, seemed to diminish in importance when he realised at last that Véronique was destined to marry René.

Married – to René! Paul could not imagine why he had not realised it before. Perhaps he had known, deep inside him, and not wished to recognise it. As his grandmother, Sal Compson, would have said, there were none so blind as those who did not wish to see. Whatever the reason for his own blindness, now that the fact had been presented to him at last, he knew that his whole being cried out against it.

He had not even been able to use the time to show Véronique how he felt about her. Immediately after Christmas, she had been ill and when she was recovered she had been sent away to stay with another uncle and aunt, far away in the south where the climate was kinder. Paul could do nothing but write letters – letters that were full of affection but could give no hint as to his real feelings. And her replies, though equally filled with affection, were no more expressive; he searched in vain for any hint that she might be coming to love him.

And it had been decided that she was to go straight to Lorraine for the annual family visit, meeting Marc and Cécile there before returning to Paris with them.

And now they were about to go. To the château where René lived and worked. And at eighteen, Véronique was no longer an adoring child; she was a woman, a flower in full bloom, a fruit ripe for the picking. This summer, surely, would see the announcement of their betrothal.

Paul could not let Véronique go. He could not let the enchanting butterfly leave him. From the moment he had arrived in Paris, she had fluttered around him, sprinkling him with affection, showering him with delight. He had taken it all for granted, treated her as a little sister, knowing that someday there would be something more but complacently putting her to one side while he allowed the headier influence of Annette to overpower both mind and body, to draw him into a dark inferno of sensuality, a vortex of sinister passions from which there had seemed to be no escape.

Night after night, Paul lay awake, cursing himself for having wasted so much time. How could he have been so blind, so stupid – drawing back to 'let her grow up' when he could have been binding her to him, succumbing to Annette's sultry attractions when he could have been concentrating on Véronique? And now it was almost too late.

After the Christmas visit, when Gabriel had so unmistakably displayed his jealousy and hatred, Paul had made up his mind not to go to Lorraine again – at least not this year. Clearly, he would not be welcome. And if he stayed in Paris, there would be no danger of his sinking once again under Annette's influence.

But now he knew that he must go. Gabriel would be there; Annette would be there. But so would Véronique – and René.

As he had expected, Paul's welcome was not effusive. Only Annette seemed pleased to see him, giving him warm kisses on both cheeks and Paul, aware of Gabriel's cold eyes on them, wondered if she were deliberately flaunting their relationship in front of her husband. There had never, he knew, been much love between them, and he suspected that Annette had other lovers to alleviate the boredom of her life at the château. He looked at her ripe figure, her luxuriant black hair and gleaming eyes, and felt nothing. He did not know how he could ever have been seduced by her.

'And here,' Cécile cried as quick, light footsteps sounded in the passage outside the room and the door was flung open, 'is our lovely Véronique! Ah, *chérie*, how we have missed you! Never, never shall we allow you to leave us for so long again.'

Véronique ran into the room as if she were still no more than a child of twelve. And Paul, turning with a great leap of the heart, could scarcely believe that she had grown by a single day since he had first met her. The same shimmering gold hair, flying loose; the same dancing blue eyes; the same laughing mouth. It was Véronique as she had first entranced him, weaving the same gossamer web of delight.

'Tante Cécile! *Mon oncle!* And Paul, my dearest cousin – oh, it's so good to see you all again!' Kissing them all over and over again, she danced from foot to foot and clapped her hands. 'I have been so lonely for you, down there in the south. Oh, it is very nice, very warm and pleasant, but not like Paris, no, nor like the dear château.' She captured Paul's hand and led him to a low couch. 'Now, sit here with me, Paul, and tell me all that has been happening, every little thing, mind you. What are you engraving now? Are you the best engraver in Paris yet?' Her laugh rippled through the room. 'Oh, I can't tell you how good it is to see you again!'

'And it's good to see you, Véronique,' he said quietly, keeping her hand in his. 'I've missed you very, very much.'

Véronique's eyes met his. For a second or two, he was sure that the laughter faded from them, that something else took its place – something serious, something questioning. And then she glanced past him and her expression changed again; became wary.

The impression was over in a flash, and then she was laughing again and withdrawing her hand from his. And Paul, turning to see what she might have been looking at, met several other pairs of eyes.

Gabriel's. René's. And Annette's. And all with varying degrees of hostility.


'So!' Annette hissed. 'You try once again to make a fool of me! Well, we shall see who is the fool this time.'

Wearily, Paul walked away to the window and stood gazing out. He saw the château lawn, bathed in the light of a full white moon, the lights of the factory beyond. The houses of the workmen were in darkness. An owl floated across the face of the moon; nothing else stirred.

'Annette, please. It's over. Can't you accept that? You knew it would end someday. Why not let it do so with dignity?'

'Dignity!' She spat the word at him. 'And what is so dignified about this situation?' She gestured at her lace nightgown, every frill designed to seduce. 'You did not even undress for me tonight,' she said bitterly.

Paul glanced down at his own clothes. He had not

made ready for bed because he was sure that Annette would come and he wanted no mistake made about his intentions. And because, undressed, he felt at a decided disadvantage – as, no doubt, Annette herself did now.

'Can't you see how humiliating this is?' she went on bitterly. 'As if I had to come begging! I tell you, I have *never* begged.'

'I'm sure you haven't,' he said soothingly. 'And you're not begging now. At least . . .' He stopped, sighed, began again. 'Annette, this affair can't go on. I've tried to stop it before . . . this time we must. The risks are greater all the time and –'

'Risks? Risks of what?'

'Well – of Gabriel finding out, for one thing. And my grandfather – can't you imagine how hurt he and my grandmother would be? They trust me –'

'Wrongly. They should know what you are really like. And as for Gabriel, do you imagine that I will not tell him?' She smiled and in the moonlight her smile was evil, cruel. 'I always tell Gabriel when I discard a lover. It amuses me to see him, realising what has been going on under his nose.' She moved across the room. 'And of course, you will never be welcome here again. I would imagine my uncle will prefer you to return to England at once.'

'You wouldn't,' he said tonelessly as her threat sank in, and Annette laughed.

'Wouldn't I? Are you going to risk it?'

He stared at her for a moment and then turned away. Had she really defeated him again, and so easily? If he gave in now, wasn't there a chance that she would tire of him and discard him, as she had evidently done with so many others? Or would she, simply because he wanted so badly to be free, take a wicked delight in holding him, binding him even more firmly by the cord that held him to her side . . .?

The thought of lying even once more with that luscious body, of kissing those ripe lips, sickened him.

He turned back.

'Do what you like, Annette,' he said coldly. 'I've told you, it's over. If you're wise, you'll go back to your own bed. And I don't think you'll tell Gabriel. It would make life unpleasant for you, as well as for me.'

She stared at him. Her cheeks blanched and her eyes grew huge, dark wells in a face that was suddenly shrunken, as if the skin itself had cringed. She opened her mouth, but made no sound. She lifted both hands and held them out, the fingers extended like claws.

And then, with a suddenness that shocked him, she flung back her head and let out a scream like that of a wounded animal. At the same moment, she launched herself at him, raking her nails down his cheeks, clawing for his eyes. Screeching, crying, shouting obscenities that he had heard only in the roughest quarters of Paris, she kicked and scratched and fought, intent on damaging him, intent on both crippling and blinding him.

After the first second's shock, Paul caught her by the wrists and held her away from him, but her strength was a match for his and the struggle was fierce. Already, he could feel the sting of blood on his cheek and knew that one of her long, sharp nails had gone perilously near his eye. And the soft flesh was surprisingly strong; perhaps rage was lending her extra power. He doubted whether he could hold her off for very much longer.

'Annette! Annette, stop – calm down, listen to me, please . . .' But his voice was drowned by her screams. It could be only a matter of time before someone arrived to investigate, and he could only pray that it would not be either of his grandparents. The sight of Annette in her nightgown, struggling with him, would be too great a shock.

In the event, it was Gabriel who arrived first. He burst into the room like an enraged bull and gripped his wife by the shoulders, tearing her away.

'Leave me alone! Let me have him – I'll tear his eyes out, I'll ruin his pretty face for life, I'll – I'll –' Restrained by her husband's massive strength, she

311

suddenly collapsed, weeping, against his chest. Gabriel held her tightly, his fingers biting into the softness of her shoulders, and jerked his head at Paul.

'Close that door! We don't want the whole family here.'

Shaking with shock, Paul went to do as he was told. Astoundingly, no one else seemed to have heard the noise, or if they had were not coming to investigate. He looked quickly up and down the passage, then shut the door. Annette was now lying on the bed, crying almost as loudly as she had screamed. With one swift movement, Gabriel slapped her hard across the face.

'Stop that noise!'

Annette stopped in mid-sob, her mouth still wide open as she stared up at her husband. Her face was ugly now, blotched with tears, distorted with hate and frustration. The marks of Gabriel's fingers stood out on her cheek, first white and then a dark, angry red. There would be bruises there in the morning.

Gabriel glared down at his wife. He was breathing hard. His small eyes narrowed and his face hardened. He lifted his hand again, bunched it into a fist.

Paul started forward. 'Don't strike her again!'

Gabriel swung his whole body round. His face was as distorted as Annette's, venom twisting every muscle, shining from every pore. The fist was directed at Paul now and, as if once set in motion the blow had to be delivered, he aimed it directly at Paul's head. Too late, Paul put up his own hand to ward off the blow. It caught him on the side of the skull and he staggered.

'Gabriel – look, it's not what you think. I didn't attack Annette –' What else could it look like, with Annette in a lace nightgown, torn half away from her body in their struggles, and himself still fully dressed? 'We simply had an – an argument. It was nothing –'

'Do you take me for a fool?' Gabriel demanded scornfully. 'I can imagine just what the argument was about! Annette never takes refusal kindly. Especially when the favours have been accepted so readily before.'

312

He continued with a bitterness that said everything. 'The gardener, the lackey, any glassmaker who cares to take her . . . You have not been given anything unique.'

Paul stood silent, rubbing his head. The anger seemed to have died out of Gabriel now, leaving him sad and empty, a shell of a man. They looked at each other and then at Annette.

She was crying again, but quietly now, her face buried in Paul's pillow, her hair spread in a dark tangle over the white linen. Her body trembled. Even now, she still looked desirable, but Paul, staring at her, felt nothing. It was over. He knew she would never stir him again.

'I'm sorry,' he said to Gabriel, knowing how inadequate the words were. Gabriel shrugged.

'If it had not been you, it would have been another. And always it ends like this. One day, I imagine I will kill her.' He said it almost as if remarking that it was likely to rain within the next week. 'I tell myself she is not worth suffering for, but you can imagine . . .'

He left the sentence unfinished, but Paul understood his meaning. Marriage to a woman like Annette must be the most exquisite torture ever devised. Knowing what it was like to hold her in your arms, possess her; knowing that she shared her favours with any other man she could find. And no possibility of ending the marriage; only death could do that.

'You will return to Paris, of course,' Gabriel said in a tone that was almost conversational. 'You are not welcome here any more. Not that you ever were, except to her. What excuse you will give, I do not know, neither do I care. And if my uncle does decide to make you his heir, I warn you that I will not work with you. Neither will René.'

He did not wait for Paul's reply, but went to the bed and lifted Annette bodily in his arms. Her sobs had diminished now and she clung to him, her arms round his neck, tears still running down her face. For a moment, he stood looking down at her and Paul, seeing the expression in his eyes, suddenly understood. In that look, there was love, sadness . . . and a deep frustration. As if he had only rarely, and a long time ago, enjoyed the favours that Annette gave so freely to other men.

Was Gabriel impotent? Was this why Annette left his bed so often, why she needed a constant reassurance of her own desirability?

And if so, what of the five children that she had, apparently, borne him . . .?

Paul closed the door and went to the window. The moon was still high, shrouded slightly by a wisp of cloud. He looked down at the garden, the row of small houses, the long building of the glasshouse.

Suddenly, for the first time in many months, he was pierced by a longing for Stourbridge, for the narrow streets, the crowded roofs, the rearing bulk of the cones. For his mother with her tenderness and fire, for Joe and his robust good sense. For Sarah, gay and smiling; for Emily . . .

But Emily was to be married. The letter telling him of her engagement had come some weeks ago. To the earnest, bespectacled minister.

He felt cold and lonely. And for once, he was unable to warm himself with thoughts of Véronique.

He did not sleep at all that night. Instead, he sat at the window, watching the moon in its lonely traverse, seeing it sink out of sight before the sky first began to lighten; watching the sky warm with apricot before the sun appeared, a distant glow beyond the mountains; listening to the first bird before the full chorus began.

He was under no illusions. Gabriel had hit him only once, but it had been enough to show Paul that he was murderously angry. Only his own pride had prevented him from rousing the whole house and denouncing the pair of them. But Gabriel was the kind of man who would never admit that anything he possessed, including his wife, could have fault. Forced to do so, he would almost certainly commit murder.

Already, Paul had caused him more humiliation than

314

he could be expected to tolerate. It could not have been easy to come to Paris in the winter to demand to know Marc's intentions. And he had been treated as little more than a servant, an employee – valuable and trusted, yes, but still merely an employee. Not an heir.

He had told Paul that he must return at once to Paris. And Paul was in no doubt but that he must comply. If he did not, Gabriel would either kill him, or betray him to Marc.

Almost certainly, it meant the loss of Véronique. He would return alone to Paris – with an excuse he must concoct very quickly – and her betrothal to René would take place while he was powerless to stop it. He supposed it must be his punishment.

Sometime after dawn, he rose from the chair and changed his clothes. He washed in the cold water left in his bowl last night and cleaned the blood from the scratch Annette had left on his cheek, hoping that the family would believe it had been inflicted by a briar. Then he went softly down through the quiet house. He was reminded sharply of his first morning here – a lifetime ago, it seemed – when he had looked down and seen Véronique amongst the roses. What had happened to him since then? What had happened to the innocence?

They had been talking of war for weeks. It should not have come as a surprise. Yet, on that morning when Paul came to breakfast knowing that he must announce his return to Paris, it was a shock to them all.

'War!' Marc said, and stared around the table. 'So they have done it.'

They looked at one another. Only Annette was absent; she had suffered a bad dream in the night, Gabriel said, and would stay in bed for a few hours. She might even have been heard crying out . . . Cécile nodded and said she thought she had heard something. René looked down at his plate. Véronique accepted the explanation with no more comment than a little murmur of sympathy for her aunt.

315

Gabriel's eyes had been fixed on Paul ever since he had come into the room, waiting for him to announce his return to Paris. Now they smouldered a little, as a grate of ashes does when a spark catches in its depths.

'War!' he exclaimed. 'Well, I, for one, am glad! It's time those Prussians were taught a lesson. I shall be glad to help teach it.'

'You? You can't go to war – you're too old, and besides you are needed here.' Marc said.

'But I could go!' René broke in, his eyes alight. 'Look, it says here they are calling for volunteers. And I might never have the chance again.'

'The chance? Chance of what?' Cécile, jerked for once out of her usual placid calm, turned on him. 'War is not a game. It is serious, deadly. You could be killed.'

'Oh, nonsense,' René said, laughing. 'Why, it will be over in a few weeks. Nobody believes the Prussians have any chance of winning. Gambetta has not even thought it necessary to cancel his holiday in Switzerland over it. Germany is a joke! I shall consider it a holiday. Imagine what an experience it will be.'

'Oh, yes, and the uniform – so romantic,' Véronique chimed in, her eyes resting on René's slim figure with admiration. 'Do become a soldier, René!'

Paul looked at her in dismay. Woman she might be, in the low-cut gown that revealed the swelling young breasts and the fresh silkiness of her skin, but she was still as impressionable as a child. René's becoming a soldier might well be enough to persuade her to fall in love with him completely. So far Paul had not believed her to be in love with the young Frenchman, only with the idea of a romantic wedding. Given enough time with her – time that Gabriel would not now allow him to have – he had been convinced he could win her love. But if René should come home in soldier's uniform, if he should go striding off to war, even return romantically wounded . . .

The whole family was now discussing René's proposal, but the argument was brought to an end by Marc, who had been sitting silently at the head of the table, his grey eyes moving from face to face, his expression unreadable. Now he brought his hand palm downwards on to the table with a small, light slap, and instantly all voices were stilled and each head turned in his direction.

'Enough,' he said, and his quiet voice held sufficient steel to command attention from every person present. 'This is idle talk. There is no question at the moment, René, of your joining the army; you are needed here. Gabriel, war is no game. I am surprised to hear you talking as though it is. And Véronique, you are no more than a foolish child, speaking of things you do not understand. Cécile, my love, you must make ready for us to return to Paris immediately. We will take Paul and Véronique. This war will, I fear, take a great deal more winning than any of you seem to imagine. Bismarck is a clever man. He has engineered this situation to further his own ends, and he would not have entered any war which he did not think his own side capable of winning.' He rose from the table and Paul was shocked to see that he seemed to have aged even during the meal. 'Paul, we must think about your immediate return to England. But nothing can be done until we are back in Paris and can learn the truth of the matter.'

He moved slowly towards the door, his tall figure stooping and suddenly old. The rest of the family sat still, stunned, watching as he went. René was looking mutinous, Véronique near to tears. Gabriel was frowning and Cécile, her plump face creased with bewilderment, was touching her lips with her napkin, over and over again as if some mechanism had been set in motion and would not run down. But as her husband reached the door, she flung down the napkin and pushed back her chair, rushing after him as fast as she could.

'Marc! Marc, you cannot simply walk out without explanation . . . Why must we go back to Paris? Wouldn't it be safer to stay here, in the country? The Germans will surely make for Paris, they will want to capture our capital city. Or do you think we will win before they can come so far, is that it? You think they will never reach Paris at all. Marc, I only want us all to be *safe*.'

He stopped and looked down at her. His face softened with pity and he took her plump little hands in his, cradling them gently in the long, tapering fingers that were so like Paul's. And Paul, watching him, remembered the old story about Marc and Aunt Susan, back in Stourbridge; how, long ago in their own youth, they had fallen in love and been parted. Perhaps Marc had never really loved Cécile, had married her only for convenience and for the sake of the family business, but they had been together now for over half a century and they were a part of each other. And Paul could see his grandfather's emotion for this fat and aged Frenchwoman warring with the streak of practicality which was entirely French and which had probably led him to marry her in the first place.

'Safe?' he said thoughtfully. 'Where is safety to be found, *ma chérie*, can you tell me that? Yes, I know you want to be safe – but we are old, and perhaps safety is no longer important for us. And we have a business still to run. There is no one competent in charge in Paris. I must go back. As for the countryside being safer – I do not know. Wars are waged over fields and through villages more than in the cities. But you may stay here if you wish.'

Cécile raised her eyes to his, and Paul saw that even hidden as they were in the mass of wrinkles that surrounded them, his grandmother's eyes were still those of a girl; and still filled with the emotion she must have known then, the love that she had always borne for her tall, elegant husband.

'No,' she said softly, and Paul wondered why anyone ever believed that love must die as it grew older. 'No, if you go back, so will I. I shall go and make all the necessary arrangements at once.'

They seemed to have forgotten the family, still sitting around the table watching and listening. Marc inclined his head and smiled a little; Cécile looked up at him with all the adoration of a child bride. And, her hand on his arm, they went out of the room together.

Napoleon's offensive against Saarbrucken, carried out soon after the Thietrys returned to Paris, succeeded and there were scenes of wild celebration. But the jubilation of the French was short-lived; the victory was followed by a series of humiliating defeats and from then on the French were in retreat. By mid-August the army was little more than a starving rabble, wandering miserably through the countryside, barred from the doors of farms and villages, and threatened with shooting if they didn't move on, like unwanted dogs straying in the fields. The Prussians were moving ever nearer to Paris, and people began to speak fearfully of siege.

'You must leave while there is still time,' Marc said to Paul. His face was haggard now, drawn with the deep-etched lines of age and anxiety. 'If Paris is blockaded, God knows what will happen to us all. But it is no quarrel of yours, Paul. You are English, you must return to your own home.'

'I am half French,' Paul said stubbornly. 'And have you not always said that this is my home? How can I leave you now? There is no one else to look after you.'

'Pierre is here, and Marie. They are good people, good servants, they have always been loyal to us.'

'And that is all they are – servants. I am your grand-son. Besides, there are the showrooms and the studios. I can take those burdens from your shoulders – I know exactly how you like things done. I can look after everything for you.'

'The showrooms and studios!' Marc said. 'And how are we to obtain glass to engrave, to sell? The fighting has stopped all transport. The château itself is in danger of being occupied – may be full of Germans at this very moment. God knows what is happening to Gabriel and Annette and the children! And René – nothing has been heard of him since Metz was taken. There will be nothing to do at the showrooms but watch men starve.'

'And that I shall not do!' Paul exclaimed. 'Haven't you told me how Thietrys have always looked after their men, even in times of great trouble? And we shall do the same now. If there is no work to be done, I shall arrange for food to be distributed – bread, enough for each family, and soup or coffee to dip it into. You may leave it all to me.' He paused, looking at his grandfather and seeing him for the first time as an old man, his face shrunken, his hands trembling. 'I shall not return to England, *Gran'père*,' he said gently. 'This is my place, here with you and *Gran'mère*. And I am worried about her too – she isn't looking at all well.'

Marc sighed and shook his head. 'No, you are right. My poor Cécile is taking this trouble very hard. She has been constantly ill since we came home. She worries about Gabriel and Annette and the children, and she complains of pains in her chest and back . . . Oh, these are sad, troubled times. I do not know what is to become of us all.'

Later Paul went out into the city. It was crowded with people, the shops and markets filled as the inhabitants of Paris piled their baskets high with provisions. He stood at the top of one of the steep, narrow streets of Montmartre and stared down at the seething mass; at the jostling shoppers who had lost all their customary good humour and were pushing at each other, panic-stricken in their attempts to get food. The stallholders had no need to shout their wares; they were kept busy replenishing the fast-disappearing stock that they had brought from their storehouses. How soon would those storehouses be emptied? Paul wondered. And from where would fresh supplies come?

He became aware of a man standing beside him, a stocky Frenchman in a loose blue jacket and dark beret. He was chewing on a pipe as short and stubby as himself, and staring as Paul was staring, down at the heaving throng.

'So this is what we have come to,' he grunted. 'And

what will they do when there is no more food to sell, *hein*? Tell me that.'

'I don't know,' Paul said. 'Do you think there really will be a siege?'

'Oh, it is certain.' The man turned and looked at him, eyes narrowed in a face so creased it seemed to have been folded a thousand times. 'Me, I intend to leave as soon as it is possible.'

'Leave? But where will you go?'

'Oh, I have a son in Bretagne, he and his wife will take me in. Why should they not? And it is a quiet place, away from the fighting. I am on my way now to the Préfecture of Police, where I shall obtain the *visa de passeport* which will allow me to leave the city.' He smiled cynically. 'It will be like swimming against the tide, I think – they say there are many thousands of people even now trying to get into the city.'

'But why are you leaving? Surely it will be safer inside.'

'You think so? Safe, perhaps – for a while.' The man turned his head aside and spat expressively. 'But then what? Starvation, hardships, and finally, the enemy. The Prussians will wait, my son. They can afford to, after all.' He nodded contemptuously down at the milling housewives. 'Meat – vegetables! They will be fighting like this over dogs and rats before the end of it all, mark my words. And me, I do not wish to be here to see that.'

He gave Paul a brief nod and turned away. Within moments, he had clattered down a steep flight of steps and was lost to sight amidst the pushing, shoving crowd. And Paul, his heart sobered, turned in the opposite direction.

During the whole of that long September day, he walked all over Paris. He walked to several of the main entrances to the city and at each one it was the same story: armies of men extending the fosse that ran around the outer walls, containing the moat, with every wagon and cart that could be commandeered filled with earth

321

and stones and dragged by teams of straining horses to build up the banks; trees being felled and hacked to pieces to form rough and ready fences; masonry, torn from nearby buildings and jammed into position to block the roads, so that there was only a small gap left to admit those who poured in from the countryside.

When the news finally broke, it was as if everyone had already known it in their hearts. Pierre came in with it late in the afternoon, when darkness was already beginning to creep about the gaslit streets. Sedan had fallen, with scenes of brutal carnage. The Emperor himself had been taken prisoner, the Empress had flown into a rage and locked herself away in her room. The streets were filled with people, the air alive with rumour . . . The old servant stared at them, his broad, honest face puckered like that of a baby about to weep, and Cécile gave a faint cry and pressed her hand to her heart.

'The Germans – they are coming! Oh, we shall all be killed!'

She collapsed, unconscious, in Marc's arms and Paul rushed forward to help his grandfather lay the heavy body on the chaise longue. Véronique was ready with smelling salts and they held the little bottle to the old woman's nose, but with no effect. Marc stared down at the face that was already changing colour and then turned quickly to Paul.

'Quickly! Run and fetch the doctor – you know where he lives. Tell him it is urgent, that Madame Thietry is suffering *une crise cardiaque*. Hurry, boy, hurry!' He turned back to his wife, murmuring softly, stroking the wrinkled forehead, and Paul gave them one last glance and flung himself from the room. Without stopping for hat or coat, he raced out through the door and into the street.

The doctor lived a good half-mile away, up and down two or three of the flights of steps that joined one street to another in Montmartre's hilly tumble of houses. And the streets were filled with people: shopkeepers and concierges stood on doorsteps, conversing anxiously;

newspaper kiosks were almost under siege themselves by the crowds who snatched the sheets and gathered under street lamps in small crowds to read and discuss the news. Dogs ran unnoticed between the feet of the people, stealing food from the stalls that had been left forgotten; children sat in doorways, bewildered and crying; and those who would never miss an opportunity, the pickpockets, moved stealthily between, filching freely from coat and counter, making it in their own way a night they would always remember.

The doctor was at home and came immediately, running with Paul since there was no use in taking out the pony and trap in these crowded streets. They arrived breathless at the door, to be admitted by Pierre; but with one look at the servant's face, Paul knew that it was almost too late.

'She is sinking fast,' the doctor told them after his examination. 'I am sorry . . . The past weeks have been too much for her, I fear, as for many other people. But at least she is spared whatever is to come. It will not be long, I think,' he said, his kindly eyes dark with compassion. 'Tonight, or perhaps tomorrow . . . And she will not suffer. She will simply sleep until it is time to go.'

Cécile lay throughout the night in a heavy sleep. Neither Marc nor Véronique would leave her side; they sat one on either side of the bed, each holding a plump little hand, not even trying to hide their tears. Véronique was persuaded to rest only when Paul agreed to stay with her, and they sat close together in the salon, their heads leant wearily on cushions, listening to the sounds outside, isolated in their own small world of death and grief.

'Oh, Paul,' Véronique sighed at last, 'what is happening to the world? It was so lovely – everyone was happy, everything so wonderful. And now there is nothing but talk of war and killing, and there is poor Tante Cécile upstairs dying . . . I don't know how to bear it!' She buried her face in her hands, her shoulders trembling, and Paul moved across and took her in his arms. How light she felt, her bones no more substantial than a butterfly's wings. He held her as if she might break, touching her with fingers accustomed to handling exquisite fragility, and she turned her face into his shoulder and wept.

'What is it like to be in a siege, Paul?' she whispered, and he shook his head.

'I know no more than you. But I know this.' He put one fingertip under her chin, raising her face so that her eyes, as blue as two flowers in the calyx of her face, looked up into his. 'It is not nearly so bad when you are with people you love.'

'Nothing is as bad when you are with people you love,' she said, and smiled a little. 'Don't you wish you had gone back to England while you had the chance? You have your family there; wouldn't you rather have been with them, safe and happy?'

'Knowing that you were here? No!' He gripped her tightly against him, knowing that this must be the worst of all moments to make any kind of declaration, with the old woman dying upstairs and the sounds of a city's fury beating at the walls; yet knowing too that there might be no other. 'Véronique, I must be here because only here can I be with the one person I love most in all the world. Because *you* are here – and you mean more to me than my own heart.' He caught her hand and pressed it against his breast. 'You *are* my heart.' There was a silence while they stared into each other's eyes. He saw Véronique's widen, the pupils large and black, saw her face blanch, heard the quick intake of breath. 'I know I shouldn't speak to you like this,' he said, in a low, urgent voice. 'But these are strange times, Véronique, and I have loved you since my first day in Paris. I thought to give you time to grow up – perhaps I needed time myself. But this year, hearing them talk of your marrying René . . . I knew that I must speak. And now I dare not leave it any longer. Tomorrow, who knows what may happen? I can't let you live another day without

324

knowing at least that I love you – even if you can never return my love.'

Véronique's eyes searched his face wonderingly, as if she had never seen him before. Slowly, she reached up and touched his cheek, stroked away the brown hair that fell in loose curls across his brow. Her hand still resting on his hair, she pressed gently against his head, drawing him down to her, and to his amazement Paul felt her lips touching his, a gentle brushing of sensuous warmth that was barely more than the flutter of a moth's wing.

'Véronique . . .' he murmured blindly, but even as he sought her lips again she withdrew from him and held up two slender white hands.

'No, Paul, you are right, this is not a good time. But it is the only time we have had . . .' Her eyes were still wide, glittering like stars on a frosty night. 'I thought you would never speak,' she said softly. 'I thought you would let me go to the altar with René and never say a word . . .'

Cécile died at eight o'clock the next morning, September the fourth; a sunny Sunday on which one might have expected the city to be quiet, with only churchgoers to be seen and only church bells to be heard. But when Paul went out to make arrangements for the laying-out of his grandmother and her funeral, he found crowds assembling. Their chant was one word: a word they repeated over and over again as they marched through the streets, a word that became more menacing as the crowd grew more massive.

'*Déchéance! Déchéance!* Abdication, abdication!' The voices became one, a swelling roar. Paul was drawn by it, as was every man who heard it. As it grew, he followed it, seeing the women and children gradually melt away, leaving only men who marched with grim purpose towards the Palais Bourbon, where the government was protected by a cordon of soldiers. Then the air began to vibrate with a low, deep throbbing that finally resolved itself into the steady beat of drums approaching from the Place de la Concorde. Instinctively, the crowd made way for the marching body of the Paris National Guard. Silent except for the beating drums, the marchers approached the cordon and indicated their intention to pass through into the Palais; the regular soldiers, uncertain as to what to do, half-heartedly resisted and in the ensuing confusion Paul found himself swept nearer the gates, crushed against the iron fence and finally, to his astonishment, carried by the milling crowd into the building itself.

He could see the government deputies, their faces frightened, trying hastily to pack papers, snuffboxes and other paraphernalia into their cases. And their fear communicated itself to him. What would this mob not do to gain its own ends? Who was safe any more in the mad bedlam that Paris had become?

Two men were trying to make themselves heard above the noise of the crowd; one of them, too short to be seen above the milling heads, climbed a stepladder, and shouted loudly in his efforts to be heard. 'That is Cremieux,' a man near Paul said to nobody in particular. 'He and Picard are both Republicans – we should listen to them.' But nobody was in a listening mood; the mob, angry, frightened and bewildered, could carry only one thought in its corporate mind: Down with the Empire! Long live the Republic!

People pushed and strained against each other, scrambling to reach better points of vantage, clambering on to desks, tables, windowsills, shouting abuse at the government. In a moment, Paul thought, they will begin to fight and kill each other, and a cold fear gripped his body. What was he doing here? How had he come to be in this place, where he had no right to be, the seat of government in a country which was not his? In that moment, he forgot his proud claim to be half French and thought only of Stourbridge and of the family there; of his mother, small but indomitable, her tawny hair flung back, tiger's eyes flashing; and of Emily, dark and vulnerable behind those grave brown eyes, turning away from him to hide the love in her heart, married by now, perhaps, to the minister's son.

Now another man was on the platform and this time the crowd listened. Paul, crushed against a wall, heard only a few phrases. '. . . the end of the Second Empire . . .' much cheering '. . . the beginning of the Third Republic . . .' louder cheers '. . . must be proclaimed at the Hôtel de Ville . . .' the loudest cheers of all.

'The Hôtel de Ville! Of course it must be there – why did we not think of that ourselves?' As one man, the mob turned and thrust its way towards the doors, again carrying Paul with them. They shouted to each other as they struggled to leave the chamber they had so recently invaded, and once again the throng made its way through the streets to a new venue. Paul had given up all hope of ever escaping now; feeling that this nightmare would never end, would be the pattern for the rest of his life, he went along too, strangely isolated in this mass of people. Half French? he asked himself with bitter cynicism? He was not one particle French. If he were, he would be at ease now, in sympathy with the chanting men who were so closely knit in ideals and desires. Each one of the men around him had a history at his back, a history he knew, had absorbed through his skin and into his very bones since the moment he was born. The call of Favre to the Hôtel de Ville and the Place de Grève had struck a chord in every man's heart; none of them had needed an explanation, though each had been ready to give it. But their history was not Paul's history. It might have been his father's, but it was not his. He had not imbibed stories of revolution with his mother's milk; his history was rooted in the English Midlands, in the Black Country where glassmakers had settled generations ago and become as English as the people already there. His ancestors had not clung to their past; they had snapped the cords that might have bound them and gone freely on into a new future.

And perhaps, Paul thought as he struggled to keep his feet in the crowd that stormed the streets and boulevards of Paris, that is what I should have done too. I should not have tried to become what I am not; shouldn't have renounced my real life for glitter, a shimmering surface that covers nothing but an echoing hollow. I should have gone home long ago, back where I belong.

And now, it was too late. He was trapped in a city that was under siege. And there was Véronique; a silken cord that bound him now more firmly than any history.

The mob had split now into many parts, one crossing the Pont de la Concorde to make their way along the opposite bank of the river beside the Tuileries and the Louvre, others streaming along the quays of the left bank and joining them by way of the smaller bridges that spanned the river between the Palais and the Île de la Cité. And here, at last, Paul was able to find respite; swept up to the very doors of the great Cathédrale de Notre Dame, he found his hand groping instinctively for the great iron ring. In a moment, he felt it between his fingers, hard and cold. He gave it a twist, a push, and was inside; and the door slammed shut behind him, leaving him in sudden darkness.

Outside, the roar of the crowd swelled and crashed against the great stone walls like the thundering breakers of an angry sea. Gradually, it died away; gradually, too, Paul's eyes became accustomed to the darkness and he began to perceive tiny points of light, glimmering in the soaring shadows, and then to see the towering shape of the columns, growing like slender trees endlessly towards the vaulted roof.

Slowly, he moved forwards. The glimmering points revealed themselves as candles, taken from the stand just inside the door and placed before the effigies of various saints. And now a new light began to glow before his eyes, a light so dramatic and powerful that he could not understand how he had not seen it at once. He stood perfectly still, gazing upwards, allowing it to take shape, marvelling in its colours: celebrating in his heart the brilliance of the reds, the blues and the greens that made up the great Rose Window and which were lit now by the sun itself, shining through the coloured glass.

The colours flung themselves like jewels at his feet, scattering over the cold stone floor, and he bent to touch them. This was the enchantment of glass, the magic that could take the sun's rays and transform them, flooding the world with the iridescence of a rainbow. This was the wonder that could equate beauty with function; that could be useful and lovely at one and the same time, strong enough to keep for thousands of years the pristine condition of its first conception, yet so fragile that it could be shattered by the touch of a child.

Glass. It was his life. But he knew now, as he gazed up at the great, glowing window, that his work here was finished. He ought to be back in England.

The sounds outside had died. Inside the great cathedral, all was silent. Paul went to the door and opened it, looking out into the dazzling sunshine.

The mob had disappeared, though he could still hear it in the distance, a muffled roar that told him they had arrived at the Hôtel de Ville. Presumably they were even now carrying out some kind of chaotic election. But here, on the island in the middle of the Seine, there was an oasis of silence, of peace.

He must go back to the house in Montmartre where his grandmother lay dead and his grandfather mourned. He would be needed there now. He must live through the days, the weeks, even perhaps the months of siege. And when it was over, he would return to England. To his home.


Over the next few days, Paris began to settle down to its new, strange existence. In many ways, little seemed to have changed. In spite of the panic buying of the beginning of September, housewives still set out each morning, their baskets over their arms, to do the marketing. To be sure, some of the vegetables were losing their freshness and certain items did become less easy to find. But during those early, heady days when the new Republic had been declared and would, everyone felt sure, soon put things to rights, these signs went unnoticed or ignored. It could not last long, the Parisians declared, and went on with tasks such as changing street names to fit the new regime: rue du 10 Décembre, Paul noticed, became rue du 4 Septembre overnight, and there were other changes which could, he felt, have been well left until later. Was this country at war or wasn't it?

'I don't think even the Parisians could answer that,' Véronique said sadly as they sat together on the evening of Cécile's funeral. The sad ceremony was over and everyone had left the house; Marc had gone early to his room, a broken figure of a man, and Pierre and Marie were in the kitchen. There were no other servants in the house now; the maids, two young sisters, had asked permission to go to their home outside Paris, just before the barricades were set up, and the lackey Édouard had simply vanished; whether he had been killed in the street, or had been dragooned into service with the guard or army, or had merely left of his own accord, nobody knew. 'Everything is so confused. People are celebrating and saying it must all be all right now that we have deposed the Emperor, and that as it was his quarrel, not ours, with the Prussians, they won't need to fight us now that he is gone. Why should they?' She paused for a moment, then added tonelessly: 'That is what the people are saying, anyway.'

'But it isn't true, is it?' Paul said quietly. 'Germany wasn't simply fighting Napoleon. She was fighting France. And she still is, Véronique, she still is. Look at the soldiers still coming into the city, with nowhere to camp but the Champs de Mars.' He thought briefly of the glorious days of the Exhibition, when he had first come to Paris and seen it in all its glittering pride. And now that exotic showground had been turned into a dusty encampment for battle-stained soldiers, wounded and weary, who did little but sprawl about their tents by day and grow steadily drunk by night. 'There are thousands of them, Véronique, thousands upon thousands, and all needing to be fed . . . And sailors, too, even

Bretons who have never been trained but just gathered together as hastily as one might snatch up a handful of nuts to chew on a journey . . . How many can be left in the rest of France, tell me that? Who is there outside the walls to fight the battle for us?'

She shook her head hopelessly, and he looked at her with compassion. The brightness had gone from her face, even her hair had lost its sun-gold shimmer and looked dull and lifeless. He leaned forward and took her hands. 'The last few days have not been easy for you, my darling,' he said gently. 'And whatever is to come may be harder still. But remember, we are together. Nothing will part us now. And together, we can face anything.' She lifted her face towards him, a trace of her old brightness returning with the hope he was giving her, and he gathered her close against him, feeling the slightness of her brittle body, the trembling of her heart against his. 'I love you, Véronique,' he whispered, and touched his lips tenderly against hers.

'Oh, Paul,' she breathed, 'what would I do if you were not with me?' She drew away a fraction and looked into his eyes. 'How could I ever have thought of being married to René? Imagine if you had not spoken . . . Paul, I cannot bear to think of it!'

'I would never have let you marry him,' Paul declared. 'If I had known earlier, I would have spoken. But I thought there was plenty of time – I wanted you to have time to grow up, time to know your own mind.'

He looked at her lovingly, thinking of the contrast between her and Annette – the one so ethereal and untouched, the other so devious and earthy. Holding Véronique was like clasping a rare and exquisite bird; he was almost afraid to hold her too tightly. He could scarcely believe that they would spend the rest of their lives together, could not even envisage Véronique grown old. Véronique, old . . . the idea was almost laughable.

Véronique saw the twitch of his lips and laid her finger against them.

'What is so funny, Paul?'

'Nothing,' he said tenderly, stroking her hair. 'But don't ever change, Véronique. Just stay as you are today, my sweet, lovely Véronique . . .'

The house in Montmartre became an oasis in the turmoil of the city. Each day brought fresh chaos. The stream of people entering the city seemed to be as great as that of people trying to get out. Most foreigners, including Britons, were leaving while they could. Every road was blocked by coaches piled high with furniture, clothing and treasured possessions, making for the country; at each of the exits from the city, the traffic was met by new herds of bewildered cattle, fresh flocks of panic-stricken sheep.

'There are soldiers everywhere now,' Véronique remarked one day. 'Every square is a parade ground, and every stranger a Prussian spy. You must take care, Paul, when you go out. You still have an accent in your speech – and not everyone will recognise it as English.'

And then, all at once it seemed, the Prussians were at the gates and the last few battles fought. Panic-stricken Zouaves, surprised and defeated by the well-ordered Germans, fled into the city and the last blockades went up. The first distant sound of cannon was heard in Paris, and people anxious for news gathered again on street corners. Their attitude at first was one of bravado: let them come, we've waited long enough! And then they saw the first wretched deserters stumbling in, soldiers who had fled before the Prussian advance and made for safety, and the truth began to dawn. The Germans were indeed stronger than they. They had driven France's proudest army into humiliation and defeat; and they were outside the walls now, waiting as patiently as a cat outside a mouse's burrow, to complete their bloody victory.

Paul, seeing the miserable soldiers spat upon, grasped by the arms and forced at rifle-point to march through the city, felt that the beginning of the end had come. The men before him – boys, many of them younger than himself – were the scapegoats of a nation. They were doomed to humiliation before their own countrymen, condemned to die the death of traitors. And yet, who was there amongst the jeering crowd who could have done better?

Sick at heart, he turned away. The nightmare had only just begun.

# Chapter Fifteen

'So,' Jeremy said thoughtfully, 'your brother is caught in Paris. Well, well, well.'

Roger stretched his length out in Jeremy's chair and blew a lazy ring of cigar smoke towards the ceiling. He was elegant in pale grey twill trousers and a black jacket, his blue plush waistcoat fitted closely to his slender body. If his hair had been the colour of corn rather than sand, and his eyes a true blue rather than hazel, he could have passed for Jeremy himself, twenty years or so before.

'So it would seem,' he answered coolly. 'Tragic, isn't it?' And he caught his cousin's eye and grinned.

Jeremy laughed outright. 'Well, you never did expect him to come back. Wasn't there some talk about him and the pretty young wench old Thietry took in as his ward? You told me Emily was very purselipped about it all.'

'She never wanted him to stay in the first place,' Roger observed. 'Wanted him quietly at home, where she could keep him under her thumb. It's a good thing she's a girl, Jeremy, or she'd have been in that glasshouse taking charge before she was twenty, like Mother herself.'

'Unlikely, I think, while your mother's still alive. If Christina's anything like she was as a girl, she'd not countenance any master but herself in that glasshouse, other than your father, of course.'

'You're right. For all their talk about the rights of women, neither Mother nor Father would be willing to let Emily take over. Not that she'd want to anyway, especially now she's married.' Roger took the cigar from his mouth and flicked ash derisively into the fireplace. 'In any case, it would never come to that, would it? We'd see to that. You know, I really believe we're in sight of our goal at last.'

The two men regarded each other thoughtfully. Ever

since their first meeting, each had seen the other as a way of attaining his own goal. Jeremy had seen Roger as an instrument of gaining revenge on Joe and Christina for the events of over twenty years ago. And he had also seen a second chance of doing what he, his father and uncles had wanted so badly – merging Henzel Crystal, Christina's business, with Henzel Brothers.

It could be done. And Roger was as willing as he. From the first, he had harboured a barely concealed jealousy of Paul, an indignant grudge against the boy who had no legal claim to any part of the business, yet bore the Henzel name and through his skill had won approval and respect. Jeremy knew that in Roger's eyes, the business should be his, with Paul no more than an employee. Not only that, he badly wanted to outstrip anything that his father or mother had achieved; he wanted to prove to them that he was their rightful successor, the man who could take Henzel's into the future. And the idea of combining the two biggest glasshouses in the Black Country appealed more than anything else to a nature which always wanted to be top.

'Father and Mother are living in the past,' he said, over and over again. 'They don't realise that the day of the small family business is coming to an end. I tell you, Jeremy, in the future, only large concerns will survive. They'll devour the little man. And Henzel Crystal and Henzel Brothers are both little men, large and important though they may seem. Imagine if we were to combine – the resources we would have. We could afford to be so much more competitive – we could reduce our prices, take all the trade for ourselves.'

'Our competitors would be pushed out of business,' Jeremy said, his eyes gleaming. 'And then –'

'And then we could step in and buy them up too – at a low price. Within ten years, Jeremy, we could be the biggest glass manufacturer in the country – the biggest in the world.' He smiled. 'We might even move into France itself, and buy Thietry Cristal, if it still exists!'

He fell silent, thinking again of Paul. The siege of Paris

had been reported in all the newspapers. The city was completely barricaded in. No other country seemed disposed to come to France's aid – most, indeed, seemed to side positively with the Germans – and it looked as if the siege might last for many months. It was not difficult to imagine the growing hardships that would be suffered inside those impenetrable walls.

It seemed even less likely that Paul would ever return to Stourbridge. And that would leave Roger, as the only son, the natural and rightful heir to the glasshouse. He smiled. Who would have thought that such unlikely characters as Louis Napoleon and Bismarck would have come to his aid! Yet even that would not have availed him much if he had not been working steadily for the past two or three years to persuade his parents that he was a fitting successor. The ruby crystal that Ben had been working on was now the best to be had, and in full production; orders were coming in daily. The black, admittedly, had not enjoyed such success – the few pieces that had been made were now gathering dust somewhere in the showroom – but Roger still felt sure that there would be a place for it. Meanwhile, he was content to live his double life, enjoying himself at Oxford in all the ways that Jeremy had shown him, and returning to Stourbridge to act the part of dutiful and industrious son . . . Yes, life was working out well for Roger at present, and with Paul trapped in Paris seemed set fair to continue to do so.

Emily too was thinking of Paul and imagining what might be happening to him. With each meal she sat down to, she wondered what he was eating that day. It was like the days of the lock-out all over again; she remembered how she had smuggled food into her handkerchief to give to the families of men who had no wage. But now people were locked in, thousands of them, and there was no way of smuggling food to their tables. How much would a city the size of Paris have in reserve? How would it feed the thousands who had streamed into the city, the soldiers and sailors who had been directed there? And what would happen when that food began to run out?

'It won't last that long,' Stephen declared. 'Even the Prussians won't let a whole city of innocent people starve. It would be inhuman.'

'But war *is* inhuman.' Emily paced the room in a torment of frustrated anxiety. 'And it's always the innocent who suffer. What do the men who order these things care for ordinary people? They sit in their palaces and move us about like pawns on a chessboard – this army to come here, that one to go there. What do the soldiers in France, or even Prussia, care who sits on the Spanish throne? What do the people in the villages and towns, the people in Paris, care? All they want is to live their ordinary lives, just as we do. But they're not allowed to, are they? They have to fight, or be overrun, or starve. And the men who ought really to be doing the fighting, Napoleon and Bismarck and the rest of them, they simply sit comfortably at home and laugh at us all.'

'That's not quite fair,' Stephen said. 'Bismarck goes to battle, and so did Napoleon.'

'But did either of them fight?' Emily demanded. 'Was either of them wounded? No – they paid others to do that work for them. And paid them poorly, too,' she added bitterly. 'Have *you* ever seen a rich soldier? And the people whose only crime is to live in the places these madmen choose for their battleground – what compensation do they get? Nothing but a ruined home, and death or injury into the bargain. And Paul – our Paul – is there, and there's nothing we can do to help him.'

Stephen looked at her for a moment. When he spoke again, his voice held a trace of coolness.

'I imagine Paul can look after himself. After all, he has done so for – how long is it now?'

'Three years,' Emily said tonelessly.

'Quite. So it is not as if he were a stranger there. Not as if he did not stay from his own choice.'

Emily flinched. She turned her head away quickly, but knew that he had seen the change in her expression. His voice was colder still as he said: 'I think you must learn to accept, my dear, that Paul is likely to spend the rest of his life in France. He clearly likes it there. And when this present business is over . . . didn't you say there is a young woman there, someone he seemed interested in?'

'Véronique, yes. But that may have changed – nothing has been said, and he's been there so long –'

'She *is* very young, though. I imagine he's simply waiting . . . In any case, it is hardly any concern of yours, Emily. Paul has chosen his own course and must be allowed to follow it. And you have far too much to do yourself to worry about him. Are the account books ready?'

'Yes.' Emily went to the rolltopped bureau and took out a small pile of household ledgers. This was a regular procedure every Friday night, when she and Stephen went through the weekly expenditure together. Or rather when Stephen went through it and Emily stood at his side, ready to answer queries and offer explanations.

And there were always some to be offered. Stephen was not mean – he gave her sufficient money each week to pay all the bills – but he expected every penny to be accounted for. And if Emily had spent money on a new ribbon, something extra special for a meal, or some small gift for her grandmother or Florrie's baby, she found herself having to justify it. 'My old ribbon had begun to fray . . . I thought your father would enjoy the fish . . . It was little Frank's birthday, and he did so love the top . . .'

'All the same, we cannot afford to be constantly spending money on extras,' Stephen told her. 'I know you have never had to do the housekeeping before, Emily, but you are quite intelligent enough to learn. Next time you want to buy something extra, come to me and we'll decide together whether it's really needed and whether we can afford it.' His tone was reasonable enough, but Emily knew that it could mask a cold anger; if she did not obey him, the anger would come to the surface.

She knew, too, that as her husband Stephen had every right to expect her to account for the way his money was spent. And it was *his* money; now that she was married, she no longer owned a thing. But she had never been accustomed to hearing Christina taken to task over money or accounts. Joe had always trusted her.

Stephen was not, however, like Joe.

She had begun to realise that on their wedding night.

Even now, the memory of that night could still bring a flush of humiliation to her cheeks. And she had approached it with such eagerness! Such happiness in the thought that at last she was to know the married love that Christina had said was so precious, the union of two bodies that the Church held so sacred.

But it seemed that Stephen had never seen it that way at all. He had been shocked by Emily's first tentative approach. He had called her . . . Even now, she did not like to remember it.

She still did not understand why he had not made the first advance. Why he had lain there in the big bed, stiff and silent at her side. Until then, everything had appeared normal – their return home to the house beside the chapel, where a supper had been left for them to eat alone in the parlour, the shy awkwardness that had gripped them afterwards until Emily finally gathered her courage together and said she was going upstairs; her hasty wash in the bedroom, trying unsuccessfully to keep her eyes averted from the bed itself. Stephen's tread on the stairs half an hour later when she was beginning to wonder if he had fallen asleep by the fire; his eyes avoiding hers as he undressed in the shadows, the movement of the mattress as he climbed in beside her at last.

And then – nothing. Not even a whispered goodnight. Just his body lying, carefully not touching hers, only inches away; rigid.

At last she turned towards him. Her heart was beating rapidly. She stretched out a timid hand, touched his body, felt him flinch and quiver. It was shyness, nothing else. Stephen was a clean-living man, a minister. He had never had any contact with women. He was as virginal as she.

'Stephen,' she whispered, and moved closer, feeling

340

the chill of his body against hers. 'Stephen, you're cold
. . . Come close.'

She had no doubt that he wanted her. The memory was
still clear of that day when he had caught her against him,
kissed her with such passion, torn himself away in an
agony of shame. Was he remembering it too? Was that
why he made no move now?

She wrapped her arms around him, felt the leap of her
own heart as their bodies pressed together, only the fabric
of their nightclothes forming a thin barrier between
them. Instinctively, she moved against him, feeling her
breasts swell, the nipples harden. The restraints of the
past months quickened her responses and she moaned a
little, letting her mouth move over his neck as she sought
his mouth. 'Stephen, Stephen . . .' She held herself close
and one hand moved almost involuntarily over his body.

Stephen gave a sudden deep groan and turned in her
arms. He gripped her body between his hands, his fingers
hard on her flesh, and his mouth met hers in a kiss that
was as savage as it was unexpected. Emily responded with
joy, but then he tore his mouth away and, wrenching at
the neck of her nightgown, laid bare her breast. He bent
his head and sank his teeth in its softness. Emily cried out
with shock and pain, and he lifted himself above her in the
bed and looked down at her. In the dim, guttering light of
the candle, she could see his face, distorted, his eyes burning and glittering. For a moment, he stared down at her;
and then he began his relentless assault again.

She could only be thankful that it was soon over.
Stephen was quickly roused and as quickly satisfied. He
had dragged up her nightgown and forced her legs apart;
there were a few moments of struggle, when Emily was
convinced that it was impossible, and then he thrust himself brutally inside her. She was conscious of a sharp,
tearing pain, and then a series of agonising jabs, which
she thought would never end. At last, after a final thrust,
he collapsed on top of her and it was done.

Emily waited, afraid to move, afraid to speak,
enduring his weight on her body, aware of the pain of his

entry, of the wetness between her legs. When he finally moved away from her, she could barely move. She felt stiff and bruised. Her breasts stung, her arms and legs throbbed and there were tears on her face that she had no memory of shedding.

So this was the married love that Christina held so precious. So this was what the Church considered a sacrament.

Even worse than Stephen's lovemaking was the aftermath.

That first night, as he moved away from her, she had caught his eyes on her again, the expression in them unreadable. Still uncertain, thinking that perhaps she had done something wrong, that it was her fault it had been so painful, so frightening, she reached out a hand and touched his face. Perhaps he would give her comfort, tell her it would be better next time. Christina had warned her that the first time might be painful . . .

But Stephen jerked his head away from her hand. His eyes darkened with contempt. And as Emily stared unbelievingly at him, he spat his words at her as if she had just done him an injury.

'So it's true! Like mother, like daughter. I hoped it might not be so, Emily, I gave you the benefit of the doubt – took you on trust. But blood will always out, won't it? You're as big a whore as your mother was!'

Emily stared at him, appalled. 'Stephen, what are you saying? How can you –'

'Oh, don't play the innocent!' he rasped. 'No maiden would behave so on her wedding night. Touching me, pressing your body against me . . . How else would you have learned such tricks, hey?' He gripped her shoulders and shook her. 'Tell me! Tell me the truth – tell me who he was!'

She shook her head, the tears falling on the pillow. 'Stephen, it's not true. I've never – I promise you, I have never known another man. Look – on the sheet – there should be proof.' Thank God Christina had told her so

342

much. She drew back the bedclothes and they gazed together at the stains. 'Please, Stephen, please believe me!'

He stared at the blood and then looked at her bruised and bitten body. A change came over his face. He closed his eyes tightly, as if in pain. His hands touched her shoulders again, but gently this time, and he laid his head on her breast. His shoulders trembled and to her astonishment she felt the wetness of his tears on her skin.

'Stephen . . .' she whispered, and he lifted his face.

'Emily, my love. How could I treat you so? How could I behave with such – such brutishness?' His voice was agonised. 'My God, what are we but animals after all . . .?'

Emily listened in horror as he went on, crying, castigating himself, his God and all mankind for the curse that had been laid on them. 'Debasing . . . Why women, the most delicate of creatures, should be forced to tolerate such depravities . . .' He shook his head and raised his head at last to stare at her with wild eyes. 'Emily, my love, can you ever forgive me?'

She gazed at him, unable to speak. His face was distorted, unrecognisable. Where had her Stephen gone, the gentle, kind, caring man she had agreed to marry? Where was the minister who listened so patiently to the troubles of his feckless parishioners? How had he turned into this wreck of remorse? And where was the happiness of physical union which she had expected, and desired?

Perhaps it's my fault, she thought with sudden dismay. My fault because I married him knowing that I didn't really love him – that my heart is still with Paul . . .

But Stephen must never know that. Somehow, she had to make him see that what he had done was not sinful – even though her body still ached from his assault. Somehow, she had to destroy the shame before it destroyed him.

'Stephen, please . . . It shouldn't be like that. We shouldn't feel guilty afterwards, we should feel happy, contented.' She sought for words to express what she knew instinctively, what Christina had tried to explain to her. 'Love between husband and wife ought to be a pleasure – a joyous thing.' Timidly, she touched him. 'Stephen, stop thinking of it as a curse . . . think of it as a blessing.'

His eyes seemed almost to retreat into his head. He looked coldly down at her hand, and then roughly he brushed it away.

After that, the pattern was always the same. The slow arousal, taking several days as Stephen visibly fought the desire he was so ashamed of. The final succumbing, degrading to them both. And the remorse that was even more degrading, mixed with the anger that he directed at Emily because he could not resist her. Because she made him lose control.

And she was coming to understand that control meant more to Stephen than almost anything else. That was why he so rarely, in his daily life, lost his temper.

Autumn drew slowly into winter, a winter as bitterly cold as the summer had been hot. Emily and Stephen reopened the soup kitchen. They were busier than ever now, for the new school had been enlarged and Emily was there each afternoon, helping with the teaching. She was also working tirelessly for an improvement in sanitation and had extracted promises from several of the local councillors to help. And she still kept up her visits to anyone who might need help, whether it be a birth, a death or sudden illness. And Stephen was equally indefatigable. It was known in the Lye that you could call on the young minister and Mrs Em at any time, day or night, and they would come at once.

But all the time, at the back of her mind, waiting for any opportunity to come to the fore, Emily carried the thought of Paul. How was he faring in the besieged city? Was he keeping warm – was there enough fuel? Was he eating enough – as the weeks dragged past, they heard horrific tales of domestic pets and zoo animals being eaten, even rats caught from the streets and stewed. Emily served soup to the hungry people of the Lye and wished with every spoonful that she could be serving it to Paul.

'They're sending balloons out,' she told Stephen one day. 'They're taking letters to be sent anywhere in the world, just like the ordinary post. We may soon hear if he is well.'

She went to the window, staring out at the bleak landscape. There was a drift of snow mingling with the sooty fog that hung like an old, tattered blanket in the air. The trees and bushes that grew on the hill were bare and shrivelled, standing humped and miserable like old men with nowhere to go.

'I pray that he is well,' she said in a low voice.

Stephen came to stand by her side and she glanced up at him and saw with dismay that his eyes had the peculiarly intent look that she had come to dread. Again – and so soon? It was only a few nights . . . the bruises were not yet faded. But she knew she would not refuse him; he had reminded her once of the vows that she had made, and she had not dared to protest again.

She had noticed that speaking of Paul seemed to have an effect on him. As if he had divined her secret thoughts; as if he were jealous. As if he needed to prove himself to the other man, even though Paul was far away in Paris, even though he did not care for Emily himself.

'We'll go to bed early tonight, my love,' Stephen said quietly, and Emily bowed her head. But her heart cried out against him. Oh Paul, Paul, where are you? Why could it not have been you?

She could not, of course, prevent herself from mentioning Paul's name again. And a week or two later, looking out of the window at the surly sky, she heard herself remark unhappily: 'This dreadful, bitter winter . . . What must it be like in Paris?'

Stephen was silent for a moment. Then he said carefully: 'I imagine it is not very easy.'

'Not very easy!' Emily turned on him. 'Stephen, have

you any idea what they're going through there? Mamma had a letter from Paul only this morning – by the balloon post, if you please. In this day and age, with modern transport and communications – trains, the telegraph, an efficient postal service all over the world – one of the most advanced cities in the civilised world must descend to using balloons and pigeons. The very same kind of pigeons that the men of the Lye race at weekends!' She paced about the small room, her eyes glimmering with anger. 'Of course, being the French, they miss no opportunity for making money, even out of each other. The letter bears a stamp, properly franked, and Paul tells us that each balloon makes a handsome profit in postage alone, even though it can never be used again. The pigeons, of course, may be used as many times as is feasible.'

'I think it all sounds very ingenious,' Stephen said mildly. 'And is Paul well?'

'He says so. Madame Thietry has unfortunately died and old Monsieur Thietry is growing frail, but that's understandable. But what life is like!' Her eyes filled with tears. 'Stephen, they're starving! Those stories we heard a few weeks ago – they were true. They've been reduced to eating cats and dogs and animals from the zoo! Everything that walks, flies or swims – they're all being killed and sold for meat.' She sank down in a chair and rested her elbows on the table. 'Can you imagine what it must be like? Even here, in the Lye, people have never been reduced to eating *rats*. And Paul – my Paul –' She laid her head on her arms and wept.

'*Your* Paul?' Stephen's voice was cool; too cool. Emily bit her lip, knowing what would follow. The jealousy, the lust that must be satisfied, the bruises, the remorse. If only Stephen could be made to see that love was no matter for shame, that it could be beautiful . . . In spite of her experiences, her bitter unhappiness, Emily still tried to believe that what Christina had told her was true. It *could* be enjoyed. It *could* be precious. If only he would allow himself to believe it too . . . But her attempts to explain this only made matters worse. To Stephen, no lady would ever admit to such feelings. No lady could ever enjoy such a degrading process. Only whores . . .

'Your Paul,' he repeated thoughtfully. 'That really is how you think of him still, isn't it? In spite of the fact that you haven't seen him for three years. In spite of the fact that you're a married woman. In spite of the fact that he is your *brother*.' His lips curled. 'You disgust me! You're shameless, unfit to consort with even the lowest gipsy of the Lye.' His eyes were dark and wild, his fingers cruel on her shoulder. 'You deserve to be punished – and I shall see that you are. You must be made to see the error of your ways – made to understand the depths of the depravity to which you have sunk – to which you have dragged me!' He was pulling her towards the stairs and Emily, terrified by the feverish gleam in his eye, the note of fanaticism in his voice, tried to draw back, begging him to let her go, to resist, to remember how unhappy he would feel afterwards . . .

'Unhappy?' he cried. 'Ashamed? Why should I be ashamed, when I am carrying out the will of the Lord? At last it's all made clear to me – at last I can see the reason – it's a punishment; a punishment for the day when woman caused the Fall. It's the curse of Eve, laid on men to remind women of that day in Eden . . .' He was ranting now, his voice loud and hectoring as if he were addressing a congregation, and he dragged Emily up the stairs as if she were a sack of coal. 'Ashamed? I am *proud* . . .'

Emily, helpless against his strength, felt herself flung on the bed and knew that Stephen was now beyond reason. He had persuaded himself that what he did to her was justified because it was God's punishment. For the first time, as she lay beneath him and tried to will her mind, if not her body, somewhere else, she faced the fact that he was mad.

Mad. And Paul, the man she loved, the man who would have handled her with gentleness and care, was far away in a beleaguered city. And might never escape.

# Chapter Sixteen

Within two days of the final investment of Paris, Paul saw a new spirit rising among the people. It was as if they were happier in a state of positive adversity than in the uncertainty that had preceded it. Now, they seemed to say, we have a job to do; let us roll up our sleeves and get down to it.

'Blockade!' Pierre snorted as he cleaned the fireplace. 'Huh! Who do those Prussians think they are, *hein*? They will not keep Paris under lock and key, I can tell you that. Already we are sending dispatches out. They may be well trained and disciplined to the last inch, but they have reckoned without the brain of the Frenchman.'

'What do you mean?' Paul looked up from the book in which he had begun to keep a diary. Possibly nobody would ever read it, but he had grown accustomed to writing letters and missed the exercise of putting his thoughts and his experiences down on paper. 'How are dispatches being sent out? Surely the Prussians won't allow –'

Pierre sat back on his heels, his peasant's face creased with satisfaction. 'Allow! They have no choice, I tell you.' He held up a broad hand, counting off on the stubby fingers. 'For one thing, there is the *boule de Moulin* – it looks like a bomb which is thrown into the Seine and allowed to float downstream. Naturally the Prussians will be afraid to touch it, thinking it to be filled with explosives, but in fact it will be stuffed full of letters. Letters that anyone can send. You, I, anyone with the price of a stamp. And before they reach the sea, some good Frenchman will retrieve them from the water and post the letters for us *et voilà!*' He chuckled and bent to rake out the ashes of last night's fire. 'But even better, of course, are the balloons.'

'The balloons?' Paul felt his heart quicken. 'You mean

the balloons that were flown at the Exhibition? Nadar's balloons?'

'But certainly. Already the *Céleste* herself has been taken out of storage, and the *Neptune*. No doubt they will both need to be renovated, but what is that? Within days – hours, perhaps – we shall see them flying proudly out of Paris, over the heads of the helpless Prussians who will be able to do nothing to prevent them.' Pierre laughed. 'Oh yes, I tell you, they have reckoned without the brain of the Frenchman.'

Paul glanced involuntarily towards the window, half expecting to see the great coloured sphere of the *Céleste* go floating past before his eyes. There was nothing, of course, only a scurry of white clouds high in the soft blue of the September sky. But Pierre's words had stirred him; he could sit still no longer. Hastily, he blotted his page and thrust it aside, and within minutes he had snatched up a jacket and a hat and swung eagerly out into the sunshine and shadows of the hilly streets.

'The balloons,' he asked everyone he met along the way, 'have you heard about the balloons? Is it true they are using them for dispatches? Where can I find out about the balloons?' He felt curiously excited, almost light-headed, as if somehow the city had returned to the carnival atmosphere of the Exhibition. He thought of the summer he had spent here then, his first weeks in Paris with Emily at his side and his mother and Joe behind them. How he had longed to make a flight in one of those balloons! But Véronique had been little more than a child then, and emphatically determined never to leave the ground. And although Emily's dark eyes had reflected his own excitement, pleading with him to take her, he had ignored their message. It had been Véronique he wanted at his side . . .

But there was no question of either he or Véronique flying in a balloon now. The balloons would, if they flew at all, surely be retained for persons of importance; for dispatches to French generals somewhere out there in the country; for messages overseas. How fortunate, he

350

thought, that there were balloons already in Paris; how fortunate that there were pilots like Nadar, able to fly them.

'The balloons?' someone answered him at last, just when he was despairingly making up his mind that Pierre must have been mistaken. 'Why, yes, m'sieur. They have already tried to inflate the *Céleste* but the poor old lady, she is more like a sieve than a balloon. And two others have been tried also – *l'Impérial*, which is certainly far too old since it was constructed at least twelve years ago in order to be used as an observatory over the war in Italy, and *l'Union*, which is only three years old but equally useless.' The man spoke rapidly, eager to impart his knowledge. He sighed, shook his head and added, 'It has been badly looked after, or perhaps the varnishing was poor, I do not know, but neither of these balloons could be inflated.'

'And are those the only balloons in Paris?' Paul felt his heart sink, his excitement dwindle. 'Are there none at all that are fit to fly?'

'I have told you, the *Neptune* is to go this afternoon, and let us hope she has better luck. As for other balloons, I know nothing.' He spread his hands. 'But they say the government has already signed a contract with Nadar himself to build a whole flight of balloons. Somehow, communication must be made with the defence delegation at Tours, and what other way can one devise?'

To Paul's chagrin, his informant, who seemed to know so much, could not tell him from where the *Neptune* would fly. Frustrated, he wandered aimlessly about the streets, craning his neck and making for all the highest parts of the city in the hope of finding the launching place. But he saw nothing until it was too late; and then his heart was cheered when, as he turned into the last street before reaching his grandfather's house, he lifted his eyes and saw the great globe wafting past overhead, followed by the cheers of all who watched. He stopped dead and stared upwards, longing as he had never longed before to be in that fragile basket, drifting

351

through the sharpening air of autumn. What must it be like to be up there, floating high above Paris, looking down on the city? He thought of the squares and gardens, filled with soldiers, the rows of huts and tents that had been pitched under the trees and in the open spaces. As he watched, the sphere drifted further away; now it must be over the fortifications, now approaching the Prussian lines. A sudden burst of gunfire announced its arrival in the enemy's sights and his heart kicked as he imagined the bullets piercing that thin skin, igniting the coal-gas within. The whole thing would become a ball of fire within seconds . . . He shuddered and closed his eyes, then opened them again. The balloon was still in sight, a tiny speck of colour now in the distant sky, and the gunfire had become sporadic.

'I mean to find out where the balloons are being constructed,' Paul said that evening as he and his grandfather and Véronique sat at supper. 'Perhaps I could help in some way. I feel useless here. There must be something I can do.'

'You are help enough here,' Marc said. He roused himself to speak only rarely now. His silvery eyes rested on his grandson with a dullness that caught at Paul's throat. 'Véronique and I need you. And there is the business, the showroom . . .'

'*Gran'père*, nobody is coming to the showroom now,' Paul said gently. 'Nobody is buying glass. And even when all this is over, we will still have to build up our reserves again. I cannot sit idly here while others are working. I must do something. And the balloons interest me.'

'You will not fly in one?' Véronique asked suddenly, and he saw that her eyes were wide with fear. 'Promise me, Paul, that you will not fly in one.'

He smiled gently. 'I promise that as long as you are in Paris I will not fly in any balloon. But that need not stop me helping to construct them, if my help is accepted.' His eyes gazed tenderly into Véronique's. Since the night of Cécile's funeral, there had been a strange, calm contentment between them. He no longer felt an urgency in their love; it was as if the acknowledgement of it were enough, a jewelled gift to be treasured in secret and not yet worn for all to see.

Even the story of his affair with Annette, confessed before the fire while they listened to the dull thump of the bombardments sounding from the city walls, had not tarnished their love. It was not so much after all, Véronique had declared with that French realism to which Paul had never quite grown accustomed. Did not all young men take mistresses? It was quite natural, before marriage.

'But with Annette?' Paul said wretchedly, and she gave him a smile that was half rueful, half understanding.

'My *Tante* Annette is a certain kind of woman . . . I have known it for a long time. And you, my Paul, so English, so far from home . . . I am glad you told me, *chéri*, and now let us forget it, *oui*?'

The balloons were being made, he discovered, in the railway stations. Only there, in the great silent vaults that covered platforms and rails, was there room for the new monsters to be built, for before they could be trusted to the air they must be partially inflated where there was no wind and no danger of their breaking loose from their moorings. Paul made his way at once to the Gare du Nord and offered his services. He was put in the charge of a thin Frenchman with blinking eyes behind small round spectacles. His name, he said, was Georges, and he took Paul around the great echoing cavern that had only days ago been filled with the steam and the bustle of a railway station and explained what was happening.

'The balloons are made from taffeta mostly, the kind that is used for ladies' dresses,' he began in the flat, toneless voice which he employed for every word he ever uttered. 'That is why they are such bright, gaudy colours, of course; only a showman like Nadar would make his balloons as colourful as the old *Céleste*, and even he would never have employed such bright fabrics for balloons that were intended for military use.' He glanced with disfavour at the brilliant reds and greens and yellows of the balloons, their gores in sharp contrast with each other as each new bale of taffeta was used. But although Paul could appreciate the advantage of a balloon that was dully coloured, to match the clouds, or perhaps the blue of the sky to avoid detection from below, he could not help feeling that balloons ought, by their very nature, to be as bright and gay as flowers, a happy flaunting of themselves as they floated overhead. He kept these sentiments to himself, however. Georges, he suspected, would be unlikely to share them, even if he understood.

'But how is the coal-gas kept inside?' he asked. 'Surely it would escape through the fibres of the taffeta.'

'No, because the balloons are varnished with flax-oil. They must also be netted with a cord of tarred hemp, as you see there, and equipped with a basket to hold four people and all the essential apparatus – the safety valves, the anchor, sacks of ballast and so on.'

Paul moved closer to a balloon that was being inflated, watching with fascination as a long canvas tube was fastened to the valve in the circular oak hatch at its mouth. The tube led directly to the main gas pipe in the station, Georges told him. All gas supplies from now on would be conserved for the balloons; there would be no more in the streets for lighting, nor in homes for cooking and heating. Everyone would have to use oil or wood, as they had done before gas had been laid on. *'C'est la guerre.'*

The balloon lay like a discarded ballgown on the platform, its colours shimmering under the flickering lights. The men inflating it made certain that all was in position and safe for the inflating. A signal was given to the man who stood by the main, and as the gas was turned on, Paul heard the hiss as it began to flow.

For a few moments nothing happened. Then there was a trembling of colour, little more than a glancing change in the shades of light. A movement rippled along the

shining fabric; a bulge appeared, vanished, reappeared
further along, as if some small animal were inside,
running frantically to and fro in an effort to escape. The
bulge grew bigger, swelled, burgeoning like the stomach
of a pregnant woman. Other bulges appeared; the fabric
between them shuddered and then lifted so that they
joined together in one large dilation. The brilliant stripes
of taffeta glowed incongruously in the shadowy vaults of
the station. The balloon began to rise from the platform
like a vast dowager on her way to a ball, and Paul
stepped back. He craned his neck, staring upwards as the
great pear-shaped balloon tugged gently at its moorings
and trembled slightly in the draught.

'Magnificent!' he murmured, awed.

Georges shrugged. 'Yes, I think it will pass. There is
four thousand francs' worth of balloon there, you know,
so it must fulfil all the conditions.'

'But who pays for the balloons?' Paul asked. 'Who is
in charge of all this?'

Georges looked at him in mild astonishment. 'Why,
the *Directeur du Poste*, of course, who else? The balloons are to carry mail, *non*? You buy stamps to send
your letters by them. Then who else should pay?' His lips
moved slightly in the nearest semblance to a smile that
Paul had seen. 'The money will not be paid until the
balloon has proved itself, you understand. Only when
the balloon has risen and is out of sight will the money be
handed over. Four thousand francs,' he repeated, 'and
of that five hundred is for gas and the pilot. It is a good
enough price.'

Paul followed him round the rest of the factory, so
quickly transformed from a railway station. The engines
were still there, some inside and some in the yard, their
lamps used for lighting. He marvelled at the organisa-
tion, the hardheaded practicality which could have
arranged all this with such rapidity. Why had the army
been so unprepared, when this balloon factory could be
set up with such ease? He thought of something else and
turned to Georges.

'This is all very well for getting dispatches out of Paris. But what about getting them back in? Isn't that just as important? Is anyone outside going to attempt to fly balloons back? Surely the winds aren't that reliable.'

'Indeed not, though I have no doubt it will be tried. But we have a better way.' The little spectacles gleamed. 'Many Parisians keep pigeons. They take them out of the city and release them to fly back home. The pigeon can carry –'

'Messages! Of course they can! And they'll be back in no more time than it takes the balloon to fly out.' Paul's face glowed with excitement. 'But how much can one pigeon carry? The messages will have to be very short.'

Georges smiled again. 'This would be true – but we have another trick or two up our sleeves yet, my friend. Have you not heard of *microfilme*?'

Paul shook his head. The word was new to him; he could not imagine what it meant.

Patiently, Georges explained. The art of microphotography had been invented by a Frenchman, here in Paris itself. He had perfected it to such a degree that a whole page of a newspaper – such as, for instance, *Le Figaro* or the English *Times* – could be photographed and then reduced so that its size was no more than a few centimetres in each dimension. These minute dispatches could then be fastened to the pigeon's legs in the ordinary way and sent back into Paris, where the same man had built a special lantern which would enlarge the photographs and display them on a screen where they could be read. 'It is ingenious, *n'est-ce pas*?' he finished proudly, and Paul could only nod his head.

'Naturally,' Georges added, 'he will be one of the first to leave Paris once we have the new balloons ready. Or who out there would know what to do?'

Paul looked at the little Frenchman. His eyes gleamed behind the round spectacles and although his voice was as flat and emotionless as ever, it was clear that inside he was as excited as any of those who had rampaged through the boulevards only three weeks ago, chanting for the fall of the Empire. Indeed, he had very possibly been one of those men, transformed perhaps by the moment, his spectacles flashing in the sunlight, his flat little voice raised in a scream of passion. Whatever he did, he would do as wholeheartedly as any other Frenchman. And now his business was building balloons.

'What do you do normally?' Paul asked. 'What is your trade?'

'Me? I am nothing. A sleeve-setter in a tailor's workroom, that is all. But I know about fabrics, you see, I know how to cut and how to sew. That is why I am here.' He moved on, demonstrating the quality of the taffetas that were being used. 'There will be no fine gowns for the ladies in Paris this winter, I fear! They will have to become accustomed to seeing the season's colours floating out of reach above their heads. I do not know what the great couturiers like Monsieur Worth will do, I am sure.'

'Well, what does it matter?' asked a man who stood nearby, applying varnish to a mass of scarlet material lying like a vast pool of blood across the platform. 'He is English, after all. What right does he have to come here and tell our women what to wear?'

'Only the right the ladies themselves give him,' Georges answered. 'They desire his creations . . . But we are not here to chatter. Jules, this is Paul Thietry. He has come to work here and I want you to take charge of him. He is to work with your team.'

'With us?' Jules was thin and dark; he looked at Paul with suspicious eyes. 'And have you any experience in this type of work, m'sieur?'

'None at all,' Paul said, 'but I'm willing to learn.'

The eyes narrowed further. 'You are not French, *hein*? But you have a French name.'

'My mother was English.' He felt a curious sense of betrayal as he said this, as if he were implying that she was the less important of his parents, almost as if she were dead. Jules stared at him for a moment, then turned away. He spoke from the corner of his mouth, giving Paul curt commands as to what he was expected to do. Clearly, he resented having a man who was half English in his team. And Paul, picking up a brush and beginning to follow his lead in applying the varnish to the silky red material, wondered for the first time if he had done right in coming here.

'So that is the end,' Marie declared, coming into the kitchen and throwing her basket down on the table. 'The meat ration is now down to an ounce and a half a day. That rumour of who knows how many thousands of cattle being brought into the city is nothing more than that – a rumour. Soon we shall be eating the horses.'

They were gathered in the big, gloomy kitchen under the house. It had been decided as soon as the weather turned cold that protocol would be forgotten; fuel would soon become short and it was only sensible to conserve as much as possible. So some of the more comfortable furniture was brought down and evenings were spent before the kitchen range and around the big scrubbed table.

'Where is Véronique?' Marc asked fretfully. 'The child is never here. You should be caring for her, Paul – she is allowed to run the streets until all hours, I cannot imagine what my dear Cécile would have said about it.'

'She is working, *Gran'père*. You know that.'

'Working?' The old eyes looked bewildered. 'Véronique, working?'

'As a nurse, helping to tend the soldiers wounded on the fortifications.' Paul answered with a mixture of reluctance and pride; he did not, any more than his grandfather, like the idea of Véronique making the dangerous journey to the outskirts of Paris, where the bombardments were at their worst, to attend to the needs of soldiers. But she had been determined to help and had volunteered at once. 'I want to be useful too,' she declared. 'You are working in the balloon factory, Paul. Why should I not occupy myself as well? And I shall be a good nurse, this I know.'

'She will be home soon,' he remarked now, and at that very moment they heard Véronique come in and clatter down the basement stairs. She pushed the door open and flew in, her hair streaming behind her like the bright tail of a comet, her eyes alight in her glowing face.

'Véronique – child –' Marc began, but she interrupted, her voice high and excited.

'Come outside, everyone, come and see. Such a sight! I have never seen anything like it, never – you must come, quickly, before it disappears.' She grabbed Paul's hand and reached for Marc's. 'Please, *mon oncle*, come at once.'

'But what is it? What has happened?' The old man began painfully to struggle from his chair and Marie threw down her knife and pressed her hand to her heart. 'The Prussians – they have given in, abandoned the siege! Is it that?'

'No, it's not that. They're as active as ever out there. But please come, you must see.' Almost in a frenzy, she urged them all towards the stairs that led out of the basement to the door. 'Look! Look at the sky.'

The old man, the servant woman and Paul stepped out on to the footpath and stared upwards. Beside him, Paul heard Marie gasp; he felt her clutch tremblingly at his arm and, on his other side, he found the shaking hand of his grandfather seeking his.

The sky was filled with a fiery glow of colour; a jewelled canopy, the brilliant reds and golds of rubies and topaz streaked with the green of emeralds, the blue of sapphires and the shimmering white light of diamonds. There was no sound, no echoing thunder or roar of cannon, no explosion to accompany this burst of light and colour that spread over the city. And the light was not still; it moved, slowly, unceasingly, changing constantly like the colours in a child's toy kaleidoscope. The blue merged with the red to form a vibrant, tremulous colour, the red shaded into gold to become the glowing orange of a furnace at full heat. The movement was gradual but continuous, a steady shifting that was almost imperceptible, yet transformed the sky and brought a different scene with every moment.

'What is it?' Marie breathed. 'Mother of God, what can it mean? Is the whole of France in flames out there?'

'I've heard of such a spectacle,' Paul murmured, his voice awed. 'They call it the Northern Lights, or the Aurora Borealis. They see it in the furthest islands of Scotland, but I had no idea it could be seen from Paris.'

'We thought at first it was a fire,' Véronique said, 'but it was soon realised that it must be something else. Something natural. Look – people are going to the top of Montmartre to see better. May we go, *mon oncle*?'

'You may, if Paul will take you,' Marc said. 'Marie and I will stay here. I am too old to climb hills just to look at the sky . . . I am glad to have seen it, however. It must be a good omen. It must mean that God is on our side.'

He turned back into the house and Véronique caught at Paul's hand. Her face glowed under the bright colours that played above them, her eyes sparkled like the stars that had been hidden by the brilliance. As she brushed back the pale curls that clustered about her small head, she looked again like the child Paul had first met close to this very spot, and he felt once again the thrill of delight that had accompanied that first glimpse of the fairylike creature that she had been.

'Shall we go to the top of the hill?' she asked, tugging at his hand. 'It must be a wonderful sight from up there! Come quickly, Paul, before it fades away. Or will it last all night? How long do these – what did you call them, Northern Lights? – go on? Will we see them again tomorrow? What causes them?'

They hurried up the hill, through streets now thronged with others who had been at first terrified and then awed by the manifestation, and were now as anxious as Véronique to see as much as could be seen. Paul racked his brains and did his best to answer Véronique's breathless questions, but found that he remembered only hazily the brief mention of the Aurora Borealis that his science masters had made at school.

Véronique, however, was not a demanding pupil. She seemed content with whatever he could tell her, and was most interested in the colours and the sheer, awesome beauty of the display, and her only concern was to find the best possible vantage point. 'After all, I may never see such a sight again.' Together, they passed the small bomb factory where only a few days before an explosion had killed one man and wounded three more; an occurrence that had become all too common during the past weeks. And at last, at the top of the hill, on the open space by the Solferino Tower, they joined a huge crowd of people, gazing out at a city burnished under a luminous radiance that only the heavens could display.

'I should like to be in a balloon tonight,' Paul breathed in Véronique's ear. 'Floating up there amidst all that colour. Can you imagine it, Véronique? Surely even you would venture up on a night like this . . .'

He felt her shiver against him. 'Me? But I would be terrified! This is beautiful, Paul, yes, but who knows what it is like up there amongst it all? The gases – one could not breathe –'

'But there aren't any gases! It's simply light – something that's happening thousands of miles away. Véronique –' He caught her by the shoulders and twisted her round to face him. 'This is a night for magic, don't you feel it? A night we shall remember all our lives.' He stared down into her moon-pale face, feeling the urgency of desire rise within his heart. 'Véronique, these are not ordinary times. The rules we have always lived by . . . they are changing. We must change with them. We belong to each other, you and I, and who knows what will happen next? The siege, the balloons, all this –' He flung his arms wide, encompassing everything that they had experienced together. 'Véronique – darling – let us make this night complete with our love.'

She stared at him, her eyes like midnight. 'Paul – what are you saying?'

The light was in his head, filling it with a blinding iridescence. 'I'm saying I want to love you, Véronique, here and now.' He pulled her against him, hungry for the touch of her skin against his. 'None of us knows what is going to happen to us. None of us knows what all this means. Grandfather called it an omen – but couldn't it as easily be an omen for the Prussians? They must be watching it too . . . Véronique, don't deny me this. Tell me you love me – tell me you'll be mine.'

Again her eyes searched his, half in rapture, half in doubt. Then she gave a little excited laugh and tugged at his hand. '*Oui*, Paul, *mon cher* – yes, I love you, I love you, and I'll be yours. Let's go home at once – we can slip into my room with nobody noticing and we'll leave the shutters back and the curtains drawn and the night will be ours, all the colour and brilliance of it for us to remember when we are old and have only memories . . . Come, quickly – there's no time to lose!' And with all the eager urgency with which they had come here, they now raced together back down the tumbled streets of the hill until they reached the Thietry house, where the garden was lit only by the shimmering radiance above and nothing but a single oil lamp burned in the dark and shuttered house.

Silently, Véronique slipped down to the kitchen and lit a candle from the stub that guttered in the middle of the big table. Marc, Pierre and Marie appeared all to have gone to bed; the house was quiet as she made her way back upstairs to where Paul waited breathlessly at her door.

'Come in, my darling.' She closed the door behind them and slipped the bolt across, turning to him and lifting the candlestick so that the flame lit her eyes with tiny stars and set a glow on the curve of her ivory cheek. 'Oh, Paul, Paul . . .'

He took the candle from her and set it on a small table. His arms slid round her and drew her close as he looked gravely down into her upturned face.

'You are sure about this, Véronique?'

She nodded. 'I am sure. It is the right time for us, Paul.'

Slowly, reverently, he began to undress her. She was

still wearing the plain, unadorned clothes she used for going to the ambulance; they slipped easily away from her body and within a few moments she stood naked before him, a slender wand in the shifting colour that still flooded into the room. He stepped back and worshipped with his eyes. He had been afraid that in this moment he would remember Annette, that the vision of those sultry nights would sully the virginal beauty of this girl. But it was Annette's image that suffered by comparison. Before him stood a woman who had never been touched, her stomach flat and her waist slender, the curve of her breasts sweet and firm. In the quivering light that fell on her like the jewelled colours of the windows of Notre Dame, she was ethereal and unreal. He knew that if it had been only lust he felt for her, as it was for Annette, he could never have touched her. But the emotion that filled his heart now was the rapture of love; a love as pure as if he too were a virgin and had never known a woman's touch before this night.

'Véronique . . .' he murmured huskily, and moved towards her.

But she held him off, and to his astonishment he heard her laugh; a soft laugh, as silvery as the note of a crystal bell. 'But no, Paul – not in your rough jacket, it would scratch me to pieces!' And, a little shamefacedly, he stripped off his own clothes and stood for her own frank inspection.

Only then did she hold out her arms, and he went to her as hesitantly as a boy, hardly daring to touch the slender limbs, the narrow waist and small, rounded buttocks. It was as if, in the strange, unearthly light, she had shed her worldliness and become insubstantial, a fragile trick of the light herself, liable to vanish at the slightest brush with human warmth.

But when the tips of his fingers rested at last on the silky skin, he found a warmth that came almost as a shock; a warmth and softness that told him she was indeed real. With a low, muttered cry, he gathered her against him, wondering at the perfection of her curves, the strength and passion in the arms that came around him and the urgency in the hands that moved sensuously over his back. All fears forgotten, he lifted her into his arms, looking down at the face that opened like a flower in the pouring light, and bent his lips to hers. And then, with a swift step across the room, he laid her on the bed and slid down beside her.

With infinite tenderness, he laid kisses on each of her eyelids, closing them over the questioning eyes. He held her head between his palms and kissed every particle of it, teasing the soft hair, breathing in the scent of fresh air and smoke and battle, for she had come straight from the field hospital and had had no time to wash before their headlong rush up the hill. But that was a part of this new Véronique, this bewildering mixture of fairy child and grown woman, of innocence and hard, bitter experience. A part that went with her sudden violence as his hands moved over her in gentle caress: 'No, no, not like that, Paul – like this, like this, like *this*!' And her own hands thrust with energy against him, her body twisted and strove beneath his and he understood that for Véronique at this moment tenderness was wrong; she needed a passion that would lift her from herself, exorcising the terrors which she saw each day by the fortifications, a rousing, soaring lovemaking that would raise her beyond the present.

And he wanted it too. With a joyous leap of his heart, he abandoned all restraint and lifted her against him, his lips and tongue seeking hers, his body stretched against the silk of her skin, searching and thrusting, his blood pounding, demanding release.

'Paul, Paul . . .' Her voice was no more than a thread but the message was unmistakable. She clung to him, her body arched to his, her palms flat against his back, fingers moving convulsively on his shoulders. He could feel the insistent writhing of her hips under his and knew that he could hold back no longer – knew that she did not want him to hold back at all. Her legs parted, twisted around his body, clasped him hard against her; and with a stifled groan, he thrust and thrust again. There was the faintest resistance; he felt Véronique jerk a little in his arms, recoil momentarily then return to him. And then he was there, moving firmly and smoothly in the rhythm that came as naturally as a heartbeat; the rhythm of life itself.

The relief lasted for no more than a few seconds. Then the urgency returned, with a violence that was almost frightening. Paul felt Véronique's trembling and held her hard against him, unable to stem the passion that surged like a tidal wave between them, compelled to give way to it, to abandon his body and hers to the wild storm that assailed them both, as helpless in its grip as they would have been in a raging sea that tossed them with careless power from wave to wave.

And then they were high on the crest of the giant wave, the peak of the mountain, the breast of the cascade. There was a moment's breathless pause, an eternity of blissful, agonising suspense . . . and then at last they lay sated in each other's arms, washed by the now muted lights of the silent sky; slowly returning from the world in which they had been to the world they had left, and found themselves wrapped together in a tumble of sheets, in Véronique's bed in the house on the hill of Montmartre; in a Paris that was besieged, where nobody knew what the future might bring.

A long time later, they revived. And this time Paul brought Véronique to him with a tender reverence that was in complete contrast with the violence of their first encounter. The enchantment died only with the coming of dawn, when they fell asleep at last, their arms still flung about each other, and a smile on their lips.

# Chapter Seventeen

Christmas that year was a sombre festival. Even Marie could not make a festive meal from the provisions available, although she tried; but nobody, remembering the antics of the little dog Funette, could relish their dinner, nor even make the standing joke of how she would have enjoyed the bones . . . 'There will soon be not an animal left in the city,' Marie said through her tears. 'Dogs and cats are fetching six francs a pound in the markets now, and rats fifty cents. And now they are talking of killing the animals in the zoos at the Jardin des Plantes and the Jardin d'Acclimatation. Mind you, it should have been done before, that. Those animals are no use and they are eating valuable feed which we could have been giving to our horses.'

'But will they be eaten too?' Véronique asked. 'The antelope, and the beautiful deer, and the tigers? Even the elephant, old Pollux, that we saw when we went there in the spring? Surely they won't kill him.'

'He eats more in a day than our poor Funette did in her whole life,' Marie declared, attacking the pudding she had made with dried fruit obtained during the earliest days of the siege. 'And an elephant is a big animal, m'selle, he will feed many hungry people.'

The Thietry showroom had closed for the duration. Paul did his best to keep track of the men who had worked there, the women who had cleaned; he made sure that they had sufficient money to buy food, that they could afford a doctor for their sick children. But he was too busy at the balloon factory to do more; and even there, he felt troubled and uneasy.

'I am sure they think I am a spy,' he told Véronique one evening as they shared a bowl of Marie's vegetable soup. 'It's the way they look at me. Even Georges has

367

become cautious, and Jules has never liked me. He is suspicious every time I send a letter home, yet why should I not? That's what the balloons are for.'

'He hates you because you are half English,' Véronique said wearily. 'There are many like him. Take no notice, Paul. He cannot hurt you.'

She leaned her head on her hands and shivered suddenly. Paul glanced at her in sudden concern. He leaned over the table and took her wrists in his hands.

'Véronique, what is it? Are you ill?'

'It's nothing – a headache, that's all. I'm tired – I'll go to bed.'

'You work too hard,' he said, watching as she got up stiffly from the table. 'I wish you would leave the hospital. It's too much for you.'

'It's too much for everyone,' Véronique said, but her face was pale, with a flush on it that disturbed him. 'Why should I be the one to stay away? It would only make more work for the rest.'

'All the same, you don't look well. Perhaps I should call the doctor.'

'The doctor? Nonsense – it's nothing, I tell you, a chill or something. I'll be better in the morning, after a good night's sleep.'

But she was not better in the morning. She came down to breakfast late, looking like a ghost, dragging herself down the stone steps into the kitchen and shaking her head wearily at Marie's offer of food. As she lifted the bowl of coffee to her lips, her hand shook and she spilled drops down the front of her dress. Paul stared at her in dismay and then looked quickly at Marie.

'Marie, she's ill! We can't let her go to the hospital like this. She needs a doctor herself.'

The stout Frenchwoman moved quickly from the fire and felt Véronique's forehead. 'It is burning! You are right, this is something more than a chill. Tell me, *ma petite*, have you any pain? A headache, yes? Anything else? Tell Marie.'

'I don't know – it hurts all over.' Véronique's teeth

were chattering and she shuddered against Marie's broad bosom. 'My back aches . . . I feel strange . . .' She turned her face into the comfort of the black, cushioned breast and a few tears trickled down her ashen cheek. 'Let me drink my coffee, Marie. I must go to the hospital.'

'You are going nowhere,' Paul said sternly. He stood up and took the thin frame in his arms, disturbed at the brittleness of the slender body. He had not held it like this since the night of the great lights, for they had both agreed that the magic of that night must stand alone. 'Marie, she must have been losing weight for weeks, there is almost nothing of her.'

'And is that so surprising, considering what we have been forced to eat?' the housekeeper demanded. 'Let me take her back to her bed, M'sieur Paul. I will look after her. You have your own work to go to.'

'I wish I could stay at home,' he said miserably, hesitating as Marie supported Véronique to the steps. 'But we are already behind with the new balloon, and if it is late there will be a fine of fifty francs a day . . . I'll be home as soon as possible tonight, Marie.' He looked at the shivering girl and felt his heart torn with the desire to stay with her. 'And I'll tell them I can't possibly go tomorrow, if she is no better.'

He worked like a maniac that day, determined that the balloon should be ready on time, stopping for nothing, speaking to no one. Several times he saw Jules watching him, but he ignored the suspicious Frenchman. Even when Georges came to offer him a drink, he refused to stop, and the eyes blinked behind the round spectacles as the little man went away. For a few seconds, Paul felt remorse for his rudeness; but then the picture of Véronique, shivering in Marie's arms, as thin and pale as a wraith, rose to haunt him again and he flung himself back into his work with renewed determination.

At last the balloon was declared ready. The men downed their tools and grinned at each other, relieved that the job was over for tonight at least. Tomorrow

there would be a new balloon to begin, but meanwhile
. . . 'Who's for a drink?' Jules called, and the team
cheered and followed him out through the door.

'At least there is one thing Paris will never run short
of,' commented a fat, jocular fellow at Paul's side.
'There will always be a drink for a thirsty man! What,
not coming?'

'No – I must get home. We have sickness there . . . I
may not be able to come tomorrow.' Paul saw the man's
eyes narrow and added desperately, 'It's my fiancée,
Louis – I can't leave her.'

'Oh, your fiancée!' The voice was knowing, and
Louis gave a short laugh. 'Then of course nobody would
expect you to leave her. I didn't even know you had a
fiancée, Thietry.'

'What's that? What are you talking about?' Jules was
beside them now, his small eyes darting suspiciously
from one to the other. 'Aren't you coming to the tavern?
I suppose we're not good enough for you, *hein*?'

Paul shrugged helplessly. He felt a desperate urge to
get back to the house in Montmartre. He shook his head
and turned away, but Jules reached out and grabbed him
by the shoulder.

'Tell me what you've been saying! I've had my eyes on
you for a long time, Thietry, so speak up or it'll be the
worse for you. What were you talking about to Louis?'

'Nothing. I was simply saying that I might not be able
to come tomorrow, there's sickness at home and –'

'Not come! You don't look sick.'

'I'm not. It's my fiancée –' Paul was desperate to
escape, but Jules's hand was heavy on his shoulder and
he knew that the older man had an uncertain temper. 'I
have to go now,' he repeated.

'So, you have to go now, do you? Very well.' The
leering face came close to him, the small eyes staring into
his own. 'But see that you come back tomorrow, or there
will be trouble, you understand? There is something
strange about you, Thietry, something out of place, and
I would very much like to know just what it is . . .' He

held his gaze for a moment, his fingers biting into the flesh of Paul's shoulder. 'Go, then!' he added with a sudden thrust. 'But don't expect me to offer you a drink when the next balloon is finished.'

Paul turned, hardly hearing the jeering laughter that followed him. He stumbled through the dark, icy streets, half lost in the maze of ill-lit alleyways, bumping into men and women who loomed unexpectedly out of doorways, tripping over dogs and cats which had so far escaped the predatory knives of their owners. At last he was climbing wearily up the last steep street. He saw the house ahead of him; the wall of the garden, the door that opened on to the street. And outside, he saw a carriage and recognised it as the doctor's.

Fear drove him the last few yards. He pushed open the door and fell into the hall. An oil lamp glimmered on the table but the only other light filtered down from upstairs. He took the stairs three at a time and flung himself into Véronique's bedroom.

The bed lay in a pool of dim yellow light. In the middle of it, her body making scarcely a ripple in the sheets, lay Véronique. On either side were Marie and the doctor.

'What is it?' Paul asked, his voice cracked and dry. He came to the bed and stared down at the pale face, at the small, prickly rash that had begun to appear on her scalp and forehead. 'What is the matter with her?'

Marie buried her face in her apron. The doctor turned. His face was grave, his eyes sombre.

'I have to tell you that she is very ill indeed,' he said quietly. 'She has smallpox.'

Only Paul and Marie were allowed into Véronique's bedroom during the course of her illness. Marie had suffered from it as a young woman and recovered; Paul had received one of Dr Jenner's vaccinations when he was a child. But neither Pierre nor Marc had ever been in contact with the disease, and both were therefore kept from her side.

Paul gave up the balloon factory. He stayed beside the

371

bed constantly, leaving only reluctantly to eat meals which had no taste, or to sleep in an exhaustion which brought only unpleasant dreams and left him feeling more drained than before. He sat for hours staring at the wasted face, the mass of tiny red spots which grew larger each day, turned yellow with pus and finally burst. The pale, ivory skin which had been so silky under his lips was an ugly, crusted mask; the body he had worshipped was grotesque with running sores, the golden hair as grey and wispy as old hay. The blue eyes rarely opened, and when they did it was to stare at him without recognition; the voice that had rung in his ears like a bell was now as cracked as a broken bucket.

But it was still Véronique who lay there, and he held her hand and prayed that she would be restored to him; marked, perhaps, her ethereal beauty gone for ever, but alive and well again, able to laugh and sing and make love. Passionately he prayed that one day they would again make love.

'There is little hope for her,' the doctor told him gravely. 'You must realise that, m'sieur. She has never been strong, and the recent hardships – too little food, too much work – have taken a heavy toll. You must prepare yourself for the worst.'

'Prepare myself – how does one prepare oneself for the worst?' Paul demanded. His tortured eyes stared at the doctor. 'Why does she have to suffer like this – is there nothing you can do for her, nothing? She's so young – so lovely. We had our lives before us. Why does Fate have to be so cruel?'

'Fate is cruel to many people,' the doctor said quietly. 'I see it every day. None of us has the right to be exempt, m'sieur. All you can do is try to make her comfortable, and be with her. Who knows what she understands, in whatever world she inhabits now?'

Paul moved closer to the bed and gazed down at the ravaged face. Did Véronique know he was there? Did she know that her hand was held in his, that his lips brushed her poor, mangled cheek? When she spoke in that high, rambling voice, her words making no sense, was she talking in her head, trying desperately to release words that would only emerge as a jumble? Did she even know that they were incoherent?

'I love you,' he said over and over again, and pressed the thin hand against his face. 'I love you, my darling. *Je t'aime, je t'aime* . . . Véronique, my little love, get better for me, get better, please. All this will end some-day, this siege, the war, and we can live again, if only you'll get better.'

He stayed beside her throughout the night, praying, exhorting, begging. But Véronique had gone into a world beyond hearing. Just before dawn, she opened her eyes for the last time. They rested on Paul's weary face and his heart jumped: she knew him, she understood, she had begun her recovery! And then they closed again, slowly, as if she were unutterably tired. And she gave a little sigh; and died.

Véronique was buried quietly beside her Aunt Cécile, in the big cemetery of Montmartre. And Paul sat listlessly in the house, drained of all energy, all desire to move. 'He is exhausted,' Marie said to Pierre as they ate their supper in the kitchen, aware of the silent figure upstairs. 'But he will have to recover himself. There is no time for grief these days.'

'He should go back to the balloon factory,' Pierre agreed. 'There is nothing like work for helping a man through bad times.'

But Paul did not go back to the balloon factory. Instead, it came to him, in the shape of Georges.

The little Frenchman arrived one evening, just after dark. Snow was falling outside; he came nervously into the house, holding his cap between his hands, brushing the flakes from his spectacles. Pierre brought him down to the kitchen, where Marie was urging Paul to drink some soup.

'It is good soup,' she said anxiously. 'The rats were fresh this morning . . . Try it, m'sieur, try it. You must eat.'

They looked up as Georges came uncertainly down the steps, and Paul's eyes opened in surprise. 'Georges! What are you doing here?'

'Is this Georges from the balloon factory?' Marie asked. 'There! I knew they would be needing you there and see, this poor man has had to walk all this way to fetch you. Now aren't you ashamed?'

'No, it isn't that,' Georges said nervously. 'It's something else – something worse.' He gave a quick glance round the big, dim kitchen at Marc, Pierre and Marie, then addressed himself to Paul. 'They are to be trusted, *oui*? M'sieur, it is serious, Jules is making trouble for you. He has reported you as a Prussian spy – he has been making inquiries and he says your name is not Thietry at all, and that you are English and have been consorting with a woman in the country who has been found to be a collaborator. Someone told him she was related to you. She has been arrested, this woman, and taken to Tours – the news came in by pigeon only a week ago, and –'

'Woman? What are you talking about? What is her name?' Paul stared at him, his mind buzzing. What did Georges mean?

'Her name is the name you have been using,' Georges faltered unhappily. 'Thietry – Annette Thietry. She has given much trouble – she has been the mistress of one of the Prussian generals . . .' He glanced miserably around the room. 'I do not know all the details, m'sieur, all I know is that Jules has reported you and even now the police may be on their way . . . M'sieur, there is a balloon leaving Paris from near here within the hour, and I have arranged for a place to be kept for you. You must leave at once – it is imperative. Or assuredly, you will lose your life!'

Marie gave a cry, and Pierre turned swiftly to Paul. 'Do you hear that? They are on their way! Quickly, get some warm clothes – it's bitterly cold outside, and worse in the sky. Don't just stand there! Don't you understand what Georges is saying? There is no time to lose.'

'But I can't leave Paris,' Paul stammered. 'There is my grandfather – he is an old man, he has suffered so much.' He turned, indicating the wraith-like figure crouched in the chair by the fire. 'I am all he has left.'

'And he will not have you at all if you stay here!' Pierre exclaimed. 'Listen, the police are coming for you. Have you not heard what they do to suspected spies? You will be imprisoned, beaten, starved, and very likely shot into the bargain. What good will that be to your grandfather?'

'But can't you hide me somewhere? In the attic, perhaps, or a cupboard somewhere, just until they've gone –'

'And do you not think they will search the place from top to bottom? They would find you at once.'

'Oh, stop all this arguing!' Marie broke in. Her face was red with exasperation. 'Quite obviously, the best thing is for you to leave at once, and here is Georges who has taken the trouble – and at some risk to himself, I daresay – to arrange a place for you in the balloon. Do you not trust Pierre and me to look after your grandfather? We have been with him for years. Are we going to leave him now, just because of a few Prussians?'

Paul looked doubtfully at her. There was a brief moment of silence. Outside, shouts could be heard, coming nearer.

Marc's thin voice, the dry, quavering whisper that had been all he could manage since Cécile's death, was as startling in that silence as the blast of a trumpet.

'Paul . . . my grandson. Listen to me.'

Paul turned quickly and knelt beside him, his hands reaching out for the wrinkled fingers that moved restlessly on the old man's shrunken lap. His heart filled with love and pity. Only a few months ago, Marc had been strong and commanding, walking straight and tall, his age a matter for admiration. Now he had collapsed into pathetic helplessness, his life tumbled in ruins about him: wife and niece dead, business shattered, and who knew what happening to his family in Lorraine. Annette

375

selling herself to the Germans, Gabriel in God knew what state, the children . . . where were the children now?

'I won't leave you, *Gran'père*,' Paul said intensely, clinging to the old hands. 'I'll never leave you. I'll stay with you until the end.'

'Which will be any moment now,' Pierre said, but neither of the two figures by the fire took any notice of him.

'No,' Marc said, and he drew one hand from Paul's grasp and raised it to touch his grandson's face. 'No, you will not stay here. It is certain death if you do – death for us both. Paul, I am going to die soon anyway, and that does not disturb me. I have little to live for now. But you – you have a life before you. You have grown since you came to Paris as a young, hesitant boy. You are a man now, a man who has something to give the world, both in your work and yourself. You cannot waste that. It would be wrong.' He paused, his voice failing. The shouts had come closer; the animal sound of a lynching mob, closing for the kill. 'Leave me now, Paul. Take the way that has been offered you and go back to England. That is your home; it is where you belong.' He drew a last difficult breath and ended in a voice that could barely be heard: 'I command you, Paul.'

Exhausted, he leaned back in his chair. His hand fell back to his lap and lay there, white and limp. Paul stared at him, terrified. But the shrunken chest still rose and fell, though very lightly. He was simply asleep.

Slowly, Paul rose to his feet. He turned and stared into the circle of faces lit by the guttering yellow lamp.

'The balloon, Georges,' he said in a dull, flat voice. 'Where does it leave from?'

It had stopped snowing. The sky had begun to clear. Between the tossing clouds could be seen a half moon. It shed a pale, wavering light on the scene near the Solferino Tower, where the balloon was being prepared. Already a crowd of people had assembled to watch its departure, even though the practice of displaying notices of each balloon's departure had ceased because of the fear of spies.

It was also partly because of this fear that the open space at the top of Montmartre was being used; the railway stations were too well known and the hill gave the balloon a better chance of leaving the city without crashing into some of the higher buildings.

Paul and Georges arrived breathless. Once the decision had been made, everyone in the house had burst into action – everyone with the exception of the old man who had forced it and who now slept peacefully in his chair. While Paul had knelt to give his grandfather's brow a last kiss, Marie and Pierre had bustled about as if they were making ready for a picnic. 'Bread,' they cried to each other as they rushed from cupboard to table, up the stairs and down again. 'Chocolate, there's a block of it hidden behind the vegetables . . . Take that old fur coat, he will be frozen up there without something warm, and the mistress does not need it now . . . Look, here is a bottle of good red wine . . . It is all we can manage, I'm afraid,' Marie said apologetically as she wrapped Paul in the folds of his grandmother's fur coat and handed him a bulging bag. 'But hopefully you will soon be back on land and anyone will help you then.' She stared at him, her lined face working suddenly, and the tears spilled from her eyes. 'Good luck, m'sieur,' she said, giving him a hasty kiss on both cheeks. '*Bon voyage . . .*'

There was no time for more. The clamour outside had grown louder, the police, if police they were, had almost reached the door. Paul gripped Pierre's hand hard and then turned to Georges. The little man's spectacles glinted in the dim light; he picked up Paul's bag and urged him to the basement door. Already they could hear fists pounding at the front of the house, and cries of 'Open up! Open up!'. At the last moment, Paul hesitated. How could he leave these good people now – what would his pursuers do to them? But Marie read his thoughts and shook her head angrily, and Pierre splayed his big hand on Paul's back and gave him a push that sent him stumbling through the door and out into the yard beyond.

The voices sounded louder; they were angry, yet at the same time excited, as if they were confident of discovering the traitor inside the house and looking forward to dealing with him. Even now, Paul wished he could stay. He felt himself to be running away, leaving three old people to bear the brunt of his own wrongs. But Georges urged him on. 'They won't hurt your grandfather, not once they find you have gone. He's a well-known man in the city, everyone respects the glassmakers. But if they do find you here – being sheltered by him . . .' His meaning was plain. With a last look at the house that had been his second home, Paul turned and followed the little Frenchman over the garden wall and into the next street.

A few moments later and they would have been caught. But there was enough start for them to be round a corner and swallowed up by the darkness before their pursuers realised that Paul was not in the house. It was long enough for them to make for the space from where the balloon was to be launched; long enough for them to arrive, panting, just as the balloon's inflation was completed and it rose upright into the air, held by its mooring ropes and reaching yearningly towards the purple sky.

Paul stopped and stared at it. For the first time, he realised exactly what was happening. In a few moments he would be in the small round basket suspended from the base of the great swaying sphere, crammed tightly together with perhaps three other men, a basket of pigeons, sacks of mail and all the other paraphernalia that was taken on each flight. In a few moments, he would be soaring into the air, floating over Paris, drifting who knew where over the Prussian lines and into the unknown France that lay beyond.

Ever since he had first arrived in Paris, he had longed to go up in a balloon. But now the moment had come, he felt flat and uncaring. The excitement had drained away.

But Georges was urging him on again, pushing him forward into the circle of light around the balloon. The scene was almost brilliant; all around the cleared space were large lanterns, their faces pointing inwards so that everyone could see what they were doing. Long mooring ropes trailed from the balloon itself, and Paul could see that the canvas tube leading from the gas main was still in position as the pilot, still wearing the uniform of a sailor, assessed whether inflation was complete. The basket was being stocked with provisions, for nobody knew how long the balloon would remain aloft, nor where it would land. There had been tales of balloons that drifted as far as Norway and landed high up in the mountains. A man was coming forward with a basket of pigeons; as he drew nearer, Paul could hear their soft cooing. The sailor who sat nonchalantly on the edge of the basket, a pipe clenched in his mouth, took them and stowed them inside. Paul looked at him in alarm – didn't the man realise that there were two thousand cubic metres of coal-gas floating just above his head? But he saw that the pipe was unlit and then, looking into the already tightly packed basket, he wondered if there could possibly be room for human passengers as well.

Georges approached the sailor and spoke to him, gesticulating towards Paul. They both turned and the pilot came over, looked him up and down and nodded briefly.

'You have been in a balloon before?'

'No, I have only helped make them at the Gare du Nord.'

'There is nothing to be afraid of,' said the pilot, who had probably never been up himself either; the only experienced balloonists in Paris had all left, except for Nadar himself, who had remained to oversee the factories and train new pilots. 'We simply go where the wind takes us – there is no question of control, you understand.'

Whether his words were intended to be reassuring or not, Paul could not be sure; but at that moment there was a clatter of hooves and the mail van rushed through the crowd and stopped as near the balloon as the horses could be persuaded to approach. Several bulging sacks were carried over and thrown in; there could surely be no more room now.

'That is all,' the pilot said suddenly. 'We must go now.' He began to give orders in a loud voice and Paul turned to Georges, now the only friend he had to see him off on this strange adventure. He gripped the little man's hand hard and kissed him on both cheeks; behind the spectacles, he caught the glint of tears. But there was no time for words; the sailor was in the basket, and another man was climbing in as well. 'There will be no room for me,' Paul exclaimed in sudden panic, but they grabbed him and hauled him aboard, squeezing him down between them in the cramped space. The rim of the basket was barely halfway up his thighs; he stared out, holding tightly to the rough, tarred cords that stretched up to the net covering the whole shimmering sphere.

The crowd was silent, as if holding its breath during these last dramatic moments before the balloon was launched. All around the basket men stood with their hands on the rim, holding it down as the mooring ropes were unfastened. Paul looked down and saw the anchor hanging over the side, just below him, while far away at the edge of the brightly lit circle a man untied the long, trailing rope that would be used as an extra method of slowing the balloon in its descent. The sailor drew it in, coiling it efficiently over his arm, and now the balloon shifted above them, tugging at the last restraints. The men holding the basket staggered under its sudden pull; the basket lurched and swayed. Already the cords were straining as the huge globe yawed above them. The pilot detached the gas pipe from the valve and tossed it away. He shouted his final command to the men to let go, and they fell away. Paul stared at them and saw them grow smaller before his eyes, dropping away below him as if the earth had fallen back rather than the balloon taken flight.

'We're up!'

The pilot's voice was jubilant as he too leant over the side of the basket to stare down at the rapidly diminishing circle of light below. Already the balloon was at least fifty feet high, but the voices of the crowd could still be clearly heard, shouting farewells and calling out last-minute messages to those aboard. It was like looking down a well at a world that existed only at the bottom; the darkness was all around them, like sheer black walls, and there was only a disc of light to show them the life that would go on now without them, while they were taken at the mercy of the winds into unknown territory, into dangers that could not be envisaged.

'Only two balloons have not been heard of again,' the pilot remarked conversationally. 'And there must be – oh, forty or fifty at least, sent out. All we have to do now is wait until morning. By then we shall be well out of the way of the Prussians.'

Paul stared out into the darkness. Paris lay below, a very different sight from the glittering city he had first known, the streets unlit because the gas was needed for balloons. In the centre, safe from possible bombardment, there were lights spilling from restaurants and houses where people lived who scarcely knew there was a siege on, where a menu offering antelope steak or sliced elephant trunk was a matter for laughter rather than dismay. But on the outskirts, close to the fortifications, where there was always the danger of a falling shell, where houses had been torn apart and looted, where people still lived amongst the ruins because they had nowhere else to go – here, there was no light, only a cold, heavy darkness, a chilly despair. Drifting over here, sensing the despondency of life below as if it were a miasma reaching up through the bitter air, it was easy to believe that Paris was dying.

Paul drew his grandmother's fur coat closer around him. What purpose was he serving, high in this balloon, taking this crazy adventure? What could life possibly have to offer him now? His grandmother dead; Marc dying; Véronique's body, decaying in a cemetery;

Annette, selling herself to the enemy . . . He would have been better to have stayed, faced the mob and taken whatever punishment they chose to mete out to him.

Stourbridge was another world, a dream he had once had. Christina, Joe, Emily and the others – they had no existence in reality. There was, in fact, no reality; only this swift, onward rush through the icy air into a darkness that must surely lead only to Hell.

# Chapter Eighteen

January passed away like an old tyrant, a cold, dense fog wrapping the mills and foundries of the Black Country like the shreds of a rusty black cloak. Susan Henzel passed away with it, drifting almost unnoticeably into perpetual slumber. They buried her in the churchyard of Holy Trinity near to her brother Joshua; and Emily, standing at the door of the yellow-bricked church and gazing down over the grim landscape that stretched away on every side, thought of the day when she had come here to marry Stephen and shivered in the icy wind.

It seemed impossible now that she could ever have believed such a marriage could be happy. The vows she had made – to love, honour, obey – rang falsely in her memory. How could she have given such promises, knowing as she had that the feeling she had for Stephen could never be love? Liking, yes – she had liked him then. Respect – she could still give him that, for he was a tireless worker and would not spare himself to bring his people to God. And there had been that other strange emotion, too – that leaping of the senses when he touched her, the breathlessness when she had caught his eye upon her.

Had she mistaken that for love?

She had known, or believed, that he loved her. There were those who held that this was enough; that to a woman, love came after marriage. Well, she could certainly tell them differently! For her, the only emotions that had followed marriage were fear, disgust and . . . her mind flinched away from the word hate, but not before it had been formed. Definitely not love. As for honour – how could any woman honour the man who treated her with such brutality, even though he was invariably racked with shame afterwards? No. The only vow she could carry out now was the last, to obey. And in that, she had no choice.

Emily had read of the effects on a woman of leaving her husband. Justified though she might be, society took the view that as a wife she was little more than a chattel, to be used as her husband pleased. Even servants, she thought bitterly, had more rights. And although Christina and Joe, never ones to allow convention to stand in their way, might take her in if she left Stephen, the barrier between herself and her father was still too high to allow her to ask his help. Besides, there were those vows. Made before God, and only one of them possible to keep. Didn't she deserve to be punished for such sacrilege?

Stephen would certainly have thought so. And would have had no hesitation in carrying out the punishment himself.

The family began to proceed slowly down the path. It was one of the few occasions when they all came together. Emily, silent beside her husband, looked at them. Old Joshua's cousins, Harold and Samuel, aged now, their vitality gone. It was difficult to believe that they could ever have been a threat to Christina. Samuel's son, Rupert, attended his father, keeping a solicitous hand under the thin elbow. His elder son, Jeremy, had not come; Emily supposed that he had not been invited, although there was no reason why he should not have come to the church if he had wished.

She thought of her Uncle Harry, Christina's brother, still in America. He and his wife Ruth made regular visits to Stourbridge now, coming over almost every year. Harry was a prosperous engineer, much in demand for building railways and bridges all over the rapidly expanding continent. When they had first gone, Emily had felt sorry for Ruth, having to leave her home when she so clearly did not want to. But now she saw her as a contented woman, plump and smiling. Clearly, she and Harry had found the love to be treasured in their marriage. She wished they were here now, thinking that perhaps she might have confided in Aunt Ruth.

It would have been such a relief to talk to someone. There was so much trouble in her mind: her marriage, the vows, the punishment Stephen seemed to find pleasure in inflicting these days. And her constant thoughts of Paul. The fears for him that never left her mind.

It was several weeks now since his last letter, although the balloon posts had still been operating. Something must have happened to him. They had heard with fear of the capitulation of Paris, of the Prussians entering the gates of the starving city. It was impossible to imagine what might be happening there; it was impossible not to.

'He'll be all right,' Joe said when he heard the news. 'He's young and strong. He'll be all right.'

But as time went on, as February marched rawly into a chilly spring, and the news from Paris became worse instead of better; as tales spread of continuing starvation, with Parisians begging for bread from their well-fed victors, as Britain and America loaded ships with flour, fish and fuel; as news came through of riots in Montmartre, of suspected spies being cruelly tortured, thrown into the Seine and stoned until they drowned; as the Commune took over and the streets ran with blood as they never had during the war, as the city itself began to burn and great buildings such as the Tuileries and the Hôtel de Ville were reported to be in flames, and there was still no word from Paul . . . all hope died. And the family admitted that they believed he must be dead.

'There seems to be nobody in the house at Montmartre now,' Joe said dispiritedly when Emily called at Henzel Court to see if there had been any news. 'We've had inquiries made of everyone we can think of. The old man died, apparently, and nobody knows what became of either Paul or the servants. As for the family in Lorraine, only Gabriel is left. His wife disappeared early on – executed, some say, for collaboration with the enemy; taken to Germany, others believe, as the mistress of one of the generals. It's nigh on impossible to get a true account from anyone. I doubt if anyone even knows it.' He sat at the head of the table, his strong face lined with worry and grief, and even Emily, feeling the same grief, could look at him with pity.

'But what of Gabriel and Annette's children?' Sarah asked. 'What happened to them?'

Joe shrugged. 'Who knows? One tale is that Gabriel sent them out of the country – to America, perhaps. Apparently he won't say. Afraid, perhaps – I don't know.'

'And Véronique?' Emily asked quietly, thinking of the fairy creature who had played and laughed with her in Paris, the child who had grown to womanhood and stolen Paul's heart. 'Does anyone know what happened to her?'

He shrugged. 'Another set of tales: she fled with Paul; they both escaped by balloon; she died; they both died. What can we believe? There must be hundreds, thousands, who have disappeared and nobody will ever know why or how. And Véronique and Paul – well, I'm afraid they're just two of them.'

Christina covered her face with her hands. 'Oh, Joe, it's so dreadful. So young, such a waste.'

'Yes,' Emily said with a quiet savagery. 'Such a waste. And all because of a vain, ambitious Empress and a stupid, weak Emperor. Neither of them worth one tenth what Paul was worth, not even one tenth of what the worst soldier in the ranks was worth. And where are they now? In England – living in comfort, sheltered by our own Queen. While Paul . . .' Her voice trembled and broke, and she pushed back her chair and stood up. 'I'm going home, Mamma. Down to the Lye. Where I, at least, can do something useful.'

Roger, home for the Easter vacation, found it hard to conceal his glee. With his parents and Sarah he was forced to maintain a straight, sombre face, to pretend to a sadness that matched their own. With Emily, he scarcely knew how to behave; since her marriage, she seemed to have imprisoned herself in an iron cage which nobody could unlock. She stared out defiantly at the world, daring it to pity her, daring it even to acknowledge any cause for pity. She refused to join in the endless discussions about what might have happened to Paul. 'There's no point in talking about it,' she said angrily. 'We just go round and round in circles. We don't know anything – we're never going to know anything. So why waste our own lives in wondering about it?' And then she dragged a jacket round her shoulders and stalked out, pain in every line of her body, disappearing to the Lye where people had their own troubles, troubles that could sometimes be assuaged by a cup of broth or a spoonful or two of medicine.

'I worry about Emily,' Christina told Roger on his first evening at home. 'She is growing thinner and more pale every day. Are she and Stephen really happy together, I wonder? If only she would talk to me . . . But she'll say nothing. And she's obviously just as worried as we are about Paul, yet she refuses to admit it, she won't even discuss it. All she will say is that she has always known he would never come back and the rest of us must live our own lives without him. It's almost as if she's angry with him for – for whatever may have happened.'

'I shouldn't worry too much, Mother,' Roger said with the easy assurance of a man who knows the world. 'You know Emily, she's always had a funny temper. I daresay she'll get over it in her own way. But as for saying that the rest of us must go on with our own lives – well, don't you think she's right? There's nothing we can do about Paul. He's almost certainly dead – I'm sorry, Mamma, but we do have to face it. And in that case – well, shouldn't we be taking certain actions?'

'Actions? What actions?'

Roger gestured with one hand. 'Well – about the glasshouse, for instance. It's always been understood, surely, that Paul would take a large part in running it if anything should happen to you and Father. Not that anything is going to for many years, of course,' he added hastily, seeing the fire ignite in Christina's eyes. 'But it's only sensible to consider these things in good time. Your own father did, after all,' he finished tactfully.

Christina, on the point of a quick retort, paused and bit her lip. 'There's some truth in what you say,' she agreed reluctantly. 'But what are you suggesting?'

'That you make certain provisions, that's all. Giving me, for instance, full powers of decision. It could be very difficult if something happened to both you and Father, and I could do nothing because Paul was still nominally entitled to a say and could not be found. It's often years before any legal decisions can be made in those circumstances, you know. A man at Oxford was telling me – his great-uncle was lost in the Napoleonic wars, and because nobody knew what had happened to him it was years before his grandfather gained full control of the family business. By which time it was almost bankrupt.' He gazed earnestly into Christina's eyes. 'You wouldn't want anything like that to happen to Henzel's.'

'No, I wouldn't.' She hesitated. 'I'll talk to your father about it, Roger. You may be right. But it seems so cruel, with Paul missing only a few weeks –'

'He might well have been dead for those weeks. It's no more cruel than if we knew for certain,' Roger pointed out slowly. 'And, of course, if he did come back, everything could be changed back, to be as it was before. I don't want to rob Paul of anything, Mother.'

'No, of course not. Of course you don't.' Christina reached out quickly for his hand. 'I never meant to suggest anything of the kind, Roger. I know you're thinking only of doing the best for us all now . . . It just seems so hard – we've hoped so much . . . Well, I'll talk to your father.' She released his hand and got up, her face pale and set. 'And, Roger – if you could talk to Emily too? She's so unhappy. I feel that if she would only talk to one of us . . .' She gazed at him with entreaty in her eyes.

'I'll try, Mother,' he agreed. 'But I can't promise that she'll listen. Emily's always gone her own way, and I believe she still looks on me as a little boy, hardly out of the nursery. And she does have a husband now to support her.' Roger thought with scorn of the young minister with whom he had exchanged barely a dozen words. A cold fish, that one, if ever he saw one. 'Well, I'll do what I can. As you say, she is my sister.' His lips smiled but his eyes were calculating. And when he recounted the conversation later, to Jeremy, he made no attempt to conceal the contempt in his voice; or the glee.

'Expecting me to comfort dear Emily!' he sneered. 'What comfort has she ever been to me, pray? Set over me in the nursery, a bigger autocrat than any nanny – put on a pedestal as my big sister, who must be looked up to and obeyed. And all the time, a bastard, the brat of some slut out of the gutter. Well, it will do her good to suffer a little. She's had life too easy, too easy by far. And Paul, the same – a bastard, given every considera- tion, treated as the first-born when really *I* should hold that position, standing to inherit the family business in equal shares with me!' His eyes glinted and he gave a short laugh. 'Well, that's one thing that looks like being put right! I've sown the seed in Mother's mind – she's almost ready to give him up for dead now, and he'll be cut out completely. And with Emily safely wed to that fool of a minister, and Sarah, thank God, content to behave as women should, that leaves me in complete charge – just as I ought to be.'

'Apart from your parents, of course,' Jeremy mur- mured, and Roger snorted and snapped his fingers.

'They won't be too much trouble! This business with Paul has taken its toll. They're both losing heart – they'll be only too pleased to hand over to me by the time I've finished at Oxford.' He leaned forward, eyes gleam- ing. 'And then I'll be able to work out my own ideas, Jeremy. Give me two or three years and they'll see that I can run the place. They'll be glad to hand over and take a rest. And then . . .' He smiled. 'I can do as I like.'

'And that is?'

Roger gave him an oblique glance. 'We've discussed this before, Jeremy. You've a thriving factory. You've already got a trade in flat glass. With your connections there and ours in tableware, we could combine to form the biggest glassmaking business in the country. And I don't just mean the Black Country – I mean in Britain.'

Jeremy stared at him. His eyes narrowed. He turned his head very slightly away, still keeping his gaze on the younger man's face, and his hand came up involuntarily to his chin and began to stroke it thoughtfully.

'It's the way we have to go,' Roger said intensely. 'We're doing well, Jeremy, both of us.' He spoke as if the business were already his. 'Together – pooling all our assets – we can do even better. We can afford to cut out the dead wood – produce more and better glass. Look – I've thought a lot about it. Until now, it was always the manufacturer who made the decisions. The working glassmaker like my father and grandfather. But what did they know about costing, about markets, the business of buying and selling? *You* know that once the glass is made it's the brain that's needed – not a pair of clever hands. It's the man in the office, handling the money, who ought to be making the decisions, Jeremy – and that's the man I intend to be. And now that Paul's out of the way –'

'The road's clear for you. But are you sure you can persuade your parents? They'll never agree to this, you know. They'd go under rather than let Henzel Crystal combine with Henzel Brothers.'

'But they won't realise. Not until it's too late.'

Roger spoke quietly, but with a certainty in his voice that caused Jeremy to give him a sharp glance. The younger man was stretched back in his chair, his hands folded across his chest, smiling slightly. He let his eyes move slowly, lazily, around the room before resting them once more on Jeremy's face, and then his smile widened and he gave a little laugh.

'You surely don't imagine I've learned nothing from you in all these years?' he said lightly. 'This is my great chance, isn't it! The only son left to them – at last they'll appreciate me. Value me. I tell you, I won't be able to put a foot wrong from now on. All the planning of the last few years – it's coming to fruition at last. They'll fall over themselves to give me whatever I ask. Responsibility – a partnership – sole charge. It'll be as easy as falling into a furnace.' He laughed again, not noticing the shadow that crossed Jeremy's face at those words. 'Have no fear, Jeremy. I'll leave nothing to chance. I'll make sure that things are tied up so securely that by the time they do realise what's happening, it'll be too late to do a thing about it. We'll be able to join forces, as we've always planned – merge the two businesses as they should have been merged years ago, and run the whole thing in an efficient, up-to-date manner. After all –' he snapped his fingers '– what does the feud amount to anyway? A silly quarrel twenty years or more ago, and I daresay there's not one amongst the three of you who can say what it was about. It's more than time it was forgotten – more than time.'

He rose and shrugged into his jacket. Jeremy watched silently. He rang the bell for his servant to let Roger out, and bade the young man a thoughtful goodbye. He went to the window and stood, stroking his chin, watching as his cousin walked jauntily off down the street.

Something in his own demeanour struck him with an odd familiarity. For a long time, he could not think what it was. And then a picture flashed into his mind – a picture of his Uncle Reuben, years ago, standing at a window in just that way, his fingers moving thoughtfully at his chin.

Down in the Lye Waste, Emily worked with fierce concentration. She was everywhere, teaching in the school, working with the women in the soup kitchen, visiting and tending the sick, listening to the troubles that were poured out to her, campaigning for better houses, better sanitation, better everything. It was as if there were no other place on earth but the Lye Waste; certainly no city of Paris.

But it was only by working that Emily could tolerate

391

the life she led now. The people of the Lye, with their constant problems, their poverty aggravated by fecklessness, their too-large families, their housing that was still poor in spite of all efforts, their sickness and disease, were all that stood between her and utter hopelessness. At least she could look at them and, thinking of her own home, comfortable, warm and dry in spite of its shabby furnishings, realise that she was in many ways fortunate. On the other hand, she could see contentment and happiness in even the poorest of homes where love was; the treasures of marriage were not confined to the rich. And seeing that, she knew herself to be infinitely more poor.

Nevertheless, she could at least feel herself to be useful. And it seemed that this was all that was to be left to her now. She was even denied children; there had been no sign of a baby in the months since her wedding, and this, Stephen told her, was yet another sign of God's displeasure.

Stephen worked with her, but he spent more and more of his time these days in prayer. Since his father had died, not long after they had married, he seemed to have retreated into a world where she could not follow, a strange, narrow world bounded on all sides by sin. It was sinful to laugh, to sing, to dance. Sinful to drink alcohol, sinful, Emily thought sometimes, to be happy in any way at all. She could not understand where this God of Stephen's had come from. He seemed to be the product of a dark and twisted mind and nothing at all to do with the stern but benevolent figure she had always imagined.

It was not sinful to make love – that had been ordained by Stephen's God. But it was sinful to enjoy it. And, she thought with wry bitterness, Stephen certainly made sure that there was no risk of that particular sin . . .

Stephen accepted her labours without comment. He never, as Christina did, told her that she was wearing herself out, that nobody should be expected to work so hard, that she owed herself time off from her toiling.

'Time off?' Emily would echo as if it were some strange new concept. 'What would I do with that? And who gives the people here time off from their troubles?' And out she would go again, knowing that Stephen would accept every ounce of effort she gave, never expecting her to give less than she could. And knowing too that there was relief in being out of the house, even though she might exchange it for the meanest mud cottage in the Lye.

She still visited Henzel Court, partly to see her sister Sarah, whose gentleness never failed to soothe her troubles for at least an hour or two, partly to keep contact with Christina, for she had come to realise that the accusations that she had flung at her stepmother had been largely unjustified and they were brought close by their anxiety over Paul, feeling their way back to friendship. Her father she still could not feel at ease with; neither of them could forget Maggie Haden and her ghost hung between them like a dark, impenetrable shadow.

Most of all, she went to the house to seek news of Paul. But always she came away disappointed.

'I can't bring myself to accept that he's dead,' she told Ben and Florrie as she sat in their warm kitchen with young Frank on her lap. 'I tell Mamma that we must, but in my heart I can't believe it. How could he be dead, with all the talent, all the skill he possesses? Surely God could not be so wasteful, so cruel.'

Ben sighed and shook his head. 'Don't see as it works that way, Em. After all, Paul's own dad was a fine engraver, by all accounts, an' look what happened to he. No, things like war an' accidents an' such don't pick an' choose.'

'Well, you're a fine one to give comfort,' Florrie said sharply. 'Why not keep quiet, Ben Taylor, if you can't say nothing cheerful? Tek no notice of him, Miss Emily. He don't know nothing about it. I'm with you – I don't believe as Master Paul's dead either.'

Emily looked down at the baby on her knee. Her eyes were blurred with tears. There was a short silence and then Ben cleared his throat.

393

'Hevn't seen you down the cones lately, Em. Why don't you come in sometime? The men'd be glad to see you, hev a word. Might cheer you up a bit too, like. Nothing like old friends in times of trouble.'

Florrie gave him a quelling glance but Emily smiled gratefully. 'I may do that, Ben. Thank you.' And then, taking a breath: 'Tell me how you're getting on with the new glass. I hear the ruby is a great success.'

'Aye, it is. Master Roger was right to keep on trying for that. Best in the business now, I reckon. We're using it in three pots, full time.'

'That's very good. And the black?'

'Well, that ent so easy, I got to be honest. Folk don't seem to want black crystalware. Most of it's stuck away out of sight now an' we don't mek no more. I got the recipe still, just in case, but no, I don't reckon that'll ever be much of a seller.'

'Well, I don't suppose Roger's too disappointed, if the ruby's successful. He seems to be taking a lot of interest in the business now – home from Oxford whenever he can manage it, so I hear.'

'Aye, he is that,' Ben said, his tone so flat that Emily gave him a quick glance.

'Why, what's the matter? Don't you think he knows what he's doing?'

'Oh, he knows what he's doing all right, an' what he's talking about. He just don't know how to handle the men.' Ben hesitated, looked at her and then said: 'I'm sorry, Em, if I'm talking out of turn, but he puts their backs up. They don't like him an' that's the truth of it. An' when he teks over, there'll be trouble on the way, mark my –'

'When he takes over?' Emily broke in. 'But Roger's not taking over.'

'No? Well, he acts as if he is, an' most of the men reckon it won't be too long at that. Your ma an' pa seem to hev lost heart since this war business . . . I reckon they mean to hand over to Master Roger soon as he comes back from that college he's at. You really mean to say they've said naught to you about it?'

'Nothing,' Emily said slowly. 'But why should they? I only call in to see if they've news of Paul. We don't really talk at all . . . Ben, are you *sure* of this?'

'Look, I don't *know* nothing. Only what me mates say, see. But that's what everyone reckons, an' – well, they ent usually wrong.'

'No, indeed.' It was true that there seemed to be a kind of grapevine in the glasshouse that carried news from cone to cone faster than a Henzel could walk the distance. Christina had sometimes declared that it travelled through the underground passages used to bring coal from canal barges to the furnaces, but Joe only shook his head and laughed. 'It's in the air, my love,' he declared. 'In the air and in the bricks. Or mebbe floating on the smoke . . . Whatever it is, you'll not stop it, so better not waste your time trying.'

Emily sat thoughtfully for a few minutes, playing with the baby's toes. Did her parents really intend to hand over the business to Roger? Or was it Roger's intention to persuade them while they were still numb with grief and worry over Paul? Did they even know of the gossip that was going through the cones?

Florrie placed a cup of tea beside her and she smiled her thanks. She drank it as quickly as she decently could and then, with a kiss for Florrie and the baby, she declared that she must go. It was earlier than usual, but if she were to reach home at the time Stephen expected her, there was not a moment to lose.

Roger, taking over the glasshouse? Roger, in charge? And had nobody considered Paul's rights in this matter? Paul, who was *not* dead – Paul who, one day soon, would come home?

The pony clopped steadily through the dusty streets. Emily sat in the trap, the reins held loosely in her hands, acknowledging almost without realising it the greetings she received as she clattered along. Past the tall, red-brick cones of the glasshouse, through the hazy smoke and the dust of a warm spring day. Back to the tall gates and driveway of Henzel Court, where she had lived since she was two years old.

And there, at the gates, she saw a tall, shambling figure. A man, shabby and unkempt in rags that seemed to be falling from his gaunt frame. A man whose hair straggled round his unshaven face, who moved slowly, as if too weary to take another step yet driven on by some desperate inner need; a man who turned at the sound of her pony's hooves and looked at her with eyes that begged for help.

A tramp. A rogue and a vagabond. One of the many who had been driven to roam from place to place, seeking shelter in the casualty wards and the lodging houses, sleeping under ditches and in woods, begging at doorways and along the way. A man without home or work; a man without hope.

She looked down at him with pity; looked down into eyes that were rimmed red with fatigue.

Grey eyes. Eyes the light, soft grey of a pigeon's wing. The silvery grey of the stars on a misty night.

Silver eyes . . . Could it be true? Could it be possible?

'Emily . . .' he whispered, and his voice was cracked, like an old, broken bell; but his voice, all the same.

'Paul . . .' she breathed in answer, and then tumbled from the trap and into his trembling arms. *'Paul . . .'*

# Chapter Nineteen

Summer came to the Black Country and slowly, as the sun's warmth grew, Paul regained his strength.

'He's almost well again,' Emily said jubilantly to Stephen. 'Goodness knows what he's been through. The terrible things that happened in Paris – having to escape a lynching mob, taking off by balloon at night, not knowing where he might come down again. And when they did land, having no idea where they were, who was friend or foe . . . The French people in the countryside had had as terrible a time as those in Paris, you see. First the French soldiers, lost and starving, desperate for food – then the Prussians, demanding everything they had, sacking their homes – battles fought in tiny villages, women and children shot and killed. By the time Paul and the other balloonists came, they were suspicious of everybody. And then they were almost caught by Prussians . . . We still don't know how he got to the coast, or who brought him to England. He doesn't seem to remember. And since then, he's been walking – just walking, begging for food and shelter, until he found himself back home.'

Her eyes filled with tears at the thought of his sufferings. And Stephen listened patiently enough the first time, though without much comment. But at the second telling, and the third, his patience began to give way.

'He must be well again now. Does he really need you at his side all the time? You are spending all your time at Henzel Court now. You're neglecting your work here.' His eyes hardened. 'I have needs too, Emily. I am your husband, after all.'

She stared at him and a deep tide of colour washed up into her cheeks. 'I know that, Stephen – I could hardly forget. But there is less to do here now that the soup kitchen is closed for the summer. And you could do more if –' She paused, frightened by the look in his eye, and then went on '– if you spent less time praying.'

'*Less time praying*?' he repeated in a terrible voice. 'Emily, do you know what you are saying?'

'Yes, I do. What do you think would be done here if we all spent our days on our knees? This isn't a monastery, Stephen, it's a living village with real people in it. They need your help –'

'They need my prayers.'

'They need your help as well,' she said stubbornly. 'The kind of help you used to give them.'

'They would not need it so much if you were here, instead of at Henzel Court playing nurse to your brother!' he said quickly.

'Stephen, it is only for a little while, just while he regains his strength. Can't you understand that? He's been through so much, and –'

'Oh, I know just how much he's been through! The siege, the starvation, the lynching mob, the balloon – I could recite it in my sleep. And what does it signify? He stayed there of his own volition, didn't he? Nobody forced him. And now he's home, living a life of pampered luxury once again under his mother's wing. *He doesn't need you*, Emily. Nor do you need him. Leave him alone!'

'And what would you know about my needs?' she asked quietly.

Stephen stared at her. His eyes were cold and hard, like pebbles, and she wondered how she had ever thought them warm and loving. And once again she felt that stab of guilt, that it was in some way her fault that Stephen had changed, it was her lack of love that had embittered him so. But I did try to love you, her heart cried out.

'Your needs?' he said. 'I think I should know more about your needs than anyone else, Emily. Let me remind you again, I am your husband.' As she tried to speak again, he lifted a hand to silence her and said: 'Paul is home and therefore everything has changed. The Lye and its people, even your own husband, no longer interest you. We were nothing but a – a way of passing the time. Of filling an empty mind. An empty heart.' He stared at her and she saw the burning emotion deep in his eyes. 'Isn't that true?'

'No!' she cried. 'No, it's not true! Stephen, how can you say such things? You speak as if I were just playing with you – as if you and the Lye and all the people here were just toys. You know it isn't so. What we've been doing is important – important to me. You must know that!'

'And I?' he asked. 'Am I important?' Suddenly, he gripped her arms, his fingers hard on the soft flesh. 'Answer me, Emily! Does it mean anything to you that you are my wife – or is our marriage no more than a diversion, to be tossed aside the moment you saw your beloved Paul again?'

'No, it's not like that, it's not!' Distressed, she looked up at him. 'Stephen, you're hurting me . . .' He let go so suddenly that she staggered and had to steady herself against a chair. She rubbed her arms, her face pale as she stared at him. 'Of course our marriage means something to me. It means a great deal. But I told you –'

'Paul came home,' he mocked bitterly. 'And everything changed.'

His bitterness shocked her. Her wide eyes travelled slowly over his face, seeing for the first time the harshness of the lines that ran from nose to chin, the tightness of the finely chiselled lips.

'Stephen, please forgive me.' She spoke quickly, her voice low. 'You're quite right. I've neglected you.' She touched his arm, tentatively, and felt it tremble.

For a moment, she was afraid. His body was as tense as a tightly coiled spring. She was aware that lately the iron control he had always exercised was beginning to slip. He had lost sight of the dividing line between good and evil and was more and more under the influence of his emotions. The humility she had once admired in him had evolved, become deformed; he now saw himself, not just as a man of God, but as a prophet, one who could do no wrong. All his actions were justified by the most frightening reasoning she had ever heard: everything was 'God's will'.

Once again, she wondered if he were mad.

'Stephen,' she said quietly, now anxious only to calm him down, 'if I promise not to visit Paul so often, will you feel happier? If I spend more time here, as I used to – if we work together – will that make you feel better?' She watched his face, and to her relief saw his taut expression relax a little. 'It'll be just like the old days,' she said softly. 'Remember? When we used to walk round the streets together, calling in at the cottages? Let's do that again, shall we?'

His eyes slid round to meet hers and he smiled slowly. 'Very well, we'll go immediately.'


Paul was only vaguely aware, in those early days, of Emily's visits, and there were times – entire days – when he barely noticed her. He sat for hours at the window, staring with sightless eyes over the blackened roofs, striving to penetrate the eddying smoke and see beyond the range of normal vision, into a world that was out of reach. He felt as if he had concentrated his entire being into one minute speck so densely protected that its defences could not be breached. He was afraid to let himself open out; afraid of the pain that must follow.

Over and over again, in his mind, he relived those last few weeks in Paris. The grim streets, the persistent, gnawing hunger, the slavery of the balloon factory, the constant thump of the bombardments. He saw his grandfather ageing before his eyes, shrinking to a skeleton. He suffered again the torment of Véronique's death.

Had he known that she would die? He remembered finding it impossible to imagine her growing old, he recalled his tenderness as he made love to her, as if she were almost too ethereal for such earthly delights, as if he were afraid that she might break in his arms like spun glass. It was as if he had always been aware that she was too delicate, her span too brief. A fairy being, a butterfly, made to flutter for only a day or two under the sun, brightening the lives of all those who caught a glimpse of her and then . . . gone. But did her passing have to be so cruel?

He lived in a trance, mind and body slowly learning to accept. And Christina, who had suffered in just the same way before he was born, let him alone and waited for him to learn to live again. And Emily, snatching whatever time she could from her tasks in the Lye, sat patiently by, and wondered whether he even knew she was there.

But although he seemed hardly to notice her, Paul was aware of her presence. He was aware of her compassion, reaching out to him across the void. He was aware of the strength which she willed to him, and there came a day when he looked at her fully for the first time, and smiled.

'Emily . . .'

'Paul! Paul, you're better – thank God, you're better!'

He considered. 'Have I been ill?'

'Not ill, no.' She was laughing with relief, seeing his eyes clear again instead of that frightening, muddy grey, his face open and frank rather than shuttered and wary. 'But very unhappy. Paul – you don't have to talk. But tell me – do you feel better? Do you feel you'll be able to start life again?'

'Start again? Here in Stourbridge, you mean?' To her dismay, his eyes clouded again, but this time with a pain she could recognise. 'I shall have to, shan't I?' he said quietly. 'It's the only place left to me, after all.'

'Did you love Paris very much?' she asked. 'Did you . . . love Véronique?'

He nodded simply, knowing that there could be no subterfuge. Emily had once offered him her love and he had refused it. Now she was married and the offer must, perforce, be withdrawn. But the old closeness, the old bond was still there and he could not deny it again.

'I loved Véronique, yes. But in a strange, unearthly way. It was like a dream – it seemed so real at the time.

But now I can see . . . there was something about Véronique that would have been always a child, Emily. She would never quite have grown up. She would never have been a – a *wife*.' He glanced at her, half apologetically. 'It had a sort of magic, Paris – it cast a spell over me. I can't pretend it didn't happen – but the spell's broken now, for ever.'

'You've come home,' Emily said softly, and he nodded.

They sat quietly for a while, both aware that this moment must mark a change in their relationship, both pierced by the sadness of it. From now on, Emily would have to withdraw from him; their bond must be set aside. From now on, they must be no more than brother and sister.

Paul reached out and laid his hand on Emily's. She felt the roughness of his skin, not yet recovered from the work of making balloons and the hardships of his journey back to England. She looked down at the long, sensitive fingers and saw them through a blur.

'Thank you for coming, Emily,' he said. 'Thank you for being here.'

From that day on, his recovery was steady. As his body grew stronger, nourished with Mrs Jenner's good food, Paul seemed to return to his old self. He went to the glasshouse again, studied the cameo blanks made by Ben and began to experiment with the carving. He had lost none of his skill, it seemed, and even Joe was impressed by his expertise. The delicacy, the exquisite tracery which he could achieve in even the finest crystal was far beyond anything that had been done at Henzel's before. His time in France had been well spent; he had learned to apply an elegance that gave Henzel's glass a unique quality, a quality that was quickly recognised. His confidence reasserted itself and, with it, the strength of character that he had attained while he was away.

It was with Ben that Paul was most at ease. Perhaps it was because Ben was simply glad to see him, did not

402

question him about Paris. Perhaps it was because they worked together, because glass was their absorbing common interest.

'You're the finest engraver Henzel's ever had,' Ben told him frankly. 'Streets ahead of when you went away. Mind, you were good then, but this work you're doing now – why, it's so fine you'd think it's bin whispered. Aye, if anyone can do cameo work it'll be you, Mr Paul. When d'you reckon to start on the first blank?'

'Next week,' Paul said, smiling. 'I've done a mass of drawings and I've been to London and studied the Portland Vase again, so we'll see how it goes then. I just hope I don't let you down.'

'You let me down? I don't reckon it's that way about! I just hope they blanks are all fused together right. If there's any stresses, they'll crack first time you cut into 'em.'

'Oh, we'll be lucky if a few don't go. There's a lot of carving to be done there. But I've got the main design drawn. Once the vase has been soaked in acid to deaden the opal surface, I can mark it out, paint it and then apply the bituminous varnish. All we need to do then is dissolve the rest of the opal glass in acid, and I'll have my relief pattern. Then all that's left is to carve it!' He grinned, knowing as well as Ben did that the carving was the slowest and most painstaking part of the entire process. John Northwood, using the same methods, had been said to reckon on taking at least two years to make his replica. Was it possible that Paul could do it more quickly?

It was not a task that could be rushed. The pattern, detailed and intricate, would be carved using hand tools – instruments that looked simple, even primitive, but were the best for the job. There was no aid to be had from wheels here, nor any other kind of machinery. And a single slip could mean total failure.

Paul stood in the room that had been set aside from the rest of the engraving shop and looked at the blanks that lined the shelves. Each one looked alike, each one looked perfect – yet some of them must contain hidden stresses, faults that would come to light only when he began to work. Or might stay hidden until the very last moment, cracking as he made the last tiny chip into the white surface. His eye strayed a little further.

'What's that?'

'Oh, that's Master Roger's black crystal,' Ben said. 'We were experimentin' with colours – we did the new ruby too, remember? It was about the time you first went to Paris. The ruby went well but the black never caught people's fancy. I'll tek it away.'

'No – don't.' Paul reached out and lifted down one of the vases that had been made. 'It's interesting. A true, dense black. I must ask Roger about it. It might help him to feel more friendly towards me.' A shadow crossed his face. Roger's welcome had been frosty, to say the least; he had shown blank dismay in the first moments and then done his best to ignore the brother so recently returned from the dead. He spent little time at Henzel Court now and no one knew quite where he went.

Ben looked sceptical. He had come to know Roger Compson quite well during the past few years. Taking an interest in his black crystal wasn't likely to thaw that one out. If you wanted his opinion, the fires of Hell wouldn't be hot enough.

Anyway, it didn't much matter. The important thing was that they were going to see those blanks being carved at last. He couldn't wait to get home and tell Florrie.

'Alive! And back in the bosom of the family, petted and made a fuss of just like the prodigal son!' Roger paced Jeremy's drawing room, his face white with fury. There was no attempt now to conceal his rage. 'Just when my plans were going so well. They would have agreed to anything, I know it. By the time I left Oxford, we could have done exactly as we pleased. And now –' He gestured hopelessly. 'That – that *bastard* comes back to ruin it all.'

'So what do you intend to do about it?' Jeremy asked

coolly. 'Allow him to take over, just as if he'd never been away? I thought better of you than that, Roger.'

'What?' Roger ceased in mid-stride and wheeled round to face him. 'You don't imagine I'm giving up now, do you? I tell you, I had my future planned – we both did. I'm not going back on our plans. I intend to run Henzel's as it should be run, and without the help of a namby-pamby French bastard, too. By rights, this is *my* inheritance and I'm not having it snatched away under my very nose, not by anyone.'

'I'm very glad to hear it,' Jeremy said. 'But it won't be easy. Paul's back, he's working and both Christina and Joe see him as the natural heir. I'm sure they intend you should have equal shares in it, but that's all you can hope for. You can't even discredit him – he's very much the hero. Why, I hear nothing but his name all over Stourbridge. His return makes a highly romantic story, and it loses nothing from the fact that he either won't or can't remember most of the journey. People are never at a loss to fill in the gaps – I've heard a dozen versions already, and each one more fanciful than the last.'

'Oh, I'll do something, never fear!' Roger flung himself down in a chair and stared moodily at the empty fireplace. 'I shan't stand by and see him take everything. And he'll try, you know! He has all the advantages. He's here in the glasshouse, while I'm away at Oxford. Not only that, he's doing good work – it can't be denied, I wish it could. And he's doing something new, something that could make him famous.' He shifted restlessly in the chair. 'He's got the whole place eating out of his hand, and Father and Mother will give him anything he asks for. Unless I act quickly, he'll be the one to take over, and I'll be nothing more than a clerk.'

'I agree,' Jeremy said slowly. 'It's most unsatisfactory. As you say, Paul does hold the advantage.'

'If only he weren't working on that new glass. The cameo . . . He's trying to outdo Northwood in copying the Portland Vase, you know. Whoever does it first is going to attract a lot of attention. And Mother and Father are putting all their trust in Paul.'

'And if he should fail?' Jeremy lifted one eyebrow. 'What happens to their trust then?'

'Mother and Father would lose faith in him. And in his present state he'd lose faith in himself.' Roger leaped to his feet, his eyes bright, the colour flooding back into his face. 'That's the answer, Jeremy! All I have to do is ensure that he fails. He'll be so disheartened that he won't even want to try again, and they'll be glad to let me take over. And then we can proceed with our own plans.'

Jeremy looked up at him. The young man's excitement was infectious. But still Jeremy was not sure. The idea was too vague, too nebulous. How could Roger ensure that Paul failed? And Paul himself, by all accounts, was different since his return – stronger, toughened by his experiences. Was he likely to be easily disheartened? In Jeremy's opinion, stronger action was needed. He remembered his own action over his own rival, the Frenchman who had taken Christina away from him. Was Roger prepared to act as drastically?

Jeremy's whole life now was centred around Roger and the determination he had formed to make this young man the instrument of his revenge on Christina and Joe. To that end, he had taught him, moulded him, shown him a side of life from which his parents had sought to protect him. He had, coldly and deliberately, changed him from a spoilt child to a man as grasping and calculating as himself. Was he also as ruthless?

Until now, the revenge he had planned had taken the shape of turning their son into a traitor, using him to wrest away their glasshouse. But now a sweeter, and even more appropriate revenge was presenting itself.

He leaned forward, his blue eyes gleaming.

'Listen,' he said. 'I have an idea . . .'

The summer was hot and dry. In the cones, the glass-blowers stripped to the waist and laboured with sweat-shining bodies in the surging red shadows. In the engraving shops, the wheels screamed like lost souls as the men crouched over them, the muscles standing out in their arms as they held wineglasses, bowls, even heavy vases against the spinning copper to carve the patterns into their shimmering surface. And in the small room set aside for Paul, the blanks stood along the shelves, the basic shape of the designs uncarved and white on their smooth blue sides as he worked.

It was work that would have driven a less patient man out of his mind. But Paul had trained himself for years to be able to sit for long periods at this painstaking task. With the vase itself resting on a large moleskin pad filled with bran and his elbows supported by two similar, smaller pads, he worked patiently, meticulously, using one small tool to chip away at the fragile glass. Over the vase, he had arranged a large magnifying glass so that he could carve the minute details of the design; every fold of clothing, every shivering leaf on the trees, every subtle shading of expression on the faces of the gods and goddesses, every single hair, all were to be shown as clearly as in some great sculpture. For this was what Paul was really doing; a sculpture, seen in three dimensions, of white glass on deepest blue.

And it could not be hurried. As John Northwood, working at the Red House, had already discovered, the carving of one vase could take months; even years.

For Paul, it was a time of adventure, of discovery, as he proceeded further with the carving, taking delight each day in the achievements of yesterday, setting out to do more. But for everyone else, it was a time of waiting.

For Christina and Joe, seeing their son take his place once more as an acclaimed artist. For Roger and Jeremy, biding their time, for their plan would be all the more successful if left until the vase was nearing completion. And for Emily, living through her own private nightmare; seeing Stephen retreat daily a little further into his world of distorted prayer and fanaticism, suffering his 'punishments' at night. Recognising that their marriage was a travesty, knowing that the man she loved was as far away from her as he had been during the days of the siege, yet accepting her lot with the stoicism she had been born with and endeavouring always to keep those vows she had made.

Yet, although Stephen kept her almost a prisoner now at the Lye, objecting to every small foray into the wider world, she refused to yield the only small pleasures that were left to her: her weekly visits to Henzel Court and to Florrie and Ben. And her occasional appearance in Paul's workroom.

'It's beautiful,' she said wistfully as he dropped his tools on the bench, set the vase carefully on its base and stretched his aching arms. 'Such exquisite work. And surely there can't be much more to do now.'

He turned his head and stared at her as if he were slowly returning from another world.

'Emily. I didn't know you were there. Have you been watching me?'

'Yes.' She came closer, leaning forward to examine the vase he had been working on. 'Paul, it's wonderful. An exact copy. Do you think this will be the one? Have you heard if Mr Northwood has got so far?'

He shrugged and flexed the wrists that had held the heavy vessel. 'How can I tell? Even if he hasn't, he could still finish his first. I could make a slip with the very last cut and ruin the whole thing. I could make a mistake in the pattern – anything.'

'Oh, surely not – you've been backwards and forwards to London, looking at the Vase in the British Museum. How could you make a mistake?'

'It seems to me I can always make mistakes,' Paul said gloomily. 'And Northwood has been to the museum too . . . He's a fine craftsman, Emily. He could win this race for fame. Perhaps he deserves to – after all, he hasn't spent years in Paris, wasting his time and others' lives.'

'Paul, how can you say that! You weren't wasting time – you were learning, and to good effect. As for lives – what have you ever done to hurt anyone, let alone waste their life?' She caught at his arm, looking up into

408

his shuttered face. 'You mustn't say such things.'

He returned her look sombrely. 'And you have no idea what you are saying, Emily. How do you know what I did with my years in Paris? How do you know what I did to others?' He drew himself away from her and paced moodily towards the narrow window. 'Things happened in France that I've never spoken of to anyone. Things that will haunt my dreams for the rest of my life.'

'Then perhaps you ought to speak of them,' Emily declared passionately. 'Don't you remember how we used to have nightmares, when we were children? The only way to forget them was to share them.' She came swiftly across the littered room to his side. He turned away but she caught now at both his arms, forcing him to face her. 'Paul, don't turn away from me. Share it with me as you used to do – have you forgotten?' Her eyes were wide, beseeching, almost black with entreaty. In that moment, her life seemed empty, hopeless, with Paul as the only bright, shining star in an endless sky. 'Don't shut me out of your life, Paul. Don't shut me out of your heart.'

He looked down at her and her heart twisted at the expression in his eyes. For months now, they had been avoiding this moment, turning away from each other in the knowledge that their hearts would not deny. But they could not turn away for ever. The moment had come; it was inevitable. She closed her eyes, almost unable to bear it. How would it be possible to go back to Stephen, once she and Paul had admitted the truth?

'I have to shut you out,' he said in a low voice. 'Emily, you know that. We have to shut each other out . . .' He turned and looked at the bench, at the vase, the few small tools he used. 'All this . . . this is what I live for now. What I *have* to live for. What else can I do now but work? What else can I do but strive to produce beauty, for it's the only good thing there is left to me now. The only justification I can have for living.'

Emily's hands were still on his arms. She lifted her face, searching his eyes for the truth. Her hands tightened on his arms; she let them creep up, up until they rested lightly on his shoulders. She lifted herself on to her toes, drew his head down to hers, and kissed his lips, firmly, steadily, and with purpose.

Paul's body stiffened. She could feel the resistance in him, and then the thread of response. His lips softened against her mouth, then hardened again in a new way. She felt his arms come round her, holding her hard against him, felt the vibrations of his groan deep within her own trembling body.

'Paul,' she whispered against his mouth. 'Paul, I love you . . .'

He held her against his body, kissed her again, wildly, violently, and her heart sang. She felt the hard, lean length of him and ran her hands down his back, rejoicing in the sinewy strength that he had regained since that day when she had met him, starved and weak, at the gates of Henzel Court. Now his lips were on her cheeks, her eyelids, in her hair, on her ears and seeking down her neck, and she moved and twisted in his arms, arching herself towards him, offering her body with abandoned disregard. She had waited so long. Could it be wrong to give herself now, even in this drab and cluttered room with glass standing all about them and tools on the dusty bench? Paul, Paul, her heart cried, and she was astounded that he did not hear it. But perhaps he did; perhaps his own heart was crying out too.

And then, so suddenly that she almost fell, he thrust her away. She stumbled against the bench, staring at him in dismay. His hair was dishevelled, his necktie loosened, his eyes wild.

'*Paul* . . .' she whispered. 'Paul, what is it? What's wrong?'

'What's wrong?' he groaned, both hands at his brow, the fingers moving desperately in his hair. 'What's wrong? Emily, how can you ask that? Everything's wrong – you, your husband, I – the whole world is wrong! I should never have come back, never even dreamed that I could take up where I left off.' His glance roved about the room, as if he dared not meet her eyes. 'Go away, Emily, for God's sake. Don't come near me again.' He looked at her at last and she recoiled from the expression in his eyes. 'It can only bring harm to you. Can't you see, I bring bad luck to any woman who comes near me? Can't you see, I carry some kind of doom within me! Perhaps it comes from my father – perhaps it's even earlier than that, I don't know. But I'm cursed, Emily, cursed, and you'll do well to keep away from me.' He shook his head as she moved nearer to him, raising his hand as if to ward her off. 'Go away now, Emily, and for your own sake, don't come near me again – ever.'

# Chapter Twenty

'Almost finished?' Jeremy repeated the words slowly and gave Roger a cautious glance. 'You say the copy is almost complete? Then he'll have beaten Northwood.'

'He will,' Roger said grimly. 'And we know what that means, Jeremy. Henzel's will be set fair to be the leading glassmaker in the country. Possibly even Europe. And Paul will be the great hero of the hour.'

'Then the the time has come,' Jeremy said quietly. 'You have your preparations made? There is not a moment to lose.'

Emily sat back on her heels and surveyed the finished grate of their bedroom fireplace. Blackleading and polishing the fireplaces in the house daily was hard work, work that would have been done by the maid. But for the past two months, the Corbett household had been without a servant of any kind. Stephen, ever seeking new ways to keep Emily occupied, had decided that she should do all her own household work and dismissed both the cook and the little scullerymaid, and now Emily's day began before six and ended at midnight. And except for the visits she still made to those who needed help in their own troubles, she rarely set foot outside the house.

How much longer could she bear it? Even now, it was not Stephen's tyranny that kept her at home, but her own conscience. Whatever he did, she was his wife. She had made those vows, and she must obey him. Even though it went against every grain in her body; even though she was guiltily aware of the hatred she had felt for him throughout almost the whole of her marriage.

Even though she yearned more each day to be with Paul.

A sound at the door warned her that Stephen was coming, and she scrambled hastily to her feet.

'What, idle again?' he demanded as soon as he came through the door. 'Shouldn't that have been done an hour ago? How can you worship the Lord in that state – look at the filth on your hands, on your face! Here, wipe yourself – it's time for our prayers.'

They prayed now several times a day, or rather Stephen did, dragging her to her knees beside him while he harangued his God in a loud, hectoring voice. He no longer asked for help; he offered advice and even commands. Emily, crouched beside him, wondered what God thought of His not-so-humble servant; and although she added her Amens, her own prayers were of a very different kind.

Oh God, if only all this were over. If only it were a dream. Let it be a dream. Let me wake up in the old room at home and find that none of it ever happened. Let us be back in the nursery together, innocent and happy . . .

But her prayers were never answered, and she wondered whether it was not even a kind of blasphemy to offer them. God had presumably sent her these troubles for a purpose, or so Stephen would have said. Who was she to question them?

'And now,' Stephen said, having issued Heaven with his orders for the day, 'you can tell me exactly what you were doing at Henzel Court yesterday.'

'I went to see Mamma. I go every week, you know that.'

'You go on Tuesdays. Yesterday was Monday.'

'Does it matter? I thought I would be too busy today – I had a spare hour, so I –'

'A spare hour? You mean an idle hour. Did it not occur to you to consult me about what you should do with that hour? Did you not think to offer it for a greater good than your own idle amusement?' The feverish glitter, now so familiar, was in his eyes and her heart sank. 'Don't lie to me, Emily! I'm not such a fool that I don't understand the significance of a Monday to the glass

414

industry. You went to Henzel Court because your brother Paul would be there – and because in spite of all my efforts, all my prayers, you still harbour an unhealthy affection for him. Well – isn't it true?'

'Stephen, of course it's not true! And Paul works on Mondays – he works every day. He wasn't at home yesterday.' If only he had been. It was weeks since she had seen him and she hungered for a sight of his face.

'I don't believe you! You're lying to me again, Emily, as you lie every time you look at me. What sort of a wife are you?' His voice was filled with bitter scorn. 'Lusting after another man, and that your own brother! You disgust me! When I have given you all that I have, when I have striven to bring you to God, to show you the love of a husband for his wife.' She closed her eyes as she thought of what form his love had taken. 'Do you know what love is between a man and a woman, Emily? Do you understand what it means?'

'I think so,' she said in a small but steady voice.

'Do you? I wonder . . .' He moved suddenly and she gasped, but he was still again, looking down, his face shadowed now. 'It's a necessity,' he said harshly. 'A necessity for men. Men have needs, Emily, needs that may seem strange but cannot be denied, needs that a modest young woman can never understand. It's all part of God's purpose that it should be so. Procreation springs from these needs, and it's a woman's duty to submit herself to them. Do you understand that, Emily? Do you have any idea what I'm talking about? Or do you still cherish that whore's notion that it's something to be . . . enjoyed?'

'Not since I married you!' she flashed, feeling a sudden surge of spirit. 'But it's not I who was wrong about that, Stephen. It's you – you and your twisted ideas about religion. Don't you see, they've poisoned your mind – driven out any real feeling, any real love. *You* are the one who doesn't understand. It isn't just a matter of needs and submission. There should be sharing – and delight – and –'

'That's enough!' His voice was like a whip. 'It is as I feared,' he went on more quietly, and now he moved close, leaning over her chair with a hand on each of its arms. 'This is your mother coming out in you, Emily. She was a fallen woman, you've always known that. And I'd hoped that you – but what chance did you have, when your stepmother herself was no better . . . But don't despair, Emily, my dear.' He was speaking loudly again now, his voice vibrating with the same thrill as when he raised it to preach to his congregation, threatening them with the brimstone and flames of Hell, exhorting them in the ways of righteousness. 'I am here to help you. Together, we'll conquer this dark side of your nature. Together, we'll vanquish the devils that beset you. And lo, even though you may lead me into temptation –' His face was close to hers, his nostrils flaring, eyes ablaze '– we'll rise again together . . . together . . .' He lifted both hands and ran them down her body; his fingers left a flaring trail of scorched nerves from shoulder to wrist. She tried to turn her face, but found his lips on hers, parting them, his tongue forcing itself into her mouth. And then he had pushed her on to the bed and his hard body was covering her own, pushing the breath from her lungs, and his hands were searching, pulling, tearing at her clothes. When he removed his mouth, she heard with horror his voice raised in a kind of black, distorted prayer; a constant justification of himself in the temptation into which he declared that she was leading him and against which he was too humanly weak to struggle.

'Stephen – Stephen, please . . .' But he seemed unable to hear her cries. His ears were closed to her protests, his eyes blind to her struggles.

'It's Paul Henzel – he's the one who has spoilt our marriage. And he deserves to be punished, as you shall be punished. He shall be burned in Hell!' He lifted his voice again, declaiming with a voice that seemed to hold the knell of doom, a voice Emily had never heard before in all his rantings. A cold shudder ran through her body as his hands fell away from her. His eyes were wild, unfocused. He turned towards the door.

She spoke through dry lips.

'Stephen . . . Stephen, what are you going to do?'

'I am the instrument of the Lord, and on his head the Lord's wrath will fall . . .' He was at the door, fumbling with the lock. Emily ran to him, tried to stop him, but his strength was too much for her. He thrust her aside and strode downstairs and out into the street, with Emily still clinging to him. Her trap stood at the door, with the pony already harnessed; he must have used it already that day on the few visits he still carried out.

Stephen put his foot on the step and Emily, thoroughly frightened now, pushed with all her strength. Taken off balance, he staggered and fell. Before he could get up, she was in the trap, gathering up the reins. The tears were thick in her eyes now and her heart was thundering so fast that she felt faint. There was a churning sickness in her stomach and her limbs were trembling, her whole body shaking and cold. Stephen clawed at her clothes, trying to drag her down out of the trap. His face was white and contorted, a mixture of dark passion and furious hatred. She had to get away from him, at once. She had to warn Paul.

'Let go of me, Stephen. Let go, or I swear I'll hurt you.' She raised her whip, sickened by her own action but knowing it was essential if she were to escape. She tried to tear her skirt away from his grasp. 'Let go at once!'

His fingers clung tighter. The pony was turning its head now, puzzled, wanting to move as it had been commanded and yet aware that the man's strength was holding it back. Desperately, Emily raised the whip. With a feeling of nausea, she brought it down hard on Stephen's knuckles and heard his cry as he snatched his hand away and lifted it to his mouth. Within seconds, he reached for her again, but the respite was all she needed. The whip was laid across her pony's back and, shocked by the unaccustomed assault, it leaped forward in the shafts.

The trap jerked and moved quickly away, and Stephen staggered back and stumbled to his knees in the mud of the road.

Emily let the pony trot as fast as it could up the narrow road out of the Lye Waste. She sat holding the reins loosely in her hands, sobbing quietly, feeling the tears run endlessly down her cheeks. Every now and then she raised her hand and wiped them away, leaving her face and hair wet. The tears ran down her neck, dripped on to her torn and draggled jacket. She felt a coldness at her breast and realised with a shock that she was still partially exposed; she pulled the tattered fabric across and held it with trembling fingers.

At last she neared the drive of Henzel Court and strained her swollen eyes through the dusk. The gas lamps had been lit and a pool of yellow light fell on the footpath. A shadow moved, left the surrounding darkness and stood for a moment outlined, revealing itself as a man, his head lifted at the sound of the pony's rapid approach.

Emily gave a sobbing cry. It seemed barely a moment since she had come up this very road and seen Paul, weary and exhausted, returned from the dead, under that same lamp. And now he was strong and well again, yet as far away from her as ever. And she cried out to him in supplication, begging him to take her back as she had taken him.

'Paul! Oh, Paul . . .'

She saw him stare, then move quickly forward. He caught at the pony's bridle and brought it to a halt. The animal stood panting from its long run, and Paul came to the trap and stared up at her.

'Emily! What in the name of Heaven . . . ?'

'Oh, Paul . . .' she said faintly, and fell into his arms.

'So this is the famous cameo,' Jeremy said, and lifted the vase from its shelf. 'It seems to be completed.'

'It does,' Roger said. 'And tomorrow Mother and Father and the rest of the family are coming to see it. And Paul will be a hero all over again.'

'Tomorrow? And is it to be displayed to the public?'

'It is. Not immediately. Northwood has not completed his copy, and so Henzel's have time to arrange as elaborate a ceremony as they wish.' Roger's lip curled. 'Can you imagine the trumpeting there will be? Or would – if it were allowed to go ahead.'

'Allowed?' Jeremy looked at the vase in his hands and tested its weight, smiling. 'Do I see what is in your mind, Roger? One slip of my fingers and . . .' He let the vase drop an inch or two, catching it again with a laugh. 'Shall I?'

'Most certainly not!' Roger took the vase and examined it in his turn. 'That's a pleasure I have reserved for myself. But not before Paul comes. I want him to share the pleasure with me.' With exaggerated care, he set the vase back in its place and turned to lift the bundle he had brought in with him. He untied it and let the cloth fall away, revealing a mass of rags from which rose a thick, familiar stench.

'Oil.' Jeremy smiled. Together, they began to disperse the rags around the room. Roger opened the door and went out into the passage, then through into the main engraving shop. He drew a box of matches from his pocket and lit the gas, then moved on through the long room, dropping rags as he went. 'We'll make sure of this, Jeremy. Just smashing the vase wouldn't be enough – he has others already partially carved, and there are new blanks as well. We could smash them all, but he would only start again. But if we burn the place down, they'll all have too much to think about to worry about a mere frippery like a cameo vase. Rebuilding – keeping the main production lines going – no, I don't think Paul will be spared to sit for hours chipping away at one vase. And they'll need a brain to help them, too – someone who can assess the damage, calculate the sums needed for starting again, someone who understands about money.' His voice had faded as he moved about beyond the door but now he reappeared again, a demoniacal glint in his pale eyes. 'That's when *I* become the hero, Jeremy. We shall see our plans come to fruition at last.'

He lit the gas in the showroom. Together, they gazed at

419

the array of glass set out on the long benches. The soft glow of the gas reflected back at them from thousands of cut and polished facets. Wineglasses, decanters, bowls – they were all here, the result of years of design and planning, months of work.

Roger moved forward. He laid his hands almost reverently on a huge punchbowl. With a ceremonial gesture, he lifted it high above his head. And cast it on the floor.

The bowl shattered into a thousand, a million shining fragments and the two men stared at it. Never before had either of them willingly smashed a perfect piece of glass. They looked at the shimmering splinters, and then at each other.

'Well!' Roger said in an excited voice. 'We may as well have some fun.'

He turned back to the bench and lifted another piece, a decanter this time, made to the first design Joe Compson had ever drawn. With a laugh, he flung it at the wall. The sound of the crash was piercing, the high, ringing notes of pure lead crystal echoing through the room. And as they died away, Roger turned and began to walk swiftly back and forth, passing down the length of the tables, sweeping the glass to the floor as he went. He laughed again and again; the high, excited laugh of a naughty child up to mischief. And Jeremy joined in, following him as he went, tossing aside the glass that Roger's sweeping arm missed, throwing tumblers, goblets, jugs to the floor and crushing them under his boots as if he were crushing them to death.

Gently, with infinite tenderness, Paul laid Emily on the chaise longue. He remained beside her for a moment or two, on his knees, his hand cupped beside her cheek. His eyes moved over her face, seeing the grime, streaked by tears, seeing the bruises that were already beginning to form. He looked down at her slender neck and the tattered blouse, falling away again to reveal breasts that displayed blue marks left by cruel fingers. His eyes hardened. And when Emily looked up, it was to see an expression of white-hot fury.

'Paul, don't look at me like that.' She turned her face aside and the weak tears slid from under her lashes.

'Darling, I'm not angry with you.' Quickly, he lifted his hand to her face again, his fingers gentle against the bruised skin. 'Only with him – whoever he was. Who did this to you, Emily? Who hurt you?'

She shook her head wearily. 'It wasn't his fault, Paul. He – he loves me, I'm sure, but –'

'*Loves* you? You – you mean – *Corbett* did this?' He was half on his feet, but she reached out a shaking hand and caught at his arm.

'Paul, no. Don't leave me – don't go away. He – he's so strange. He wants to love me, but he thinks it's wrong. He thinks loving is wrong, sinful – he can't help himself, it's all tangled up inside him, but I know he'll suffer for this, he –'

'Suffer! And so he shall suffer – I'll see to it myself!' He was up again but Emily clutched his sleeve and shook her head again.

'Please don't. Don't leave me now, Paul. I – I need you with me . . .' The tears began again and he stared down at her, his face softening. Slowly, he knelt again, reached out and took her very tenderly into his arms. She turned her face into his shoulder and wept, the heartache of years flooding from her breast. She felt his lean hardness against her, felt it relax slowly, felt his own tears begin. For a long time, they clung together, like the two children they had once been, like the adult lovers they had almost become. And when she lifted her face at last and their eyes met, she knew that for Paul, too, this had been a release, and that there would be no more restraints between them.

'Paul, I love you so much,' she said shakily, and he smiled and touched her tear-soaked face with tender fingers.

'I love you too, Emily. I've always loved you.' And to his surprise he realised that it was true. Even in the darkest moments with Annette, the brightest with Véronique, he had never, in his deepest heart, stopped loving Emily.

He looked into her eyes and saw the warmth in the dark brown velvet, the glow of a love that had never been sullied. He remembered the passion with which she'd declared her love, the brightness of her delight in Paris during those first few days, the joy they had shared on so many occasions. And he saw that in Emily there was all that had drawn him to both other women: the sultry fire he had found in Annette; the tenderness in Véronique.

'All this time,' he said wonderingly, 'I've been searching for you. Even after I turned you away . . . oh, Emily, my darling, can you ever forgive me?'

Emily turned her face into his hand and kissed the palm lingeringly. 'Just love me,' she whispered. 'That's all I ask. Love me now.'

Paul gazed at her. His eyes travelled down her body, seeing again the marks, the bruises. Gently, his fingers parted the torn blouse and he bent to kiss the soft breasts. His lips were tender, barely whispering across her skin, and Emily closed her eyes, a great sigh shuddering through her. But she would not let him draw away; when he lifted his head, she slid both arms around his neck and drew him close, drew him back to her breast.

'Love me,' she whispered again, and it was a cry from the heart, a cry that could not be denied.

Paul went to the door and turned the key. He moved to the fire and replenished it with a log from the basket. He came back to the chaise longue and knelt at her side.

'Emily . . .'

For a brief second, as he slipped her clothes away from her trembling flesh, Emily stiffened. Was Paul's love-making, after all, to be as savage, as painful, as Stephen's? Was it always like that? But at his first reverent touch, she knew that her fears were unfounded. The long, sensitive fingers that could carve beauty into a

422

piece of glass were no less delicate in making love. It was as if he had already known her, as if he understood her every desire. And, feeling him tremble against her, his bare skin touching hers, she knew that this moment was as precious to him as it was to her. She knew that Paul would never hurt her; only bring her joy.

In the final moment, soaring over a pinnacle of rapture that neither had ever known before, they looked into each other's eyes. There was no smile; the moment was too intense. But Emily knew, and Paul knew too, that they had found each other at last.

Afterwards, dressed again, they lay curled together before the fire. They made no plans – the situation was too complicated for that. Emily was a married woman and Stephen a jealous and vindictive husband. He would not let Emily go lightly, and to live together would mean having to leave England. The family had been unconventional enough in the past, but even Stourbridge society, accustomed to their foibles, would not countenance such a departure from the rules as that. And Stephen would go to law . . .

'Would you go to France with me?' Paul asked tentatively. 'Or . . . perhaps America? Oh, why was I so foolish in Paris? Why didn't I *see* . . .?'

'Hush, my darling.' She laid her fingers on his lips. 'It was too soon for us. Don't let's think about it now. Let's just be happy together – for an hour, at least.'

'An hour . . .' Paul said. But even as he spoke, there was a knocking at the front door. They heard Rose come panting up the stairs from the kitchen to answer it. Hurried voices. The quick tap of heels – and then someone tried the locked door.

'Mr Paul!' Rose called. 'Mr Paul, are you there? There's a boy brought a message – says it's urgent, there's someone in the engraving shops. He saw a light –'

'The engraving shops!' Paul sat up quickly. 'The cameo . . .'

\*　　\*　　\*

423

There was no piece of glass left whole when they left the showroom. And then they began on the engraving room too, throwing the half-finished pieces to each other, investing each vicious crash with the bitter hatred they had both harboured for so long: Jeremy for the humiliation he had suffered twenty-five years ago, Roger for the wrongs he believed to have been done him by his half-brother. And at last they came to the door of Paul's workroom, where the cameo vase still stood. It was almost the only piece of glass untouched in the entire place.

'*What's going on?*'

The two men whipped round. Paul was standing behind them, staring into the room. He saw the cameo vase, already in Roger's hands, and started forward.

'Put that down! You'll break it –'

'Break it?' Roger cried in that high voice. 'So I shall! But not here – come with me and let's do it in the engraving shop. We've got something else to show you there, Paul, my dear bastard brother.'

'Roger, don't be such a fool –' But he dared not wrest the vase from his brother's grasp. He stood helpless as Roger and Jeremy went past him through the door and down the passage. His eyes fixed on the vase, anxiety pumping through his body, he followed them. And saw the chaos of the engraving shop.

'What in Hell's name . . .?' He stared wildly from one to the other. 'Roger! *Jeremy!* What are you doing here? *What have you done?*'

'My dear boy,' Jeremy said urbanely. 'You don't mind my calling you that, I hope? I should have thought it was perfectly obvious what we've done.'

'You mean – you mean *you* did this? The two of you?' He stared aghast at the smashed glass all over the floor. 'But – why?' His eyes moved along the room, saw the door at the far end standing open. 'The showroom –'

'In there, too,' Jeremy said pleasantly, and Paul gave him a wild glance and ran through the crunching splinters to see for himself.

'My God . . .' He came back slowly. 'You've gone mad. You've both gone mad.'

'Not mad, no.' Roger set the cameo vase down on one of the littered benches and faced him. 'Simply tired of having to play second fiddle to a half French by-blow who should never have been here in the first place. Henzel Crystal is mine by rights, Paul, mine. But I'll never get it while you're here, dazzling Mother with your pretty face and your pretty glass. So I've decided to get rid of it all. They'll never recover from this –' He gestured around him at the destruction. 'They'll be happy enough to let me take over. And then Jeremy and I will merge our two companies and build something really worthwhile. You see, it's all quite simple, once you understand it.'

'And you imagine I shall stand by and say nothing?' Paul demanded contemptuously, and then saw the expression on their faces.

'Of course we don't,' Roger said smoothly. 'But you won't be here, will you, Paul? You'll die in the fire. And everyone will remember the boy who came to you with a message that there was an intruder here. It will all seem very easy to understand.'

While he was speaking, he and Jeremy had moved in close to Paul. Gradually, they edged him away from the door; nearer and nearer to the showroom itself.

'There's no way out from here,' Roger remarked cheerfully as Paul stared in horror at the smashed glass all around. 'And they say that death by fire is not nearly so bad as you imagine. The smoke puts you to sleep quite early on.' He took out his matches again and struck one.

At the same moment, Jeremy lifted his head and sniffed. Roger paused, watching him. With a quick glance around, Jeremy went back to the door and stared down the engraving shop.

'Roger! Look – the rags – they're on fire!'

'Already? How can they be? I've not begun to –' But he turned and saw that Jeremy was right. The bundle of rags nearest the door, where he must have thrown the first smouldering match after lighting the gas, was already bursting into flames. And immediately they spread to other rags. The flames seemed to leap along the walls, licking along the oil that had dripped as Roger carried his bag through the building, bursting into life as they reached each soaking pile. And the fire was spreading outside too, into the narrow corridor and through to the engraving shop. The air filled with black, acrid smoke; they began to choke as they tried to make their way through it. Within moments, they could hear a dull roaring; they glanced wildly at each other through the flaring darkness and knew that the engraving shop, with the wooden benches and tables that had stood there for so many years, as dry as tinder, was ablaze.

Stephen, left staggering in the mud as Emily's pony trap clattered away up the street, stared after her with a mixture of rage and dismay.

How dared she! How *dared* she! The hussy – attacking him with a whip, daring to run away like that. Making a fool of him in front of everyone. And no doubt gone running to that posturing, effeminate half-French bastard who was as near her brother as made no difference, whether or not there was blood shared between them. Well, he would soon see about that! He'd follow her, here and now, and bring her back at once. He was in the right, after all. The law was on his side. He might even take a policeman along with him, should he see one on his way. And when he brought her home, he would make her understand just what a wife's duty was. It seemed to be a lesson she was reluctant to learn.

'I'll make him burn in Hell,' he muttered over and over again as he toiled along the dark, muddy roads between the Lye Waste and Wordsley. Burn in Hell . . .

He arrived at Henzel Court just after Paul had left. And Rose, coming to the door for the second time in half an hour, looked at him with surprise. She knew Mr Corbett, of course, but he rarely came to the house. And he was in such a state! Muddy, dishevelled, wild-eyed . . . she'd half a mind not to let him in at all, especially as none of the family were here. But Mrs Corbett was, of course, and in not much better condition. Whatever had been happening? An accident of some sort?

'Miss Emily – Mrs Corbett – she's in the library,' she said, wondering if Mr Corbett was quite well. He looked so strange . . . 'Is there anything I can bring you, sir?'

'Nothing, thank you.' He thrust past her and through the library door. And Emily, lying on the chaise longue with her eyes on the fire and a head filled with dreams, started up with a cry of fear. But Rose had gone, back to the kitchen.

'Stephen!'

'I've come to fetch you home,' he said grimly, and started towards her.

Emily scrambled up, keeping the heavy piece of furniture between them. 'I shan't come! I'm never coming home with you again, Stephen.'

They stared at each other in the flickering firelight. Slowly, Stephen took in her appearance; the wild hair, the streaks of dirt on her face, the torn clothes she had put on again after her lovemaking with Paul. He saw the bruises already making shadows on her skin, the swelling beneath one eye.

'Emily . . .' His voice was bewildered. 'Did – did *I* do that?'

'You know you did.'

He moved towards her, and she saw that the remorse had begun. 'Emily, how could I? How could I hurt you – the woman I love? You know I'd never willingly hurt a hair of your head –'

'Since you've frequently torn several of them out by the roots, I find that difficult to believe,' she said sharply.

He shook his head. He looked like a puzzled child. 'No. No, it's not true. That was someone else – a devil. It's the devil that gets into me and does that, Emily, you know it is. Don't we all have to fight with the devil? I fight him day and night, but I can't always win.' He came to her, hands outstretched. 'Come back to me, Emily, I beg you, come back home with me now.'

'No,' she said in a low voice. 'Never.'

The room brightened suddenly and they both glanced at the fireplace. But the log Paul had laid on it some time ago had smouldered away to nothing, and the glow was dim. With fear leaping suddenly in her heart, Emily ran to the window and dragged back the curtains.

'It's the glasshouse! The engraving shops! They're on fire! Oh, my God – Paul – the cameos . . .'

Stephen came to her side. Together, they stared appalled at the conflagration below. The whole of Wordsley seemed to be lit by it; already they could hear the shouts and cries of people running from all sides to see what was happening. Emily turned, her face white and agonised.

'I must get down there at once. Paul –'

'I'm coming with you,' he said, and followed her down the stairs. In the hall, Rose was standing irresolute, her face pale and frightened. She saw Emily and stared, but Emily silenced her questions with an imperious gesture. 'Get me a coat, Rose. Quickly, girl! There's no time to waste. Where are the master and mistress?'

'They're out, miss – visiting – I'm not sure –'

'Well, they'll know about this soon enough. A *coat*!' Emily's voice cut sharply through the girl's terrified voice and she grabbed at the garment that was held out and pulled it round her shoulders. 'Get help at once,' she flung back as she ran out of the door. 'Get Parker – he'll know what to do. And *hurry*!'

The flames were leaping high from the roof of the engraving shop as Emily and Stephen ran down the hill. Against them, clearly outlined, they could see the towering black silhouettes of the three cones. Already there was a crowd of people – women, children, the men who worked in the cones, the engravers themselves – all were scurrying from different directions, their faces lit by the crackling glow, eyes wild in the leaping light.

Joe and Christina arrived at the same moment as

Stephen and Emily. They looked at each other, Emily's dishevelled state barely noticed. Christina was as white as death, her green eyes enormous, her hair loosened, as bright as the flames themselves as it flew about her head. Joe's face was dark with anger as he snapped out orders to the men who strove to douse the flames. Impatient with their attempts, he grabbed a bucket himself and joined in, exhorting them all to greater efforts, but it was clear that the fire had gained too great a hold.

'Paul!' Emily cried above the din. 'Paul, where's Paul?' She searched the faces, ran here and there through the crowd, but nobody had seen him. She found her father again. 'Papa, Paul's inside – he must be, someone came with a message – oh, my God!' She stood appalled as long red tongues of flame licked through holes in the roof. 'Papa – *Paul's in there*!'

'You're sure?' He gave her a quick, comprehensive glance, then turned and plunged through the door. Christina screamed and reached out a hand, but too late. He was gone, swallowed up in the billowing black smoke. And he was followed by a second figure, a figure Emily barely recognised in the tumult, a figure who turned and gave her a look of deep, heartbreaking remorse before disappearing into the inferno.

'*Stephen* . . .' she whispered.

Ben was at her side, tall and solid, a bucket in each hand. 'Come here, Em – help with the buckets. Tin't no use just standing there when there's work to be done.' He handed her a bucket of water and, moving like an automaton, she stepped into the line, standing shoulder to shoulder with the men as they passed the slopping buckets as quickly as possible from hand to hand.

All around her, she could hear the voices, rising and falling like waves of sound.

'We'll never put it out – it's going to gut the entire foundry!' 'My God – if the cones go too . . .' 'They won't! We won't let them!' She worked energetically now, snatching each bucket from the man beside her, passing it on to be filled, reaching for it again as it returned, slopping water from its sides, and thrusting it into the waiting hands. 'What about the new fire engine in Stourbridge – has anyone sent for that?'

'They'll hev seen the flames,' another man said, looking up at the blazing sky. 'They must be able to see 'em from Brierley Hill . . . They won't come if you're not insured though . . .'

Insured? Emily had no idea if they were insured. She remembered vaguely being told of the new fire engine, supplied by one of the insurance companies, which would come out to help its clients. It had a high-pressure hose, even one of the new fire extinguishers. Was it coming even now to their aid? Would it be of any use when it did arrive? Each window of the glasshouse was now a square of brilliant, searing light and flames were beginning to lick through the roof. Surely help could only come too late. *Where was Paul?*

The clanging bell of the fire engine sounded in her ears then, and the clatter of the horses' hooves, the whistles and shouts of the men as they tried to clear a way through the press of frantic people. The human chain was moved further along the bank while the engine came to a halt in front of the blazing building. While the crowd still passed their buckets from hand to hand, the firemen uncoiled their long pipes and began to train them on the building. Great jets of water rose from the hoses and curved like fountains over the flames. A hissing filled the air and the stench of soaking ashes permeated the smoke that still billowed from the timbers. The flames were still there, burning fiercely, but they were now having to fight their own battle and those watching could see that for the first time there was a chance of winning. A cheer went up, and then everyone set to and worked harder than ever.

Paul, she cried in her heart, Paul. And Papa – her father who was in there too – surely neither of them, nobody, could survive in that seething furnace. She thought with despairing remorse of the coldness she had displayed towards her father. And now, when he was lost, she knew that her anger had been a trivial affair, based on her own mistaken ideas. Who was she to say how her father ought to have behaved all those years ago? Who was she to sit in judgement on anyone – she who had driven Stephen to the verge of madness, she who had once turned on Christina in bitterness and repudiated the love of twenty years and more?

'Miss Emily! Miss Emily! You're needed over here – quick, quick!'

Her head jerked up at the cry and she stumbled towards the man who was shouting her name. Who he was, she had no idea, for everyone looked alike in this fearfully lit darkness, every face was black, only eyes and teeth shone white, yet gave no clue to identity. She reached out and took the hand that was offered her, feeling a rough, warm clasp that was only a momentary comfort, and then she was being hurried along, taken past the smouldering building to a clear space that was lit by a few lamps. And she stopped and drew back, for there on the ground was a huddle of bodies, bodies that looked charred and blackened in clothes that were little more than crisp shreds.

'Paul . . .' she whispered faintly. 'Papa . . .' And she looked up at the man who had led her there. 'Who – who are they? Are they . . .?'

Even in his grimy face, she could read compassion, see the gravity in the red-rimmed eyes. He looked down at her and his voice was sombre as he said, 'I'm sorry, miss. It's your brother. And –' He shook his head, unable to say any more, and Emily moved slowly forward to the knot of men who surrounded the crumpled black heap.

'Paul . . .?' she said, her voice infinitely sad. And one of the men kneeling there looked up and then lifted himself to his feet and stood close and put his arms around her.

'It's all right, Emily. I'm here. I'm all right. Hardly burnt at all.' He smiled from a blackened face as she stared up at him, unable to believe that it was true, and then his smile faded and he looked down soberly at the pitiful huddle at his feet. 'It's Stephen, I'm afraid,' he said quietly. 'Stephen . . . and Roger and Jeremy. They broke into the building and smashed all the glass. They were going to leave me to burn . . .' He shook his head and passed his hand across his brow. Emily listened in horror. *Roger*? Her own brother . . .? But Paul was speaking again. 'It went wrong . . . none of us could find the way out. Stephen came in and tried to drag me to the door – his body protected me from the worst of the heat. He's dead . . . and Jeremy too. And Roger . . . Roger is very near it.'

An arm was laid across Emily's shoulders from the other side and she looked up to see her father beside her, his heavy shoulders bowed, his head bent in grief. She lifted her hand to his face and held it there, willing all the comfort she could summon into his sorrowful heart. And then she heard the rattle of a trap approaching. The doctor leaped out and knelt by the injured men. Over Stephen and Jeremy, he shook his head; over Roger he looked grave, but gave orders for the burned and blistered body to be lifted into his trap and taken home as quickly as possible.

'Aye, and you must go too,' Joe said heavily, his voice flattened by weariness and shock. 'Find your mother, Paul, and tell her what's to do, and take her and your sister home. God knows what's been going on here tonight. At the moment, I don't even care. I just want to see this mess cleared up.' He looked at the engraving shops, their ruined timbers standing out black and stark against the reddened sky. The fire had died down now and the firemen were picking their way carefully among the embers, dousing the final glimmers.

It had all happened very quickly. Two men were dead; another probably dying. And all Paul's labours, all his patient care, had gone for nothing. The cameo vases were no more than cullet, gritty black ashes amongst the ruins.

# Chapter Twenty-One

Once again, the glassmakers were holding a picnic, and once again it was towards Prestwood Park that the procession wound its way through the streets of Wordsley and Stourbridge. The sky was bright and clear; the smoke from the factories rose straight up and then dispersed in a breeze that was just enough to keep the day from being sultry. The brilliant colours of the banners glowed like church windows, their silk rippling gently in the breeze, and the sun glittered and reflected like a thousand rainbows from the hundreds of pieces of glass that were being carried so proudly: the old favourites, brought out year after year, like the crown, the bellows, the barrel and the doves. And new pieces brought gasps of admiration and nods of approval from the onlookers: a massive cut-glass decanter, a great vase of cased ruby, engraved with classical motifs, a crinoline figure complete with lacy flounces . . . Almost before you had had time to look at one, another was passing by, and the brief passing glimpse was enough to set most bystanders following the procession, eager to get into the great marquee where they could gaze their fill.

Emily and Paul had been married that morning, in the yellow church on the hill at Wordsley. They had bowed to society in the matter of mourning; after such a tragedy, the family must wait a year at least before beginning a normal life again. And it had been a year filled with anxiety, with problems. The engraving shops had to be replanned and rebuilt, new glass made to fill the showrooms that had been set up in a cleared space in one of the warehouses. There were orders that could not be fulfilled, others that must be held over. The full cost of the fire had not yet been calculated, but the family knew it must be enormous. It was only thanks to the reserves

Christina and Joe had built up, and the respect in which Henzel's was held, that they were able to survive at all.

And, in a strange and ironic way, the plans that Roger and Jeremy had made were coming to pass after all. For the shock of Jeremy's death had killed his father, Samuel. Harold, aged and frail now, had lost heart and decided to retire altogether. Alfred, up in Newcastle and childless, had declined the offer to take over the Stourbridge part of the business, and it had been left to Jeremy's younger brother Rupert to come to Christina and suggest combining the two businesses. Which, after due consultation with Joe, she had decided to do.

'How strange,' she said as they left the church and looked down over the busy town. 'How strange that after all these years the two Henzel glasshouses should become one at last – and in such a way. I wouldn't have wished it, Joe – not like that.'

'Neither would I. But we can take comfort in knowing that the old rivalry is over now. And with Paul and Emily to follow us, the glasshouse is in good hands.' He looked at the couple leading the procession down the path to the carriages. 'We were wrong about them, my love. They're well matched.'

'I don't know why we ever doubted it,' Christina said, smiling.

After the wedding breakfast, the whole family crowded into the carriages again and went to the picnic. And Emily and Paul, feeling themselves to be children again, wandered hand in hand over the springy grass for the rest of the day. They watched the cricket and the children's races, joined in the kiss-in-the-ring, marvelled at the conjurer, laughed at the comic songs and smiled at the sentimental ones. They stopped at the refreshment stalls and ate their own picnic under the spreading branches of a great oak.

'How fortunate we are,' Emily said at last as they gazed out over the colourful scene from the hillock where they sat. 'We could not have had a better day if we'd had the making of the weather ourselves. And everything seems to be coming right at last. Almost everything, anyway.' Her face clouded a little. 'I still feel sad whenever I look at Roger.' She thought again of those terrible days when he had hovered between life and death, the weeks when he had still been in danger of losing his sight. And even when, eventually, he had recovered, he was horribly disfigured by his burns; his smooth good looks had gone for ever, leaving a blistered mass that strangers turned away from, and the sinews and muscles of his body had tightened and distorted so that his strong, lean body was left grotesque and tortured. 'It was a terrible lesson to learn.'

'Yes. And it's decided now – he's to work in the office of the glasshouse. He already knows most of the business – in a few years he'll become chief clerk. I'm afraid there'll never be any more for him than that, and I pity those who have to work under him, for his temper's become a nasty thing to experience. But he's clever with figures, and what else can we do?' Paul lifted his shoulders. 'He's still our brother.'

'Yes.' They rose to their feet and walked slowly down to the great marquee. It was almost empty now; the thousands of people who had thronged the park and filled the tents were now wending their way home. Paul and Emily strolled at ease amongst the tables, glancing at this, examining that, laughing over some of the exhibits, admiring others.

The Henzel display was as glittering as ever. The setback suffered through the fire had been overcome in the past year; there was an array of engraved and cut glass, fresh from the new workshops, which gave testimony to the determination of every man to bring Henzel Crystal once more to the forefront of glassmaking. The Compson Chalice, blown by Joe Compson and engraved with the entwined initials of C and J by Paul's father over twenty-five years ago, stood as always in pride of place. Emily stopped and looked at it. She put out a finger and touched it gently.

'The Compson Chalice. We had hoped that your first piece of cameo glass would be shown here too, Paul – the first copy of the Portland Vase. And now John Northwood has made his. Will you try again?'

Her husband glanced down at her from his slender height and shook his head. 'No. It's been done now, and Northwood deserves his success. He made a fine job of the Vase – as fine as anything I could have done. And he's brought cameo glass into favour again – now that the secret's known, all the glassmakers will be trying it.' He stared absently at the exhibits: the shimmering green, bright as new ferns, the ruby that glowed like a crimson heart, the crystal that gleamed with its own brilliant light. 'Except for Henzel's.'

'Except for Henzel's?' Startled, Emily looked up into the face that she had grown to love so well, so completely. 'What do you mean? Surely, after all your work, you're not going to abandon cameo glass? Surely we can make it as well as – *better* than – anyone else? Paul – what's in your mind? Tell me!'

He smiled. 'Don't worry, Emily. Henzel's aren't bowing out of the race. No – we intend to lead it.' He took her hand and led her along to the end of the display. 'I've thought about this a lot. I've talked it over with Mamma and Papa, and they both agree with me. And I've talked with Ben.'

'*Ben*? But what –'

'Henzel's have never followed the crowd,' Paul said, and she heard the throb of passion in his voice. 'We've always led. I'd hoped to lead in this, too, but dear Cousin Jeremy put a stop to that, as no doubt he meant to. Well, he reckoned without me and he reckoned without Ben. Between us, we can produce something quite different, something no one else has thought of.' With his other hand, he picked up a small piece of glass. A vase. Black, with the density of ebony, the smooth gleaming polish of jet. 'Ben's black crystal. He's perfected it now. Nobody else has exactly this recipe, nobody else can produce exactly this degree of colour. With white, it looks highly

effective – with red, it looks dramatic. With gold . . .'
His eyes were shining like newly polished silver. He set
the vase back on the table and turned to her, his hands
gripping her shoulders. 'With Ben's crystal, we can lead
the world, Emily. We'll make vases such as have never
been seen before. Cameo vases in sheer jet black, with
handles shaped like huge, fiery dragons. Decanters with
golden lions' heads, flagons with exotic birds – eagles,
peacocks, birds of paradise . . . We'll make ordinary
cameo, made with blue glass, look ordinary, a copy.
*Ours* will be something new.'

'Black crystal,' Emily said slowly. 'Paul, it's wonderful. Black crystal.'

'No,' Paul said, and gave a quick glance around the
empty marquee before laying his lips firmly and tenderly
on hers. 'Black Cameo.'